DRAGON'S SONG

DRAGON'S SONG

Sara Stern

iUniverse, Inc.

New York Lincoln Shanghai

Dragon's Song

iUniverse books may be ordered through booksellers or by contacting:

iUniverse
2021 Pine Lake Road, Suite 100
Lincoln, NE 68512
www.iuniverse.com
1-800-Authors (1-800-288-4677)

ISBN-13: 978-0-595-34592-2 (pbk)
ISBN-13: 978-0-595-79339-6 (ebk)
ISBN-10: 0-595-34592-1 (pbk)
ISBN-10: 0-595-79339-8 (ebk)

Printed in the United States of America

For Mom and Dad

CONTENTS

▼

Acknowledgements

Since the summer following fifth grade, when I first put pencil to paper and began to chronicle Selah's travels through Alcaron, many have provided words of encouragement that spurred me onward when my fingers became cramped and weary from writing for too long. Generally, acknowledgements of those who have helped along the way are saved for the end of a series—however, Selah's first book brought forth vast amounts of assistance that allowed it to finally reach publication. To leave my gratitude unspoken would be a crime, as this book could not have been published without a community of help—my family, friends, teachers have all contributed efforts, no matter how small, that have shaped Selah's journey into what it is today.

My parents provided the support I needed as Dragon's Song became less of a hobby to work on in times of boredom and more of an occupation. Mom, my "manager", was the constant encouraging voice in my ear when I neared the homestretch and needed a little push in order to finish. Dad, while challenging me intellectually, taught me 'big picture' lessons that I tried to incorporate into the story. My sister, Kaylee, read over my shoulder as I wrote and thanks to her, grammatical errors were virtually nonexistent in my first typed draft. My little brother, Brian, must be thanked for sacrificing the computer and respecting my space when I was "on a roll".

Friends, too, have helped Dragon's Song on its way to publication. Erin Gibson, best friend, bona fide editor, and talented writer in her own right, has been at my side throughout the whole process of writing, from helping with a first sentence from which to begin Selah's journey to reading each draft and tactfully telling me where I needed more work. Her mother, Ann Gibson, created the wonderful cover art that fits Selah and Windchaser so perfectly.

Each of my teachers contributed to this effort by improving my prose, whether through exposing me to more of the English language or instructing me on the blandness of linking verbs. However, I must give special acknowledgement to Arlene Naganawa, Advanced Writing teacher. Besides educating me on the basic elements of fiction and challenging me creatively, she convinced me that my writing and stories were good enough to be a book, taking my dreams of publication and making them that much more tangible.

Lastly, I must thank Selah and Windchaser, who have shaped me as much as I have shaped them. They have stayed with me, patiently, as their adventures transformed from three scruffy spiral notebooks filled with a loose scrawl to a typed manuscript. Selah, over the three years that I have known her, has become her own person, leading me through her story instead of the other way around and reminding me that there is so much more to her life still unsaid, that there are more books still to come. Without her, I would have no path, no adventure, to share with others.

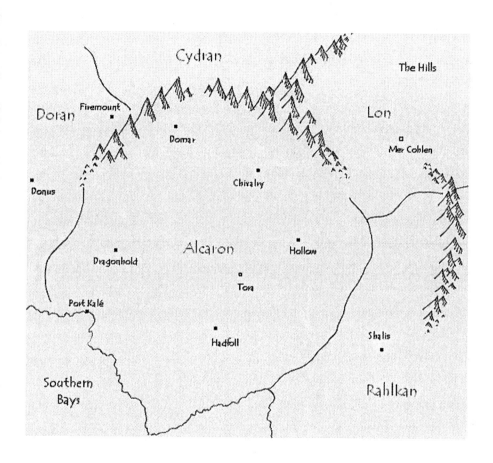

Cydran

The Hills

Doran   Firemount

Lon

Domar

Mer Coblen

Donus

Chivalry

Alcaron   Hollow

Dragonhold

Tora

Port Kalé

Hadfoll

Shalis

Southern
Bays

Rahlkan

PROLOGUE

▼

The air was thick with the haze of summer, the kind of languid heat that seemed to muffle any sound. The very sky reflected the furor of the afternoon, an intense, sharp blue that had banished all clouds from the horizon. The sun looked down like an unrelenting eye, silently watching the battle that unfolded below it.

Fief Domar, the protector of Galdrid's Pass, was under siege. The steel of armor and blade flashed in the blinding sunlight, screams and battle cries of man and horse alike mingling on the smoky breeze.

Louder than all the others was the mighty roar of the dragon. The light scales that had earned him the name Sandrunner stood out sharply against the lush greens of the Pass, making him an easy target. Still, the Cydran invaders could not fell him.

Sandrunner launched himself at a knot of red-clad soldiers, moving with a grace uncanny for a body easily the length of two warhorses. The dragon was just as dangerous on the ground as in the air, his claws striking at the knights like lightning.

Men tried to climb onto his back and slash at the vulnerable flaps of his wings; he rolled, crushing them into the churned dirt. They did not get up.

Once he had dispatched the remainder of the group, the dragon scanned the battlefield. The Guards of Domar were turning back the Cydran soldiers, but there was a small skirmish beyond the burning homes of those who had been caught unaware. Sandrunner loped toward them.

Something made him stop as he passed one of the blazes. A presence tugged at his mind, insistent. The battle forgotten, Sandrunner moved closer to the burning home. A moment later, a scream split the air; not the yell of a grown man, but the squall of a human child.

Without another thought, Sandrunner rose to his haunches. Reaching forward, he gripped the edges of the door and ripped it off its hinges. With the door gone, there was enough space to fit his head through.

The fire that had begun on the roof was creeping down to the floor; already the pallet in the corner was alight with tongues of flame.

A woman lay in the center of the one room home; Sandrunner nudged her body, but there was no response. His senses told him that she was already in the next world; it was not the woman that had screamed. It was a moment before he caught sight of the two babes huddled close to her body, wailing piteously. Reaching forward with a paw, he gently scooped them into his arms, wincing as they screamed even louder at his touch.

He was about to pull out of the house when another tug at his mind stopped him. A soft pattering drew his attention past the dead woman, toward the back of the room. Another child drew toward him, staring intently. She could not have seen more than four seasons, but already brown locks framed her hazel eyes. No tears clouded them; she was not afraid of him. Nor did she fear the fire that raged around her in fury. She crawled forward until she was close enough to touch the stunned dragon. Reaching out with a small, pink hand, she laid her fingers upon Sandrunner's nose.

"Dwagon," she said quietly, reverently, as if it was a beloved maxim. "Dwagon."

The beams above them shuddered and groaned, sending a shower of sparks to the ground. Sandrunner gently took hold of her, pulling out of the house. The moment he was clear, it collapsed into a pile of burning timber. Sandrunner quickly recited a prayer to Stormhunter, the dragon god.

Throughout the remainder of the battle, the dragon guarded the three babes like they were his own brood of precious eggs. The Cydran that dared to come close met their end with a strike from his claws. The two children that he had first rescued continued to wail. They were males, but the female did not sob or weep. She, if anything, was comforting the other two, holding them in a small but strong embrace.

Gradually, the Cydran soldiers surrounded the dragon, seeing that he was unwilling to move from his position. Sandrunner snarled and snapped with his jaws, but the soldiers backed out of range, continuing to harass him with spears.

Pain pierced his shoulder, tearing a roar from his throat. He spared a moment to look at it; an arrow was buried deep into his scales. Usually they were strong enough to protect him, but at this range…

"Domar!" A warhorse plowed into the ring of Cydran soldiers, the rider on his back striking the mob with his broadsword. Distracted, the soldiers swarmed on the rider. A Cydran knight tore him from the saddle. A strike from Sandrunner's good paw sent the knight flying.

The rider leapt to his feet, fighting his way to Sandrunner's side. "Why aren't you moving?" he asked as he parried a blow.

Because Sandrunner's dragon tongue could not form the words of the human dialect, he used his telepathic mind-speech. Only the flicker of the rider's eyes in his direction confirmed that the man 'heard' the dragon's voice within his mind.—*I found babes in one of the houses, three of them. I cannot move, or they will be exposed.*—

For a moment, the rider blanched, but he quickly returned his attention to the men in front of him.

Sandrunner could not accurately say how long they fought, pushing off wave after wave of Cydran soldiers. The sun was beginning to sink below the horizon when a horn call filled the air, a horn call of victory. The rider let out a cry of joy. "We turned them back! They're retreating!" He turned to the dragon. "I owe you my life."

Sandrunner shook his head slowly.—*It is I who is in debt. Had you not come, I would have been slain. I am Sandrunner.*—

The rider bowed. "I'm Flyn, a lieutenant in the Guard."

—*You are not a knight?*—

Flyn shook his head. Sandrunner nodded in respect.—*You fight like one.*— Minding that he didn't hurt the babes that were beneath him, the dragon stepped to the side.

Flyn paled when he saw the children. "Those are Bendain's triplets." He crouched down, looking closer at them.

—*You know their father?*—

"Yes." Grief clouded the young man's face. He wiped tears from his gray eyes. "I knew him very well. We are…were…friends since we were young children."

—*Were?*—

"A Cydran knight stabbed him in the back." The gray eyes smoldered in anger and bitter sadness. "They have no honor."

"Flyn!" shouted a feminine voice. A woman dressed in light battle gear ran toward them, slowing to a stop when she drew near. "Thank the gods you're alive. When I saw Bendain's body, I thought…"

Flyn shook his head. "No. I'm all right. This is Sandrunner," he gestured to the great dragon. "He found Bendain's triplets, Firmin, Kavan, and Selah." The names were spoken for Sandrunner's benefit alone—the humans seemed to know them well.

The girl was already crawling about, bending her head back so she could see all of Sandrunner. She was fascinated with the dragon.

The woman, who introduced herself as Beda, picked up the brown haired male. He quieted under her soothing touch. "What about Cassandra?"

Sandrunner bowed his head.—*There was the body of a woman next to the babes. I…could not drag her out. I do not know if this is the Cassandra you speak of.*—

"Which house?" Forgetting his wound, the dragon pointed to the pile of burning timber that had once been the home of the babes. His bleeding shoulder couldn't take the strain, and he collapsed, a muffled roar of pain slipping from his throat. His multiple wounds, so easily pushed aside in the face of crisis, had returned to his attention with a vengeance.

"Sandrunner?" asked the guard captain, kneeling beside the great beast. The girl child, braced against Flyn's hip, sucked on her fingers. Her eyes did not leave Sandrunner for a moment.

The dragon shook his head.—*I will be all right…we dragons bleed slowly.*—

Flyn came around to the front of Sandrunner so the dragon would not have to crane his neck to look at him. "We'll get one of our healers to look at your shoulder." Sandrunner attempted to place weight on his injured limb, wincing when his shoulder burned.

Selah began to whimper, gently stroking the dragon's face with her small hands. Her fingers, damp from being in her mouth, traced lopsided circles along his scales. "Dwagon…dwagon…"

Sandrunner looked at the human babe that comforted him. She was barely the size of his forearm, but there was a strange look of intelligence in her eyes that should not be present in one as young as she.

—*Guard this child well,*—the dragon told Flyn, touching a gentle claw to the babe.—*She will leave a great mark upon the world.*—

SELAH

Selah walked slowly down the hall, tracing the stones that made up the wall with a lazy finger. The bell rang again, reminding the inhabitants of fief Domar that dinner was served. The girl needed no further urging.

Firmin was already at the table. "What took you so long?" he asked as she slid into her seat. "Usually you're here before the bell even rings."

Selah ladled herself a bowl of stew. "I was thinking," she admitted, stirring her spoon absently.

Firmin looked at his sister oddly. Selah wasn't one to brood, and "I was thinking" was becoming more and more common as an excuse.

"Okay. Pass the pitcher."

Flyn came to the meal far after everyone else. The past eleven years had hardly changed the guard captain; less could be said for Beda, who was beginning to sport a few gray hairs in her black mane. The two had taken it upon themselves to raise Selah, Firmin, and Kavan; Selah loved them dearly, just as much as she would have if they were her real parents.

"Good evening, everyone," he said, pausing to ruffle Selah and Firmin's brown hair. "What's for dinner?"

"Stew," Firmin told him, still watching his sister curiously.

Selah's gaze lingered on the empty place at the table. Kavan had stopped eating with them years ago, joining the Lord and his Lady in the dining hall reserved for nobles after they had informally adopted him. A disdainful sneer was usually his only greeting to his siblings, although Kavan had several snide comments up his sleeve for Firmin. When he spoke to Selah, it was with a voice choked with hatred and scorn. Selah could not remember what she had done to him to deserve such loathing, but it had apparently scarred Kavan deeply.

Flyn poured himself water from the pitcher, unable to keep a broad grin off his face. "I've got some good news for you two."

Selah, broken from her reverie, looked up from her meal. "What?"

Flyn winked at Beda as if sharing a great joke. "Wingleader Averon and Sir Mendel should be here within the week."

Selah thought she should know the names, but they were only slightly familiar. "Who are they?"

Beda swallowed a mouthful of the meaty stew. "Mendel is the recruiter for the Knights of Alcaron. Averon you've met before…don't you remember? The summer equinox five years ago." Domar was a protector of Alcaron's northern border; Selah and Firmin had both seen their share of knights and dragonriders, but few with the rank of these two.

Selah searched her memory. "Is he tall?" Flyn nodded. "Dark hair?"

"He's grown a beard since you last saw him. It's Averon's job to find promising youths in the northern fiefs. He looks for boys, and girls," he amended, seeing Selah's frown, "to try to be Chosen by a dragon."

"They're coming here?"

"Averon's an old friend of mine. He always makes sure that Domar is on his list."

Selah almost leapt out of her seat in excitement. It was her dream to be a knight, and her childhood had been spent rescuing imaginary damsels in distress with her brother. "Firmin, you and I are going to be knights!"

She didn't see the look that passed between Beda and Flyn.

Firmin quickly finished the rest of his meal. "Beda, can we go and practice?" The woman nodded, staring at Flyn. Once the two were out of earshot, she spoke.

"You know Mendel doesn't allow girls. He'll never let her be a knight."

Flyn's face was forlorn. "I know. I just…I couldn't tell her when she was so happy. Not with the way she has been lately." Selah had been quiet and withdrawn for weeks. She had even confessed to him that sometimes she felt an aching emptiness in her heart that festered like a sore when there was nothing to distract her. "She hardly ever smiles anymore. I worry about her, Beda."

"She's bored, Flyn. Her dreams are too big to stay in Domar. Maybe training is what she needs. I know Averon will like her."

"He will. I don't worry a bit about Firmin. He's good enough to keep some of my guards on their toes. So is Selah. But even the dragonriders are reluctant to accept females into their ranks."

Beda rose, automatically clearing the bowls that Selah and Firmin had left behind. "You know her better than anyone else. She'll make it into the dragonriders, or the knights, gods willing. If she doesn't make it into knights, it might be a good thing for her to be on her own with the dragonriders. She's been inseparable from Firmin ever since..." Flyn frowned at a bad memory, and was reluctant to talk about it. Beda changed tacks and continued to console him. "We've sent boys with half her talent and they got in. So stop moping or I'll sign you up for kitchen duty."

Smiling, Flyn picked up his own bowl. "You're right. I just hope they don't wear themselves out."

Beda chuckled, shaking her head knowingly. "Oh, they will. In an hour they'll be back here, asking for seconds."

*   *   *   *

Averon of Northford had risen far too early that morning. The hours before dawn were not a time he was often up and about. Yawning, he made his way through the hallways of Dragonhold, nodding to fellow dragonriders he passed. By the time he reached the dragon dens, he was fully awake. Marching down the row of slumbering dragons, he reached one with blue scales and gave its tail a hard yank.

The dragon started, whipping the tail from Averon's grasp. The dragonrider laughed as his dragon, Farsight, glared at him.—*You know I hate that.*—

"That's exactly why I do it, Farsight. Now hurry up. Daylight waits for no dragon."

Farsight stretched, the tips of his outstretched wings brushing the ceiling of the dens.—*All right, all right. I am up.*—

By the time Averon had harnessed Farsight and led him out to the courtyard, Mendel was waiting for them. "It's about time," he muttered, hauling his pack onto a shoulder.

Averon looked at the horizon, where the sun was just beginning to peek over the far off mountains, and struggled to contain a sigh of exasperation. Sir Mendel was not one of his favorite people. Farsight muttered something to himself aloud, only the gentle rumbling and slightest twitch of his muscular tail revealing his dislike for the knight.

"What did the beast say?"

Averon laid a restraining hand on Farsight's neck as the dragon growled softly. "It's nothing," he said nonchalantly. "Farsight just hates going on a long flight without a meal first."

The remark had its desired effect, and Mendel looked considerably more uncomfortable. Farsight sent Averon a mischievously glance, licking his jaws meaningfully. Mendel began to rub the back of his neck. "Well, let's, let's be off then. It's a good four day flight to Domar." The two men climbed onto the back of the dragon, Averon taking the front seat.

—*We have far too much fun,*—Farsight told him privately.

Patting the dragon fondly in reply, Averon made sure that the straps that secured him to the saddle were pulled tight as Farsight began to pump his great wings. They lifted into the air, flying ahead of the rising sun.

*   *   *   *

Four days later, Farsight glided into the inner fief of Domar, the sun already high in the sky. The guards rushed forward to unsnap the packs from Farsight's harness. Averon leapt from the saddle with ease, leaving Mendel fumbling with ties that had been pulled a little too tight.

Flyn greeted him with a firm handshake and a warm smile. "It's been a while, Averon. Has it been two years?"

Averon smiled, pulling off his riding gloves. "Too long, Flyn. Got any good ones this year? Bendain's children should be of age now." Averon could trust his old friend to be honest with him.

"The triplets just turned twelve. Only two, Selah and Firmin, are going to try out. The other wants to be a mage; Kavan, don't you remember?"

Averon nodded, raising his eyebrows in recognition to Flyn's words. To be a mage, a wizard with the power to conjure forces with a murmured incantation, was no small dream. "Didn't he move in with the Lord and Lady?"

Flyn sighed. "Four years ago, I think. He's impossible." He looked at Averon's intent face and smiled. "I'm rambling, aren't I? Sorry. Most of the lads wouldn't leave the fief if you paid them a cartload of gold pieces, although many say they want nothing more than to be a knight or a dragonrider. Not much of what you're looking for, though. Most of our best boys you took last recruit." The guard captain eyed the struggling knight, still atop a chuckling Farsight. "I see you and Mendel are continuing to get along well."

"Like brothers." Averon returned his attention on his friend. "I would like to start as soon as possible, if that is all right by you. I find it's easy if the youngsters have a while to say goodbye to everyone."

"I'll get them," said Flyn, nodding to the guardsman stationed next to the bell tower. The guard pulled the rope, sending a sonorous ring throughout the fief. Within minutes, all the interested children of age had arranged themselves in a line.

It was not hard to find Flyn's foster children among the group; for one thing, they were taller than all the others. The boy was stockier than his sister; she had more of a slender build that gracefully suggested her strength. She was dressed in an outfit of tunic and breeches, her hair tied back in a simple ponytail. Her hazel eyes regarded him intently for a moment before dropping to the ground; out of respect or shyness, Averon could not tell.

Smiling to himself, he launched into his speech. "You have been called to here to attempt to become a knight or a dragonrider. Neither path is easy. You must face two years as a page then four years as a squire before you are knighted. A dragonrider must be Chosen by a dragon and spend two years as a pallon and four as an apprentice. Those who no longer wish to do this may leave at any time; I will not hold it against you. The life of a warrior is not for everyone."

None moved. Averon sighed, knowing that more than half of the twenty youths standing in front of him would have their hearts broken today. "Very well. Let's begin."

He split the group into two. The first half went and rode horses for half an hour, demonstrating their mastery of simple horsemanship. The second group went for ride with Farsight; those afraid of heights could not hope to be a dragonrider. Most came back a little pale, but the girl, Selah, had only excitement in her eyes after the brief flight.—*She was not afraid, not once.*—Farsight reported. He frowned.—*In fact...I think she even liked it.*—

Selah was not nearly as comfortable on horses. The girl held the reins with an iron grip, unable to trust the beast that was prancing beneath her. Mendel marked down something that looked remarkably like an X on his paper.

There was little else to measure—if a youth wished to be a warrior, they would receive most of their training at a respective fief. Each was asked to handle a small dagger—those that seemed comfortable with the proximity of razor sharp metal were given a nod of approval. Simple archery was tested—both of Flyn's charges performed well.

The last test was one of Averon's favorites. He favored a broadsword for his close range weapon, and one by one, asked the would-be pages and pallons to lift his blade.

A boy named Otto went first. Averon's blade was made for battle, not beauty, and had the weight to reflect it. After a brief struggle, Otto managed to get it into the air. He looked at Averon and smiled.

Averon returned the grin, although his reasons for smiling differed from the boy's. "Now hold it there. Lower—so that your arms are parallel with the ground."

Otto blanched but obeyed. Averon leaned against the wall and said nothing. After thirty seconds, Otto lowered the point of the sword to the ground. Averon winced when his broadsword grated against cobblestones. He took the blade back. "Thank you for your effort, Otto. Try again next year, if you wish." Otto, hearing the dismissal and rejection in the dragonrider's voice, fled in shame.

Selah was several after Otto. She too had difficulty raising the blade into the air but was successful and looked to Averon for further instruction.

"Hold it there."

The girl did not reply. Silence surrounded them, and Selah focused all of her attention on the sword that she had to hold up. It was magnificent despite being devoid of the intricate carvings that forgers often used to decorate their creations. The wire-bound hilt was easily to grip, and the interesting texture it created seemed to bring Selah closer to reality. She realized, quite suddenly, that she held the power to take away life within her hands.

Her arms were beginning to burn with exertion—how much time had passed? Averon observed her intently, his facial expressions hinting that he was making mental notes for future reference.

After what seemed like an eternity, her arms began to shake with strain. Averon left his leaning position and took the sword from her. "Well done. Selah, isn't it?" The girl nodded, her shoulders aching even without the weight of the blade. Averon nodded in respect. "That was certainly long enough. Well done," he repeated.

Averon asked her what path she would take, knight or dragonrider. She looked him directly in the eye. "I would like to be a knight." There was a slightly apologetic manner in her voice, but it was clear that her mind was made up. Averon sighed only when she had gone to speak with Mendel. She had shown such promise.

Mendel's laughter split the warm, summer air. "You must be joking!" Selah was standing before him, a look of hurt filling her eyes. "Girls can't be knights! I doubt you could even *lift* a lance, providing you managed to get on the horse. No, I think your brother is much better suited toward the life of the sword. Let go of this foolish dream before you hurt yourself."

"I…" the girl angrily wiped away the tears that were beginning to form in her eyes. "You…"

"Please inform your brother that I would like to speak to him. He needs to provide a horse for a ride home; the dragon cannot carry them to Fief Chivalry," Mendel turned away from her, returning his attention to the gelding he was inspecting for his own mount.

Selah couldn't suppress the choked sob that burst from her throat. Running blindly away from the knight, the girl fled for the inner fief, a single tear sliding down her cheek.

Averon looked at Farsight, his eyes relaying an unspoken request. Rising, the dragon followed Selah. She headed past the barracks, suddenly slowing to a stop. Farsight's keen ears could pick up snatches of conversation that emitted from the small alleyway created by the barracks and stone wall next to it.

"Don't, Kavan…please…"

"We didn't mean it…"

Selah marched into the alleyway, her hands clenched at her sides. As silently as he could, Farsight peered his head around the corner.

Two younger boys were backed up against the wall. A third boy, faintly resembling Selah, stood before them, his jaw clenched so rigidly the muscles along his face were visible against the sun kissed tan of his skin. His hair was black and thick as underbrush, nearly hiding his sea green eyes. His irises, circular pools of the ocean, were as hard as a coastal storm in the throes of winter as he considered his younger adversaries. Curled about his hands were tongues of flame, flickering about menacingly. Farsight's nose wrinkled as he sensed the faint aroma of the boy's magic.

A startled anger was receding from Kavan's eyes rapidly as a tide change, to be replaced with relieved superiority as he realized he had the upper hand in the situation. "I told you not to bother me while I was meditating. I *told* you to…" he reconsidered his words, his voice returning as he caught up with his thoughts. "Leave me alone, or I'll…do magic on you!" The boy feinted with his flaming hands, his face relaxing as the other two pressed as close to the curtain wall as the stone would allow.

Selah reached forward and grabbed Kavan by the back of his tunic, spinning him around with a rough jerk of her wrist. "What do you think you're doing?"

Her hazel eyes were hard as steel, only a faint mistiness betraying the hurt Mendel's words had inflicted upon her.

Selah was taller than Kavan, but the affronted glint in his eyes seemed to make him larger than his body. "My business is my own; it's not your concern." His voice was dark and full, with the eloquence of one who read often. "Go back and play with your little weapons."

Selah, used to the usual scorn that filled his voice, refused to back down. "Leave them alone, Kavan." She and Firmin generally policed Kavan's actions, but it seemed that she was on her own for now.

"Right, sister. Just because you say so, I will return to my room until Flyn gives me permission to come out." His words were saturated in sarcasm. The anger flooded back into his eyes. "Don't take it out on me just because you failed in your tests. Don't think I don't know," he said as Selah opened her mouth to protest, "the tears on your cheeks give it away."

Selah stepped forward in anger, raising her fists in a universal threat that was easy to understand. Kavan's eyes widened in fear for a moment, and the flames around his hands burned brighter. "Touch me and I'll burn you."

Selah was unfazed. "Come on, Kavan. It's nothing but a few strands of light magic. Did you think that I wouldn't know what you can and can't do?"

The two other boys, forgotten now, snuck around the pair, dashing away as soon as they were clear of the barracks. Kavan flushed in anger. "So what if it is, sister? I can still control it."

Farsight noted with interest that the term of endearment, "sister", had become a veiled insult—Kavan had yet to address Selah by her birth name.

"Unless you want to light a room or make an illusion, it's useless."

"Fight me, then," Kavan snarled. His words trembled, and not from the voice fluctuations that plagued boys of his age. "Do you really think that brute strength can beat magic?"

Selah dismissed her brother's aggressive stance with an unimpressed sigh. "I don't have time for this." Selah turned and caught sight of Farsight. She paused for a moment, surprised by the dragon's presence.

"Selah!"

"What, Kavan?" As the girl faced her brother, searing light shot from his hands, illuminating the dark alleyway. Selah shut her eyes quickly, but the damage was done. Farsight started forward, but stopped himself. He wanted to see how the girl reacted.

"Useless?" The boy expertly trained a beam of pure light on his sister's face, preventing her from opening her eyes. His hands were aglow with bright magic.

"Don't open your eyes or I'll blind you." His voice was cold and harsh—he had controlled the tremble that had plagued his words just moments before.

Selah winced, lashing out with her fist wildly. He dodged it. "Don't you see Selah?" His words were cruel—there was more than just a simple argument here. The rivalry between brother and sister had been a full-scale vendetta for some time. "You'll never be a warrior. You'll get married to some wall guard and amount to nothing more than a wife and housecleaner." The words shot from his mouth like needled barbs—a harsh tongue, it seemed, was the only weapon in which he was superior to his sibling. "You're nothing, Selah. Nothing." Slowly, he withdrew his palm. "Nothing," he repeated, his voice a mere whisper. Farsight wondered if he was trying to convince himself of the truth in his own words.

Selah felt her cheeks grow red with rage. Something stirred within her, sending a tingling sensation racing through her veins. Opening her eyes, the girl lashed out.

Kavan's face snapped to the side with a sharp *crack* as Selah's hand struck his cheek. Blood began to well in three deep cuts on his face. He touched his cheek and stared at the red liquid on his fingers.

Selah glanced down at her hand, shocked that she had drawn blood. For a moment, there almost seemed to be a golden sheen to her skin; her nails shone silver. The girl pulled her hand out of the sunlight, and it was gone.

Kavan's eyes were burning in hatred, one hand pressed to his wounded cheek. "Why?" he demanded. "Why do you take everything from me?"

Selah said nothing, her chest heaving as she tried to control her anger. He riled her more than anything in the world. Then she saw red blood flow from between Kavan's fingers; the cuts were far deeper than she had thought.

"Sorry, Kavan. I...didn't mean to." Even as she spoke the words, she knew they were a lie. Her apology was for the benefit of the dragon that was watching them.

"Yes, you did." His eyes were cold. "Yes, you did." Kavan shouldered past her, ignoring Farsight. He looked back at her one more time, hatred written all over his features. Selah felt the blood drain from her face. The boy turned away, disappearing around the corner.

—*Why did you scratch him?*—demanded the dragon. He was not impressed; scratching, like biting, was a low form of fighting for humans.

Selah looked down at her hands. She felt sick to her stomach; Kavan's blood was under her fingernails. "I didn't mean to," she said, hanging her head in shame. She wanted to be a warrior, and all she could do was fight like a common animal.

Words of reprimand perched on the tip of the dragon's tongue, but he reminded himself that the girl was only a child. Humans not connected to dragons such as himself, especially younger ones, were often prone to rash actions.—*It is all right. I believe the scratches are not that bad. You should, however, work on your technique.*—Farsight was regretting the harshness of his words as the girl seemed to cower under his massive size and disapproval.—*My name is Farsight. You are Selah, correct?*—She nodded.—*Tell me about yourself.*—

"Me?" The girl was surprised. "Why?"

—*I am interested.*—It wasn't a lie—while the girl had proved herself worthy of dragonrider training through her skill with weapons, Farsight wanted to catch a hint of her personality. A dragonrider's heart was much stronger than his sword.

"Well, I've never been very far from home...I've stayed at Domar for my whole life. My real parents died when I was very young. Domar was under siege by a Cydran army...I would've died too, if Sandrunner hadn't saved us."

—*Sandrunner?*—

"A dragon. Somehow, he managed to figure out where Kavan, Firmin, and I were, and got us out of the house before it burnt to the ground. Flyn and Beda adopted us, and they've been good parents."

—*I am sorry. Do you remember much of them?*—

"My parents? Not really." The color was beginning to return to her cheeks. "I know that my father had a great, deep voice, but I don't remember my mother at all. I remember that day, though. There was a lot of yelling, and burning...then Sandrunner saved us, protected us."

—*You speak of him fondly.*—

"I like dragons."

—*Why?*—

The girl paused, glancing from side to side furtively, as if about to reveal a great secret that was not intended for other ears. "I...feel better, around them. Sometimes I feel as if there is this great empty part of me, like half of me is missing. I've asked Firmin about it, but he just laughed and told me it was my stomach." She smiled a little. "Around dragons...it doesn't hurt so much."

—*I am glad I can help. Perhaps...*—Farsight trailed off, unsure of whether it was his place to voice what he was thinking.

"Perhaps what?"

—*Many future dragonriders display the same feeling of loneliness, although not as strong as you describe. Perhaps this means that you are searching for a dragonet to be your Chosen.*—

"Maybe." The girl looked thoughtful. "I've never told anyone that...dragons making me feel better."

—*Thank you.*—

"Do you think I could be a dragonrider?"

—*Yes,*—said Farsight.—*However, it is not my opinion that matters. It is yours. Do you think that you could be a dragonrider?*—

"I think so."

—*Then you should talk to Averon. My Rider would be more than happy to tell you everything about being a dragonrider. It is not something you should do on a whim, though. Training takes discipline that is not required here in Domar. But, unlike the Knights, we dragonriders do not discriminate based on gender.*—Farsight looked her straight in the eyes.—*There is, too, the chance that you will not be Chosen by a dragon. You must be prepared for that.*—

Selah nodded. "Yes. I've been disappointed before." No other words were needed as she looked over to the courtyard, where Mendel was still examining the horse. Her eyes narrowed once—so quickly, the man who she wanted to impress desperately had become a hated enemy. "I'll need a night to think it over. Is that all right?"

Farsight, still thoughtful from the previous incident with her brother, was impressed by the girl's maturity in asking for more time.—*A decision such as this should not be rushed. Averon and I can stay for three days at the most, as Mendel will not be flying back with us. Take your time.*—

Selah peered out of the alleyway. "I better go back before Flyn starts looking for me." She looked back at the dragon, a slight smile lifting her lips. "Thank you."

—*For what?*—

"For listening to me." The girl disappeared around the corner. Farsight trotted toward the place where he had left Averon, interested in both her cryptic words of farewell and the events he had witnessed. He and his Rider had much to discuss.

*　　*　　*　　*

Mendel, loath to stay any longer in Domar, was quick to make excuses for a speedy departure. "The Knights expect new pages within a fortnight. It has already been four days since I was sent—we should head out soon."

Averon raised an eyebrow wryly. By now, he was aware of Mendel's true motivation for leaving. The Knight-Recruit bristled. "Besides, if we make it to Ranvaile by nightfall, I can start instructing the boys on the requirements of a page. They would be too distracted here."

Averon knew it was pointless to argue, so he didn't. As Captain of the Guard, Flyn had been informed that the youths might have to leave on a moment's notice. They had been instructed to have their possessions gathered by the time the dragonrider and knight arrived. If Mendel was determined to depart as soon as possible, so be it.

Mendel had purchased one of the horses, while each of the soon to be pages received a sturdy highland pony as their mount. The pages would be staying at Chivalry for the next two years at least—Domar could not afford to send away good warhorses that would not be returned each time boys were selected by the knights. Firmin lost the battle to keep the joy of his face and grinned cheerfully, despite the downcast features of his sister. Selah still felt the sting of Mendel's rebuke and hung in the shadows as the man mounted up.

As Firmin mounted the stocky bay he was to ride, Selah thought it time to give him the gift. She thrust strips of leather into his hands. "What are these?" he asked incredulously.

"Wrist bracers," Selah explained. They had taken her several days, both to make them and to convince the tanner to let her have good leather. "You put them on your wrists…see, they lace up here," she pointed, "so you don't sprain anything."

"Thanks," said Firmin. He looked about awkwardly—it was obvious that he had nothing for her.

Selah tried to ignore the hurt that was growing to be a constant companion as Firmin searched his pack for a quick present. "Here," he said hurriedly, tossing a square of cloth to her, "my emblem, fair lady."

It was a handkerchief. Selah held it up by one corner, hoping it was fresh. "A handkerchief?" she asked.

Firmin nodded, a lopsided grin adorning his face. "Keep it close to your heart, lest I fall in battle." His tone was humorous.

Selah's was not. "You blew your nose into this!"

"Which should make it all the more dear to you, Selah." Firmin smiled. Selah returned the gesture but did not having any feeling in it.

Mendel signaled that it was time to move out. "Bye, Selah." He kicked his pony forward, pausing only to shake Flyn's hand and receive a hug from Beda.

As she watched the procession of new pages and Knight-Recruit pass beyond the gates of Domar, Selah wished she could follow. She had never felt so alone in her life.

*   *   *   *

Selah was very late to dinner. The meal had already been served by the time she arrived, a thoughtful look on her face.

Averon, seated across from Flyn, did not press her on for a decision. She would tell them when she was ready.

Midway through the meal, Selah set down her fork and looked her guardians straight in the eye. "I've decided that I would like to be a dragonrider."

Averon covered a sigh of relief with his hand. "Good."

Flyn did not ask the girl if she was sure of her decision. He trusted Selah to be thoughtful in a choice that would shape her future.

Beda was not as confident. "Are you sure, Selah? This is a great part of your life we are taking about."

The girl nodded. There was no hesitation in her eyes, no flicker of uncertainty. "I'm sure. This is something I want to do."

Averon swallowed a bite of venison. "There is the chance that you will not be Chosen by a dragonet. That's a baby dragon," he added when he saw Selah's look of confusion. "There is no guarantee of success."

"I know. Farsight told me."

Selah looked at the empty seat at the table. Without her triplet, Selah felt lost and alone. *You should be used to it by now,* the girl told herself. *Not even Firmin can make me feel whole.* She glanced once to the high table, where Kavan sat next to the Lord and Lady as if they had brought him into the world. One side of his face was swathed in bandages. Selah huffed softly—he would bring her no comfort.

"Well, if it's all right with you, Selah, I would like to leave tomorrow morning." Averon was looking at her curiously.

The girl nodded.

*   *   *   *

The next morning, Selah was already in the courtyard when Farsight and Averon arrived. The man chuckled. "Did you sleep at all?"

Selah shook her head. "I...had a lot on my mind."

A sudden thought struck Averon. "Do you have a flight jacket?"

"No. I've never been on a long flight before, so I never needed one."

"That's all right. I brought several extras, although you'll have to get one tailored to your size at Dragonhold."

"Dragonhold?" Selah had heard Flyn mention it before.

Averon smiled. "The fief of dragonriders. That's where most of your training will take place."

Selah began to tie her packs to the harness. Averon noted with a small measure of satisfaction that she knew several dragonrider knots and was making good use of them. As well, she had packed lightly. Averon appreciated the courtesy toward Farsight.

"What?" he asked. Selah had said something.

"I asked you what it was like, Dragonhold. I've only been to another fief once." She took the flight jacket that he offered her.

Averon smiled. "Well, you can see it from miles away—the walls are whitewashed every five years. There's always at least a thousand dragons stationed there. The hallways are large so that if the dragons need to come into the inner fief, they can, although they prefer to be outside."

Selah tried on the flight jacket. "What's the training like?" She struggled with the sinew ties that kept the jacket impenetrable to the heavy top winds—Averon helped her secure them so that the jacket could fit her as best it could, being several sizes too large.

"Hard. For the first few weeks, you'll go to sleep sore and wake up sore. Once you get past that, it's challenging but extremely beneficial."

By this time, Farsight was all ready to go, Selah was suited up, and the sun was beginning to clear the Ryshea Mountains.

Averon pretended not to notice the tears that were glistening Selah's eyes. The girl kissed Beda on the cheek, listening for a moment as the woman whispered in her ear. Selah held Flyn's embrace for a long time.

"Don't forget to write." Selah felt a drop of wetness hit her cheek and slide down. Flyn was crying. Seeing the man that had always been a tower of strength giving into his emotions only made her own grief that much more acute.

"I won't," she assured. "I'll come back in the summer."

Flyn held her a moment longer and then pushed her gently forward. "Go on. The dragon's waiting."

Selah froze, the words stirring a chord deep inside her. It was like she had caught sight of something important only to miss it. Then Flyn nudged her again, taking her stillness for reluctance, and the spell was broken.

Selah mounted Farsight, feeling the sharp emptiness inside of her heart again. Turning in the saddle, she took one last look at the fief that she had called home for all of her life. Farsight flapped his wings, lifting into the sky.

Selah turned away, facing southwest and the future that lay there. The wind tore the last tears from her eyes, the drops falling to rest on the stones of Fief Domar.

$$* \qquad * \qquad * \qquad *$$

The ground moved beneath them like a stream as Farsight flew. Selah could not take her eyes from the land below them. It would have taken days on horseback to travel as far as they had in several hours. She didn't mind the heights; it was a little frightening, but she trusted Averon and Farsight.

"Put your arms around my waist," the dragonrider advised. "We're about to go into rough wind."

Selah obeyed, glad for the warm flight jacket that kept her comfortable even at this altitude. "How do you know?"

"Dragonmagic is connected to the wind. Farsight can read wind currents better than most dragons."

Selah suddenly tightened her grip, bracing herself. Averon looked back. They hadn't even hit the roughs yet. Was she...

A great buffet of wind slammed into them from the side. Farsight, startled, dropped several feet of altitude before recovering his flight. Averon rocked to the side, the ties that held him in the saddle cutting into his waist. Selah quickly reached out and pulled him upright.

—*I did not sense that one,*—explained Farsight apologetically.—*I was too focused on the roughs in front of us.*—

"It's all right," said Averon, checking the saddle ties. "Let's fly low for a while. That was a strong crosswind."

—*I agree.*—

Averon turned back to Selah. "Thank you."

"For what?"

"Pulling me up and not losing your head."

Selah was a bit bemused by the compliment. "Um...you're welcome."

The rest of the day was passed in comfortable silence. Selah never tired of looking at the land they flew over, and no words were needed between Farsight and Averon.

The sun was beginning to sink lower on the horizon when Averon spoke. "That clearing looks good."

—The one by the river?—

"Right."

They landed quickly in the small clearing. Averon looked around intently before dismounting. Selah followed, and had to clutch Farsight's side as the feeling returned to her legs. The saddle had been comfortable, considering, but her whole body ached from sitting for so long.

Averon chuckled when he saw her. He had no problem. "Walk around a little bit. It helps if you move your legs around during the flight to keep them limber."

Selah looked at Farsight, who made no move to remove his tack. "Are we taking off your harness?"

—It takes too long to put it on in the morning. Besides, it is not that uncomfortable. Will you be all right?—

Selah nodded quickly, standing away from Farsight's side. Folding back his wings, the dragon got a drink from the river, the water sloshing as it entered his great belly.

Averon handed Selah her bow and a quiver of arrows. "We do camp work in shifts. I'll set up camp if you catch something for dinner. Don't get lost."

Hooking the quiver so that it hung at her hip, the girl strung the bow with a practiced air. Nocking an arrow, she set out into the forest, moving quietly.

By the time that Averon had completely set up camp and had a fire going, Selah returned, holding two dead rabbits by the feet. "Will this be enough?" she asked. "I wasn't sure how much Farsight would eat."

Averon smiled. Selah was probably unaware that she had passed one of his personal tests. "Thank you. Farsight ate before we left Domar, but I am sure he would appreciate a snack."

Farsight was eyeing the rabbit with interest. Once Averon had skinned and cooked them, he handed Farsight one. It was gone in a single bite.

Selah didn't mind not having any plates or utensils. She was glad, too, when Averon didn't seem to care that she licked the last juices off her fingers.

She had liked Averon when she first met him, and over the next several days of traveling, she only admired him more. "When Farsight was still a dragonet, there was a big state dinner; several Lords came with their wives. Farsight took one look at the roast boar, and dove at it. I was talking to a…er…lady, and I didn't notice. By the time I figured out where he was, half of the boar was gone and Farsight was moaning because he had gorged himself so badly." Selah laughed, both from mental picture the story had created and the actual look of embarrassment on the great dragon's face.

Selah woke late the third morning, weary from the flight the day before. Rolling over, she stopped, ignoring the sharp twig that dug into her shoulder through the bedroll.

Averon and Farsight were standing beside the river in silence. One hand on the dragon's back, the man was watching the sun clear the horizon. Selah felt as through she was intruding on a private moment between the dragon and his Rider. She couldn't tear her eyes from the pair.

They did nothing, and yet the love between them was obvious. Startled, Selah realized she had seen it earlier and had not realized it; Averon scratching the small of Farsight's back, the dragon reaching out his wing to shield his Rider from a quick shower of rain. It was almost as if Averon and Farsight were extensions of each other, one shared soul in two bodies.

Selah looked away, swallowing the sadness that choked her. She had no one to stand beside a river with. Maybe Farsight was right; perhaps her empty heart could be filled by a dragonet.

*   *   *   *

It was the middle of the fourth day when Averon pointed to a white gleam on the horizon. "There's Dragonhold!" he shouted over the wind.

As they came closer, Selah's jaw dropped in awe. Domar was, proportional to other fiefs, fairly large. It was nothing compared to this.

Dragonhold was perched at the top of a large cliff, far enough away that it wasn't dangerous for inhabitants but close enough that the natural rock formation provided protection against attack. The cliff overlooked a large plain that was spotted with trees and knolls. Behind Dragonhold rose a great forest that covered the southern landscape in a blanket of firs and cedars. Beyond and above the trees loomed the imposing figures of the Three Watchers, a clustered trio of mountains that could be seen from all directions.

Even as the girl watched, a Wing of dragons flew from the battlements of Dragonhold, wheeling in a circle until they were heading west. Farsight bugled a greeting to them; the leader roared back in acknowledgment. The whitewashed walls glinted in the sunlight like marble, giving the effect that the entire fief had been cut from one block of stone. A red flag flapped from each of the four towers.

Farsight craned back his head to look at her. His sea-green eyes twinkled with a smile.—**Welcome to Dragonhold.**—

DRAGONHOLD

Farsight glided down toward the fief. He seemed to sense Selah's curiosity and slowed his flight, allowing her to gaze in wonder at the whitewashed walls of Dragonhold. The girl's eyes were wide with awe and excitement.

Smooth metal spikes as tall as a man protruded from the battlements like jagged fingers. It took several moments for Selah to realize that they were to keep enemy dragons from landing on the walls. Guards patrolled back and forth ceaselessly, some manning machines that resembled giant crossbows.

"Those are ballistas." Averon had followed her gaze. "It takes more than a normal arrow to take down a dragon."

Once Farsight had identified himself with the guards, he was permitted to land. Selah's stomach lurched as they dropped, and she took the rough pull in her hand to steady herself as Farsight landed. Averon untied himself with a practiced air and slid down from the saddle. Selah lingered on the dragon's back, looking around. The newfound confidence of being accepted as a pallon had fled at the sight of the dragonriders around her. Many had stopped to gaze at her in interest, and it was difficult to look them in the eye.

—*It will be all right,*—reassured Farsight. His eyes shone with encouragement.

—*You belong here. Let us go.*—

The girl smiled at him as she struggled down from the saddle and grabbed a few of her bags. "Thanks."

"Wingleader Averon!" A voice cut across the comfortable serenity of the courtyard and grated against Selah's ears. A man dressed in the colors of Fief Lord was approaching them rapidly, his frame rigid with indignation. "Where have you been?"

Selah was the only one close enough to see Averon's jaw tighten briefly before he turned to address the Lord. "I was at Domar, Holdleader." He looked at Selah meaningfully, his eyes a silent order to behave. "I thought you have been informed of my absence."

"Of course," snapped the Lord. His brown hair, typical for the regions, was worn long in the fashion of nobles. His tunic and breeches were obviously working clothes, but they were of a fine make that made Selah self-conscious of her own attire. "I *was* the one who sent you out to recruit in the first place. I did not order to take your sweet time on the way back. You have a patrol in two days, and your dragon hasn't even fed yet."

"Farsight ate some on the way," Selah argued and flushed as the Holdleader's black eyes turned on her. She had forgotten where she was. At Domar, she had not been required to show excessive respect to anyone save the Lord and Lady and was always allowed to speak her mind.

The Holdleader's cheek twitched in agitation. "I beg your pardon." His tone was mocking, and Selah blushed a deep shade of red. "And who are you, to know so much about the amount of a dragon requires before a long flight?"

"Selah of Domar, sir." The girl bowed from the waist like a boy would; her tunic and breeches, as well as the bags she held in both arms, would have made a curtsy look ridiculous. The man snorted, seeming to notice her violation of custom.

Averon bowed quickly to him, taking one of Selah's bags with a second warning glance. "I need to show Selah her rooms. If you don't mind, I'll come back and speak with you about that patrol in a quarter of an hour."

The Holdleader sighed. "Very well. Meet me in my office."

Once they had entered the fief and were out of the earshot of the man, Averon laid a hand on Selah's shoulder to slow her pace. "You must be very careful around Sean, Selah."

Selah hoisted her pack to a better position under her arm. "Who's Sean? The man you talked to?"

Averon nodded. "He is the Holdleader, our equivalent of a fief Lord. He has higher rank than everyone else here. Everyone," he added for emphasis when he saw Selah's gaze wander to the tapestries that adorned the Great Hall they stood in. The girl returned her attention to his face with difficulty.

It was a challenge not to be distracted. The main entrance of Dragonhold was as grand as the outside. The wide hall was large enough for several dragons standing abreast to enter without too much trouble. Smooth panels of interlocking stone made up the floor, and even the hard claws of countless dragonkind generations had not been able to scratch it. The air was clean and fresh, free of the pungent wood smoke generally created by torches. Rather, light came from chunks of glowing crystal that had been placed in brass niches. As a result, the hall was brighter and far more pleasant.

"Selah! Selah, are you listening to me?" A slight hint of annoyance was beginning to creep into Averon voice.

The girl jumped. "Sorry. I was looking at the Hall."

Averon glanced at their surroundings. "Yes, it is very nice. The rest of the fief tends to be a bit more practical, but Dragonhold was built during the Golden Era. Not many places really match up to it."

He continued down the hall, Selah hurrying to catch up with him. The girl's interest was perked. "What's the Golden Era? I've never heard of it."

Averon shook his head with a smile. "To tell you everything about it would take weeks. Basically, it was the time of heroes like Gonran and Stormhunter and Alihan the Great…you know, heroes that ended up being gods. The world was literally saturated with magic and kings built things like this," he gestured to the grandness around them, "on a whim."

"Oh." They walked onward in silence; Selah was too busily staring at Dragonhold to ask any more questions. True to Averon's word, the section of the fief he led her through wasn't nearly as impressive as the Great Hall, but it retained a measure of its splendor. No hallway was without a tapestry or wall carving, most displaying some sort of fire spewing dragon, just as no room was without the reassuring light of a crystal cluster.

Averon stopped at a large chamber that was filled with mahogany tables and chairs. The walls were lined with shelves of books, and an unlit fireplace completely took up one corner. "The common room," Averon explained. "This is where you'll do all of your coursework and such. That's what all the books are for."

Selah eyed the shelves skeptically; the words "coursework" and "books" had filled the girl with apprehension. "Averon," she started uneasily, "when you say—"

"Was your room on the east or the west wing?" he muttered. The dragonrider was preoccupied with his own thoughts and hadn't heard her. Selah didn't press him.

After a few moments, Averon made up his mind and led her down the east half of the two hallways branching off from the common room. Selah, by this time, was completely lost. This corridor was filled with doors. Most were closed;

the girl could hear sounds of conversation emanating from the open ones. It took Selah a second to realize that these were the pallons' rooms.

The girl jumped at a sharp rap; Averon had knocked on one of the rooms. "Just a minute," called a voice from inside. There were several noises of things being shuffled around, as well as a bump and a sharp yelp. The door opened, and a boy about Selah's age peered out at them.

He was tall and lanky, an inch or two taller than Selah. The boy had a pleasant face and wore his dark brown hair short. From first glances he appeared ordinary enough, but a look into his eyes made Selah reconsider. His eyes were the color of emeralds and shined with the gem's intensity and luster. They were dancing with intelligence and curiosity.

The pallon raised his eyebrows in slight bemusement. "Hello. Can I help you?" His voice was as rich as his eyes, an eloquent pitch that hadn't begun to crack with age yet.

"Um...I...uh..." She looked at the dragonrider beside her for help.

Averon spared her the difficulty of having to think of something to say by greeting the pallon with a grin. "Hello, Landon. This is Selah. She's one of the new pallons; we just got in a half hour ago. I know you're busy, but would you mind showing her around for a few days, until she gets her bearings? I'd do it myself, but I have a sweep flight in two days and I need to take Farsight hunting. Would it be too much trouble?"

Landon shook his head. "I wouldn't mind showing you around for a few days." Selah smiled, grateful that he had addressed her rather than Averon. The boy's eyes twinkled with humor. "I'll protect you from all the evildoers."

With Firmin, Selah would have retorted with a jesting comment. Instead, Selah struggled to keep a red tinge from coming to her cheeks and thanked him softly.

"Selah is in the third to last room at the end of the hall." Averon placed a comforting hand on her shoulder. "Will you be all right?" Selah nodded. "Remember, you can always come talk to me if you need any sort of help at all." The dragonrider looked at Landon. "That goes for you too." He returned his attention to Selah. "Well, I better go before Sean has half the fief looking for me. Good luck." With one last, reassuring pat to her shoulder, the man disappeared down the hall. Selah watched him go, suddenly feeling very alone.

"Here, let me take that." Landon relieved her of a pack, flashing her a warm smile. "Dragonhold's a really nice place, once you get used to the coursework," he told her as they made their way down the hall.

Selah opened the door to her new room and tried to hide her dismay. Her quarters were smaller than a servant's room at Domar. A bed took up much of one half of the room. The only furniture, besides the bed, was a clothes dresser. A wooden screen concealed a small alcove, apparently the washroom. A small cluster of crystals glowed on the nightstand beside her bed. Other than that, the room was as bare as a prison cell. None of the lavishness of the Great Hall or the other corridors was apparent in her room.

"I know they're not the loveliest quarters," said Landon, breaking her thoughts. "But the apprentice quarters are much nicer. It's only two years, and it's not like we do much more than sleep here. That's why the common room is so nice." He had read her mind.

Selah rubbed the sunburn she had acquired on the trip from Domar. "Oh, its fine. I'm...just...used to more space." Selah hung her quiver on some pegs that had been hammered into the wall.

Landon nodded, a wistful look entering his eyes. "I used to have a big bed...enough for a few of our hounds to sleep in and not be uncomfortable." He shook his head. "I supposed we haven't been properly introduced. I'm Landon of Boran."

Selah took his offered hand. "Selah of Domar."

*   *   *   *

Selah lay awake long into the night, listening to the pounding of her own heart. The crystals had faded to a dim blue that cast the furniture in slight glow that would have been comforting in normal circumstances. Now, it just seemed to accentuate the eeriness of her new chambers.

More than once, a tear slid from the corner of her eye as the girl thought of home, but she didn't sob. Nevertheless, it was a long while before she drifted into a fitful slumber.

A loud roar awoke her with a start the following morning. For a moment, she didn't know where she was and looked around in panic for the source of the sound. It took a while for all of yesterday to catch up with her. The roar must have been the watch dragon. Yawning, the girl stumbled to her lavatory and straightened up for the new day. Quickly, she pulled on tan breeches, trying to get her white shirt on simultaneously. It didn't work, so she slowed down and took one article of clothing at a time. Her hands were trembling with nerves. Selah struggled to calm herself. *It's just training...why am I so afraid?*

"Selah? Selah, are you up?" Landon's voice broke through her thoughts.

"Just a minute!" the girl called, struggling into her earth brown overtunic. Tying her belt about her middle, Selah opened the door. Landon's fist was ready to knock, and he was shifting from side to side in impatience.

"Come on," he urged as she stepped out into the hallway. "Breakfast is in five minutes, and I'm starving." Without another word, he set off down the corridor.

"What's the rush?" Selah asked in confusion. Even with her long legs it was hard to keep up with Landon's pace. "Its just breakfast."

"Just breakfast?" Landon demanded in mock disbelief. His emerald eyes were ringing with a silent laugh. "My dear, what you so blatantly called 'just breakfast' is crucial to our very survival."

"Why?"

Landon chuckled. "Because, Selah of Domar, if we don't get there, we aren't fed, and it's a long time 'til lunch!"

Despite the fact that Selah slowed whenever she saw an interesting wall carving, they were on time to breakfast. The Mess Hall was equally as large as the Great Hall. Already, plates of steaming food were set in the middle of the long tables that filled the room.

Selah stared in wonder. There were easily several Wings worth of pallons in the Mess Hall. There were a scattering of girls; some had clustered together, while others, like Selah, were with boys.

Landon led her over to a table near the center of the room. The pallons seated there called out greetings when they caught sight of him. Selah's face fell as she saw the number of Landon's friends. Once again, she was acutely aware of how few people she actually knew at Dragonhold.

She was considering sitting at one of the empty tables when Landon gave her a slight push forward. "This is Selah, everyone. I'm showing her around for a few days. Come on, Marcus…shove your backside and make room for two."

The black haired boy sighed and scooted over so that they could sit down. Once the pallons had uttered the daily devotion to the gods, Landon made sure that she had a bit of everything on her plate. The food was simple but nutritious.

Selah was too nervous to feel hungry and pushed her food away. A blonde pallon seated across from her reached forward and returned the plate back to its original position. "You need to eat something," he said, his blue eyes kind. "I'm Bern, and this is my twin brother, Aswin." He gestured to the dark haired pallon on his right.

Selah took a bite of bread, swallowing before she spoke again. "You two are twins?" They nodded. "Really? I'm a triplet. I have two brothers."

Bern smiled. "I'm sorry. I mean, it's hard enough having one twin, let alone two." Aswin cuffed him on the shoulder lightly and they chuckled. Selah felt her heart stop for a moment and a wave of homesickness pass over her again. Just then, Aswin and Bern had reminded her of Firmin.

Landon managed to get her to eat a bit more before the cook ushered them out of the Mess Hall. The boy was carrying three books and several sheets of paper under his arm; Selah hadn't noticed them before. When she asked him what they were for, Landon chuckled. "This is last night's work. Don't worry, you'll get some soon enough."

"That's what I'm afraid of," muttered Selah.

"What did you say?"

"Oh…nothing."

*   *   *   *

Her first class was mathematics. The Master was well beyond the prime of his life and stuttered over his *s* sounds. "Plea-s-se be s-s-seated." Selah chose a seat next to Landon.

So commenced an hour of complete confusion for the girl. She had been given a decent amount of education at home, but the math that he covered was well beyond her experience. To make matters worse, the girl was far behind; Selah didn't even understand the concepts that appeared to be fundamental to everyone else. When the master peered over her shoulder, he snorted in disapproval. "How do fifty-five and thirty-s-s-s-six make eighty-one?"

Selah blushed crimson, ashamed to be caught in so simple a mistake. The girl knew how to add, but had been so focused on the rest of the problem she hadn't noticed. She heard snickers behind her; some of the other pallons found her situation extremely amusing. It seemed like ages before the bell rang and they were allowed to leave.

Landon saw the look of frustration on her face and didn't ask her any questions. Selah frowned at the worksheet the Master had given her to complete that night. She had never, ever had to do homework.

Her second class was, unfortunately, led by the Holdleader, Sean. He didn't look pleased when he saw her enter the room.

"Welcome to the Care of Dragons, for those of you who are new." All the pallons turned to stare at Selah, who flushed red to the roots of her hair. "Now, please get out the diagram I assigned you yesterday. I'll be collecting it."

Sean stopped at her desk, his hand held out expectantly. "I...uh," Selah stuttered, "don't...have it."

Sean raised his eyebrows. "That's right, I remember you. The expert. Well, you can fill it out and give it to me by tomorrow."

Selah opened her mouth to protest but shut it quickly. She had learned her lesson in the courtyard.

"You should be able to find the terms in here." Selah took the book the Holdleader handed her with numb fingers. She'd only been to two classes, and already she had more than an hour's worth of work.

Sean returned to the front of the room, frowning at the floor as if trying to gather his thoughts. "The Knights are the fighting force of the ground. They can navigate through forests when our dragons would be unable to fly through tree cover. They deal with bandits, Cydran armies, and the occasional highwaymen."

Selah sent a bemused glance over in Landon's direction, but he was looking at Sean. Why was the Holdleader telling them this?

"As dragonriders, we deal with the more common threats as well, but are often called into action when war breaks out on the border. Our Knights would not be able to defend themselves against enemy dragonriders if we were not there to help them. However, there is one group that we and we alone must combat." He looked to his pupils, gauging whether or not they were truly paying attention to him. "I'm sure that you have heard of dragonhunters."

Selah had heard of them before, in whispered conversations between Flyn and dragonriders that were staying at the fief for the night. The stories she had overheard were terrifying, usually involving some sort of torture or slaying of dragons. Now that she was a pallon, the word sent a shiver of fear down her spine.

"They are a cult that hate us, have hated us, for centuries. Long ago, when the decision was made that dragons would chose who would have the privilege of riding them, there were a group of warriors that were angered by the decisions. Many of them were Knights or captains in the army who thought their deeds deserved a dragon as a mount. They could not accept that dragons were sentient beings in their own right."

Sean paused to clear his throat. "They are a group of hatred—the very sight of a dragonrider or dragon will cause a Hunter to attack them. Dragonhunters are very good warriors, almost as well trained as us." Sean looked each of them in the eye. "The dragonhunters are a very real threat. They will kill you if you do not fight back first."

Selah felt apprehension creep into her mind. The idea of being a dragonrider was starting to have very deadly drawbacks. "That is why we have so many patrol sweeps. That is why dragons only fly alone when a patrol has recently cleared the area."

The girl remembered her flight to Dragonhold. Had there been eyes, watching them in the shadows? She shivered.

Sean looked directly at her. "The dragonhunters will hunt you for being a dragonrider. If you are unable to handle that possibility, then Dragonhold is not the place for you. There is still time to back out, but it is now. If you are Chosen by a dragonet, then it is too late."

There was silence in the room. No one moved. After several moments, Sean dropped his eyes to the floor. "Good. Now that we have that out of the way…" he looked at the hourglass situated on his desk, "it is time for your next class."

Her next class was Strategy and Tactics. The master, after a brief rundown of what they had currently been studying, handed her a box of blue pebbles and told her to arrange them in battle formation. The idea was to engage in a skirmish with your partner. Within minutes, Landon and his force of red pebbles had completely surrounded Selah's "troops". The Master saw the end result, sighed, and assigned the girl a chapter on simple tactical theories. Although the class left Selah with a headache, it banished thoughts of dragonhunters from her mind.

Selah exited the room in a daze. She had taken a peek in the book she was to read, and it contained enough complicated terms to choke a dragon. *When am I going to have time for this?* she thought as she stared at the growing pile of books under her arm.

She crashed into the person in front of her; the girl had been so wrapped up in her thoughts that she hadn't been aware of her surroundings.

"Watch where you're going!" snapped the boy.

"Sorry," Selah mumbled, moving the side. He blocked her, leering down with eyes that were like round chips of ice. When Selah stepped aside again, he positioned himself in front of her a second time.

"What are *you* doing here? Servants aren't allowed in this corridor." His voice was dripping with disdain, and he sneered. His black hair fell in front of his eyes but did not hide their intensity. Selah was taken aback and blushed crimson.

"Corith!" Landon's emerald eyes were crackling with annoyance. "Selah's just as much a pallon as you are. Besides, the hallway is for everyone's use. I don't remember the Masters making you a toll collector. Move."

The boy, Corith, shook his head in obvious scorn. "You're wasting my time." He shoved by them, knocking Selah to the side. The girl instinctively reached out a hand to steady herself, and her books came crashing to the floor, drawing the attention of everyone in the crowded hall.

Corith chuckled darkly. "Coordinated." He disappeared down the corridor, his laughter ringing in the girl's ears. Selah reached down to gather her books, wishing more than anything that she was back home.

*   *   *   *

Aviation passed with less difficulty than her other classes. The Master, Loman, had them pouring over maps that were marked with a lattice of permanent wind courses. There was no let up on work, however; Loman expected a full report of how the wind had affected their flights to Dragonhold by the next day. Selah struggled to keep herself from moaning out loud in despair.

Lunch was a well-needed break; the girl consumed her meal voraciously, her mind on the work she would have to do after training. Landon caught sight of her dejected expression and read her thoughts. "Don't worry," he said, trying to cheer her up. "We'll help you out on your work, if you need any."

The girl looked down quickly at her meal. "That's okay. I'm fine." It was a blatant lie; Selah felt completely overwhelmed. She was still recovering from the sting of Corith's comments.

Selah tried to get some of her work done over her meal, but only made it through a few pages of the tactics book before the cooks ushered them out of the mess hall. Selah rushed to her room to change. Her quarters didn't improve her mood; the bare walls made her feel isolated. The girl bit her lip to hold back the tears of homesickness that touched the corners of her eyes. *Oh, Firmin, where are you when I need you?*

Landon's insistent knock on her door broke her out of her sad thoughts. Giving one final straightening tug to her exercise tunic, the girl opened the door, already dreading the rest of the afternoon.

*   *   *   *

Despite Landon's constant urging, they were late to training. The master looked Selah up and down, a slight smile playing on his lips. His spry and muscular figure belied his gray beard and hair, now only showing a slight dusting of brown. The master's eyes were deep, golden amber, and alight with intelligence.

"You must be Selah of Domar." His words were quiet and he spoke slowly, but his voice commanded the girl's attention. "I am Garrett of Dalbrook, the training master. Wingleader Averon informed me that you had been given primary instruction with most weapons. However, a pallon must show advanced proficiency." He chuckled as Selah blanched. "Don't worry. You have two years to convince me that you have mastered the weapons of a dragonrider. Today we will cover the basics of staves. Have you ever practiced with them?" Selah shook her head, feeling a knot clench in her stomach. How far ahead of her were the others?

Garrett walked over to a stack of the long wooden poles and tossed one to Selah. He walked her through the basic blocks and strikes before gathering the rest of the pallons for the warm up.

He had them run twice around the inner fief, jogging beside them and shouting encouragement to those who were lagging behind. Selah was fit from her constant races with Firmin and managed to stay with the middle of the group through most of the run. Still, it was more than she was used to, and the girl was breathing hard by the time they stopped.

Garrett's idea of a warm-up was Selah's idea of a workout. Her muscles were already burning by the time they had finished an exercise that included push-ups, sit-ups, running in place, falling to ground and leaping quickly back to their feet, and a myriad of other small tortures.

Garrett ordered them to find a partner for staff work, and Selah scrambled to Landon's side. He was the only familiar face among the pallons, and one of the only friendly ones. The boy grinned. "I'm glad you like my company so much." Despite her nerves, Selah smiled back.

Garrett walked up and down the line, barking out directions in a voice that was quite different than his soft-spoken greeting. "High block, low block, low block, low block, high block...Coyle!" A heavyset boy who looked to be a year older than Selah jumped. "It's a staff, not a club! Show some skill! High block! Low block!"

Selah was struggling to keep up with Garrett's tempo when Landon's staff slammed into her fingers. The girl yelped, dropping the staff and cradling the injured hand. Landon immediately lowered his guard and apologized.

Selah's fingers were swelling already; it would be a bad bruise. Blood welled in a small cut on her ring finger. Garrett walked over, alerted by Selah's outburst. "Everything all right?"

"My hand..." started the girl, showing the training master her smarting fingers. Garrett took her hand and examined it with an expert eye.

"It's not broken," he reported, as if that ended the matter. He bent down and picked up Selah's discarded staff. He handed it back to her, his golden eyes slightly reproachful. "Never drop your weapon. Your opponent might be *aiming* for your hand next time. Continue." He turned back to the rest of the pallons.

"But—" The rest of Selah's sentence froze in her throat at Garrett's raised eyebrow. Thoughts raced through Selah's head. Flyn stopped the exercise at any show of blood. Beda would've been sympathetic. Even the most ornery old guards at Domar would have shown more concern than Garrett had. Selah opened and closed her mouth, but no sound would come out.

"Is there a problem?" Garrett's golden eyes narrowed.

Selah struggled to find her voice. "N-No, sir." Blushing deeply, she returned to the line, trying to ignore the throbbing of her fingers and the stares of her peers.

Selah's hands were smacked several more times during the exercise, leaving them peppered with small cuts and bruises. She almost groaned when Garrett announced they would continue to work with staffs for the rest of the day.

Garrett changed partners, pairing Selah with a sturdy boy named Renton. He was good, blocking most of Selah's blows with ease. Selah saw the opening she had left a moment too late and reeled back as Renton's staff smacked into her arm.

Selah retreated. Renton's staff collided with the girl's stomach, driving the wind from her body. "What's your problem?" Selah snapped, irritated by the second attack.

"Selah of Domar!" Garrett's voice cut through the hazy summer air. The pallons around her ignored him and continued sparring with each other; only Renton and Selah froze at the training master's command.

Garrett's golden eyes were burning with exasperation. "Your opponent won't ask you if you're all right after he's landed a blow! He'll follow up! Why is this so hard for you to understand?"

"But—"

"Continue." He stepped back, watching them expectantly. Renton immediately crouched down in a guarded position. Selah took a second longer, and was punished for her delay with a hard smack from Renton's staff.

"Recover!" Garrett shouted as Selah faltered. "Strike!"

Selah obeyed, but Renton caught her blow with one end of his staff, striking out with the other. Selah leapt out of the way, the wooden pole inches from her abdomen.

"Good!" cried Garrett. "Try again."

Garrett always seemed to be watching her, his voice looming over the clack of staves whenever he caught Selah slacking or making a mistake repeatedly. The girl was at her wit's end by the time the training master called a break. She had hardly landed a blow throughout the entire day. At Domar, she had always bested everyone but Firmin. Now, it was all she could do to block a few of the eminent blows.

They had been training for over three hours when Garrett told them to take two laps as a cool down. Selah could hardly keep up with the others, she was so exhausted. Her legs were burning, and each place a staff had struck her ached horribly. Garrett jogged beside her on the last lap; she was one of the last ones. "One more time," he encouraged. "Come on."

Selah picked up her pace, unable to refuse her training master's challenge. He easily kept up with her, hardly breathing heavily as they rounded the last corner.

Once they reached the training courtyard, Selah came to an abrupt halt, supporting herself on her knees. She was trembling with exertion.

Garrett dipped his head slightly in approval. "Well done, for your first day. I will see you tomorrow." Selah couldn't speak; she nodded in acknowledgement, struggling to control her ragged breathing. She had never been so tired in her life.

Landon, looking far better than she did, slapped her on the back. "Nice job. I felt like I was going to die after my first day. Well, you survived Garrett."

Selah finally found her voice. "Barely."

Landon chuckled, giving her arm a slight tug. "Come on. We have to wash up before dinner."

"Wash up?" Selah was considering the possibility of going to straight to bed. The farther they walked, the better of an idea it seemed.

Landon nodded. "Yeah. The cooks have a fit if we come anywhere near the Mess Hall without taking a bath first. Don't worry," he reassured as he saw Selah look at him incredulously, "they have a separate bathhouse for girls."

After grabbing a clean pair of clothes from her room, the girl gratefully sank into a hot bath prepared by one of the servants. The warmth eased the ache in her sore muscles, but did nothing to loose the knot in her heart. Another wave of homesickness washed over her, and Selah blinked tears out of her eyes. The white walls of Dragonhold, as beautiful as they appeared from the sky, were cold and unfamiliar. Landon, despite his kindness, was no substitute for the memorable camaraderie that she had shared with her brother. She and Firmin could have finished each other's sentences if they desired, and without him the girl felt lost and alone.

Selah washed herself down, wincing as the soap entered her half-healed scratches, stinging painfully. She was covered in bruises; her skin was as speckled with purple marks as a fawn's back was dusted with white spots. Every movement brought forth a new wave of pain—muscles she didn't even know she had were sore.

Selah sat in the bath for a long while, watching the water lap against the sides of the tub whenever she shifted. It was the first time she had stopped to rest all day, and the girl relished not having to move, wrapped up in her melancholy thoughts.

The bell announcing the hour finally summoned the girl from the water. Without Landon's guidance, it took her twice as long to find the Mess Hall. She was late to dinner.

The blonde haired boy, Bern, offered her the plate of meat when she arrived at the table. He seemed to understand the reason for Selah's silence. "Here. How much work do you have tonight?"

Selah frowned at her plate. "A lot." She sighed, stabbing the meat with her fork irritably. It was the only thing that she could take out her frustration on.

Another pallon seated two down from Bern snorted. "Good luck," he said, his tone indicating that he was not sympathetic at all.

Selah ignored him, chewing her meat slowly. By the gods, even her jaws were sore.

Landon was in deep conversation with Bern's twin, Aswin. "The Choosing isn't supposed to happen for a month or two...I heard that the eggs aren't even laid yet."

Selah, her interest perked, leaned toward the boy. "What's the Choosing?" The girl blushed as she realized that she had interrupted.

Landon didn't seem to notice. "It's where the dragonets pick their Riders. Those who aren't picked by a dragon get sent home."

"Oh." Averon had mentioned something like it the day he had recruited her. The girl turned back to her meal, thoughts returning to the work she had yet to do.

It took her three hours to fight through the assignments. Worse, much of it the girl didn't understand—the tactics language was over her head and beyond her comprehension. Her report could have been more detailed, but Selah was exhausted and didn't feel like holding a quill for much longer.

By the time she was finished, the other pallons in the common room were either talking in groups or playing some sort of game. None of the pallons spared her a glance; even Landon was in the middle of a game of Dragonstones with Roswald and hardly ever looked up from the board. Feeling the familiar ache of lonesomeness in her chest again, the girl gathered up her things and retreated to the refuge of her room, shutting the door quietly behind her. No one noticed the girl leave.

*   *   *   *

The next few days were as miserable as the first. Loman was disappointed with her report, marking it heavily with corrections and informing her that she would have to redo it as well as finish the assignment for that day. Sean continued to challenge her with difficult questions. Her other masters did not let up on the work.

The work Selah could deal with; while it was challenging, she always had enough time at night to finish all of her coursework, even with her extra assignments. It was training that had her exhausted and frustrated.

They continued to focus on the staff, much to Selah's vexation. After a week, she managed to block most of the blows her fellow pallons threw at her; however, the physical demands of training left her worn out every time.

Harder than Garrett's constant criticism was the terrible isolation she felt. Landon, while genial and agreeable, did not make friends easily. He would show her around and his group of friends would help her out when she needed it, but Selah knew that they hadn't accepted her as one of them.

At least they were better than some of the other pallons. A few couldn't resist throwing some scathing remark related to her gender whenever they saw her. Worst of all was Corith. He had taken a special interest in Selah, going out of his way to be rude and "accidentally" trip or run into her in the hallway. Gradually Selah found the easiest way to make it in Dragonhold was to remain invisible and keep out of everyone's path. Deep inside, she knew that she didn't want to live like this.

So the day marking her three weeks as a pallon, she found herself hugging to the side of the hallway, trying not to draw the attention of the others. By the time she saw Corith out of the corner of her eye, it was too late.

He collided into her, knocking her to the ground. "Oops. Sorry." He smiled down at her maliciously. Selah looked down at the floor, catching sight of a book he had dropped.

Corith nudged her forcefully with his foot. "Pick it up." When Selah hesitated, he kicked her a second time. "Now."

Reluctantly, Selah reached for the textbook, her blood boiling in hatred. She yelped as his boot came crashing down on her hand. Corith grinned savagely, twisting his heel slightly. The girl bit her lip to keep down a cry of pain.

Slowly, Corith lifted his foot. Selah cradled her hand, eyes glistening with tears of rage. Corith hauled her roughly to her feet. "Pick it up!"

Selah snapped. Corith staggered backward as a right cross, backed up with all the fury and pain Selah had kept inside, slammed into his face. The hallway froze, everyone turning to stare. The newest pallon was finally fighting back.

"Don't touch me," Selah ordered, trembling in anger. Corith removed his hand from his face; she had bloodied his nose.

He recovered quickly, slamming her into the wall. The pallon drew back his fist, his ice eyes burning in rage. Selah ducked in the nick of time, feeling the bottom of Corith's fist brush the top of her head as his hand slammed into the wall.

The boy howled in pain and fury, backing away from her. Landon leapt between the two combatants. "Stop," he commanded, putting a restraining hand on the girl's shoulder. "Selah, he's not worth the trouble." The boy turned to face Corith, but the pallon had fled with the remainder of his pride.

Landon looked at Selah with a new level of respect in his deep green eyes. "What's gotten into you?"

Selah was still trembling, both with the adrenaline that had filled her veins when she had struck Corith and uncontained anger. Her hazel eyes were crackling with a new energy and determination. "I'm sick of letting him walk all over me. I'm sick of people telling me that I don't belong here." Retrieving her books from the floor, the girl continued down the hall, no longer walking on the side.

When Landon and his friends offered her a seat at their table in the common room, Selah didn't refuse.

*   *   *   *

Selah knew that Corith would not allow her defiance to go without retribution. She wasn't surprised when the pallon stalked her the next day, spilling her ink jar during mathematics and glaring at her savagely whenever she met his gaze.

Landon knew as well, and seemed to be keeping an eye on her throughout the morning. It seemed that Selah had redeemed herself for her previous dependence on his protection from Corith and his fellow tormentors by standing up for herself. The girl felt more included in mealtime conversations and her comments were listened to with more interest. Still, Selah was aware that she was still considered an outsider; the esteem of her fellows would not be gained easily.

Garrett seemed to sense the tension between Selah and Corith and, thankfully, did not partner them together. They had moved on from staves to hand to hand combat, and Garrett drew Selah aside to discuss her footing. However, he only briefly pointed out her mistake before changing the subject. "You know, Selah, that skill counts greatly in a battle of any kind. Still," Garrett folded his arms and looked out into the distance. "Even though one combatant may be stronger, faster, smarter, it all counts for nothing if their opponent is willing to get up."

"Sir?" Selah was unsure where her training master was going with this.

"I'm saying that you shouldn't resign yourself to defeat so early on." With a slight smile, Garrett ushered the girl back to the lines. Selah pondered on his words as she sparred with Landon, wondering if there was a hidden double meaning to his suggestion.

Corith was waiting for her after training. Unfortunately for him, she was surrounded by Landon and his friends. As the girl passed them, he reached in and grabbed her arm. "You can't hide behind the others forever," he hissed in her ear. "You'll be sorry that you were ever born." Selah pushed him away. Corith shot the girl one last venomous look before exiting the training courtyard.

By the time Selah had been a month at Dragonhold, the girl felt like she had gotten her bearings. She could navigate the hallways without another pallon's assistance and only rarely had to ask for directions. She had caught up with her coursework and was slightly less sore each night.

For the first time, Selah was smiling when she finished training that night. Landon had stayed late to work with Garrett on his archery, and the other pallons had already left. The girl was rounding a corner when Corith's hand shot out of the shadows and pulled her against the wall.

The boy was flanked by three others, all of which Selah had observed during training to be strong and skilled with weapons. They leered at her, and the girl's heart leapt up to pound in her throat.

"What do you want?" Selah struggled to contain her fear, but her voice trembled, and Corith smiled in satisfaction.

"You hit me in the hallway."

"Finally figured it out, did you?" The words flowed out of her mouth as if someone else was speaking them; the real Selah was frozen with terror. "It must have taken you a good night or two."

Two of the boys beside Corith frowned, the other beginning to crack his knuckles in an attempt to intimidate her. Selah tried to swallow the lump in her throat. It was working.

"I don't like your tone," snarled Corith, pushing her back.

Selah steadied herself; when he shoved her again, the girl remained firm. *Run away!* shouted one part of her mind. There was no Firmin to back her up here. The strange part of her that had suddenly taken control snapped, "I don't like the look of your face."

The boys swarmed on her, astonishing Selah with a flurry of punches. The girl rocked backwards as four fists struck her simultaneously.

Two of the pallons grabbed Selah's arms and held them behind her back. Corith commenced to beat her about her the face, pausing every now and then to drive the wind from her with a blow to the stomach.

It was minutes before the boy had finally satisfied his desire for revenge. He stepped back, breathing faster than normal. "Had enough, girl?"

Selah had gone limp; only the combined grip of the two boys that were holding her arms was enough to keep her upright. A drop of blood from a cut above her eyebrow fell to the stones beneath them. There was no reply.

Corith sneered in disgust. "Pathetic."

"N-No." The boy started in surprise. Selah's voice was rough and hoarse from crying out in pain. "You're pathetic." The girl coughed. "You had to resort to getting help to get back at me." Selah raised her head. Her hazel eyes were burning with rage and hatred. "You're not a pallon…just a coward. A sick and twisted coward."

Corith flushed in rage. "Shut up!"

Selah didn't flinch. The fear that had possessed her earlier had abated to half of its original intensity; every place that he had struck her ached terribly, but she could bear it. "Make me."

The pallon seized her collar, teeth bared. He drew back his fist, but stopped at the sound of loudly approaching footsteps. "Let's get out of here," he ordered, dropping Selah to the ground. The four boys fled, leaving the girl prone and trembling next to the wall.

A blue form rounded the corner, stopping short in surprise when it saw Selah. The girl was facing away from the dragon. Leaning heavily against the wall, Selah struggled to her feet, breathing heavily.

—*Selah? Are you all right?*—It was Farsight.

The girl whirled too quickly, and careened forward. The dragon caught her with ease. Despite his care, the rough undersides of his claws caught on the fabric of her clothing. He steadied her until he was sure that she could stand before asking,—*What happened?*—

Selah kept her face averted from him. "Nothing." Her voice was heavy with unshed tears. "I'm fine."

The dragon reached out with a gentle claw and turned her face toward his. His sea-green eyes narrowed in anger when he saw the bruises Corith and his followers had inflicted upon her.—*Who did this to you?*—

"No one."

—Tell me.—

A tear slid slowly down Selah's cheek. "A boy." She began to cry. "I'm trying, Farsight, I really am. I thought I could be a pallon." The girl wrapped her arms around herself, the salt from her tears burning in the scrape on her cheek. "I'm trying to stand up to them. I want to hit back, and I can't." Her eyes glimmered with moisture and anger. "I hate him."

*—You have done more than try,—*said Farsight.*—He may hurt your body with blows, but there is nothing he can do to your mind. He cannot convince others that you are beneath them unless you are willing to believe him yourself. Keep fighting him in your heart, Selah...someday the rest of you will catch up.—*His eyes were kind and understanding.

Selah wiped her eyes and tried to smile back.

*   *   *   *

Selah didn't go to dinner. The girl washed in her room; while the soapy water removed the dirt from her skin, it did nothing to alter the bruises that covered her face. If anything, the marks only seemed more terrible without the blending mask of sweat and grime. Farsight's words had stemmed the flow of her tears; still, it was difficult to concentrate on the night's assignments.

A cook came by after dinner with a tray of food. The girl accepted the meal gratefully. She was aching all over by the time she crawled into bed.

Her wounds had not improved in appearance by the next morning. Selah briefly considered hiding in her room, but dismissed the idea immediately. She would not give Corith the satisfaction of thinking he had beaten her into submission.

The girl earned more stares than a dragon in a ball gown as she made her way down to breakfast. While the people she passed in the hallway gawked at the extent of her injuries, they didn't seem that surprised. Selah resisted the urge to hide in the shadows.

Landon almost upset his platter when he caught sight of her face. "What happened to you?" he exclaimed as she sat down.

The girl began to eat. "I got on the bad side of a brute."

Landon was gripping his utensils so hard that his fingers were turning white. "Who? I knew I should have waited for you."

"You're not my nurse!" snapped Selah. A bruise shaped like a hand discolored one of her cheeks and made speaking a painful process. "It's not your problem."

"Of course it's our problem!" retorted Aswin. "You shouldn't be getting beat up…it's not fair!"

Selah flinched. While his words were well meant, it sounded like Aswin would fight for her because he hated bullies, not because she was his friend. "I don't need your help. I can manage on my own."

The rest of the meal was finished in silence. Selah was the first to leave.

*   *   *   *

Another month passed. Selah kept up with her training and studies. Corith cornered her three more times. By the second encounter, the girl managed to land a few blows before the boys overwhelmed her.

By the time that the heat of summer was beginning to gain the nip of fall, Selah was able to keep up with the other pallons during training. They were still on staves, but Selah was far more comfortable with the wooden pole in her hands than she had been two months ago.

"Selah, Corith! To the middle!" Selah walked to her training master. Every now and then, Garrett would call on two unfortunate pallons to demonstrate their skill in front of the others. Corith's gaze was confident. Selah gripped her staff tightly to conceal her hatred for the boy.

"Ready, begin!" Corith slammed down on her staff, testing her strength. The girl faltered, unprepared for the force behind his blow. She moved to the side, blocking another strike.

After a few moments of striking and blocking, the boy caught one of her blows and shoved her back, sending her to the ground. He stepped back, not even bothering to pin her down. "Yield."

Something inside Selah wouldn't give in to that smug look of cockiness on his face. Something inside roared in fury, and the girl gave into her anger.

Gritting her teeth, she kicked Corith's legs out from under him. With a cry of surprise, the boy fell to the ground, struggling to get back to his feet. Selah brought her staff down on his with all her strength, and it was Corith's turn to falter. The girl charged into him with her shoulder, knocking the pallon back in a way that would have made the Guards of Domar smile in pride.

Corith recovered, catching the blow of her staff and striking at her thigh. Selah ignored the pain that shot through her leg, knocking the boy down through the opening he had left wide with his attack.

Selah dived forward, placing her staff across Corith's chest so he couldn't rise. She stared down at his ice eyes. "You yield."

No one spoke. Selah was acutely aware of how her blood was pounding her ears, how her lungs were burning with exertion.

Keep fighting him in your heart, Selah, rang Farsight's voice in her mind. *Someday the rest of you will catch up.*

"Yield," Selah demanded with more conviction, pressing down with her staff to reinforce her words.

"I yield," snarled Corith. Selah straightened slowly, unable to comprehend what she had just done. She had beaten him. She had done it. Surrendering to the broad grin that spread across her face, Selah returned to the lines, her staff held loosely in one hand.

∗   ∗   ∗   ∗

It happened three days after her defeat of Corith. The Math Master was stuttering even more than usual and was barely able to announce that there was no homework for the night.

It was a burly boy named Coyle who finally figured it out. "Don't you get it?" he asked as they entered the Care of Dragons. "A dragon has laid eggs." He looked meaningfully at Selah, who pointedly ignored him, placing her books at an empty seat. "Finally, the unworthy will be…" he paused, and selected a more sociably accepted word, "…removed."

"Leave her alone," snapped Landon.

Coyle smirked. "You too. Not even nobility can fool a dragonet."

Selah looked at Landon in surprise. "You're a noble?" The boy didn't look the part; his hair was short rather than long, and his clothes, while of a fine make, were nothing extraordinary.

The boy averted his gaze, a pink flush creeping onto his cheeks. "That's…it's…not important."

Selah opened her mouth to continue but swallowed her words as Sean strode into the room, an impatient look on his face. "Sit down!" he thundered. Those unfortunate enough to be caught standing rushed to the nearest seat. Sean began to pace back and forth at the front of the room. "Farsight's mate, Snowfire, has laid twenty-two eggs. The Choosing will take place two weeks from now. Once we take you to the Cavern of Choices, you will stand in front of the eggs. You are forbidden to speak until the end of the ceremony. If you are Chosen, the dragonet will make it very clear that you are his choice. If you are not Chosen, we ask you to leave the fief; from now on, we only train pallons that are Riders to a dragonet. You can try out for the dragonriders again next time, but you may be too old by then." The enormity of his words filled the room.

"You will be wearing white shirts and tan breeches, for bright colors may confuse the dragonets' judgment. I can tell you no more, for the rest of the ceremony you must face yourself. As for today, you have the remainder of class to complete your essays on proper nutrition. Begin."

Sighing, Selah took out her half-completed essay, noting the crestfallen look on Landon's face. "What's eating you?"

The pallon fidgeted for a moment, as if debating whether or not to confide in her. "It's just…what if we don't get dragons?"

Bern, across the row, leaned toward them. "I heard that dragonets could read your future from a dragonrider. They choose whoever's future they like the best."

"I heard that too," agreed a boy who Selah had learned was Roswald.

"Back to work," Sean snapped testily, glaring at them over a pile of documents he was going through.

Farsight's the father, Selah thought as she settled down in her seat. *Maybe…no.* The girl shook her head as if to physically dispel her thoughts. *I can't depend on the fact that I know Farsight. I have to be worthy of a dragonet, but…how can I prepare my future?* Turning back to her essay, Selah decided to leave those matters to the dragons.

Choosing

Landon pounded on Selah's door, his knocking accentuated by the sound of the storm outside the fief. "Come on, Selah, come on, we're going to be late!"

Selah was tucking her white shirt into her breeches with trembling fingers. "Hold your dragons, Landon, I'm coming!" Buckling her belt, the girl opened the door. Landon, his fist raised to knock again, was shifting from one foot to the other in impatience.

"How do I look?" asked Selah automatically.

"Fine," replied Landon without even glancing at her. "Come on, we'll be late to the Choosing." He tugged her arm insistently, and the pair set off down the hall.

It didn't take long for them to reach the common room, but navigating through it was another matter entirely. All forty-six pallons had gathered in the large library, as well as many dragonriders, Masters and apprentices. All were talking to each other nervously, completely drowning out any outside noise.

A piecing whistle cut through the conversation. The Holdleader perched on a chair so that everyone could see him. "Be quiet!" he shouted, politeness forgotten. Everyone stopped talking, countless eyes turning to Sean to see what he had to say.

Sean cleared his throat before continuing on in a softer tone. "All apprentices need to leave so that we can make sure all the pallons are here." Grumbling, the older youths exited the room. Selah watched them go, her eyes locked on the dragonets that rode on their shoulders or scampered about their feet.

Sean started to speak, and the girl reluctantly returned her attention to the Holdleader. "The dragonriders will lead you down to the Cavern of Choices. Before you go, please remove your boots. You are not allowed to wear anything more than simple garments. If you are Chosen, wait in the cave for further instructions when the ceremony is completed. If you are not, come back to your room and begin packing. A dragonrider will take you home in the morning. It is time for the strong to be Chosen, and the unworthy to leave." Sean's gaze lingered on her for a long moment as he spoke the last sentence. Selah looked him in the eye, her hands balling into fists. "Do not return until your fate has been decided."

A woman tapped the girl on the shoulder as she was pulling off her boots and tossing them to the side of the room. "I'll be leading you down to the Cave." For a moment, Selah was struck speechless. She had never seen a female dragonrider before, and yet the woman wore a flight jacket that bore the same Wing emblem as Averon's.

The dragonrider extended her hand. "I'm Aerin of Molane." Her eyes, the pale blue of a clear sky in wintertime, were warm with a smile, and Selah felt some of the tension in the pit of her stomach abate.

She grasped the offered hand, returning the handshake and the smile. "I'm Selah of Domar."

Aerin brushed a stray strand of red hair out of her eyes. "Domar, huh? Well, I suppose we had better be going."

As a large mass, the pallons and their dragonriders exited the fief. Selah paused once in the Great Hall, wondering if this was perhaps the last time she would see it; if she did not get a dragon, she would be cast from the fief. Aerin looked back, a question in her eyes, and Selah hurried to catch up.

The storm outside didn't seem to bother the dragonriders, who were wearing comfortable flight jackets built for cold weather. Selah's shirt, however, wasn't half as protective; soon the girl was soaked and shivering. Her bare feet were rendered numb within minutes, but Selah was glad of it. As the trail down the cliff face became rockier, the sharp stones cut into the soles of her feet. If it hadn't been so dark, those walking behind her would have seen streaks of dark red in her footsteps.

The farther down the cliff they went, the narrower it became, forcing the pallons to walk sideways in some places. Selah's pace slowed until she was inching along the rock face; while she was not afraid of heights, the prospect of slipping and falling to her death was not a pleasant one. Aerin didn't urge her onward or goad her for cowardice, as she herself was watching where she placed each step. Selah couldn't wait to get to the cave.

As eager as she was, the girl almost missed it. Even though the cavern was a great gap in the rock face, it avoided detection. Unless Selah looked directly at it and focused her thoughts, her eyes slipped to the side as if the cave wasn't there.

The girl stopped at the threshold of the Cave of Choices, her resolve weakening at the sight of the darkness within. A wave of warmth from inside washed over her, and Selah was possessed with indecision. She had no plan if she did not succeed here; to be a dragonrider was her future. She couldn't fail. Steeling herself, the girl entered the cave, her hazel eyes set in determination.

Many of the others, including Landon, had already arrived. The boy flashed her an uneasy smile before returning his gaze to the back of the cave. Selah soon saw why.

Two dragons, a blue and a white, stood a stone's throw away from the pallons, watching them intently. Eggs with a range of shell colors were clustered about their feet. One of the dragons she recognized as Farsight—the other she assumed to be his mate. To the side of the dragons was a bubbling spring of crystal clear water; Sean had told them it was the Spring of All Tears, made from the weeping of Stormhunter, the dragon god.

As the last pallon crossed the threshold of the cavern, the dragons began to speak in mind voices so soft Selah had to concentrate to understand them. After a few lines, she realized that it was a poem.

> *Shards of stone have cut your feet*
> *Shattered your resolve*
> *And yet you are here*
> *Wind has slapped your skin*
> *Stung your eyes*
> *And yet you are here*
> *Rain has soaked your brow*
> *Washed away your courage*
> *And yet you are here*
> *You are stronger than the stone, rain, and wind*
> *You are stronger than your fear*
> *But are you strong enough for me?*
> *You are wiser than your opponent*

You are wiser than time
But are you wise enough for me?
You love the challenge of battle
You love the blade's call
But do you love enough for me?
As I choose
Ask yourself this
Are you strong enough for me?

"The Song of the Dragonet," Selah heard herself whisper, although she was unsure how she knew the song's title. The words rang in her soul, rekindling a memory; although Farsight and his mate had only spoken the verses, Selah felt as though she knew music that went with the poem. It was meant to be sung, but even without notes it sent shivers of doubt through the girl. *Are you strong enough for me?*

Farsight and his mate stepped away from the eggs, baring them to the sight of all. Selah quickly tallied the eggs; there were about twenty or so of them. Over forty pallons were waiting to be Chosen.

—*Our dragonets will decide your fate,*—said Farsight softly, looking at the pallons. His sea-green eyes paused when they reached Selah.—*As you will decide theirs.*—

The first egg cracked, sending a collective shudder of anticipation through the group of pallons. Strangely, all of Selah's fear had evaporated like water. Her heart had only room for one emotion now—hope.

The eggs began to hatch, tiny dragon heads breaking forth to cry out in the cold air. A brown dragonet rolled from its shell, drawing together legs that lacked coordination to stumble toward the pallons. It reached a cluster of three boys. Turning aside from the first two when they stepped forward, the dragonet threw itself at Landon with a trill of happiness.

—*Landon, Rider to Indio!*—announced Farsight. Sparing a glance, Selah looked at the boy; tears were streaming down Landon's face, and he clutched the dragonet close to his heart.

One by one, the dragonet picked their partners, and one by one, the names of the new pairs were called.—*Bern, Rider to Seasong! Aswin, Rider to Silverclaw! Quinn, Rider to Moonflight! Corith, Rider to Ironscale! Hale, Rider to Windstar!*—

Selah's name was not called. No dragonet came up to her. If any came close, they swerved to the side as if encountering a transparent barrier. Selah began to panic; none of the dragonets had so much as looked her in the eye. With each one that passed her, she sank deeper and deeper into despair.

The girl looked to empty eggshells. Only one intact egg remained; the last dragonet. It had not yet begun to hatch. She took an involuntary step forward, but forced herself to stop. The choice was to be the dragonet's, not hers.

The other twenty remaining pallons did not share her thoughts. They raced forward, pushing each other aside in their eagerness for the last dragonet. One boy, faster than the rest, scooped the flawless egg from the stones and raced away from the pallons. Farsight roared in rage, but there was nothing he could do; no one could interfere once a Choosing had begun. Sean had stressed this to them; deep and ancient magic that could not be wielded by mortal hands permeated the very stone of the Cavern of Choices. The enchantment of the cave prevented any outside intrusion once a Choosing had started.

The boy paused, his black hair matted to his forehead with sweat. Turning on the mob of pallons racing after him, he held the egg under one arm, reaching out with the other. "*Scroklc!*" the pallon commanded, his voice laden with magic. His hand tightened in a commanding gesture, and the boys following him froze in mid-step, their faces twisted into expressions of surprise and pain. Selah froze, although not from the spell; besides Kavan, she had never seen another mage her age.

The boy smirked. Selah suddenly recognized him; it was Marcus, one of Landon's distant friends. Marcus held the egg aloft so that all could see it. "This is mine!"

Farsight roared, the sound of his anger reverberating throughout the cave. The black stone echoed Farsight's voice back upon itself until the volume of the dragon's rage rivaled the thrashing thunderclaps from outside the cave. Selah resisted the urge to hold her hands over her ears.—*You cannot deny the Choice to others! Remove the spell, now!*—

"If they had been worthy, would I have been able to stop them?" Marcus snarled, stroking the egg in a way that made Selah sick. He looked down at it, a smile spreading across his face like a spilled glass of water. "Hatch, dragonet. I am your Chosen. Hatch!"

Fury raced through Selah's veins like molten fire, returning the life to her frozen limbs. "Put it down!" she shouted, racing toward Marcus. Closing the distance between them in moments, she reached out and grabbed his arm, wrenching it away from the egg. The blue orb clattered to the stones, rolling away from the two combatants as if guided by an invisible force.

Marcus whirled, extending his palm and shouting words of magic. *"Scroklc!"* Selah winced, expecting her body to turn to stone like the others.

Nothing happened. Marcus' eyes went wide with surprise and fear. He thrust his hand toward her face, repeating the spell desperately. Selah felt nothing. His magic had no effect on her.

Thinking quickly, Marcus dove forward, snatching the egg from the ground a second time. Before Selah could react, he uttered more words of magic. *"Toristalve! Falwen toristalve!"*

Between them, a red line began to burn itself into the stone. Selah stepped backwards in confusion, raising her gaze to the boy's face. Marcus laughed once, a short, mocking chuckle, and pointed his finger to the ceiling.

A wall of flame burst from the red streak, spreading to the edges of the cavern until there was no way that the girl could get around it. Selah rushed forward, but a wave of intense heat drove her back. "Stop!" she yelled. "Enough!"

Over the crackling of the magical fire, she heard the sound of an eggshell breaking. Her heart frozen in horror, Selah watched through the flame as the egg began to hatch, a blue dragonet tumbling from the shell after a few moments. Marcus reached forward, and the word burst from her lips. *"Windchaser!"*

Time seemed to stop. The only sound was the roar of the fire and the surprised gasps of the pallons who had already received dragonets and were watching in shock. Selah's chest heaved, her lungs burning as if she had run countless miles. For the second time, she had uttered a word that she had never heard before. The dragonet cried out in joy before she realized what she had said; *Windchaser* was the dragonet's name.

"No!" growled Marcus, reaching forward. The blue dragonet snarled. The boy's face turned ashen and he backed away.

Her foe dispatched, the dragonet began to crawl toward Selah, oblivious of the flame wall that was between them. The girl realized with alarm that the dragonet couldn't go around it; she would go through it.

"Stop!" she cried desperately, waving her arms to distract the baby dragon. "You can't go through, Windchaser, you'll burn! Wait, please, I'll get someone to take it down!" Windchaser ignored her, walking toward the fire, the light glittering in her eyes.

Panic was closing Selah's throat. "Farsight!" she yelled. "Make her stop!"

—*I cannot; she must touch you before I can interfere! The Choosing must end!*—

Windchaser was a mere spear length from the fire, and her pace had slowed, but the dragonet would not be delayed for long. Through the fire, her hazel eyes met Windchaser's violet ones, and Selah knew what she had to do.

Fear clenched like a cold fist in her stomach, testing her resolve. Selah gritted her teeth, hearing the last line of the poem ring in her mind as Windchaser paused.

Are you strong enough for me?

She exhaled slowly, banishing the second thoughts from her mind with one breath. Breaking into a run, the girl leapt through the fire.

*   *   *   *

Everything was burning. A scream split the air, going on and on and on. Her skin, her hair, her clothes were on fire. Jagged knives of white-hot pain stabbed her without mercy, tearing through her flesh. Selah rolled in the stone, tossing back and forth in an effort to quench the flames that were blackening her skin, cries of agony ripping from her throat.

Landon watched in horror as the girl screamed, tongues of flame leaping up from her body in fury. She had jumped through the flame wall so that the dragonet would not have to burn to death in an effort to reach her.

With great effort, he stood away from his dragonet, Indio, racing toward Marcus. The boy had taken down the fire wall after Selah had jumped through, putting it back up once he was on the other side. Now he was pushing the fire toward Selah and the baby dragon, his face twisted with fury and hatred.

Landon caught him in a full body tackle, Marcus's head making a sickening smack as it struck one of the stones. The firewall flickered once and shattered. Aswin and Bern dashed over the smoldering rocks to Selah. The twins took a hold of the girl and began to roll her over and over, trying to smother the flames on her body.

Landon straightened, looking down at Marcus. Red welled in a deep gash on his forehead; the pallon was unconscious. Without bothering to take a second glance, Landon crossed the fire-blackened line to Selah, wincing as the heated rocks seared his bare feet.

Aswin and Bern were battling with the fire that clung persistently to Selah's skin. Landon bent down, helping the other two to suffocate the flame. After one excruciating minute of battle, the last tongue of fire had disappeared in a whiff of smoke, leaving Selah motionless on the stones.

Her skin was blackened, and the sickly smell of burning flesh filled the cave, making the dragonriders at the entrance recoil in disgust. Her shoulder-length brown hair had burnt away until only a few strands were longer than her ears.

The blue dragonet crept forward, whimpering in disbelief. Selah's charred body lay still as death. Landon let out a sigh of relief as the girl began to stir. She was alive, but not for long. It didn't take experience in healing to know that she was dying. No one could survive wounds like the burns that had mangled her body.

The dragonet began to cry without shedding tears. She keened in a high note that made the pallons shudder, the sounds of her grief echoing through the emptiness of the cavern. Leaning forward, the dragonet touched her brow to Selah's. For a long moment, all was still.

The girl coughed weakly, the stones beneath her mouth flecked with blood. "Windchaser?" Warmth, not of pain, but of love, had blossomed at the pit of her stomach, growing until Selah was sure that her body couldn't contain it. Windchaser let out a soft cry of joy, burying her head into the folds of Selah's tattered shirt.

The Choosing completed, the dragonriders at the mouth of the cave rushed inside, most running to the pallons that were still frozen in Marcus' first spell. Averon was the first to reach Selah. A moan of pain escaped her lips. The girl was to far gone to recognize him or respond. Her hand, nothing more than a blackened claw, rested weakly on Windchaser's back; even at the threshold of Death, her thoughts rested on the dragonet that had Chosen her.

Averon knelt, gathering the girl up in his arms. As strong as he was, it was frightening how easy it was to carry her. Windchaser, her physical connection with Selah broken, snarled and whined, desperate to return to the arms of her dying Chosen. The dragonrider looked around helplessly—the fief was too far away. Selah would die before they even reached the top of the cliff. There was nothing he could do.

As he scanned the cave, Averon's eyes lingered on the spring near the back. A bronze plaque was hammered into the large boulder beside it. There were words in scripted upon it. Feeling as though an outside hand was guiding his mind, Averon began to read.

Stormhunter wept
For his Gonran slept

In death
And what but he did see
Gonran had ceased to bleed
Healed by the waters of
His heart torn asunder
These tears shall not bathe another
Unless by his consent

Rising, Averon walked to the Spring of All Tears, ignoring the stares of the other dragonriders. He stopped at the edge, looking down into the frothing waters. If he was wrong, the gods could strike him down in anger for what he was about to do. The crystalline tears glistened although there was little light in the cave.

It was Sean who realized what he would do. "No!" he shouted, running over to where Averon stood, the dying girl in his arms. "You can't!"

Bending down, Averon placed Selah into the holy Spring of All Tears. The waters closed over her and the Spring became an opaque blue—he could no longer see beyond the surface. Windchaser squealed, trying to dive in after the girl. Averon caught her in the air, ignoring the pain as the dragonet's sharp claws gouged furrows into his arms. "Wait," he ordered, fear mounting in his chest as the waters of the Spring began to churn.

*   *   *   *

Selah sank deeper into the Spring until her body stopped to rest on the smooth stones of the bottom. Opening her eyes, the girl looked up; the surface seemed miles away. Her memory seemed patched and frayed; she knew she was in a holy spring, but couldn't remember who had placed her in it. The tears around her were clear, but she couldn't see beyond them to the Cave above. She couldn't see Windchaser.

She had to get back to her Chosen. Selah shifted, trying to propel herself to the surface; too quickly. Her burns clouded her mind, and the girl opened her mouth to scream out in agony, inhaling a lungful of the sweet water. It didn't choke her, but nourished her like air, easing the pain of her charred body.

Too weak to fight anymore, Selah drifted back down to the bottom of the Spring. She would die here, alone and forgotten. The Spring was slipping in and out of focus, blurring and clearing until Selah closed her eyes. She wanted to see

Windchaser—for that one moment, when she looked into the dragonet's gaze, she had seen her future as a dragonrider. Selah began to sob raggedly, mourning the loss of a love she had only known for a few moments. She was dying, and she would never see Windchaser again.

Why do you despair? A voice pounded behind the girl's eyes, making her gasp a second time. It was terrible and comforting at the same time, thick with the sounds of a thunderstorm and the whisper of a gentle breeze. *You do not know that your fate will end here. There is much more for you to accomplish.*

Who are you? The sound of Selah's words was lost in the crystalline tears around her, but the girl was sure that the speaker could hear her.

You may call me Stormhunter, answered the voice. *Why do you bathe in my tears?*

She was speaking to the dragon god. *I'm dying,* Selah replied, wincing when she realized how frank she was. *I'm sorry...I didn't know these were your tears.*

The dragonrider did. He made a good decision. The voice did not contain any trace of accusation. *If there is anyone that can save you, it is me. The other healer gods may have tried, but the Father gods of each race are the best for their own kind.*

Their own kind? Selah repeated, confused. The tears were beginning to numb her pain, making it easier to think. *I'm human. With all due respect, you're not my Father god.*

In that, you are correct. But I have taken a liking to you, as Gonran sometimes favors promising dragons. Besides, part of you is under my jurisdiction, and I feel responsible for the nature of your soul. Therefore, I have an obligation to keep an eye on you.

What are you talking about? Selah demanded, then chided herself for her lack of respect.

The voice laughed. *You are a slow little dragon-pup. By now you should know...*Stormhunter paused. When he spoke, his voice was thick with anger, and Selah could feel his frown. *Who did this to you?*

Who did what? The burns? Selah was confused. Breathing was no longer an agony, and with second that passed, her pain was becoming dimmer.

No, the barrier.

What barrier?

The voice seemed to realize what it was saying. *This sets us back, but it is not a large problem. I thought you would have understood your true nature by now.*

Selah would have questioned him, but she began to choke. The water, once sweet, had become normal and was suffocating her. *Stormhunter, I can't breathe!*

Do not panic. You will be able to breathe once I take hold of the Spring. First, you must give me something in return for your life. Nothing in this world, or mine, is given freely, and I must have something in exchange for healing you.

Not Windchaser, Selah begged, her mind going to her Chosen. *Anything but Windchaser.*

Stormhunter thought for a long moment. *I will take your ignorance. Yes. That will do.*

My ignorance? Of what?

Of what you truly are.

A tingling sensation started at the base of her spine, traveling up to her heart. Invisible claws of the god reached into her chest, breaking through the charred skin. Selah bit her lip to keep from crying out. Although the dragon god had reached into her flesh, she did not bleed. The girl closed her eyes.

Without warning, the claws tightened and tore something free from her heart. Selah screamed. She had been beaten and burned, but she had never felt pain like this in her life. The girl twisted in agony; a fire raged inside her chest, eating away at her heart.

After what seemed like hours, the pain had faded to a dull ache that throbbed with each heartbeat. Still sobbing, Selah watched as a stormy gray dragon materialized in the water beside her. He glowed with an inner, golden light that made the water around him shine as if each droplet had captured a piece of the sun. He held something in both paws, looking at Selah with an apology in his eyes.

I am sorry I had to hurt you like that. You are stronger than I initially thought you would be without connection with your soul. It must have been agony to live with this in your heart. Opening his claws, he revealed a thin golden disk that was covered in dark purple blood on one side and crimson on the other. *Whoever placed this between your soul and your mind must have been a powerful mage...to divide without destroying is potent magic.* His eyes became sad. *You will lose much from this, Selah, but you also have much to gain. As you can see, your burns have already disappeared.*

Raising a hand to her face, Selah blinked in awe. Her blackened skin had been replaced by new, pink flesh that was able to move without pain. All of her burns had disappeared, and a few strands of new hair floated in front of her eyes. Feeling some energy returning to her limbs, the girl swam a few strokes toward the dragon. *Thank you,* she whispered.

Stormhunter smiled. *The numerous scars you have collected are gone as well. Well, all but one.* When Selah opened her mouth to inquire, he shook his head. *It is time for you to return to your Chosen…no doubt she has caused considerable dam-age in an effort to reach you. Farewell, Selah. Send Windchaser my greetings.*

The dragon god shimmered once and was gone. Selah began to push her way to the surface, acutely aware of the throbbing in her heart. It seemed forever before her head broke the surface of the Spring. Opening her mouth, the girl took a deep breath of air. Treading water, she looked around.

The Cavern was empty. All that remained of Choosing were a few shards of eggshell that had been left behind on the stone. The place was devoid of pallons, dragonets, or any other sign that an important ceremony had taken place here. The only sound was the gentle slapping of water as Selah's movement sent ripples through the Spring. A gentle light filtered in from the mouth of the cave; the sun had risen while she was underwater. She had been in the Spring all night.

"Hello?" she called, wincing as the motion aggravated her aching chest. "Is anyone here?" She swam to the side of the pool. Her dripping fingers slipped on the smooth stone, and she was weary; it took her several tries to haul herself out of the Spring. The girl lay on her stomach, breathing heavily. After a while, she sat up.

A soft, disbelieving whistle reverberated through the Cavern of Choices. A sky blue dragonet crept out from behind one of the boulders. Hope filled her eyes, and she took a step forward as if not believing what she saw. Selah's dragonet had waited for her.

"Windchaser?" whispered Selah, reaching forward with one hand. "Wind-chaser, it's me."

With a cry of joy, the dragonet leapt forward, pressing herself to Selah's chest. Trembling with relief, Windchaser snuggled as close as physically possible. A smile lifting the corners of her mouth, Selah wrapped her arms around the tiny dragonet and knew she would never, ever let go.

✴   ✴   ✴   ✴

Even though the morning was clear, it took Selah much longer to ascend the cliff than it had the night before. Windchaser's weight, while comforting in her arms, grew heavy after a while and Selah often had to stop and rest. The dragonet was exhausted from her night's vigil at the side of the Spring and slept the entire trek. The scrapes on Selah's feet had been healed by Stormhunter, but soon the stones cut new wounds on the soles of her feet. The sun was high in the sky by the time Selah reached the curtain wall of Dragonhold.

*—State your name,—*demanded the watch dragon, who had sensed her presence.

"Selah of Domar," she shouted, hoping the great beast would hear her.

—You lie.—

"No, I don't. My dragonet is starving, my feet hurt, and I'm cold. Will you just bring me over the wall? I'll explain later."

The watch dragon unfurled his wide wings and left his perch on the north tower, flying over the gatehouse until he hovered above her.—*I do not know what mockery this is, but the girl you claim to be is dead. Dragonhold does not let in every scrawny urchin that pounds on our door. Now, I suggest you leave...—*

*—Dellwing, who are you talking to?—*asked a voice that Selah recognized.

"Farsight?" she yelled. "Farsight, I need to get in, and Windchaser—"

—Selah? Is that you?—

$$*\qquad*\qquad*\qquad*$$

"Why, in the name of Gonran, did you put her in the Spring?" Sean shouted, knocking an inkwell from his desk. His face was red with fury, and he stormed about his office, taking out his anger on his numerous possessions.

Averon looked at the Lonian rugs at his feet. "It was her only chance, Sean. I thought that Stormhunter would heal her."

"And what if he didn't? I don't want her death on my hands, Averon. That boy, the one who killed her...he could say that she drowned in the Spring of All Tears. What were you thinking?"

"I thought..."

"No, you didn't think." Sean frowned, reaching into a cabinet. "Gods, I need something to drink."

There was a knock on the door, and Garrett entered, his face white with an emotion that Averon couldn't read. "Is it true?" he demanded. No one had to ask what 'it' was.

"Yes," answered Sean, uncorking a bottle of dark red wine. "We lost two pallons last night. One died of burns, the other is recovering from a head wound."

"Marcus was the one who burned her," snapped Averon. Sean's tone had implied that the boy wasn't to blame.

"Her?" asked Garrett, understanding dawning on his face. "Selah died of burns? From what?"

"Stupid wretch threw herself through a magical firewall when it looked like Marcus was going to be Chosen," explained Sean. He took a long pull from the bottle. "It's her own fault."

"She was already Chosen. Selah jumped through the fire so her dragonet wouldn't be burned in an effort to touch her!" retorted Averon angrily. While he had not been overly fond of the girl, her death was hitting him hard—especially his part in it.

"What's all this talk about the Spring of All Tears?" asked Garrett. He asked only for clarification; he was a smart man and had already put most of the pieces together.

Sean pointed an accusing finger at Averon. "He put her in it. Her body didn't come back up to the surface."

"I see." Garrett's face was sad. "What happened to her dragonet?"

"It stayed behind. There's nothing we can do. It will stay in the cave until it dies of starvation."

"So we lost a pallon and a dragonet." Garrett frowned. "When are you going to tell her family?"

Sean took another drink from the bottle. "Later."

A second knock on the door interrupted the conversation. A dragonrider from a reserve Wing peered around the corner, his face pale. "Holdleader, Master Garrett, Wingleader Averon," he said respectfully. "There is som-someone to see you." He opened the door, and Selah, cradling Windchaser lovingly, stepped into the room.

Sean choked, spraying wine all over his desk. Garrett blinked in surprise, too stunned for words. Averon sank into a chair, unable to speak for the wave of relief that washed through him. There was silence. Sean was the first to recover.

"What...you...it...what happened?"

"Well, I..." Selah blushed. She hadn't had the chance to change out of her burnt breeches and shirt, and they were in tatters. Fortunately, the shirt had survived enough to cover her modestly, although the section below her collar had burnt so that the skin above her heart was revealed. Unlike the rest of her scars, which had disappeared, a new mark of white lines was emblazoned on her skin. It was a scar of claw marks shrunk down until they marred the skin above her breastbone and nothing else. Selah suspected it had something to do with Stormhunter.

Sean leaned forward, staring intently at her. "What is that?" he asked, a dangerous tone in his voice. "What gave that to you?"

Something told Selah not to reveal what Stormhunter had taken in exchange for her life. Not now. "Um...I'm not sure." She shrugged, hoping she sounded convincing. "Maybe Windchaser did it, on accident." The dragonet glanced up at her indignantly, and Selah shot her an apologetic look, stroking Windchaser's back to calm her.

"What happened in the Spring?" questioned Averon, dark circles under his eyes. He looked overjoyed to see her alive. "Where did your burns go?"

Selah told them what had happened, leaving out most of the confusing conversation that had taken place between her and Stormhunter.

Averon looked the girl up and down. Selah was the same, and yet she was not. Her hair had grown back to its shoulder length, but it was slightly darker shade of brown than it used to be. Her hazel eyes contained traces of amber where there had been none before. Although she had not physically grown, she appeared taller and her presence was stronger, as if the girl was surrounded by an aura of importance. There seemed to be more pride in her stance, but that could be attributed to the sky blue dragonet that she held in her arms.

The girl answered each question truthfully, although it was easy to see that she was withholding information. By the way his cheeks were reddening, Averon could tell that Sean knew she wasn't revealing everything.

After her third rendition of what had happened in the Spring, Selah interrupted the Holdleader. "I beg your pardon, sir, but Windchaser is really tired, and I need to put her to bed." The girl, only twelve, spoke with an almost maternal tone, and it was easy to see that she already cared deeply for her dragonet. Windchaser was snuggled in her arms, snoring softly; the steady talking had lulled her to sleep.

Sean, as if realizing for the first time how uncomfortable she must be, gave a dismissive wave of his hand. "You may go. We are not done with this."

Bowing, Selah left the room, her bare feet hardly making a sound against the carpeted floor. Once the girl was out of earshot, Sean spoke. "Am I the only one who noticed the interesting shape of her scar?"

Garrett nodded. "That is the mark of Stormhunter. I've only seen it in temples before."

Sean frowned pensively, turning the wine bottle slowly in his hands. "Why would Stormhunter heal her? Dragon*riders* are not his worshippers...if anyone were to spare her, why wasn't it Gonran?"

"Perhaps Stormhunter deemed her worthy of his attention. Besides, the Spring of All Tears was his creation. Those who bathe in it are sure to attract his interest," mused Garrett.

At this, Sean sent another glance at Averon, who ignored it. "However, that does not answer the question of the mark." After a moment, the Holdleader turned his eyes to Garrett, a serious expression on his face. "Whether or not the gods are interested in her has no effect on her standing here. Remember Owen of Falran? The gods favored him, and he did nothing but slaughter thousands. She will be treated like all the others. Am I clear, Garrett of Dalbrook?"

Garrett frowned, affronted by the Holdleader's tone. "If you think I would favor her because of this, you don't know me very well. She will be trained equally and fairly, as I would have done whether or not this had happened."

Sean turned to Averon, who was still sitting patiently in his chair. "You may go, Wingleader, but do not think I am not still irritated with you. Get out."

Rising, the dragonrider stalked out of the room, avoiding the gazes of the training master and the Holdleader.

Once he was gone, Sean leaned back in his chair, rubbing the corners of his eyes. "Thank gods I don't have to write a letter to Domar. Gonran knows *that* would have been awkward. First the border dispute and now this; this season is off to a bad start."

Garrett took a seat, placing a letter on the desk in front of the Holdleader. "It's about to get worse. We just got word from Hadfoll…"

✳   ✳   ✳   ✳

Once Selah had reached her room, she collapsed, exhausted, onto her bed, setting Windchaser on the pillow. Rolling on her stomach, the girl looked at the dragonet.

Windchaser was small, the length of Selah's hand and forearm. She easily fit on the pillow, her sky-blue scales standing out sharply on the white fabric of the bed sheets. Her delicate ears were laid back on her head, her wings clamped tightly to her back.

Without warning, the dragonet's eyes snapped open, her violet irises turning until they regarded Selah intently. Yawning widely, Windchaser struggled to her feet. Her claws caught on the blankets and the hapless dragonet fell flat on her face. Whispering comforting words, Selah took the dragonet into her arms. The dragonet was slightly stockier than the adults of her kind, who tended to be more streamlined. She had such a look of innocence that Selah felt her insides melt. The dragonet looked up at her with adoration, reached forward with one paw and clawed her on the arm.

"Ouch!" exclaimed the girl. "What'd you do that for?"

Windchaser immediately flinched at the tone of Selah's voice, her folded wings beginning to quiver dangerously, like a pouted lower lip before a child starts to cry. The girl regretted her words, and patted the dragonet to appease her. "Sorry, Windchaser. What do you want?"

Windchaser began to whine, opening and closing her mouth piteously. It took Selah a moment to understand. "Oh...you're hungry. Can I change first?"

The dragonet moaned even louder. Setting Windchaser on the bed, Selah pulled on a fresh tunic and breeches quickly, taking a moment to enjoy the feeling of the fabric on her new skin. Windchaser whistled in irritation, opening and closing her mouth faster. Selah pulled on her boots, apologizing hurriedly. "Hold on, Windchaser, I'm coming, we'll go straight down to the kitchens, please, don't cry..."

The dragonet let out an earsplitting shriek that made the crystal cluster on the beside table flicker. Selah scooped up the dragonet and raced out of her room, a restraining hand over Windchaser's mouth.

The dragonet continued to shriek all the way to the kitchens, Selah blushing until she was a bright red. The cooks seemed to have expected her, an apprentice tossing her a warm bottle of milk the moment she burst into the room. Fortunately, the girl escaped for the Mess Hall before the cooks recognized her as the pallon who had supposedly died last night.

Selah sat down at one of the empty tables and placed the bottle of milk in Windchaser's mouth. The dragonet drank it voraciously, both paws pulling the bottle closer to her face as she chugged it down. When she was finished, the dragonet belched loudly and fell asleep.

Moments later, Landon walked in with his own baby dragon. "Selah!" he shouted, almost dropping his dragonet in shock. Selah held up a finger to her lips, beckoning him over.

The boy, taking notice of the sleeping dragonet in her arms, dropped his voice to a whisper. "What happened to you? I thought you were dead. Where are your burns?"

Getting the feeling that she would be telling this tale many times more in the future, Selah told him what had happened. Landon nodded and was silent throughout the entire story. When she was finished, he sighed. "I...I'm sorry for what Marcus did. He wasn't one of my closest friends. He's in the infirmary right now...his head smashed on a rock when I tackled him," he explained to Selah's questioning glance. "Trust me, no one is talking to him right now...even Corith thinks what he did was wrong."

Selah smirked. "Burning me? I bet Corith was angry because he didn't get to do it himself."

Landon smiled half-heartedly. "It's not just burning you...everyone hates him because he paralyzed them or one of their friends during the Choosing. I just," the boy's eyes burned with anger, his jaw clenching, "I can't believe that I ever considered him worth talking to."

Selah adjusted her grip on Windchaser. "Was it you and the twins who put out the fire? When I was burning?" Landon nodded. "Who put me in the Spring?"

"Averon."

Selah bit her lip. "Why would he do that? I mean, it looked like Sean was pretty mad at him. What if Stormhunter hadn't liked—hadn't healed me? He could have been struck down if the gods were in a bad mood."

Landon smiled. "That's the type of dragonrider he is. He got yelled at by my father for something I did when he was recruiting at my fief, and didn't say a word. He doesn't let anything stop him from doing what he thinks is right."

"I want to thank him. He saved my life."

Landon leaned forward. "I...want you to know something. Jumping through the fire...that was the bravest thing I've ever seen. I consider you my friend, as do the others."

"I'd be honored to be your friend."

"Enough talk like that—my head's big enough as it is." Landon grinned. "I need to get milk for Indio, but I'll see you later."

Selah watched him go, a smile lifting the corners of her mouth.

＊　　　＊　　　＊　　　＊

Selah awoke in the middle of the night to the soft sound of snoring. Windchaser lay spread-eagled on her back, her mouth hanging open. Smiling, the girl turned the dragonet on her side, arranging her in a more comfortable position. Propping her head up on her elbow, Selah looked at her Chosen. To her surprise, tears welled up in her eyes, and she bent down and kissed the baby dragon on the brow.

Windchaser reached out and grasped Selah's forearm, clutching it to her body. She was still fast asleep. The glow of the crystal cast her in a soft light, and Selah had never seen a more beautiful thing in the world.

Drawing the dragonet to her chest, Selah closed her eyes. She had found the love she had been looking for all along.

HADFOLL

For the next two weeks, Selah was the happiest girl in the kingdom and she knew she shouldn't be. Under normal circumstances, the constant begging and whining of a dragonet would have set her teeth on edge. Keeping Windchaser occupied should have been the least of her vexations; feeding, washing, burping, and caring for a living, fragile creature ought to overwhelm her.

It didn't. Every moment spent with Windchaser was pure joy. The Masters had given them two weeks off to care for the newborn dragons, hoping to give the pallons time to adjust to the foreign task of nurturing. Selah relished the time she spent alone with her Chosen; the other pallons were as reluctant as she to engage in conversation. They were all infatuated with their new companions.

Selah spent her days feeding Windchaser every hour on the hour. As the dragonet had demonstrated, she would be as obstreperous as possible if she did not receive immediate gratification. Generally, Selah passed the time examining Windchaser, although staring at the dragonet with an agape mouth soon lost its luster. Even though the girl considered her dragonet beautiful in every way possible, Selah quickly realized that Windchaser did not change in appearance between each meal.

Three days after the Choosing, Windchaser finished her meal and whined loudly, wanting more attention from Selah. The girl tickled her stomach, causing the dragonet to chortle, but she soon tired of the game and began to whimper again. The other pallons were beginning to look at Selah with a look of irritation. Desperately, Selah snatched the thickest book she could find on the shelf, turning to the first page and beginning to read.

"It was high summer, and the world was alive with the joy a warm season brings. The rivers were satiated with water as clear as the glass that many a family could afford in their windows. Life was rich for the poorest of the poor. It was a time of courage and bravery, eternal love and valor. The Knights of Alcaron traversed the most humble of paths, carrying torches of glory to light the few pockets of darkness in our beloved kingdom. And thus the Golden Age reached its height. By fall our climb to the heavens had stalled. With winter came our long plummet into darkness. This is the story of their mistake...my mistake...and our fall from the sky."

Slowly, Windchaser stopped grumbling, fascinated by the sound of Selah's voice. The girl, her eyes on the page, didn't notice that the other pallons had stopped making noise as well and were listening intently.

She had read for an hour when she felt the small grip on her hand go slack. Windchaser had fallen asleep, lulled into slumber by Selah's steady stream of words. A slight smile on her lips, the girl closed the book and set it on the table.

"Don't stop," Landon ordered. He had turned his chair toward her so that he could hear the words more clearly. "It's just starting to get to a good part."

Selah looked around the room, realizing for the first time that the others had been listening. "Er...all right." She opened the book and flipped to the approximate place that she had stopped. "Where was I?"

They read late into the night, Landon taking over when Selah's throat grew sore. No one left, although a few more pallons joined them, taking a seat in a chair or beside the roaring hearth. Windchaser awoke once, falling back to sleep when Selah fed her. The soothing tones of Landon's voice seemed to place a spell on the dragonets; those who were awake watched him with a dreamy fascination that was matched by their Riders. Selah was riveted to her seat and unable to tear her attention from the story.

Landon had just finished a chapter when a servant peered around the corner. "What are you all doing up?" he demanded in a low voice, hands on his hips. "You were all supposed to be asleep an hour ago!"

As if startled out of a deep doze, the pallons sat up in surprise. Selah glanced at the hourglass—all the sand had long since collected at the bottom, just as the crystals had dimmed to their nighttime intensity. The girl hadn't noticed; time had passed with a surreal quickness.

With hurried good nights, the pallons retreated to their rooms, the admonishing whispers of the servant chasing them down the hall. Selah quickly changed into her nightshirt and clambered into bed, cradling the slumbering Windchaser carefully.

Every night after the first, the pallons continued to read aloud. Over the next two weeks of their vacation, a group of ten or so regular listeners formed, each of them getting a chance to read. Bern was by far the liveliest, gesturing broadly until the dragonet in his lap, tired of being jostled and bumped, squawked loudly. The boy toned down his acting, but couldn't resist the odd facial expression when the text called for it.

Windchaser stayed awake longer and longer until she was only taking six naps a day rather than ten. Selah encouraged the dragonet when she tried to walk across the room. However, Windchaser was highly right side dominant, always stepping out with her right paw rather than alternating sides.

It was the last day of their break, and Selah was on her knees, coaching the struggling dragonet. "No, Windchaser, your left paw." Reaching forward, the girl took a hold of Windchaser's paw and pulled it out, placing it on the floor. "Like this."

Her tiny brow furrowed in concentration, the dragonet stepped out with her right paw. Pausing with her left in the air, she wobbled and overbalanced, sprawling on the floor of Selah's room. Smiling, the girl set the dragonet back on her feet. "Try again, Windchaser."

With painful slowness, the dragonet took one step forward. Reaching out with her left, the dragonet placed in on the ground, swaying for a moment but retaining her balance. Another step with her right. Left. Right. Left. Right.

"Windchaser, you're doing it! You're walking!" Selah shouted in elation. Falling down on all fours, Selah crawled beside the dragonet, verbally encouraging her whenever she faltered or hesitated. Windchaser let out a whistle of disbelief, bumbling around the room. Her violet eyes were alight with a pride and joy that Selah had never seen before. Her claws snagged on the rug, and she fell flat on her face.

Selah swept the dragonet up in her arms, rising to her feet. "You're the most wonderful dragonet in the world," the girl whispered in the tiny ear, her words thick with praise.

Bracing the dragonet on her hip, Selah picked up a book that she had left on the floor. Turning to place it on the dresser, the girl chuckled. Firmin would have thought that she was ridiculous, crawling about on the floor like that. Her smile disappeared as her brother's face swam into focus in her mind's eye. She hadn't thought about him for a long time. The girl set the book down, tracing the seam with one finger.

Windchaser struggled against Selah's protective grip until the girl set her back on the floor. The dragonet spent the next hour making her way slowly around the perimeter of the room, leaning against the wall when she was weary.

Selah watched from the bed, a strange emotion swelling in her chest. It took a few moments for the girl to locate a name for it—she was proud. Not of herself, but of something else, proud *for* someone else. It was a new feeling—she had always been in so much competition with Firmin and the other youths at Domar that many of her emotions were related to herself. She was sad when she was unsuccessful, joyful when she triumphed, angry when Kavan irritated her. She had loved others, but this kind of love, turning another being's failures and victories into her own...it was new, something that confused her. Selah didn't know what to think. She was pensively silent, brooding, until Windchaser, on her sixth lap around the room, fell and began to whine. Rising, the girl determined that her dragonet had had enough for one night.

*   *   *   *

The following Monday marked the return to her classes. Selah was up early, roused out of a pleasant dream by Windchaser's pleas for breakfast. The girl reached the Mess Hall before the others. Even with her dragonet, she felt rather alone sitting by herself at the long table that had long been designated as belonging to the group of her friends.

Selah shivered, feeling unseen eyes boring into her back. Glancing to the side, the girl noted that the cooks were staring at her. All of them. She looked quickly back at the smooth surface of the table. While most of the pallons had grown accustomed to her return from near death, the servants had not and showed it openly. The cooks were the worst; when they distributed the plates of meat to each table, they never handed it to her. The maids and menservants walked on the other side of the hallway when they caught sight of her. Normally, Selah didn't let it bother her, but without the comfortable conversation of her friends, she was painfully aware of the cooks' scrutiny.

"Morning, Selah," yawned a voice, making her jump in her seat. Landon took the chair opposite of her. "Sorry. Did I startle you?"

"No," Selah lied. "How'd you sleep?"

The boy smiled ruefully. "Poorly. Indio was hungry at midnight." The dragonet perked his ears at the sound of his name, and then looked away in disinterest when Landon continued to address Selah. "I'm not ready to return to classes yet, much less training. What are we going to do with our dragonets when we're with Garrett?"

Selah shrugged. "I don't know. I'm sure Master Garrett has something figured out."

It seemed that all the Masters had prepared for the arrival of the dragonets. A small mountain of extra milk canteens was stacked in the corner of each room. The pallons frequented the pile several times during classes, as their dragonets were eating voraciously and often.

When they reached Care of Dragonets, Sean had the look on his face that indicated a forthcoming lecture. Selah took her seat, allowing herself a small sigh. She was not looking forward to whatever he had to say.

One by one, Sean inspected each of the dragonets, proclaiming their faults or strengths to the entire class. When he made his way to Selah, a look of profound irritation briefly flashed across his face, as if she reminded him of a past annoyance. He examined Windchaser with a business-like detachment.

"Her wings are far too large. They will be ungainly when she is on the ground." He glanced at Selah as if this was somehow her fault. "She is too small."

Now that it was roughly brought to her attention, Selah realized that Windchaser *was* small—compared to Indio and Silverclaw, Landon and Aswin's dragonets respectively, her baby dragon was undersized.

Sean had taken Windchaser into his arms to test her weight. "She will be disadvantaged in battle, when attacked by a larger dragon." Selah swallowed the gall in her throat, and took Windchaser back without a word in reply. For the gods' sake, Windchaser was only two weeks old! How could he know her strengths and weaknesses before she had a chance to show them properly?

Windchaser tucked her head close to Selah, seeking the comfort of her embrace. The dragonet could not see the blush on her Rider's cheeks, but seemed to sense that she had failed somehow. Selah could hardly bear the feel of the room for the rest of the hour. Corith had made use of Sean's embarrassing comments to turn in his seat and sneer at her at every opportunity. Selah tried to ignore him.

Aviation was far more interesting—Master Loman showed them how to ensure that their dragonets were in best form for flying. Using Hale's dragonet to demonstrate, he gently massaged the wings, first along the bone and then with a lighter touch on the delicate flaps of skin. It took a while for the girl to coax Windchaser to extend hers to their full extent.

Windchaser's wings were a sight to behold. They were two-thirds the length of her body, scale-less skin stretched taut on the wing bones. It felt like the soft roll of imported cloth that Selah had once touched on a market day at Domar. As the girl massaged each wing, Windchaser craned back her head to study them curiously, as if she had just realized that they were there. The dragonet was still staring when class was over and began to examine beneath her claws, apparently hoping she might find another surprise.

Training proved to be the most challenging of all. Snowfire was put in charge of the dragonets while they exercised. Garrett did not seem bothered by the presence of the baby dragons and would not let the pallons lose their focus either. When he saw Selah pause during an attack to steal a glance at Windchaser, he rapped her smartly on the arm with a curt, "Pay attention!" Nonetheless, Selah found her thoughts drawn to her new companion and fought sluggishly. Her fellow pallons seemed to be suffering the same lack of concentration, and Garrett was not pleased at the end of three hours. After a stern lecture on how they were not entitled to sit on their heels now that they had dragons, he sent them away, shaking his head in disappointment. Selah felt a prick of guilt at his words, but her low feelings dissipated the moment Windchaser caught sight of her and scrambled into her arms.

Selah went to sleep bone tired. It was a pattern that was soon established over the following weeks; Windchaser would rouse her when it was still dark outside—the dragonet hungered early and often. The girl would drift back to sleep until the watch dragon woke them all with a great roar. She would rise, and complete the coursework she had not finished the night before over breakfast. Her three classes would pass in a fit of boredom or attention, depending on the subject. Training would leave her exhausted, too tired to even play with Windchaser, much less complete the work her Masters had assigned her. She received a day off each Sunday, but it was filled with rudimentary chores that she didn't accomplish during the week.

Slowly, Selah felt herself begin to change. She had eaten well at Domar, but most excess fat had been banished by Garrett's demanding training. Over time, she was not as tired as she had once been. The weapons she handled no longer seemed leaden after three hours of training. Garrett began to talk of beginning them on sword instruction.

Positive change was not limited to Selah alone; Windchaser grew in both mental and physical capability. Soon, the dragonet understood much of what Selah was saying and could walk beside the girl for extended periods of time.

One morning, a month after her return to classes, Selah awoke far earlier than usual. Even Windchaser, nestled in the crook of her arm, was fast asleep. The air was crisp and free of the smell of cooking; breakfast had not been prepared yet. Selah lay for a while before a strange need to be outside consumed her thoughts.

Loath to be away from Windchaser, the girl dressed and waited until her drago-net had awakened before exiting her room. The crystals lining the walls were still dim.

It was strangely chilly for an early fall morning. The sun was just beginning to peer over the horizon, casting a strange pattern of shadows on the hills that were only visible from the white battlements of Dragonhold. Breathing in the fresh air, Selah relaxed, leaning against the wall. Birds sang in the distance, carrying on a discussion with each other that was as real as any human conversation.

A guard manning one of the ballistas regarded her curiously. The helmet he wore obscured a good part of his face, but from what Selah could see, he was smiling. "What's a pallon like you doing up so early?"

Selah liked him immediately, if only because he recognized her rank, female as she was. She shrugged. "Couldn't sleep."

The guard chuckled, bracing himself on his spear. "Wish I *could* sleep in." He returned to scanning the distance. Selah joined him.

She had turned her eyes to the sky when a black speck against a cloud forma-tion caught her attention. The girl watched intently; it grew larger with each passing moment but was still small enough that she couldn't identify it. She walked over to the guard and tapped him on the shoulder. "Sir, there's something out there."

He was immediately alert. "Where?" When Selah pointed to the black speck, he shook his head. "I don't see anything." It was a long minute before he nodded. "Aye. I see."

They waited a moment longer before Selah exhaled in understanding. "It's a dragon."

The guard looked at her oddly. "Are you sure? All I see is a black spot." When Selah nodded the affirmative, he raised his eyebrows. "You have good eyesight, youngster. You need to have sharp eyes to be on guard duty, and I don't think even Caldor could have seen that one. He's probably coming in to land in an hour or so."

Selah thanked him for the compliment, turning back to the fief. The smells of cooking meat emanated from the kitchens. The girl smiled at the guard. "I need to go—breakfast is almost done."

The guard gave her another bemused look. "If you say so." The watch dragon roared the final wake up call, and Selah bid her new acquaintance farewell. Carry-ing the yawning Windchaser, the girl made her way to the Mess Hall.

Oddly, when she got there, Sean and Garrett were standing at the front of the room. Curious, Selah slid into her seat, giving Windchaser a steaming piece of bread to placate her. When all the other pallons had arrived and the food had been served, her training master began to speak.

"Most of you have not heard—there was a large wildfire just southwest of Hadfoll three fortnights ago. Some of the town burnt to the ground before they could get it under control. When Lord Myelin first contacted us, he thought that he would be able to manage without support from any of the other fiefs. Unfortunately, they need more hands to help them through the winter; many of his men died trying to control the fire. We cannot spare two Wings," here Garrett paused and sent a strange look in Sean's direction, "so we have decided to send you to help with the harvest." He raised his hands for silence when excited murmuring broke out among the pallons. "The Fourteenth Wing will accompany you, as will I. We plan to stay at Hadfoll through the winter and leave in early spring."

Selah brightened at the thought of seeing Averon, the Wingleader of the Fourteenth again. She had not had a chance to thank him for saving her life during the Choosing. "We leave in two days," finished Garrett.

The night before they left, the girl began to pack. Selah did not have many clothes; she had three each of shirts, breeches, tunics, and whatnot. That, and her formal pallon wear that she had received at the beginning of her training, constituted as her entire wardrobe. It was easy enough to jam the clothing into one of her haversacks. When she had first arrived at Dragonhold, she had been weighed down with memorabilia from Domar more than anything else. Selah scanned the room, checking to see if she had forgotten anything. Also included in the bag were Windchaser's bottle and various necessities. Garrett had instructed them to bring their weapons, but all Selah owned was her bow and the belt knife that every person carried with them at all times.

There was a knock at her door just as she had closed her haversack. "Come in," Selah called automatically.

It was Aerin, the dragonrider who had led her to the Choosing. Her ice-blue eyes widened when Selah turned to face her. The woman looked to the ground. "Well...you certainly look better than when I saw you last."

Aerin's last sight of her must have been when she was dying from horrific burns. Selah rubbed the back of her neck awkwardly, unsure if Aerin had heard the rumors that had been running amok in Dragonhold ever since the Choosing. Strange things were whispered in the halls, and she had overheard some of the stories about her return from death—they were neither becoming nor accurate. "I'm feeling a lot better. I...well..."

Aerin lifted her hands. "That's all right. I know what happened. I suppose you know that the Fourteenth Wing is taking the pallons to Hadfoll?" When Selah nodded, she continued. "Well, I'm your chaperone for the trip. You'll be riding with me when we fly to Hadfoll."

"What does your dragon look like?"

"She's bright red with emerald green eyes." Aerin smiled at the thought of her dragon. "Her name is Firegem—if you get lost, just call her or my name."

Selah nodded. "Thank you."

"I'll see you tomorrow morning then," Aerin paused as she left, turning back to regard Selah with interest. When Selah returned her gaze, the woman shook her head as if to dispel troubling thoughts. She shut the door behind her.

*   *   *   *

The watch dragon roared again, calling the pallons to the dragons that were gathered in the courtyard. Two wings, the Fourteenth and the Third, were carrying them to Hadfoll, but only the Fourteenth would stay with them through the winter.

It was no easy task to find Firegem. There were multiple red-scaled dragons gathered in the courtyard, waiting for their respective pallons. Windchaser chirped in appreciation for her older dragon counterparts; several were enormous.

When she finally saw Aerin, she made her way through the mob to the woman. The dragonrider smiled when she saw the girl that would be her charge for the next few months. "Morning, Selah," she said, taking the haversack from her. The woman quickly explained matters while she attached the pack to Firegem's harness. "We'll leave in about fifteen minutes. You have a flight jacket?" Selah nodded, extending her arms to show Aerin the jacket that Averon had lent her when she had first met him.

"It's a little big," said the girl. "And it's Averon's. I need to give it back to him."

Aerin dismissed the notion with a wave of her hand. "He has at least ten different flight jackets—you can keep this one until we get you a new one."

"Where?"

"Banor can make you a flight jacket if you want one—although you should get one made here when you finish growing."

Selah nodded, the hairs on the back of her neck prickling. Someone was watching her. Before she could try to see who it was, Aerin urged her to mount Firegem.

"Here," said the woman, offering her a rope with a miniature harness attached to one end. "Put your dragonet in the harness and tie the rope around your waist. It's for safety measures. Keep her in your flight jacket any time we are in the air." Selah did as she was told, making sure that the harness would support Windchaser's weight. After knotting the rope around her waist, she secured herself to Firegem's harness.

Once Aerin had mounted and Windchaser was tucked safely into her flight jacket, they waited for a few minutes while the others made last second preparations for their flight. When Averon lifted his fist into the air, the dragons began to pump their wings. Another hand signal, and they launched into flight.

Selah rocked back as Firegem soared into the sky. Windchaser whistled in surprise as the ground sank beneath them.

Once Dragonhold became a white spot far below, Firegem craned back her head to regard Selah curiously. The dragons around them were also looking at her.—*I have heard much about you,*—stated Firegem.

"Oh," said Selah, suddenly very uncomfortable. Firegem seemed to be able to ask the questions that her Rider, Aerin, would not.

—*Is it true that Stormhunter came to you?*—Selah was surprised; Firegem's inquiry was the most accurate that she had received. When the girl nodded, Firegem's expression became unreadable.—*It is quite an honor.*—

"I suppose," said Selah, painfully aware of Aerin's presence in front of her. The dragonrider could probably hear everything that Firegem was saying as well.

The red dragon returned her eyes to the front.—*It is not common for Stormhunter to visit mortals...especially of your kind. It is strange that he chose to visit you.*—

Selah wondered how Firegem and Aerin could have Chosen each other—from the tone of Firegem's mind voice, they had very different personalities. "I was placed into his Spring," said Selah over the wind. "I don't think it was a question of *what* I was so much as *where* I was. I don't think Stormhunter would have come to me if I wasn't trespassing on his Spring."

When Firegem spoke again, her voice had changed to a much lighter and younger tone.—*She will do, Aerin. She will do.*—

"Do what?" asked Selah, but Aerin only smiled and did not answer.

It took them three days of hard flying to reach Hadfoll. She only saw Landon and her friends in the brief moments between meals, sleeping, and flight. It was challenging to not despair in the middle of a long flight, but Aerin kept her occupied by explaining the commonsense of fighting dragonback. However, when they reached Hadfoll, Selah almost wished they could turn the dragons around and fly back to Dragonhold.

First to catch Selah's attention was the lack of people as they drew nearer to the fief. There was no call of recognition from the gray walls of Hadfoll. The flags on the pennants of the castle were at half-mast, and the purple cloth of mourning hung from many of the doors in the town that resided within the outer wall. The farms to the north and the west were full and ready to harvest—the lands to the southeast were razed to the ground. As they flew even lower, there was no baying of cattle as the smell of dragons filled the air. There was hardly a sound at all.

After the guard on the wall identified that they were friendly, the dragons were permitted to land. As Firegem landed in the field outside the curtain wall of the castle, Selah thought that if the pallons and dragonriders from Dragonhold *had* wanted to attack Hadfoll, there was very little that the beleaguered guards on the wall could have done to stop them.

A man wearing the colors of Hadfoll, deep burgundy and pale yellow, approached them, stopping in front of Garrett. As the training master, he had the highest rank of all the dragonriders present. "Welcome to Hadfoll, Wingleader Garrett of Dalbrook."

Garrett inclined his graying head as Selah started in surprise—she was not aware of that her training master had once led an entire Wing. "I am sorry for your loss, Lord Myelin. The pallons and dragonriders here will stay with you through the winter to ensure that the new spring will be hopeful."

Myelin bowed in gratitude. "We have a large barrack that some of the dragons may stay in. Work is being done to change the horse stable into a den. Please, dismount." He gestured to a boy standing next to him. "Edwin here will show you to your rooms."

Edwin had the harrowed, far-off look of one who had seen too much death. His eyes were as downcast and mournful as Myelin's. He waited while the dragonriders and pallons gathered their belongs before wordlessly leading them into the streets that surrounded the castle. He steered them away from the southwest corner, which, if Garrett had informed them correctly, was burnt to the ground. The inhabitants of Hadfoll had not had the time, or the manpower, to begin rebuilding the homes.

Edwin stopped them at an inn that had escaped the fire completely. "This is where ye'll be stayin', Riders." Something like a smile lifted the corners of his mouth when the Wingleader of the Third pressed a copper into his hand. "Thank ye."

Dusk was falling, and Garrett bid them goodnight as they made their way to their respective rooms. Each pallon was partnered with a dragonrider—thus, Aerin and Selah shared a room.

It was sparsely furnished. Two pallets adorned either side of the room—a small stand with an empty water basin and towel had been lain out for them. A stack of blankets and privacy screen for dressing were the only other items in the room.

Aerin yawned widely, taking half of the blankets and beginning to arrange them on one of the pallets. Windchaser began to explore her new chambers. Selah dropped her bag beside the untaken bed and followed Aerin's example. When they were finished, Aerin took the basin outside to fill it.

Selah was asleep by the time she returned, exhausted from the long day's ride. Windchaser had curled up in her arms, her eyes closed. Aerin smiled at the sight, knowing she must have looked much the same when she was younger. The woman shut the door and went to sleep.

*   *   *   *

"Who knows anything about carpentry?" asked Averon. None of the pallons raised their hands. "Farming, or growing things?" Two of Selah's peers stepped forward so Averon could see who they were. The dragonrider was trying to assess their skills and see what he had to work with. They were all gathered in the main hall of the inn, many fidgeting because they had not been served breakfast yet. The man made notes on a sheet of parchment.

"Sewing?" Averon looked around the room. Many of the dragonriders and pallons turned to Selah expectantly. The girl folded her arms across her chest obstinately. She had never used a needle in her life.

When no one made comment, Averon continued down the list of skills that would prove useful to the fief. Selah grew more uncomfortable as she realized that she had nothing, besides the knowledge of how to do mediocre chores, which would be any sort of help.

The dragonrider reached the end of his list, and Selah had not responded to any of his inquiries. She was not alone—Bern and Aswin, as well as several more of the pallons, had not raised their hands.

Averon shuffled the papers in front of him, pausing to dip his quill in more ink. "Those who have not raised their hands report to Garrett once we're done here."

Selah and the others did as he requested. Garrett, after asking them more specific questions about what they knew how to do, placed them under the jurisdiction of a dark man. His skin was tanned and weather-beaten—it was obvious that he spent a great amount of time outdoors. His hair was stark white; the combination of the two features would have been comical if the man's expression was not so serious.

"I am Bron, a knight of Hadfoll." He spoke cultured but plainly, as if his rank was nothing to be proud of, and did not offer them his hand. "I'm in charge of you lot. We'll be doing grunt work—nothing fancy. Are you sure you can handle that?" He looked pointedly at Nolan and Fagan, respectively the plumpest and skinniest boys in the group, and at Selah. The girl bristled at his tone, wondering why the knight was deliberately trying to provoke them. Before she could puzzle out the man's motives, he brusquely told them to get outside—they had work to do.

First, he had them muck out the dens and stables. It was a new chore to Selah, and the girl had to keep herself from gagging as they scooped up the putrid manure. It took them several hours to finish the job. Despite her training, Selah's back was sore by the time they were through.

It was only the beginning. Without so much as a rest, Bron ordered them to climb into the hayloft and feed the horses. When they were finished with that, he found another chore for them to do. The whole while, he groomed and exercised the horses, not without informing them that he had to care for the animals himself because he couldn't trust the pallons with the job. By the end of the day, the stable was spotless, and Selah had learned to hate the look in Bron's eyes when he inspected her work and found something wrong with it.

She, Renton, Fagan, Bern, and Aswin returned to the inn in a foul mood. They were hot, sticky, and dirty. The smile on Landon's face when he greeted them at the door only served to deepen Selah's irritation. "How was your day?" he asked.

Selah exploded. "It was horrible!" Landon, taken aback, blinked in surprise. "I swear, this knight has something against us; he made us work *all* day! No breaks! He's the nastiest man I have ever met."

An iron grip seized her shoulder, and Selah was enveloped by the smell of leather and horsehide. "I'm glad I left a good impression," whispered Bron's voice dangerously. Selah instantly regretted her words. The knight spun her around to face him. His eyes were narrowed in an intense anger that didn't seem to match the relatively pale measure of Selah's accusations. "Souped up dragonrider brat," he muttered, more to himself than to her. "Follow me."

Afraid not to, Selah did so, ignoring the stares of her peers. Bron did not look back in her direction once.

When they were out of the earshot of the others, he turned on her. The anger had not faded out of his eyes. "Have you ever heard the old saying, 'Men work from sun up to sun down, but a woman's work is never done'?"

Selah froze, recognizing the common phrase but unable to understand what Bron meant by it. The knight shook his head. "I want you to see something."

Bron lead her through the maze of Hadfoll, moving at a pace that forced Selah to push herself to keep up. He stopped a small building that had been recently constructed—shavings of wood still littered the ground.

The window was open; the summer had hung a thick blanket of warmth over Hadfoll that made even the nighttime stifling. Bron gestured that she come to the windowsill and gaze within. Selah obeyed.

A woman sat in the center of the one room building, surrounded by looms and bolts of fabric that formed a palisade of cloth around her. Two solitary candles provided a dim glow that faded into warm darkness by the time it reached the corners of the room.

A red band of cloth had been tied about the woman's forehead to keep her black hair back. She did not look up at her observers—all of her attention was focused on her work. Her fingers fell and rose like hawks as they guided a needle through the cloth in front of her. She was making a tunic.

"Maria woke before sunrise today," said Bron. His voice quivered with some kind of emotion that Selah could not read; was it pride? Sadness? "She stopped once, to eat at lunch. All the others have gone to bed." The knight regarded Selah with eyes that burned with intensity. "She hasn't taken a break all day. Granted, neither have you, but she does not complain. Not one word. Do you know how many people she has clothed today?"

Selah shook her head. The muscles in Bron's forehead knitted together into a frown. "You dragonriders are so choked with your own glory that you don't look at the ordinary people. There would be no clothes on your backs, no food on your table, if it were not for the common people. Life is good when you're on the back of a dragon," Bron snapped, his words saturated with bitterness, "but when on the ground, the work is too hard."

"I…" Selah started.

"If you can't stand listening to an old knight, look at Maria." Bron was almost yelling now. "She sits there and makes tunics so that the boys won't be cold in the winter. She makes shirts so that you dragonriders will be comfortable when you go on patrol. She doesn't do any fighting, but she is just as dedicated and selfless. And that is more than you can ever hope to be, dragonrider brat."

Selah turned her eyes on the woman. Maria did not look up.

*   *   *   *

Selah did not sleep well the night after Bron's lecture. She had too much to think about. Gradually, though, the insults overshadowed the lessons he was trying to convey, and Selah only hated the man more.

"Domar! Straighten that row! It's a line, not a maze."

Selah didn't say a word, bending over to comply with Bron's orders. If the crop line was not perfectly straight, Bron had a panic attack. *I'll show you dragonrider brat,* she thought. *Just because a dragon thought me worthy doesn't mean that I can't do real work. No matter what* you *say to me.*

Bron returned her sentiments, rarely speaking to her in anything but barked orders. One time, after a full day of harassment, Selah snapped and shouted, "I did my work today!" at him.

He raised an eyebrow mockingly. "To help someone or just to spite me?"

Selah couldn't give him an answer.

*   *   *   *

It's odd how destruction brings such good luck sometimes, thought the man to himself, surveying the signs of fire damage in the undergrowth around him. He returned his attention to the campfire before him. There would be little need to hide the signs of their camp. The whole wood was in ashes…a bit more from his fire would not be noticed.

The others slowly gravitated to his flame, waiting for his orders. They wore only simple leather armor; a few were lucky enough to have acquired chain mail. His own brown dragonscale armor gleamed even in the dull lighting. Others in his band had taken dragonscales and woven them together into armbands or bracers. Their constructions gave them only a slightly higher standing among the Hunters—they were made from scraps of skin that were purloined from kills after the true slayer had taken his share. His armor was real; he had skinned the hide from the dead dragon himself.

He was in command of twenty dragonhunters. They were, more or less, as disciplined as soldiers, but better trained and fearless. It took a different kind of man to battle a sixteen-foot long dragon without hesitation than it did to stand watch behind the wall of a fief.

He turned to Joaquin, the scout and spy. "What do you know?"

Joaquin was not afraid of the leader; the spy's skills prevented him from being expendable. Still, his voice was respectful. "Dragonslayer, two Wings flew into Hadfoll several days ago."

The Dragonslayer was growing impatient. "Tell me something I don't already know." His voice, although calm, contained a veiled threat.

Joaquin, taking the hint, bowed. "Apologies. One Wing left the next day, although the other remained. It appears that this year's pallons have accompanied them as well."

The Dragonslayer drew his sword and began to hone it on a stone. Joaquin squirmed, uncomfortable at the sight of bare metal. "How are the defenses?"

Joaquin's eyes lit up with fierce excitement. "Minimal, Slayer. There is the Wing I mentioned earlier, but—"

"We cannot attack an entire Wing of dragons and their Riders," snapped the Dragonslayer. "You are disappointing me, Joaquin."

Joaquin shook his head. "I am not referring to a full scale assault. Even the clumsiest of us can hide like a shadow in the forest. The pallons are sent out each day to harvest or perform tasks. There is not always a dragonrider with them."

The Dragonslayer already knew where the spy's thoughts were headed. "I see. Wait until they are isolated and pick them off one by one." Joaquin nodded. The Dragonslayer continued. "The farmlands are flat. It is far too easy for a dragon to pick up our scent or catch sight of us. We would be walking into a deathtrap."

Joaquin twitched, one side of his face scrunching unattractively. The man was balding, with shoulder length, wispy brown hair—he had never been becoming, even when he was younger. "Not if the dragons are somewhere else."

"A diversion."

"Send them on a wild goose chase. Leave an obvious mark for one of their Scouts to pick up. The Wingleader won't risk having a group of dragonhunters running around while there are pallons in a vulnerable position. Draw the Wing into a fight several miles from Hadfoll. Then send the rest of us into the farmland and kill what pallons you can."

The Dragonslayer nodded slowly. It was not a bad plan; there was a chance of causalities on his side, but he had learned long ago not to be adverse to a loss of men. Besides, once the pallons headed back to Dragonhold, there would be no getting at them—chances were, they would not have another opportunity to fight them until they were years older and more experienced. He had to strike now.

"Very well. Take the trackers and set up a fake campsite. Make sure it can be seen from the air. Leave something so that they know it was us." Joaquin nodded. "I'll take the rest of the hunters to the edge of the forest. You know the signal for retreat."

The Dragonslayer did not often allow himself to convey emotions. However, the opportunity that had been presented before them brought a cold smile to his face. Even the warm fire seemed to shudder in fear.

*   *   *   *

The next few days passed uneventfully for Selah. The temperatures had dropped until it was necessary to pull a blanket over herself when she went to sleep at night—previously, the weather had been warm enough to make covers unnecessary.

Windchaser was able to stomach a full meal of meat now, making the chore of preparing mash an ordeal that Selah only had to perform once a day rather than three times.

Bron continued to be a pain, making them work long hours. Although Selah grudgingly learned her lesson, the knight retained the inordinate ability to irritate her. Still, she was becoming stronger, no longer exhausted after a day's work.

She was out in the fields, weeding away the plants that were beginning to choke the crop rows, when the alarm bell rang.

Hadfoll had only one large bell, its sonorous tones able to reach several miles away from the fief itself. The group of six pallons that had been placed under Bron's command began to move toward the fief before he motioned for them to stop. "Wait," the grizzled old knight said, his eyes scanning the horizon. "I don't see anything. They'll send someone out to us."

True to his word, a messenger arrived a few minutes later. "There were signs of a dragonhunter camp a few miles north of here," said the servant. "Wingleader Averon is taking the dragonriders out to find them. He advises that you return to fief."

Bron shook his head. "We're not that far from the fief. There will be no trouble here, anyway. We'll head back in a few hours."

Selah glanced in his direction. "But what if—" A glare from the knight silenced her. Thoroughly chastised, the girl bent back down to hide her face in the row of berry bushes she tended.

The servant sighed. "All right. Call on the horn if you need help."

Bron waved a hand dismissively, turning back down to the rows. The servant left with several backward glances.

The sun was ruthless, burning the back of Selah's neck and soaking her brow with sweat. Her torso ached from bending over to yank stubborn weeds from the baked ground. Despite the fact that much of her attention was taken by her work, the girl could not shake the feeling that she was being watched. Shadows perched at the edge of her peripheral vision, disappearing when she turned and saw only acres of farmland. *You're imagining things,* she scolded herself. The news the servant had brought them had set her nerves on edge.

It was several hours before Bron straightened. "We should be able to finish this in a cou—" His words ended in a harsh rasp. He choked, his face frozen in a mixture of shock and pain.

"Sir?" asked a pallon named Ennis.

Bron's eyes rolled up in his head, and he pitched forward. Someone shouted at the sight of a dark-feathered arrow imbedded into his back.

The pallons stood in place for a moment, unable to comprehend what had just happened. Selah saw the arrow in the knight but couldn't make the connection. Saw the way he was no longer breathing but couldn't understand.

An oblong figure rose from behind a row of bushes, revealing itself to be a man. He wore the simple garb of a farmer, but the wicked blade he held in his hand, the steel glinting dangerously in the sunlight, implied otherwise.

Someone shouted, "Run!" Selah needed no further urging. More men were emerging from various hiding places—all of them leering with a sick delight. Selah's heart was ramming wildly in her throat. *Dragonhunters.*

Aswin and Ennis, were breaking ahead, racing toward the fief and safety. Selah's breath was ragged, her chest pained with both exertion and panic. A root snagged on her boot and she crashed to the ground, tasting harsh grit in her mouth.

She rolled over, trying to scramble to her feet. There were six or more dragonhunters behind her. Roswald squirmed in the grip of one of the men, stilling when the dragonhunter brought a blade to his throat. Selah heard the creak of wood and turned, seeing too late the man aiming his bow at her heart.

He grinned, once, and released his arrow. Selah threw up an arm to protect herself.

A sharp *crack* split the air, and the arrow shattered into a thousand pieces, shards of wood pricking Selah's face. The arrowhead struck her chest with a soft thump, lacking the force to even pierce her tunic. Unthinking, Selah scrambled to her feet, swaying as the world began to spin. Shaking her head to clear it, the girl sprinted away while she still could, not daring to look back.

The breath caught in her throat. "Someone, help!" she screamed.

*   *   *   *

Farsight surveyed the campsite. Eight dead dragonhunters lay sprawled on the ground; two had gotten away. The damages on their side had been much less severe, although Banor would have a restricting scar on his left arm for the rest of his life.

He felt the touch of another mind against his; thinking it was another dragon with instruction or inquiry, he opened his thoughts to communication.

A blast of emotion flooded his mind. Fear soaked his body, transferred to him through mind-thought. Whoever was contacting him had not yet learned to speak in words, or at least, ideas. It was strange; all the adolescent dragons had remained at Dragonhold, and the dragonets could not possibly be able to communicate with their thoughts at this stage in their life.

—*Farsight?*—That was Blackwing. The giant dragon looked at him in confusion.—*Do you hear it too?*—

Farsight nodded. A moment later another blast of fear shook his thoughts. There were words this time. *Oh, gods, someone help. Help! Please!*

—**Who are you? Where are you?**—

The voice could not hear him. It was young and female, her words choked with panic. *THEY ARE GOING TO KILL ME! NO! PLEASE!* She screamed, and the dragons of the Fourteenth Wing shuddered.

Farsight knew that voice, but could not place it. Where had he heard it before?—**Where are you?**—he demanded. His mind became choked with images of bushes, planted orderly in rows. Boys that he recognized as pallons from Dragonhold running toward Hadfoll. The view changed, looking behind into the faces of men in pursuit. He was looking through her eyes, whoever she was.

It suddenly became clear to him.—**It's a diversion!**—he shouted. It was obvious now—why the dragonhunters had engaged in combat rather than fleeing in the face of sure death, why there were only ten of them to begin with.

Averon mounted him without a second thought—the tone in Farsight's voice told him that this was serious. Farsight launched into flight before his Rider completely tied himself to the saddle.—**There are more dragonhunters,**—Farsight explained as the other dragons hurried to take to the sky.

Averon swore. He did not have to ask Farsight to know that they were too
late.

*   *   *   *

A cord wrapped around Selah's ankles, ripping her feet out from under her.
She fell to the ground for a second time, tears of pain and fear blurring her vision.
Something hard struck the back of her head, driving her face into the dirt. A
rough grip rolled her over onto her back.

She stared up at the coldest eyes she had ever encountered. They were a pale
shade of violet, harsher than a bitter winter wind. The man was tall, and as she
watched, he ripped off his tunic to reveal brown dragonscale armor. He smiled,
the expression more malevolent than if he had frowned.

"Do you know what I am?" Selah began to sob in fear, too terrified to struggle.
A dragonhunter grabbed her arms and held them behind her back.

"I asked, do you know what I am?"

"Please don't kill me," begged Selah.

The dragonhunter in armor backhanded her across the face. "Silence." The
scales that made up the protective tunic rasped against her skin, leaving a red
abrasion on one cheek.

Selah trembled, tears rolling down her face. "Can I kill her, Dragonslayer?"
asked the man holding her arms behind her back. A sudden wind had picked up,
whipping Selah's hair back and forth.

The Dragonslayer began to nod, but stopped. Her tunic had been ripped off
one shoulder, revealing the strap of her breast band and the tip of Stormhunter's
mark. Reaching forward, the Dragonslayer ripped her shirt further, revealing the
rest of the scar.

"So the rumors were true." His violet eyes narrowed. "I want to kill this one,
Gene. She has the mark of Stormhunter."

Selah sobbed. "Please!"

The dragonhunters around her began to shrink away, fear in their eyes, backing until they were a safe arm's distance away. The Dragonslayer raised his blade,
pausing when he saw the light above Selah's heart. The scar was *glowing*. He had
to end this now. "Die, abomination!" he shouted, bringing down his blade.

Selah screamed, a harsh sound that was more animal than human. The Dragonslayer felt his feet leave the ground as a powerful burst of wind threw him into
the air. The other dragonhunters yelled in fear as they met the same fate as he.

Only Selah's remained on the ground, the ropes around her feet and shins snapping just like the arrows. The girl broke out in a sweat as exhaustion claimed her bones, making her fall forward onto her hands and knees.

The dragonhunters began to pick themselves up from the ground. A roar split the sky as Farsight bore down on them—help had finally arrived. One of the dragonhunters managed to fire an arrow in his direction. The dragon shrieked, and the arrow exploded with a soft burst of light—the telltale sign of magic.

Selah watched, remembering how her arrow had shattered. It must have been a dragon. Why hadn't they come sooner? The girl began to tremble.

More arrows came, from the sky this time, as the rest of the Fourteenth Wing arrived. The dragonhunters fell, some of their bodies riddled with multiple arrows. Selah shrank down to the ground—it was so much killing. The screams rang on her ears, but she was frozen, unable to move.

She could not see the Dragonslayer. A red dragon descended upon her, covering her protectively with a wing. The wing billowed up as Firegem snorted in surprise, turning her green eyes on Selah. The grass around the girl's feet was pressed flat to the ground, and the bushes near her whipped back and forth in a powerful wind.

The dragons were landing, lowering themselves to the ground so their Riders could dismount. Aerin slid down from Firegem and took the trembling Selah in her arms.

"It's all right," whispered the woman in Selah's ear. The girl struggled to regain her composure. She wanted the dragonriders to think her brave. To her shame, she began to cry into Aerin's shoulder, her knees shaking with relief and the lingering traces of adrenaline.

Aerin touched Selah's bare shoulder, her eyes taking in the ripped cloth of the girl's tunic. "Did they…" She couldn't finish the sentence. Selah understood her meaning and shook her head.

Selah opened her eyes, looking over Aerin's shoulder. The other dragonriders were staring at her. The girl blushed, glad that Beda had insisted that she start wearing breast bands. Without one, she would have even less modesty than she did now.

Farsight approached her slowly.—*Where is the young dragon?*—

Selah wiped the tears from her eyes, thoroughly confused by the dragon's question. "What dragon? There aren't any here, 'cept you."

Farsight stiffened, his eyes widening. Selah's voice and the voice that had called for help were uncannily similar.—*Keep talking.*—

Selah stood away from Aerin, beginning to control her trembling. "Why?"

The blue dragon frowned.—*Did you call for help? A few minutes ago?*— There was an intense edge to the dragon's voice that frightened the girl.

She nodded.—*What did you say?*—demanded Farsight.

"That's enough!" barked Averon, disturbed by his dragon's behavior. "Leave her alone, Farsight. Whatever it is, it can wait. We need to find the other pallons."

Selah led them to Roswald, who was bound tightly in rope, but otherwise unharmed. The dragonhunters, apparently, were planning to take the pallons somewhere before killing them. "Dragonhunters never kill a dragonrider without torturing them first," said Averon softly as they untied Roswald. The boy was shaken, but he had not broken down like Selah had. The girl saw him eyeing the fresh tears on her face and ducked her head in shame.

To hide her embarrassment, she spoke, "They were going to kill me, though. The one they called Dragonslayer."

Averon's eyes narrowed. "There was a Dragonslayer here?" She nodded. "Do you know where he is?" Selah couldn't give him an answer.

They found the body moments later. The Dragonslayer had landed several dragon lengths from where Selah had first been. The man's body was contorted, bent and twisted in sickening ways. There was no question that his back had been broken by the fall. He was breathing still, his eyes beginning to mist in death. Averon, as Wingleader, performed the interrogation.

"Why are you here?" Averon drew his dagger and made sure the dragonhunter could see it.

The Dragonslayer laughed, an empty, raspy sound from dying lungs. "You…think that will work…dragonrider? I'll…tell…nothing…"

Averon sighed. "I know that, dragonhunter. I could make your death quick." There was a morbid respect in the eyes of both rider and hunter. Just as they hated each other vehemently, they acknowledged the extent of the other's abilities. The Dragonslayer was showing remarkable fortitude.

"I…fear…no…pain…I fear…nothing."

The Dragonslayer's violet eyes roamed the dragonriders that had gathered around him. His gaze rested on Selah, who was unable to tear her eyes away from the man that would have killed her.

The Dragonslayer inhaled quickly, his breath coming faster. Blood gathered at the corners of his mouth. "No…keep it…away."

"What?" demanded Averon.

"The…abomination."

The dragonriders turned and stared at Selah. The Dragonslayer continued. "Marked...by the god...of monsters..."

"Stormhunter," someone whispered.

The crosshatch of scars on Selah's chest began to glow a shining gold. Selah clapped her hands over the old wound in horror, but the light penetrated through her palms, refusing to be hidden.

The Dragonslayer stiffened, his face frozen in a final mask of terror. He was dead.

Selah's vision was misting, gold particles swimming before her eyes until the dragonriders were obscured from view. She swayed, lightheaded and dizzy.

"Selah?" someone asked.

The ground rushed up to meet her with sudden and alarming speed.

*   *   *   *

Listen...

Bright colors seared her mind's eye, reds and blues and greens spinning in a whirlwind of hues.

Can you hear it?

Piles of burning timber thrust dark smoke into the sky. A woman and a man looked on as a sand colored dragon gently cradled a human child, respect in his eyes.

Guard this child well...she will leave a great mark upon the world.

She knew that voice...

Listen...

A song came now, penetrating the blackness that replaced the dragon. It was triumphant and sad, joyous and powerful. Selah drifted, the music rising and ebbing like the sea. Fisherman legend told that the great whales of the ocean sang—the music sounded somewhat like the descriptions made by traveling seamen. The song was a chorus, light and deep voices, bugles and trills. Each note locked inside her as if the sounds were filling an empty part of her that Selah had not known existed.

It was dragons singing. Selah had never heard anything more beautiful in her life.

Listen...

After what seemed like hours of absorbing the music, the song stopped, leaving Selah cold and alone in emptiness.

Each dragon has their own song, composed and given to them at some point in their life. Sometimes they are sung to at birth—others do not receive their song until they die. This is my gift to you.

A gray dragon, larger than any mortal one that she had seen, appeared beside her. Stormhunter breathed deeply. *It took me quite some time to find the notes that could encompass* your *being.*

Lightning played along Stormhunter's scales. Selah was slow to understand. *I'm not a…*

Stormhunter shook his head. *Now do you understand?*

No! shouted Selah mentally. *What is there to understand?*

Sadness crept into Stormhunter's eyes. *It will be hard for you. You need more time, but there is not much more for you to take.*

Time for what? Selah demanded, confused and strangely desperate.

You must be more careful, Stormhunter cautioned, ignoring her words. *Today was too close to ending something that has yet to begin. Take your song and use it, Selah. It will help you in the days to come. Goodbye for now, little one.*

∗   ∗   ∗   ∗

Selah shot upright. Cold air caught on the sweat that soaked her clothes, and the girl shivered. A rustling of cloth diverted her attention. Aerin rolled over, apparently awakened by her movement. They were back in the inn.

"Selah? Are you all right?" It was dark, probably the middle of the night. Even if she couldn't see her face, Selah could sense the concern in Aerin's voice. "Selah?"

Selah drew her knees to her chest for protection. Her scar ached terribly. "Where am I?" she asked, although she already knew the answer.

"The inn. You fainted."

"I did." It was a statement, not a question. A warm, uneven surface touched her arm, and Selah started before recognizing her dragonet. The girl hugged Windchaser to her, disturbed by Stormhunter's second visit. What did he want from her?

"Selah, are you sure you're all right? You've been unconscious for hours. It's close to midnight right now." The dragonrider paused. "Did the dragonhunters do something to you?"

Selah remembered the blast that had thrown the dragonhunters high into the air. It had happened when she had screamed. The arrow had exploded when it surely would have killed her. Had Stormhunter saved her life a second time? If so, why?

"I...don't want to talk about it."

Thankfully, Aerin did not press her for reasons. It was only a few more minutes before the woman's even breathing drifted across the room, signaling that she had fallen asleep. It was hours before Selah joined her—troubling thoughts plagued the girl long into the night.

✱   ✱   ✱   ✱

The sun rose on a hushed morning. Even the birds seemed to sense the tragedy of the day before and were cowed into silence. The entire fief attended Bron's funeral. The old knight had made Selah's life miserable, but she was sad to see him lain to rest in the earth. The violent images of day before flashed through her eyes as Bron's sword was handed to his oldest son.

Myelin declared the day one of rest—the fief was still reeling in shock from the sudden events of the previous afternoon. Whispers hung in the corners of dark rooms, in the hallways, even in the stables.

"Dragonhunters? *Here?* I thought they stayed in the forests."

"There was a Dragonslayer?"

And finally, "I heard the girl pallon killed him."

Selah shuddered. By all appearances, yes, it looked like she was the cause for the sudden gale that had surrounded her and her alone, but she was sure it had been Stormhunter or another dragon. It had to be.

Selah's nights became restless—half the time was spent wide-awake, staring into the darkness. When she did sleep, she was plagued with dreams of dragonhunters chasing her, every one of them leering at her with violet eyes. A week after the attack, her dream changed.

The dragonhunters were there—still violet eyed and still terrifying. Their dragonscale armor was as vivid as it had been that day in the field. Selah screamed, but no sound would come out. She was back in the field, but when she turned to run, the hedges bent away as if she was staring at them through curved glass. For a chaotic dream, her feelings were oddly specific—it was less that she was fleeing from the dragonhunters than it was she was racing toward something far, far more important.

The hedges straightened, and Selah began to hear soft singing, a melody she recognized—the song that Stormhunter had given her. A dragon flew from the sky, notes so rich they felt almost tangible upon her ears falling delicately from its mouth. Sunlight, where her dream world had been stormy before, danced along the dragon's golden scales, nearly blinding Selah with their radiance.

The dragon landed—it was young, much smaller than Farsight or Firegem, and still had the awkwardness of adolescence that was apparent in Windchaser. Selah was sure the dragon was female. The distance between them shrunk until the girl was a mere inches from the dragon.

—Selah.—She looked into eyes that were the same shade of hazel as her own— Selah had never seen a dragon with hazel eyes. The corners of the eyes crinkled in a welcoming smile.

Selah returned the expression, full of joy to see a creature that she immediately regarded as a friend. She reached out to touch the dragon's face.

Pain lanced through her body as her fingers touched the dragon's brow. She screamed and heard the dragon's answering roar of pain. The girl thrashed in agony; white-hot blades drove into her flesh, twisted, and ripped out, only to drive in again. The dragon looked once more into her eyes before everything went black.

The image left her, as did the dragon; the pain did not. Selah rolled back and forth, sobbing—her skull felt as though it would crack in two. Aerin was beside her, hands shaking her shoulder.

"Selah! Selah! Wake up!"

The girl stopped shaking, only to cry out when another wave of pain descended upon her. Windchaser danced in and out of her field of vision, whistling desperately at the sight of her Rider in distress. Selah turned away from the dragonrider, hugging her sides. The coppery tang of blood filled her mouth—she had bit her lip. The girl forced herself to breathe. Slowly, agonizingly slowly, the pain that had coursed through her body faded to nothing but a dull ache in her skull. Soft paws ran through her damp hair, a gentle voice cooing in her ear— Windchaser was trying to comfort her.

Aerin was staring; the expression in her eyes could only be described as fear. Dragonriders didn't scare easily. *She must think me possessed,* Selah thought.

"Are you all right?" Aerin's voice was strained.

Selah nodded. Her throat was raw, as if she had been screaming uncontrollably.

The door crashed open, light streaming in to burn Selah's eyes. Her headache only increased. Averon stood in the doorway, an unsheathed sword at his side. More members of the Fourteenth Wing were clustered behind him.

"What in the name of Gonran is going on?" he demanded, his eyes managing to look both worried and irritated at the same time.

Selah sat up slowly, cradling Windchaser to calm her. "I had a bad dream."

"That's *all?*" snapped one of the dragonriders behind Averon. "A dream? The way you were carrying on, I thought you were being brutally murdered."

Selah hung her head in shame. Averon's eyes were concerned, but the expressions of the other dragonriders she had awoken were less welcoming. "I'm sorry."

"I'm going back to bed," declared the dragonrider that had snapped before. His black hair was sticking up on one side, testimony to his rough awakening. Without another glance at Selah, he stalked away from the doorway.

One by one, the other dragonriders left, muttering and grumbling about lack of sleep. Averon returned to his room, dousing the torch in the hallway. As inky blackness descended upon her, Selah lay back down, a strange sort of fear building in her chest. The dream had been so real, it was frightening. And she had continued to feel pain even after she had jerked herself from the dream.

The questions continued to haunt her. Slowly, exhaustion took the girl and her hazel eyes closed of their own accord.

Hedges bent away from her in every direction. She was back in the dream, although this time she knew what was coming. The dragonhunters were already gone, and the golden dragon was before her. Her feet seemed to have a mind of their own, dragging an unwilling body ever closer to the bright beast in front of her. The dragon watched her curiously, as if she remembered the first dream.

*Selah fought to break the forward motion of her feet. She didn't want to touch the dragon, not ever; the once friendly face had become a synonym for pain and embarrassment in front of the dragonriders. Try as she might, her body was determined— within moments, she was once again inches from the dragon. The hazel eyes looked deeply into hers.—***Selah,***—called the voice of the dragon again.*

"No," she cried. "No, please, don't touch me!"

A great claw that dwarfed her own hand reached out and, after a moment of hesitation, gently brushed her forehead.

Selah's scream went on and on.

"Black God," yelled a male voice. "Is she at it again?"

Her forehead throbbed as if a fiery brand had been held to it. Her sheets were soaked with sweat. A flash of shadowed blue flickered at the corner of her peripheral vision—she had frightened Windchaser again. The dragonet bawled in distress, creating a racket that would set even the most patient mother's teeth on edge. Dragonets in the rooms adjoining theirs began to wail as they were awakened from slumber. Soon, the inn was afire with the crying of dragonets, the grumbling of pallons and the cursing of dragonriders.

*   *   *   *

Selah stirred the breakfast broth with a weary hand. She had gotten little sleep last night. The golden dragon had plagued her dreams until the early hours of the morning, when she was too exhausted to sleep. The other dragonriders and pallons had the same expressions of sleep deprivation as she, and it was her fault. Even after stuffing the blanket against her mouth to muffle the sounds of her screams, she had jerked everyone from slumber at least three times. The girl felt especially guilty whenever she looked at Aerin.

The dreams haunted her, although she no longer woke up screaming. The golden dragon continued to bother her subconscious for several weeks. Before Selah knew it, the harvest was finished.

The Fief Lord, Myelin, procured an entertainer as a reward for the long work that the people had put in throughout the entire year. The artiste was a mage named Klaxon. He performed at the Harvest Feast that was a tradition at Hadfoll.

"Ladies and Gentlemen," he declared, "prepare to be stunned into amazed silence. I, Klaxon the Great, will show you things that will make you stare in awe, gape in wonder. I will thrill you, surprise you, and even shock you. So," he threw out his cape, "brace yourself for the amazing."

Selah, although unimpressed by his speech, had to admit that the mage was good at tricks. He plucked a roll from the ear of the Lord's daughter and concealed it in Averon's hair. When his audience demanded more, Klaxon swallowed a dagger and breathed fire on the suckling pig. Still, Selah got the feeling that the entertainer had not yet reached the climax of his performance.

Klaxon spun into the middle of the room, his cape flaring out behind him dramatically. "Now, Ladies and Gentlemen, I bring you my greatest feat of all." His closed his eyes, bowing his head as if he was about to reveal a well-kept secret. "Soul sight!"

The dragonriders chuckled appreciatively—some of them had encountered Klaxon before in their travels and knew what was up. Selah perched on the edge of her seat, thrilled by the rich tones of Klaxon's voice as he spoke.

The mage brought his fingers into the spell casting position, his wrists cocked. Selah blinked. Kavan would sit for hours with his hands in those positions when he was a child, ignoring their half-hearted attempts to get him to play. It had been the beginning of his alienation from them. Even the sight of a mage's robes sometimes brought Selah back to the sun-kissed battlements of Fief Domar.

"Do you want to play swords with us?" asked a Selah only half as tall as she was now. She and Firmin, armed with long sticks scavenged from the kindling pile, were utterly ignorant of their grubby faces and would be until Beda threw them into a bath with all the tenacity of a warrior woman turned surrogate mother. Kavan was seated in the middle of the battlement, his legs tucked neatly beneath him. His fingers were curled and tense, his eyes closed. When Firmin repeated Selah's request, he opened them and regarded his brother and sister with sea-green eyes that held an ocean of emotions his siblings didn't understand.

"No. I'm practicing." Without another word, he returned to his meditation.

Firmin thrust out his chest in a ploy to seem grown-up. "So are we. We're practicing swords."

"No, you're not. You're playing." Kavan's voice was as full of scorn as a seven year old could make it.

"Let's go, Firmin," snapped Selah in a voice meant to hurt. "Kavan can keep 'practicing'."

The two stalked away, convinced that they had bested their brother in the sparring of words. Neither saw Kavan's eyes open and track them as they clambered down the battlement steps. Neither saw the downward tug at the corners of Kavan's mouth, or the twitch of his cheek before he stilled his features. Neither bothered to look back.

"Do I have any volunteers?" asked Klaxon, returning Selah abruptly to the present. Windchaser, seeing that Selah wasn't paying attention, had snatched a slice of flank meat from her plate and was gobbling as fast as she could. When the girl reached down to take it away from her, the dragonet cramped the rest into her mouth.

Selah glared her Chosen, but couldn't help but chuckle when Windchaser's ears drooped in the picture of apology as her swollen cheeks bobbed up and down. The dragonet, despite her morose features, made sure to swallow the meat before Selah had the chance to do anything about it.

"No volunteers?" Klaxon said in disbelief, pacing up and down the tables. "I suppose I have no other option than to choose victims!"

Selah wanted to shrink down into her seat and disappear. After what had happened in the fields, all she needed right now was more attention. A wave of relief washed through her when Klaxon coaxed a guard to the center of the tables. The dragons, lying down next to the seats of their Riders, lifted their great heads to get a better view. The children that had been allowed to watch the mage did not have the same size advantage as the beasts and had to sit on the shoulders of their elders.

Klaxon instructed the guard to sit down and brought his hands into the spell casting position. *"Aveha nokis, quisnelatinari benew lasik,"* he chanted, weaving his hands in and out of each other as he intoned the words. The guard inhaled sharply as tree sprouted from the cobblestones before him, spreading out branches that bristled with needles. When it reached the guard's chin, it stopped growing, swaying in a wind that Selah did not feel.

"A tree," said Klaxon with a measure of surprise in his voice. "You are a person deeply rooted in your beliefs—pardon the pun." Several in the crowd chuckled. "You shelter others and are a giver of resources and comfort. Without you, the horizon of society would be bleak and empty. With enough care, you can reach your full potential easily." The guard blinked in wonder, too infatuated by the tree before him to reply.

Klaxon closed his fists and the tree disappeared, leaving unblemished cobblestones where there had once been roots. Selah couldn't tell whether it had been real magic or just a petty illusion.

The guard stood, leaving the stool vacant. Klaxon returned his gaze to the crowd. "Who's next?" he asked.

There were several more people after the guard—the Lord of the Fief, Myelin, was represented by a mountain lion, the innkeeper a stone. A merchant had the sea as the emblem as his soul. Klaxon wiped sweat from his upper lip—the soul sight, as he called it, was definitely causing exertion on his part. "One more," he said, scanning his rapt audience.

Selah breathed a sigh of relief. Too late, she saw Klaxon eyeing her. "You, the pallon with the blue dragonet. Come up here."

Selah felt all the blood in her body rush up to her cheeks. Everyone was staring at her. Windchaser, oblivious as always, whistled loudly. Selah stood slowly, leaving her dragonet in the seat with strict instructions to sit still, hush, and touch nothing.

Klaxon gestured that she should sit in the stool. Selah complied, quite uncomfortable with the eyes of almost everyone in the fief on her and her alone. Klaxon moved behind her, and Selah was painfully aware of how close to her he was standing.

"Aveha nokis, quisnelatinari benew lasik," breathed Klaxon. The air in front of Selah seemed to stretch and slide, like the waves of heat from hot ramparts in high summertime. One moment, a spark drifted in and out of the warped air, the

next, a golden dragon three times the size of Windchaser stood before her, facing the audience.

The sounds of eating stopped. The dragons snorted in surprise. All conversation ceased as nobility, guard, dragon, rider and freeman alike turned to stare. Windchaser, perched over Selah's plate with the rest of the girl's meal halfway into her mouth, froze midway in a swallow.

Selah saw none of them. The golden dragon's scales shone with all the radiance of the sun. She was smaller than the other dragons in the courtyard—she must be an adolescent. When the dragon turned to face the girl, it regarded her with hazel eyes that were exactly like her own.

"A dragon," began Klaxon, but his voice trailed off. It was obvious that he had never encountered a 'soul' like this before.

When the mage opened his mouth to continue, the dragon roared, spreading her great wings. Although she was facing away from Selah, the girl knew that she was looking straight at the dragons of the Fourteenth Wing.

And the dragon, Selah's soul, began to sing.

Selah knew what the song would be from the first note—it was the dragon song that Stormhunter had so strangely given her. Now she understood, partially, why he had.

Behind her, the girl sensed, rather than saw, Klaxon close his fists in the command to stop a spell. The dragon continued to sing its song undeterred, notes falling on her audience like the first snowfall in the high reaches. When Selah's soul paused at a rest in the song, the crystal goblets of the nobles echoed with her voice, trembling in the stillness.

The dragons of the Fourteenth gazed at the girl and her soul with expressions that Selah could not read. Before she knew it, the golden dragon had reached the climax of the song, and drew out the last note until it trembled with vibrato. When Selah began to believe that no living creature could sing without breathing for so long, the dragon let the note end, leaving the air ringing with the dragon song.

The golden dragon turned around until it faced Selah. Slowly, it bowed its head what seemed to be respect. Klaxon closed his fists a second time, and the dragon disappeared.

Selah lurched forward, grasping the sides of the stool to steady herself. Her body, soaked with sweat, felt as though she had run one of Garrett's fitness tests. She swallowed and felt the rawness of her throat—had she been singing as well?

Farsight stood, towering over the seated humans.—*Selah, who gave you a dragon song?*—

"That was a dragon song?" asked Garrett. He seemed to still be recovering from the surprising actions of Selah's soul. "What did it say?"

The russet dragon behind him shook his head.—*To translate the exact words would butcher the beauty of it—dragon songs are not meant for the human tongue.*—

"What was the basic idea?"

—*A girl with the soul of a dragon. A dragon with the body of a girl. She is both.*—

"Surely you jest," laughed Klaxon. All eyes turned to him. "That was a clever enchantment you dragons did—altering my spell. I think now that it is time this whole farce is up? There is a law for souls—humans cannot have dragons, or the other way around. They are too close a species in nature."

Firegem snorted.—*I will ignore the tactless comparison of humans to dragonkind. However, your disrespect toward the dragon song is unacceptable. Each dragon receives a song sometime in his life. That Selah has one is confusing, but not humorous.*—

Klaxon chuckled, but it sounded forced and without heart. "*I* am amused. You are all very good at acting."

"It is not acting." Only when all the dragons turned to look at her did Selah realize that it was she who had spoken. "If you say that I am a fake, then you have to say that the rest of the soul sight that you have done is a fake as well. The dragons did not do any magic on you, or the spell."

Selah shuddered inwardly, surprised by her own audacity. It was like someone else was in control of her body. She felt different, like she was a mere shell being filled. The girl trembled again, and this time it showed—she had to reach out to grasp the edge of the stool again. Since when had she been standing? All the feeling in her body had congregated to the pit of her stomach—she was sick and nauseous.

—*Selah?*—Farsight asked. The girl turned to look at him.—*Who gave you the dragon song?*—

Selah opened her mouth and closed it. The new, brave Selah was about to shout out that a god had visited her for the third time. The frightened Selah won the battle, and managed to croak out, "You know."

The dragons shuddered, closing their eyes simultaneously. The lights flickered, and one of the children, caught in the moment, shrieked. Landon, watching from his seat, flinched, and then returned his eyes to his friend. Selah's eyes closed and she rocked backward. The clack of the stool hitting the floor reverberated the room, summoning a stunned silence that made the shadows seem darker.

*   *   *   *

Selah woke from sleep like a diver reluctant to come to the surface. When she did, she wished she had never broken from her dreams.

People were clustered around her, obliterating her view of everything but the ceiling. "She's awake!" someone whispered, and Selah heard more voices echo the phrase.

The girl reached out and felt empty air. There were no blankets, and the surface underneath her was solid and did not give like a pallet.

A candle was held above her face. Selah closed her eyes; the sudden light invoked a terrible, splitting headache. Her body felt as though her bones had been disconnected from each other and resettled into new, more appropriate positions that took getting used to.

"Test her memories again. I think it is safe now."

"She's not given you consent! You can't go into someone's mind without their consent!"

"Peace, Aerin!"

"Myelin," began another voice, "She is my pupil, and as such, is my charge. I refuse to let you go through with this."

"Garrett, she might be bound, or worse. Surely there is nothing so important in her memory that warrants privacy."

Selah felt cold fingers touch her temples. A man with the white cowl of a journeyman mage bent over her and began to chant.

*   *   *   *

When Selah first saw a dragon take to the sky, she stared for hours, until the mighty beast became nothing more than speck in the horizon. Even after it had completely disappeared, the toddler watched, and wondered.

The guards let her out through the gates with a smile. Selah continued on until she found a tree of suitable height. When she was sure that no one was watching, the girl child scaled the branches with the ease of practice.

She climbed to the chest height of a dragon, seeming miles and miles for her imagination. Selah leapt, arching her back to stretch her body to its full potential. The ground was kind, considering; she landed with only a bloody knee and sore joints. Undeterred, she climbed again, and again, leaping and falling the same way each time.

Beda was sitting in her quarters when Selah trundled in without knocking. The woman took one look at the bloody and bruised child and shrieked, "What were you doing?"

Selah smiled, ignorant of her wounds. "Flying."

*   *   *   *

"Nothing."

"Keep looking."

"Myelin…" protested Garrett's voice.

"Only a bit longer, dragonrider."

*   *   *   *

Selah raced forward, bouncing off tables and chairs that were at eye level. Firmin was beside her, giggling as loudly as she. Kavan…Kavan was there as well, more subdued than her other brother, but energized all the same.

She was leading them up to the battlements. Flyn's shift at guard duty was almost over and he would be excited to see them after two hours without their company. Selah slowed, allowing her triplets to catch up. Instead of returning the favor, they sped by, determined to get a lead on the sister who always won. Selah, bored with the race, cut her pace down to a walk.

The toddler was not yet afraid of the alleyways created by the barracks and the inner wall of Castle Domar. She would avoid them for the rest of her life.

A man in a cloak was leaning against the wall. He looked lonely. "What y'doing?" asked Selah. The man beckoned her closer. Ignorant of danger, Selah proceeded toward him.

The man snatched her arm, placing a grimy hand over her mouth. "I am sorry, little one. This is the way it has to be."

He withdrew a golden disk from the folds of his cloak. Selah did not scream. Not until the disk was in place and the man was gone. Not until Flyn found her.

*   *   *   *

The scream in her memories split the air, making the people around her shrink back in fear.

"She's not letting me in!" shouted the journeyman mage. The iron grip was still on her temples. Selah jerked her head from side to side, tears leaking from the corners of her eyes. Hands pinned her down.

"There has to more. What happened after the disk?"

"I'm trying!"

The pressure in her mind was unbearable. "Get out!" Selah whispered. The volume of her words rose in a steady crescendo until she was screaming. "Get out of my mind! All of you!"

Pain gripped her head in a vise. A force probed her mind all the harder. Selah began to sob in agony.

They do not belong here. Our memories are our own. They are hurting us. Selah felt the dragon stir within her. Rage turned her lungs to fire as the pressure in her skull increased. *We are separate no longer. The disk is gone.*

Her blood was pounding in her ears.

One is two. Two is one. Our memories are our own.

Selah felt the strength that was flooding her veins lock into place.

My memories are my own.

"Get out!" A roar tore from her throat.

Windchaser, secured in the arms of Aerin, keened in pain as Selah's yell reached her ears. The dragons looking on grunted and slumped forward as if they had been struck by a mighty blow. The dragonets in the arms of their pallons bawled and trembled. Shouting filled the air.

Farsight groaned when Averon rushed to his side. "What is it?"

—*She is in our minds—release her from the memory search now!*—The dragon roared.—*Make it stop!*—

Purple blood trickled from his ear. "Farsight!" cried Averon.

—*She's using mind-speech…she must have gained it from the dragon…too much, too powerful.*—

Averon looked to Garrett. The training master ripped the mage who had been searching Selah's memories for proof away from the girl. Selah ceased screaming.

Slowly, she opened her eyes. The rage within her quieted. Her heartbeat slowed. When Selah sat up, the dragonriders stared at her with a mixture of fear and anger. They were beside their dragons.

Each of the beasts was bleeding. Purple blood flowed from their ears and nostrils. Windchaser coughed weakly, spraying Aerin's sleeves with dark droplets. Selah rushed forward and snatched her dragonet to her.

The baby dragon did not open her eyes. "What's wrong with her?" Selah shouted. "What did I do?"

The pallons and dragonriders looked up in anger from their own wounded dragons. The freemen and servants stared.

Windchaser coughed again, coating Selah's shirt in blood. "Help me!" the girl cried, panic closing her throat. "Someone help me!"

Like the crystal lighting of Dragonhold would never do, the candles that adorned the tables flickered in the cold draft that filled the room.

*   *   *   *

"I don't know what to tell you." The healer began to pull various herbs from his satchel. "Dragons have a special capability to transfer mental stress to physical pain—it's a coping mechanism that relieves pressure when their telepathic communication overloads their mind."

Selah did not know which was worse; the healer's fine words or his inability to get to the point and tell them what was wrong.

"It is rather interesting," continued the healer. "Human magic is really using mental willpower to support physical strength, while dragonkind uses the body to support the mind."

Selah bristled. She wanted the healer to help Windchaser, not stand here and give her a lecture.

The healer bent over Windchaser. "What happened again?"

All of the dragons had gathered in the dens for treatment. The injuries to the dragonets were worse—each pallon was cradling their Chosen carefully. The older dragons had suffered only bleeding to the ears; most of the dragonets were still keening in pain. Landon was holding a cloth to his dragonet, Indio's, nose—it was already stained purple. Only Windchaser was coughing.

—*The human girl was in our minds, screaming,*—explained Garrett's russet dragon.—*She was using mind speech. It was louder than any voice I have heard before.*—

Selah was choked with guilt. She glanced around the room and met the accusing stares of the pallons whose dragonets she had ravaged. Landon's eyes were burning in anger so intense that Selah had to look away.

—*Selah was in pain from the memory search—it seems that she transferred it to our minds, and we transferred it to our bodies,*—said Farsight.

"I did...this?" Selah asked in disbelief. She touched one finger to Windchaser's scales, but couldn't bring herself to meet the eyes of the dragons.

"Who else?" snapped Landon, rising to his feet. His cheeks were red with ill contained frustration. "Look what you did! You hurt them! All of them! You hurt Indio!"

"I'm...sorry."

"Are you? First you're a dragon, now you go around fainting and hurting everyone."

"Landon." Selah reached toward her friend, her eyes dropping to his dragonet. Indio was breathing heavily, the skin around his nostrils coated with purple blood.

The boy turned so that his body shielded the dragonet. "Don't touch him." Landon's voice had fallen to a dangerous level. "I don't know who you are any-more."

The back of her eyes felt warm and fuzzy. Selah tried to swallow the lump that had formed in her throat and returned her attention to Windchaser. "What..." she had to stop and force the guilt and waver from her voice, "...should we...I...do?"

The healer sighed. "There isn't much you can do. The nosebleeds will stop soon, as will the ears. It may take longer for your dragonet to heal. It may have been that she felt more of your pain because of the bond between you."

Selah nodded, stunned. *Windchaser...I hurt you.* She couldn't stop the tears now—they fell unbidden to her cheeks. Everyone else in the room seemed to dis-appear as Windchaser coughed again.

*   *   *   *

Selah stayed beside Windchaser for the rest of the night. The guilt and tears came in waves—she would sob and shake until she was spent, then be still until her emotions overwhelmed her again.

I hurt them all. Most of the dragons had recovered and left, but many of the dragonets were still here, under the care and supervision of several healers. They avoided her. It seemed that Landon had spoken for all of them with his outburst.

Windchaser's coughing had subsided until blood no longer stained the warm rags that Selah used to sooth her. The girl had to bite her lip every time she touched her Chosen; this pain was of her making. *I didn't mean to.*

Sky blue paws wrapped around her hand. Windchaser's eyes were closed, but the dragonet squeezed soft reassurances into Selah's fingers. Her tiny claws dug into Selah's skin, leaving small puncture marks. The tears on the girl's face dried, leaving her cheeks feeling taut and her eyes raw. She felt strangely empty, as if she had spilled all the tears she bore, and they would never come again.

The dragonet's breathing became steady and her grip on Selah's fingers slackened—she was asleep. Selah disentangled her fingers from Windchaser paws, settling them in a more comfortable position.

Several minutes passed. The girl drew her belt knife and began to fiddle with it, playing a few halfhearted games of mumbly-peg to pass the time. She slipped and gouged a deep red line in her palm, beneath her ring and pinky fingers.

The girl watched the dark blood well in the gash with no sense of urgency. Her hand throbbed, but she made no move to bandage it. She deserved this pain. It wasn't even half of what she had inflicted on others.

A healer coming by to check on Windchaser saw the red streaks that coursed down her hand and were beginning to drip on the floor. Selah stared into space, wrapped in her guilty thoughts.

"You're bleeding," the healer announced. He wasn't sure if she had noticed.

Selah looked down at her hand. "Oh…that. It's nothing."

The healer frowned. "You did that to yourself?"

Selah shook her head. "No. It was an accident."

The man still looked skeptical. "Don't do it again. All I need right now is more of a mess." He handed her a rag. "Use this to stop the bleeding."

Selah accepted the cloth and mopped up her fingers before pressing it against her wound. She returned her attention to Windchaser. The dragonet was sleeping peacefully, and shifted once in a pleasant dream.

Selah wished she could do the same.

✳   ✳   ✳   ✳

It seemed that the entire group of pallons made a pact against her. Each one was furious at the harm their dragonet had suffered at her hands. Selah was not spoken to at all for quite some time. The dragonriders treated her with equal disdain—she had attacked their Chosen, albeit not purposefully, and worse, was a pallon. They could not even challenge her for the offense she had committed.

When the pallons did begin to speak to her, it was in words of hatred. "Don't come near me," were the first words she heard in a long time, uttered by Corith. Her old nemesis was especially careful to be nasty to her in her circumstances.

Bern, easily the kindest person she had ever met, did not speak to her at all. That was worse than if he had actually insulted her.

The new Selah that she was not accustomed with only put up with the harassment for so long. At dinner, after someone had uttered a particularly scathing remark, Selah leapt to her feet, smashing her plate to the table with enough force to make the others jump.

"It's not my fault, all right? It was a gods-cursed accident!" Selah was surprised by the amount of anger in her voice.

Landon looked up from his meal. His face was a nonchalant, but Selah could tell it was only a mask. "Nice speech," he complimented, words dripping with sarcasm. "Remind me to write that one down in case I ever need to beg someone for forgiveness. It was quite compelling." His eyes hardened until they were as impenetrable as stone. "Get out."

Selah was so mad and hurt that she was trembling. She snatched her plate and stalked away, a now healthy Windchaser at her heels.

The other pallons patted Landon on the back.

$$*\qquad*\qquad*\qquad*$$

The pallons were sent out in the fields again, although this time three dragons and their Riders escorted them. The dragons were too large to stay in the rows, and the dragonriders stayed in the shade provided by the bodies of the great beasts while the pallons worked.

A bee flew in lazy circles around Selah's head. The girl waved it away in an equally lethargic motion—she was exhausted. They had been working in the hot sun all day.

The insect flew over to where Landon was working diligently. Selah ignored it, straightening a moment later when the boy cried out. Landon held his hand, flicking away a stinger imbedded into the fleshy part of his palm.

"What happened?" Selah asked, forgetting for a moment that she was angry with Landon, and he with her.

The boy glared at her. His memory was better than hers. "Bee stung me."

Selah snorted scornfully to recover. "That's all? Don't be such a baby."

Landon glowered. "Me, a child? Right. I'm not the one who hurts every dragon in the fief then gets angry because people are a little frustrated with her."

Selah stiffened. "No, I wasn't," she lied, knowing all to well that his accusations were true.

"Yes, you were. Or was that the *dragon* in you?"

"Shut up!"

Landon flushed in anger. "That's probably the only reason you got Chosen in the first place. Otherwise, you don't deserve Windchaser."

That was the final straw. Selah crossed the distance between them in a moment. Her right arm shot out and caught him in the side of the face. "Take it back!" she shouted. The blood was pounding loudly in her ears.

She reeled back as Landon returned her attack with his own, his fists slamming into her stomach and eye.

The girl had recovered and was about to charge her former friend again when one of the dragonriders that was keeping an eye on them and forced them apart. "That's enough!"

"Take it back!" Selah demanded.

Landon shook his head.

"She Chose me! She…" Selah couldn't finish her sentence. A dark stillness hung in the air. *My dragon…did Windchaser sense the dragon? Not me…I knew her by name! I called her! Commanded her! She answered her name, not me!*

No, she Chose me! By Choice!

I knew her name.

Selah swayed for a moment, as if struck. Landon began to regret his accusation.

"She Chose me," whispered Selah, terrible thoughts flitting in her mind like trapped doves. "She Chose…"

…Me…

*   *   *   *

Selah returned to her quarters at the inn with a heavy heart and a black eye. Windchaser squealed in delight when she caught sight of her Rider, and Selah could barely force a half-smile.

Windchaser quieted when Selah sat down on her pallet. She sensed that something was wrong and nuzzled her arm.

"What am I, Windchaser?" asked Selah aloud.

Windchaser said nothing, settling down next to Selah. The girl raised her face to the ceiling, asking questions that she knew the dragonet could not answer. "Why am I a dragon? Why did Stormhunter give me a dragon song?" She turned her eyes to her dragonet. She had to swallow the lump in her throat before continuing. "Why did you Choose me?"

Windchaser rubbed her head against Selah's leg, cooing comfortingly. She regarded her Rider with wide violet eyes.

Selah sighed, unable to control the emotions inside her. Her heart ached, but tears would not flow from her eyes. "I have the soul of a dragon...like you. How can we be Rider and Dragon? How?"

Windchaser whistled softly, leaning against Selah. *We just are,* her eyes seemed to say. *What more is there to ask?*

Selah closed her eyes, and felt the dragonet grasp her hand as she always did when she wanted to comfort her Rider. For the first time, Selah curled her own fingers around the paw, until it was hard to tell where dragon ended and human began.

*   *   *   *

Selah sat alone. It was almost too much to bear, seeing Landon and her other friends laughing and enjoying themselves. The sounds of good-natured banter around her made the spaces at her table that much emptier. Windchaser gladly split her meal, eating as much food as she could lest Selah change her mind about sharing.

When the meal was over, Garrett stood to announce who had the unpleasant duty of cleaning the dining hall. He scanned the room with golden eyes before gesturing to Landon and Selah. "You two."

Selah stood and began gathering plates and bowls, Landon a beat behind her. He seemed determined to do a better job than her, moving a fast pace in order to beat her to the kitchen. Selah let him go, devoid of her usual affronted anger whenever he was near.

Landon was not. When he did meet her eyes, it was with a frown that refuted Selah's ideas of having a civil conversation. After depositing the dishes in the care of the cooks, the two returned to the dining hall as the other pallons were filing out. Several of their peers shot Landon looks of pity. Selah pretended not to notice.

Soon it was only they in the wide chamber. When Selah opened her mouth, Landon ducked under the table to gather the rushes that caught the table scraps.

When her former friend resurfaced, Selah took a hold of his arm before he could avoid her again. "Landon." Reluctantly, the boy turned to meet her eyes. "I'm sorry. I'm sorry for what I did to Indio, I'm sorry for what I've said. I know that's not enough, but I don't know what else to say. I could spend the rest of my life repeating this and you still wouldn't know how horrible I feel. Can you please forgive me?"

Landon's beautiful green eyes softened for a moment. "That was the best apology I have ever heard." The corner of his mouth curved in a rueful smile. "However, forgiveness is something I cannot give. For the time being, I must respectfully decline your request, for all the eloquence with which it was delivered." The fine words only betrayed the distance between them—Landon of Boran, son of a nobleman, was speaking to her now, not the Landon she knew.

With a short bow, the pallon turned, grimy rushes in arm, and exited the hall. Selah braced herself for the tears, but none came despite Landon's harsh rebuke. Hollow disappointment echoed in her heart, but left her eyes dry of emotion. When she mopped the floor, it was bucket water, no more, that scrubbed the wooden slats clean.

*   *   *   *

Training resumed—in the mornings, they would continue with the various chores that had to be done, while the afternoon was devoted to weapons training.

Nolan was bedridden from fever. The healers informed them that it was serious but not fatal, and required him to sleep until the infection cleared. It left the pallons with an odd number.

Selah looked around, hopeful that at least one person would have forgiven her for her various offenses in the past weeks. She was wrong; the other pallons paired up quickly to avoid having to train with her.

Garrett saw her standing alone and frowned. "We need a group of three."

Silence. Garrett sighed. "This is ridiculous. Selah can rotate through the groups."

"She still wouldn't get as much time on the sword as us and will need time to catch up." Selah started at the sound of a voice that she had not heard in a while. Corith, however, did not even glance in her direction. "Besides—we don't know if she's safe. Remember what happened to the dragons."

The reminder of past and present guilt drove Selah's eyes to the ground in shame. Only the strange edge in Garrett's voice betrayed his feelings. "Yes, I do remember what happened to the dragons. I also feel that you boys could do to learn a little compassion and forgiveness. What happened was a mistake. Nothing more. Now someone accept Selah in their group."

Fagan, one of the more bookish pallons, raised his hand timidly. Garrett nodded toward him with forehead wrinkles that were quickly turning into a frown. "Dragonrider law states that one dragonrider may challenge another if harm befalls his dragon because of the other's actions. Since that is not permitted in this circumstance, it is unreasonable for you to force us into a situation that puts us into more stress."

Garrett started to speak, then swallowed his words and adopted a more condescending tone. "Very well. I thought that you had assumed the maturity that comes with your position, but I was wrong. Selah will train alone, as you wish."

Selah snatched a wooden sword from the pile and stalked away, her fingers digging deep depressions into her palm. Her guilt over the accident prevented her from hating her peers, but it did not stop her from being very angry. And hurt, although she didn't want to admit it to herself. She was growing more comfortable with the dragon that she knew to be part of her nature—that same dragon inside her would not cry.

She heard Garrett barking instructions and knew that she should be listening. Instead, she slashed at the air wildly, striking imaginary foes with the faces of those who shunned her.

The sound of footsteps behind her made her pause mid-swing. Selah turned to face her training master. He clutched a wooden sword in his hand that matched the one Selah had in hers.

"There is no sense in fighting the air." Garrett raised an eyebrow. "Can't get any better that way."

He lifted his blade into the "guard" position. Selah followed suit. "First of all, never take an unnecessary risk when in combat. Taking a gamble when your life is at stake is unhealthy to say the least." Selah smiled.

Garrett still did not engage her. "Most pallons go stir crazy in their first sword bout without a set pattern. Do not let the fact that you carry a large piece of metal go to your head, understood?" Selah nodded.

He proceeded to show her the high parry, middle parry, low parry, how to block on both sides. When Selah had shown him that she could perform each one without the pressure of another blade, he struck and instructed her where to parry.

"High! Middle! Low! Right! Left!" This continued on until Selah became bored, and despite herself, began to block automatically.

"Left!" Garrett commanded. Selah blocked to the left, only to feel the sting moments later when her training master struck her right side with the flat of his blade.

When Selah looked at him in confusion, Garrett revealed a rare grin. "You're falling asleep. Be aware of what I am doing and don't just go through the motions."

Selah nodded, refocusing her awareness until it centered on her "opponent". She improved throughout the afternoon, although it was obvious that Garrett could best her with his eyes closed.

Selah's arms were sore by the time Garrett called for a break. Wooden swords were not half as heavy as real ones, and Selah was glad that they did not have to handle them yet.

The rest of the afternoon was devoted to conditioning—wind sprints as well as the dreaded upper body workout that Bern had once described as "the most painful experience of my life".

Selah rejoined the rest of the group to glares and faces adverted. She chose to ignore it. She had tried with Landon, and her apology had failed. There was nothing else for her to do.

$$* \qquad * \qquad * \qquad *$$

The pallons had been lax with their personal training while they had been working at Hadfoll, and Garrett was determined to get them back into peak shape. Two-mile runs became a commonplace warm-up. Somewhere between agonizing training sessions and the warm baths for recovery, Selah's muscles quickly remembered exercising every day and adjusted to new demands.

Her peers still refused to partner with her. When Nolan returned, he was so behind in sword work that he had to be privately tutored by Garrett, which still left her without a partner. The guards wanted nothing to do with her—for the most part, they thought her possessed.

So it was that Selah found herself squared off against Averon. He was one of the few that had come to terms with what she had done and forgiven her.

Averon's blows were harder than Garrett's—he was unused to facing opponents not even half his age and had trouble adjusting to her skill level. To make matters worse, they had switched to light metal swords—waves of pain shot up Selah's arms every time their blades connected.

The pallons were still on patterns, although every now and then Averon would have her do some easy free form to get her used to not having Garrett shouting instructions from the sidelines. It was much harder when she didn't know what the dragonrider was going to do—while his blows during patterns made her arms shake, she at least knew where they were coming from.

After one such session, Selah realized that she had never formally apologized for what had happened. As Averon was mopping his brow with a rag, she said, "I'm sorry for what I did to Farsight."

Averon paused for a moment, but continued to wipe his face. "It's all right, although I think I'm not the person you should be apologizing to."

Selah took his words to heart and walked through the dragon dens that evening, expressing her apologies to each of the dragons she had hurt. It had been two weeks since the accident, and some of the beasts regarded her with only stony stares. Others seemed satisfied. A dragon named Blackwing, large enough to take up two den spaces, shook his head when she approached him.—*We have forgiven you, Selah, for the most part. I think it is time that you forgive yourself.*—

*   *   *   *

Several days later, Garrett told them that they were going to intersperse some free form fighting within the set patterns in sword work.

He called them out in pairs to have a match in front of the entire group. After several groups: "Selah! Roswald! Get out here."

Selah rose to her feet and made her way to the center. Roswald was a beat behind her, lingering a moment too long. His expression betrayed him—this was, apparently, the last place, last person, that he wanted to be fighting.

"Guard!" barked Garrett. Selah whipped her sword up perpendicular to the ground, roughly beating down the nervousness inside her with an inner calm she didn't know she had. "Begin!"

Roswald lunged forward, eager to end it quickly. Selah sidestepped to put space between them, just as she had seen Garrett and Averon neatly avoid her poorly timed thrusts. Roswald slowed, striking out a few times to test her. Selah parried one and backed away from the other. Watching Roswald was like watching a mirror of herself. He left openings in his defense that Selah could only see now because her older instructors had seen them in her and exploited them. Selah still had some of the bruises to serve as reminders.

She parried Roswald's blow and lashed at his open side, forcing him to half-jump, half-block in a hasty defense. She struck again, and again, leaving him a beat behind to try and block her next blow.

Roswald had backed up until he was only a half dragon length away from the seated pallons that were watching. He slashed at her to break her attacking streak.

Selah rushed into the opening, bringing up her own blade until it was a safe distance from Roswald's throat, but close enough to be a threat. "Yield," she demanded.

Roswald was silent. "Yield," the girl repeated.

There was something too close to fear in Roswald's eyes. "I yield."

He's afraid of you. Selah scanned the watching pallons as she lowered her sword. *They're all afraid of what you are.*

Selah returned to her place. Watching the other matches, it was easy to tell that she was not the best swordsman among them. Renton had remarkable talent with a piece of steel, and Landon had been trained in the art of fencing and swordsmanship since he was a small boy. *It doesn't matter,* thought Selah, staring at the ground. *It would have changed nothing if I were the best anyway. They would still hate me.*

*   *   *   *

Selah and Landon were assigned for clean up once again. Fate seemed determined to make them suffer each other's company, or at least force Landon to suffer hers. Selah had reached the point where it was hard to wake up each morning to know that there would be no one to talk to at breakfast, lunch, dinner, or anywhere in between.

Landon was silent as they cleared the tables. Selah cleared her throat.

"Don't talk to me," Landon snapped.

Selah flinched, but obliged and said nothing. There was a grudge in his voice, but it seemed...automatic, a tone born of habit.

It was several minutes later before his voice echoed throughout the hall. "You're not crying."

"You want me to?" Selah challenged, unable to keep an edge of anger out of her voice.

Landon shrugged, the only gesture he had made in a long time that did not contain anger or frustration. "No. You just used to cry a lot."

Selah felt a strange sadness stir within her that had nothing to do with Landon. "I don't cry anymore. Not since..." she stopped, unwilling to go on.

The silence returned, although it no longer seemed so empty.

A soft chattering drew Selah attention from wiping down the table. Windchaser and Indio were waiting for their Riders, Selah's dragonet perched on the top of one chair and Landon's on the other. They were communicating softly. Indio gave a soft trill and Windchaser chortled, spreading her wings to keep from falling off the chair. There was no sign of the enmity that lay between their Riders.

Selah met Landon's eyes. He stared back. They both gazed at their dragonets, then back at each other.

Landon sighed. "Not much you can say to that." There was no trace of hostility in his voice. He seemed to have reached a conclusion to something he had been pondering for a long time. He reached forward, extended his hand to her. "Apology...accepted."

Selah reached forward to take his hand, was surprised when he reached farther and grasped her forearm in the gesture of friendship. She returned the gesture. "Thank you," the girl whispered.

*   *   *   *

Selah was not immediately welcomed back into Landon's circle of friends. She was permitted to sit at their table, but there was not much else. Selah apologized to all, with Aswin and Bern readily forgiving her now that Landon had broken the ice. The others, however, were not so eager to forget. Roswald's poor humor toward her was only compounded by the fact that she had beaten him during the freeform exercises. Hale was reluctant to talk to her. Glenn never looked at her during mealtimes.

Landon replaced Averon as her training partner. His blows were not as heavy as the dragonrider's, but he was skilled enough to beat her every time. Selah was constantly struggling to keep up with her friend.

The green on the trees blurred to yellow and red. A thick blanket of fallen leaves covered the ground as the dirt underneath became hard with frost. Selah's breath was visible as a great white cloud escaping from her mouth. The moon had waned to a sliver when the first snow came. Sheep and cattle were urged into the stables as the icy crystals began to fall from the sky. It took only two days for Hadfoll to be covered in a foot of the snow, officially claiming the world for winter.

The pallons were sent out to hunt after the first week of dried meat. Selah was in a group with Aswin, Bern, Landon and Roswald. A dragon circled above, in case of another attempt by the dragonhunters.

The trees set Selah's nerves on edge. Without their beautiful greenery, their limbs became skeletal fingers that perpetually grasped at the heavens. The dark brown of winter wood was a stark contrast to the pure white of the ground. Selah had to keep her eyes from glancing to the sky—it seemed too large, too imposing. She could hardly wait for spring.

"This is pointless," Roswald said, breaking the silence that had fallen over the group. Landon looked up at the boy, frowning in a soundless order to be quiet. Any game nearby would be alerted by their voices.

"There isn't anything here!" Roswald snapped.

"Be quiet!" whispered Aswin fiercely.

"We've been over this area twice. There is nothing here." His eyes shot to Selah, then back to the other pallons. "Besides—Selah's face probably scared everything away."

Selah's friends commonly insulted each other in jest—in more lighthearted times, Selah had done so herself. However, the tone in Roswald's voice betrayed how serious he was.

"You wound me," Selah replied, not missing the strange looks that passed between Landon and the twins. "The thief calls the smuggler crooked," she muttered underneath her breath.

"What was that?" Roswald demanded.

"Nothing."

"What did you say?"

There was movement behind her. Selah spun, snapping an arrow to the string of her bow. She felt the feather of the shaft tickle her cheek for a brief moment before her fingers released the string. The snow hare that had caught Selah's attention was killed instantly as the projectile struck it cleanly in the heart.

Her friends blinked in surprise. They had not even seen the animal. Selah had even caught herself off guard. To cover her thoughts, the girl slogged through the deep snowdrifts to where the hare lay. Even when she was up close, it blended neatly with the snow. Shaking her head, Selah gathered up the hare.

"Nice shot, Selah." Bern seemed a little taken aback by her actions.

"How did you see it?" asked Landon curiously. "I didn't see a thing."

"It…moved." Selah felt a strange flush come to her cheeks. She actually wasn't sure how she had reacted so quickly to the hare, although the last thing she wanted to do was admit it. There was enough strange talk circulating about her as it was.

Landon gave her an odd look, but seemed satisfied with her answer.

*   *   *   *

Winter passed with an abrupt swiftness. Conversations that had once been awkward became more relaxed as Selah began to be accepted back into the community of dragonriders and pallons. Windchaser bugled for the first time, moving the pallons to tears of laughter at her absurd voice cracks. Garrett was chuckling so hard he couldn't speak.

Her training master moved them indoors with the coming of snow, and worked them until the sword no longer felt alien in Selah's grip. Because of the hatred of her pallons and her resulting training with Garrett and Averon, Selah was ahead of several of her peers and found herself the eighth best swordsman of the pallons. The girl tried not to dwell to long on the irony of the situation, and threw herself into training. When she had disliked the feeling of exhaustion at the end of the day, Selah now felt satisfied at the conclusion of a training session. She could feel herself getting stronger.

The snowfall waned and finally stopped. Patches of brown began to show through the snow. Two days later, Garrett announced that they would be returning to Dragonhold.

Selah took one last look at the fields and forests of Hadfoll from the saddle of Firegem before they launched into flight. She was glad to leave the fief, even for its beauty and kind people. Between the Dragonslayer, Bron, her dragon song and soul, she had her share of ghosts locked in the fields now bare with late winter. To be honest, she would have been content to leave them there.

DRAGONMAGIC

It did not take long for the ghosts to return to her. A day after their return to Dragonhold, Sean called her to his chambers.

Selah, usually nervous around the Holdleader, felt none of her previous emotions as she entered his office. Sean was just a man—he was no longer as imposing as before. The Dragonslayer had shown her what it truly meant to be terrified.

The Holdleader gestured for her to sit down. Selah obliged, already knowing what this was about. Sean wasted no time getting to the point.

"What's this about you having a dragon for a soul?"

Selah could not think of anything to say. Sean continued. "Garrett told me about what happened with the mage, but there was much that he did not know. I need you to tell me," he looked at her intently, "what happened?"

Selah had no desire to tell Sean about the dragon that was her soul. However, she sensed that lying would not get her far. "Klaxon...the mage," she explained at Sean's quizzical look, "did something called soul sight. He did it for several others as well...the Lord Myelin was a mountain lion." She thought he might be interested, but the impatient expression on his face indicated she had better get to the point.

"Well, when Klaxon did soul sight on me, my soul was a dragon."

"How is that possible?" interrupted Sean.

"I don't know," Selah countered, bristling at the Holdleader's tone. Despite good intentions, she was already on the defensive. "There is a lot that I don't know. I have no idea why my soul is a dragon."

"Do you have any siblings?" asked Sean, seeming to strike a thought.

"Yes, two brothers. We're triplets."

"Was there anything special about them?"

Firmin surfaced in her mind's eye. "One's training to be a knight." Her favorite brother was replaced by Kavan, his hands cocked in the spell casting position. "The other wanted to be a mage."

Sean sighed. "No, I mean, did anything strange ever happen to them? Anything like the Choosing and, more recently, at Hadfoll?"

Selah stiffened. The Choosing invoked both painful and pleasant memories, but made the doubting thoughts about Windchaser resurface. She wished the Holdleader had not mentioned it. It took a moment to return her thoughts to the question at hand. "No...not that I remember."

"So much for that notion." Sean took a second to rearrange some papers on his desk. "Basically, all you know is that you have the soul of a dragon and somehow communicated with the other dragons enough so that they were internally bleeding." Selah swallowed the knot that formed in her throat at the mention of the dragons and nodded.

Sean frowned. "Forgive me, but I have a hard time believing you. You know more than you are telling me." His eyes narrowed in distrust. "The dragons say that your soul sang. What did it say?"

Selah surprised herself by shaking her head. "With all due respect, Holdleader, that is for me and the dragons to know. To be honest, I'm not even sure what it means, but it is none of your business." She saw the Holdleader's nose flare in rage and tried to recover by adding a, "sir".

"It is paramount that you tell me everything!" Sean's voice rose in a steady crescendo that made Selah wince inwardly. "You didn't tell us everything after the Choosing...and there is no telling what may be the consequences because you withheld information!"

"Such as?" Selah inwardly winced at her impudent tone, but it was too late to take back her words.

"What if you lost control and hurt the dragons again? There are more dragons here; you could potentially cripple several thousand. Are you prepared to face that?"

Selah felt as though she had been struck. "I won't lose control."

"How do you know that?"

"I..." Selah trailed off. She didn't.

*   *   *   *

After their disastrous interview, Sean left her alone, although he seemed to enjoy targeting her with the difficult problems during class. Her other masters were panicking—they had sent work with the pallons to Hadfoll, but they were still months behind because of the trip. To compensate, her masters dumped as much work as they could on the pallons without driving the youths mad.

Selah was grateful for the new workload. After training, several hours of coursework, and everyday chores, she was too tired to think about her soul, Windchaser's Choice, or Stormhunter. It was a convenient distraction from strange, new things about herself that she was afraid to comprehend.

Sean was not the only one that she was no longer afraid of. Her other masters no longer seemed so important and terrifying—she did not cower in her seat, hoping that they would not call on her, when a question was asked.

Speaking with Garrett became easier. She didn't feel so chastised when he corrected her. She spent one night searching the ceiling of her room for the reasons to the changes in her confidence. The wooden slats gave her no answer.

Selah's soul and the occurrences at Hadfoll were seldom discussed. If anything, the fief had shown her who her real friends were; despite the time that had passed since the accident, only Landon, Bern, and Aswin would speak to her with constant civility. Even their words were laden with sharp tones when conversation came to Hadfoll.

It was fortunate that very few people had a desire to comment on her soul—Selah refused to talk. It was easier for her to avoid thinking of the changes that had come and try to get on with life as it had been before Hadfoll. Even though her waking mind refused to deal with what had happened, her dreams continued to dwell on her dragon, and the dragon song. She still dreamt of violet-eyed dragonhunters. Worse still were the nightmares where Windchaser Chose Marcus as she leapt through the fire, and she burned to death slowly.

The pallons had one free day a week—it was usually devoted to chores and catching up on coursework. Selah sat down to her work with good intentions to finish it early so that she and Windchaser could spend the afternoon relaxing. With a sigh, she pulled out the book on strategy that the tactics master had assigned them.

Despite her efforts, the words on the page in front of her blurred into a meaningless scramble of black and white. She found herself reading the same passage several times and was still unable to remember what it had said.

The chapter focused on the Battle of the Seven Ridges, the end to the last holy war. The forces of the pantheon that Selah believed in had defeated the followers of the One God, a fake idol that was the head of a bloody, sacrificial religion. Selah wondered if Stormhunter, or the other gods for that matter, had any part in the war. The thought of the dragon god immediately conjured unwanted images in her mind.

The girl tried to push any ideas concerning her soul away, but they kept coming back to distract her. After a half hour of futile efforts, Selah slammed her book shut and thrust herself away from her desk. Windchaser, startled, peeped an inquiry. The girl began to pull on the flight jacket that Averon had loaned her. "Come on, Windchaser," she urged, grabbing her cloak. "We're going for a walk."

*   *   *   *

The cold nip of late winter brought a rosy blush to Selah's cheeks but did little to clear her head. She wandered through the courtyards aimlessly, but her thoughts would not be shaken so easily and continued to pursue her.

How long until I lose my sanity completely? Selah wondered as she stirred herself into motion again. Windchaser whined, tired and cold, and the girl tucked her Chosen into the front of her flight jacket. *Here I am…running away from myself!*

Gradually, her feet lead her to the outer gates of Dragonhold. A troop of apprentices, riding on the back of their half-grown dragons, was heading out of the fief in order to practice flight on the small ledges further down the cliff. The guards had opened both portcullises in order to let them pass, and Selah managed to slip through their midst unnoticed. The apprentices, lost in the glory of riding dragonback, did not pay attention to a cowered figure at their side.

Once outside the gates, Selah was overtaken by a strange sense of freedom. She had not traversed the grounds surrounding Dragonhold since the day after the Choosing, and then it had been brief. She set off, eyes on her feet lest she encounter the many rocks and depressions that pockmarked the barren landscape. Streaks of white snow still marred the ground—Dragonhold, farther north than Hadfoll, was still within the grips of winter.

Selah was not sure how much time had passed before the flat land around her gave way to trees and saplings. She was too wrapped in her thoughts to notice much about the environment around her, despite the fact that it had been her original intention.

The girl slogged through mud that clung voraciously to her boots. Windchaser squeaked, pawing at the neck of the flight jacket. The girl loosed the ties at the nape of her throat so that the dragonet could crawl out. Windchaser dropped to the ground, bored of being in one place and eager to explore.

Selah looked around for the first time. She had been walking for longer than she had realized, and must have been a least a mile into the forest. It was time to head back before Windchaser grew extremely bored and grumpy.

She leaned against a sapling to tighten a boot that had been pulled loose by the mud. The trail wound along the side of a large ravine, and Selah stopped for a moment to admire the view.

The deep groan that rang through the crisp air was her only warning. Selah pitched backwards as the tree gave way and thrust her into empty air.

The world became a blur of green, brown and streaks of white as she tumbled down the hill. Pain lanced through her body as she came into hard contact with the ground repeatedly. Ferns scratched at her face and hands.

The ravine began to level out. Selah ground to a halt as she rolled up against a moss covered boulder. The greenery did little to cushion the impact, and the girl was stunned as her momentum was forcefully stopped. Her hands sank a few inches into muck consisting of mulch and mud. Selah rose to a sitting position, painfully aware of each place where her body had come into contact with the ground. Crashing further up the hill attracted her attention.

The sapling was rolling down the hill after her, loud cracks filling the air as branches snapped off. It was almost upon her before Selah leapt to the side.

The first sensation she felt was a dull throbbing along her lower leg. Her cheek was cold where it pressed up against the ground. The girl lifted her head.

She had escaped serious injury, possibly death, by a near margin. The tree had smashed all the way up against the boulder—it would have crushed her if she had not moved with such haste.

Pain returned her attention to the here and now. The tree had fallen sideways, so that her legs were entangled in the branches. The girl withdrew one leg from the mess without any trouble, but the other had been caught in the V of two intersecting branches. They had sunk deep into the mud, effectively pinning her leg to the cold and damp ground that was soft from the early spring thaw.

Selah could do nothing about her present situation at the moment—her thoughts went to her dragonet. "Windchaser?" she called loudly.

A plaintive cry sounded halfway up the hillside. The sky blue dragonet was easy to pick out among the dark greens and browns of the forest as she made her way down the face of the ravine. *Thank goodness,* Selah thought. *What if she had been in my flight jacket?*

It only took a few more moments for the dragonet to reach her. Selah stroked her Chosen to calm her while she observed her situation. The branches were far too thick to be broken, and looked heavier than she could lift. She tried to pull her leg out, but it was no good. Her calf throbbed painfully—the branches were cutting off her circulation.

After a few minutes of communication, Windchaser understood what Selah was asking of her and dug several hand-sized stones from the earth. The girl squeezed them between the tree and the ground so that her leg did not have to bear the full weight of both branches. The throbbing eased to a dull ache, and she was able to think clearly again.

She thought of sending Windchaser back to the fief, but soon dismissed the idea—the dragonet was still too small to be passed up for a meal by the many predators that inhabited the woods and had been hidden in her flight jacket for most of the trek—she probably had little sense of direction.

Despite the fact that it was still light out and would be for hours, the girl was faced with a chilling thought. If no one found her and she could not escape, she would be forced to stay the night outdoors—the weather was still cold enough that it was potentially dangerous, if not to her, definitely to Windchaser. She had to get back.

Selah drew her belt knife from its sheath at her hip, but knew it would do little for her. The blades that each person carried with them at all times were good for little but cutting food and menial tasks. Selah began to saw strips from the tree branches about her leg. Going straight downward would soon dull the blade, rendering it useless.

After fifteen minutes, she had made little headway. Her hands were turning numb with the bitter cold that still gripped the land. Windchaser had not stopped bawling since she had been first pinned. Selah joined her in shouting, hoping that someone would happen to be walking by and hear them. And if someone did, that they would be a friend.

Selah couldn't tell how much time had passed before her voice gave out. The light was fading, and she was beginning to panic. She collapsed backwards, giving up for the time being. She had tried everything she could think of, without success.

She closed her eyes. Farsight's face swam into focus in her mind's eye. The girl had not seen Averon's dragon for several weeks and was unsure why she had thought of him. The dragon looked at her and spoke. *You were in our minds, Selah…like another dragon.*

Selah's eyes flew open. *Mind speech?* She had been in the dragon's minds the night she had accepted her dragon soul, but had not thought about it since. She had not dared too. Last time, the dragons had all been bleeding. Windchaser…she did not want to hurt Windchaser again. No matter how dire her circumstances.

Selah wrestled with her thoughts for another half hour before she realized that she was out of options. Unless the gods were smiling upon her, there would be no traveler, coming to Dragonhold on foot, who would to see her and come to help. There was no way that she could get out the situation on her own. She had no choice.

Selah lay down so that all her concentration could be focused mentally. She closed her eyes to block out external stimulation. Windchaser, sensing that Selah needed silence, quieted.

Selah searched the space behind her eyes for what seemed like hours. She thought of Dragonhold, of various dragons that she remembered and thrust her mind at their images. Nothing. She concentrated until sweat beaded on her brow and dissipated in the cold air.

She was about to give up when she felt, or sensed, something on the edge of her awareness. It was a sensation similar to seeing something out of the corner of her eye. Selah, battling down the enormous relief that was creeping into her thoughts, forced her mind toward the sensation. It was akin to a spark seen at a great distance—the barest hint of something else.

Hello? Selah asked, hoping that this worked.

Silence.

Selah despaired for several moments before she felt the strange tingle that shot up her spine when another mind made contact with hers.—*Who is this?*—

Selah of Domar. Who is this?

—*Riveneye. How are you in my mind?*—

I don't know how long I can keep this up, Selah confessed. Her temples were beginning to throb. *I'm trapped under a tree about a mile into the forest on the old deer path at the north end of Dragonhold. I'm at the bottom of a ravine and can't get out.*

—*Keep talking to me. I am coming.*—

I'm next to a large boulder. The trail I fell from is at the lip of a ravine, at the edge of a hill. Windchaser…my dragonet…is with me.

—I'm at the start of the trail. It may take a moment to get to you—I cannot fly in trees as close as this. Don't stop talking.—

All right. Sweat soaked her face. *Is there anyone with you?*

—No. I am coming as fast as I can. How heavy is this tree?—

It's just a sapling, not much more. Heavy enough that I can't lift it, but you probably can.

—Very well. I believe I am close. Shout, so I can hear you.—

Selah's throat was raw from shouting endlessly before; nevertheless, she yelled once again. Windchaser began to cry out as well. Selah wasn't sure if Windchaser had been privy to the conversation or if she was simply following by example.

Within moments, a russet dragon appeared at the crest of the ravine. He looked familiar and Selah waved to him. Riveneye, as he had introduced himself, was down the side of the hill quickly.—*Be ready to pull your leg free,*—he instructed, taking hold of the sapling with his large claws. He pulled until the tendons in his forearms were taut and straining. With a deep groan, the tree lifted and Selah scrambled away. The dragon returned the tree to the ground when Selah was clear.

The girl massaged her calf as feeling returned to the limb. "Thank you," she said hoarsely.

The dragon nodded.—*It is no trouble. I had nothing better to do.*—His eyes sparkled with humor.—*Forgive me, but...how did you end up under a tree?—*

Selah blushed. "I was leaning up against it, and...fell. It fell on top of me."

The girl was waiting for the dragon to ask her how she had spoken with him mind to mind and steeled herself for the awkward conversation. However, Riveneye merely motioned that she should try to stand.—*Can you walk?—*he asked.

Selah stood, but her foot had been asleep for so long that it would not bear any weight. The dragon shook his head.—*The gods seem to have played quite a jest on you.*—There was a smile in his voice.—*You may ride on my back until we get back to the fief. Your leg should be better by then.—*

Because the dragon was not wearing a harness, he did not take the risk of her falling off during flight and stayed on the ground. The dragon made short work of the distance between the ravine and the gates of Dragonhold, eating up the ground with his long stride. Selah was less than comfortable—she had never ridden a dragon without a saddle, and it was not a soft seat. Windchaser, who had retreated again to the warmth of Selah's flight jacket, fell asleep momentarily. The day's events had been too much for her.

The dragon was let through the gates without much questioning—at least in words. The guards curiously observed her bedraggled state, but did not comment on it. She was damp, muddy, scratched, and bruised. It looked like she had been in the midst of battle rather than underneath a tree.

Riveneye did not stop at the dens, but continued on to the gates that led into the Great Hall. Selah slid down from his back, grateful that the ride was over; Riveneye had quite a backbone. The dragon nodded toward the doors.—*I would escort you myself, but I must finish my hunt. My Rider should be waiting for you.*—

"Who is your Rider?" Selah asked, but the dragon shook his head and turned away. Coiling his powerful hindquarters, Riveneye leapt into flight, his great wings cutting through the air as he gained altitude.

Selah shivered. She pushed aside the great doors, reflecting on Riveneye's words. *The gods seem to have played quite a jest on you.* He probably didn't know how right he was.

Selah had pulled her cloak free of the closing door when a voice she recognized broke the silence. "Selah of Domar." The girl turned to face the unreadable expression of her training master. "How was your walk?"

✳   ✳   ✳   ✳

Garrett was Riveneye's Rider. Selah knew this, of course, but had not bothered to remember it. The dragonrider marched her to Sean's office, a place that Selah had come to associate with interrogation.

Sean appeared less than happy to see her. "Selah of Domar." He echoed Garrett's words in an identically neutral tone. "For what reason do I have the pleasure of seeing you again?"

Selah did not see the meaningful glance that passed between her training master and the Holdleader. When Sean spoke again, his tone was grudgingly more respectful. "What happened?"

"I took a walk."

"And?"

"Fell under a tree."

"What?"

"I leaned against a tree, the tree broke, fell down a ravine, and the tree fell on top of me, trapping my leg. Riveneye came a few hours later and lifted the tree off of me." The dragon had apparently between speaking with Garrett, his Rider, during the trip back to Dragonhold. She hoped that he had not mentioned that she had used mental communication.

Her hopes were futile. "Aren't you forgetting something?" asked Garrett. The training master arched one brow in disapproval. Selah, sufficiently chastised by the expression, lowered her eyes.

"I used mind to mind communication."

"Telepathy?"

"Is that what you call it?" Selah had never heard the word before, but it sounded right. "There was nothing I could do. I couldn't get the branches off my leg, and there was no one coming. The night was too cold to tough out. I had too!" Her voice had been steadily rising in volume as she tried to convince the two men—and herself—that she had taken the right course of action.

"You used mental communication? After what happened last time?" Sean did not have to say more—those words alone conjured up images of bleeding dragons in her mind. "What were you thinking?"

"There was nothing else for me to do!" Selah was shouting now. "Riveneye didn't say anything about it hurting. I don't think I hurt him." She looked to Garrett for confirmation.

The dragonrider nodded. "Riveneye said nothing of pain. He told me your voice was faint but understandable, and that you sent more emotions than words."

"I was thinking words," Selah offered.

"You transmitted your emotions. More practice will prevent you from doing that."

"Practice?" demanded Sean. "What do you mean, practice? We are lucky she didn't hurt anyone this time. How can you do this?"

"I don't know, sir."

"Is that your favorite phrase?"

Selah, unable to think of anything in reply, looked away. Sean sighed, seeming to regret the harshness of his words. He did not speak for a long while. "I fear you, Selah of Domar. I am not afraid of many people," he looked into her eyes, "but I am afraid of you. What you are capable of doing. That is enough to frighten anyone. I am forbidding you from any sort of mental telepathy from this point onward. There is too much at risk here."

Garrett opened his mouth to protest, but Sean raised a hand for silence. "That is my decision, Garrett, and as my inferior in rank, you must adhere to it. Understood?"

The muscle along Garrett's jaw tightened. "Very well."

Sean returned his attention to Selah. "As for you, leaving the fief without per-mission is strictly prohibited. Your free days for the rest of the month will be spent in the armory. You will be put to work there. Dismissed."

Selah rose to leave, turning toward the door. She felt hollow. *I fear you, Selah of Domar.* Behind her, Sean spoke again. "Both of you."

Garrett followed her out of Sean's office. He did not say anything to her as he turned and walked in the direction of the dragonrider's hall. Selah, too, was silent as she made her way to the pallon's wing.

*   *   *   *

Garrett made no further mention of the strange events the next day, and Selah decided to follow suit and keep silent as well. Like matters of her soul, the girl was content to leave the occurrences behind her and pay them no further thought. However, there was a part of her that couldn't help but wonder what other abili-ties the merging of her soul and mind had given her.

Training was somewhat different that day. Garrett announced that they would be testing their endurance. Selah, thinking that it would be some sort of running, was not too worried—she was in good shape and her leg had mostly recovered from the strain of the day before.

They started with push-ups, sit-ups, and multiple other core exercises. No one faltered. He had them run twice around the inner fief, but the training master had often demanded this of them before and they were conditioned enough to handle it. He thrust swords in their hands and instructed them to fight against a partner for five minutes.

Selah's breath was beginning to catch in her throat, but she was otherwise fine. Garrett called for them to stop and told the pallons to sprint to the doors of the Great Hall and back twice. They complied, although a few pallons were a little slower than the others on their way back a second time.

Garrett did not allow them to rest for a moment, gesturing to the rack of bows and telling them to shoot from sixty paces until they hit the bulls-eye. Selah, who had always had a knack for archery, hit the center of the ring on her third try. She was preceded by four others. Landon, only a beat behind her, joined them shortly.

Garrett ran the group through a set of terrible exercises until Selah's stomach burned and her arms shook. The girl swallowed in relief when the training master told them to stop.

They were not finished for the day, however. It was just the beginning. Garrett worked them in every imaginable way possible. She came to use the times that they were doing push-ups as a time to rest—they did more running than ever before.

It was two hours into the workout that pallons began dropping out. Nolan, weakened by his fever in Hadfoll, was the first to stop during one of their many runs around the fief. Garrett instructed him to go inside.

After Nolan fell behind, others did as well—Fagan and Quinn were the next two. The group got rapidly smaller as two hours became three. Garrett showed no sign of ending the day, although he did allow them one five-minute rest.

Selah watched her training master curiously. She was still bemused by his slight defense of her the day before, and she wanted to make it up to him somehow. Therefore, she would not allow herself to stop. As Garrett called for them to stand up, she realized that before Hadfoll, she would have given up long ago. The dragon part of her was not all drawbacks. She had a new determination that had never manifested itself before her connection with her soul.

Soon, there were only ten of them left, then seven. None of the seven would break as easily as the others—Selah was the last among a group consisting of Landon, Aswin, Bern, Corith, Renton, and Hale. The wear of the afternoon was beginning to get to her, but she would not stop and show that she was not as strong as the others. Her pride would not let her.

It was another hour before Garrett told them to stop. Selah was trembling with exertion. Each breath burned in her lungs and it was hard to focus on anything. She was exhausted. The training master looked at them with respect in his eyes. "Congratulations for having the mental resolution to not quit. I applaud you. It is an accomplishment to be proud of."

Landon patted her firmly on the back. "Nice work," he said, face shining with sweat.

Selah's breath issued from her lungs in great white clouds that misted in the air before fading away. "Thanks...you too."

The corner of Garrett's mouth twitched in a rare smile. "There, of course, is the matter of a reward for your tenacity." The pallons brightened at the mention of compensation. The training master shook his head. "You have it. Imagine that each one of those who dropped behind lost their lives because they could not keep going. Imagine that each run, each exercise, was a Cydran dragonrider that you had to face in mortal combat. You lasted it out, and are alive. Those who couldn't have, theoretically, lost theirs." He looked at them, one by one, to make sure that they understood his meaning. "Each day, you have one chance to make the best of it. Your lives are the reward. Make sure that you have the resolution to defend them."

Selah was struck by the impressive truth behind Garrett's words. He was right, and although she would have appreciated a day off, she had to admit that he had a very valid point. It was a thoughtful and exhausted group that trudged off to the bathhouses.

*   *   *   *

After the dropouts of over half of the pallons, Garrett intensified workouts until Selah was so sore she had trouble walking. When several complained aloud during training, Garrett brought out suits of armor and made them condition encased in metal. Push-ups were much harder with the additional thirty pounds of chain mail alone. Those who struggled were relegated to constant work in armor—those who did not moved to plate armor on special occasions.

Once again, Selah crossed the threshold of change. As the greenery around Dragonhold surged with the coming of Spring, so did her height; the girl stretched an inch in the two months after their return to Hadfoll. By her thirteenth birthday in March, she had reached five feet and seven inches, passing the twins. Her masters no longer seemed so imposing.

Her ghosts, waylaid by intensive training and work, returned with a vengeance. The discovery of her ability to mentally communicate with dragons had instilled a new fear in the girl. If she lost control, she could have hurt every dragon in the fief. Selah vowed not to take her dragon side lightly—she would obey Sean's wishes, however much she disliked the man, and not take chances.

Despite her private resolution, she returned to sleeping uneasily. The girl woke several times a night from dreams of dragons singing her dragon song. During daylight hours, she tried to locate places that would help her find inner peace. Others moaned about the challenge of training, but Selah enjoyed it. Garrett's sessions were a needed distraction from ideas she did not want to think about.

As with before, Selah found it impossible to outrun her ghosts. When she could no longer keep her thoughts at bay during training and classes, she decided to seek divine guidance.

*   *   *   *

Selah entered the small temple as quietly as she could. Despite her efforts, the hinges creaked loudly—they had held the iron wrought door in place for countless generations and were beginning to show it. Selah winced, but those who were lost in prayer did not acknowledge her.

Incense streamed from small bowls, turning parts of the room into a smoky haze. The beams of sunlight that peeked through the small window seemed solid and tangible in the otherwise dim atmosphere.

Some god statues were littered with offerings—small wooden carvings, candles made of colored tallow—mostly trinkets. Selah passed the altars of Conway, the god of honor, strength, courage, and sacrifice, the Seer, Gonran, Matrik, the Lord of Gods, his Lady, Fael, and countless other small idols. Stormhunter's section of the altar was situated next to Gonran, his Rider. It would have been wrong to place the greatest of all dragons away from his Chosen.

Selah's knees, bruised from training, complained as she settled down in front of the statue. The dragon god's likeliness, created from bronze and hints of copper, was flawless, if not completely accurate. The god, in reality, did not have such great shoulders and a much softer brow line. The artist had depicted Stormhunter with an expression of majestic indifference, eyes lifted from the worshiper and gazing off into the distance.

Selah sat for a long while. The murmuring of other worshipers became a constant din that her mind registered but did not decipher. Words of prayer waited in her thoughts to be uttered softly as was appropriate in a place of the gods, but something in her throat locked and smothered the words in silence.

The girl gazed into the eyes of the bronze idol. Questions reverberated within her mind, all the words she would ask of the gods. *How did I become the way I am? Was it on purpose? If so, why? Why did Windchaser Chose me? What am I? Human or dragon? How can I be both? What am I?*

What am I?

Selah asked the questions in silence, knowing all too well that she lacked the answers to make them leave. She looked plaintively to the golden statue, half wishing words would spill from its delicately shaped mouth and ease her inner turmoil.

"Selah," whispered someone next to her. The girl jumped.

Talmud immediately seemed to regret startling her. It appeared that he had just returned from paying his respects to Aria, the goddess of healing. "I'm sorry, Pallon Selah, but it is almost time for the evening meal. There is a punishment for being late and I thought you might appreciate knowing the time."

Selah nodded, struggling to her feet. Blood rushed back to her legs after being in a folded position for so long, and the girl wobbled for a moment before regaining her balance. "Thank you."

Talmud smiled. "Did you come to honor the dragon god?" He nodded to the metal figurine.

Selah returned the smile, but hers was rueful and somewhat forced. "Partly."

"May I ask why else you came? The pallons rarely pay their respects to the gods on any day other than when it is required."

Selah sighed. "Soul searching." She was struck by the double meaning to her words that would never apply to anyone else.

Talmud steered her toward the entrance of the small temple. He seemed lost in thought for a moment, then spoke. "In my experience, answers generally come to those who are not trying so hard to find them." He turned to the girl, making sure she was paying attention before continuing. "Your questions will be answered when you are ready to understand them. All in due time, Pallon Selah. If you will forgive me, I have not eaten since breakfast and the table awaits." With a slight nod, he turned and walked away.

$$*\qquad*\qquad*\qquad*$$

Talmud's words were not a balm for her troubled mind—however, they did convince her to set aside the matter for the time being and concentrate on other things. Garrett had nearly doubled the intensity of workouts. Any who fell behind in their conditioning or training joined the Guild of Early Risers, a group of pallons that met the training master early in the morning for an additional session with him. Selah was loath to become a member and refocused her efforts during training as to prevent it. Others did not match the determination of their fellows and became the first honorary members of the Guild. Conversation volume at the breakfast table dropped several notches as a result.

Two weeks came and went without her truly noticing the passage of time. After regular chores, caring for Windchaser, classes, and training, she was far too tired to even think. The girl slept soundly and was outstripped only by Landon for waking late on their days off—the boy would not be seen until luncheon when he was not required to get up.

Selah was normally jerked out of dreams by the roar of the watch dragon. When she opened her eyes to silence, she was surprised. She was not an early riser unless strange thoughts bothered her, and she rolled over to try to return to her dream.

Windchaser, generally sprawled out on the pillow beside her, was wound into a tight ball, her nose thrust into her tail in the hopes that it would provide her with extra warmth. The dragonet shivered fiercely—when Selah prodded her, she stirred and revealed glassy violet eyes.

Windchaser coughed weakly. She lay listlessly on her side, and panic closed Selah's throat. Her dragonet had never been sick before.

The girl rushed out the door, her Chosen clutched in her arms. Her bare feet slapped loudly against the stone tiling, sending eerie echoes reverberating down the corridors. She had not changed from her sleeping clothes; her overlarge night-shirt hung off one shoulder unheeded.

She pounded on the door of the infirmary until her fist throbbed from the rough contact with the solid wood. She was blind to the servants preparing for the coming day; it was early in the morning, as the crystals were still flickering at their dim nighttime glow.

An apprentice healer Selah had not encountered before opened the door. The girl didn't bother with introductions. "My dragonet's sick." The words tumbled from her mouth like hasty sparrows fleeing from a hawk.

The apprentice nodded, his thick black brows knitting together into a frown. "Master Talmud should be here in a few minutes." He opened the door wider and beckoned for her to come inside. Selah glanced at Windchaser—the drago-net's eyes were still tightly sealed.

The apprentice healer gestured that she should lay the dragonet on one of the smaller tables. Selah obliged, painfully aware of how little Windchaser squirmed in her arms.

The apprentice felt the dragonet's wings for temperature. "She's hot," he said, checking swollen glands in her throat. He brought out a basin of water and small rags. "Put cool water on her forehead and sponge down her wings. We need to keep her temperature down until Darien comes back with Master Talmud." He raised his eyebrows toward another apprentice, who acknowledged Selah briefly before exiting. The first apprentice returned his attention to her. "I think your dragonet has a fever."

Master Talmud arrived shortly. His eyes were still bleary with sleep, but they snapped into focus when he caught sight of Windchaser and her Rider. "Pallon Selah," he rubbed along his jaw, "what seems to be the trouble?"

The apprentice broke in before Selah could reply. "Her dragonet has a fever, Master. Her glands are swollen and her wings are above normal temperature."

Talmud drew closer to the dragonet, examining her wings, throat and body. "What's her name?" he asked.

"Windchaser."

"Windchaser," the healer repeated. "What's wrong with you, Windchaser?" The dragonet made no reply. Talmud sighed, peeling back one eyelid to look at Windchaser's pupils. They were still glassy and feverish.

"She *is* sick. It looks like Cold Fever." When Selah glanced at him in confusion, he explained. "Did you ever have the fowl pox as a child?" When Selah nodded, he raised his eyebrow at her unblemished face. "I see that it was kind to you. Cold Fever is like the fowl pox…once you get it, you will not get it again. Dragonets develop a high fever that must be contained. When they reach the hottest point of their fever, they will 'freeze' and not move. When that happens, bring her back to me, and I will help her lower her temperature. Other than keeping her cool and comfortable, there is not much that you can do." When he saw that Selah understood, he spoke again. "She will be feverish for several days, and it can take up to two weeks for a full recovery." Selah blanched.

Talmud lifted the dragonet from the table and retuned her to Selah's embrace. "You'll have to stay in your room—Cold Fever is highly contagious the first day, and the older the other dragonets get it, the better."

Selah's spirits fell at his words; Windchaser was not yet a year old. She returned to her quarters, unable to comprehend being quarantined within their claustrophobic walls for several weeks. Talmud had assured her that her masters would be informed and meals would be delivered to her chambers, so there was nothing else to do but wait.

By the time the watch dragon roared at the coming of dawn, Selah had caught up with all her coursework while Windchaser slept. The dragonet showed no sign of improvement—if anything, her temperature was rising. Selah's hands became wrinkled from soaking the rags, wringing them out, and washing Windchaser down. Her body continued to radiate heat despite her Rider's efforts. The girl felt helpless in the face of such a potent fever—she had never been a caregiver and knew nothing of nurturing. Still, Selah murmured sweet encouragements to Windchaser she tended her. The girl was unsure if the dragonet was able to hear her words.

The day passed sluggishly. Meals were slid around the door with little talk interchanged between Selah and the server. Talmud came by at mid-afternoon, but did not stay long; he did not want to contaminate the other dragonets.

The sound of slamming doors roused Selah from her doze. The other pallons had returned to their rooms and were going to bed. A moment later, the crystal cluster on her bedside table switched from a clear light to the blue of evening.

Windchaser whimpered in a nightmare. Selah picked up the dragonet and held her gently. She felt so useless.

Her eyes ached; Selah closed them with good intentions, but was soon asleep.

*   *   *   *

She and Firmin were patrolling. As usual, her brother was in the lead with her a half step behind him. The boy knew exactly where he was going; only a few minutes of walking brought them to the threshold of their brother's chambers. Firmin pounded on the door loudly. "Come out, Kavan!"

It was a moment too long before the door opened with a creak. Sea-green eyes stared out at them untrustingly. "What do you want?"

"You were performing magic on the little kids!" accused Selah.

Kavan shrugged nonchalantly. "They asked me too. Tate wanted to see if I could turn him into an owl."

"His nose was bleeding! Explain that!" shouted Firmin.

"He thought he was an owl and climbed up to the roof of the stables! Is it my fault he fell down?"

Firmin crossed his arms across his chest. "I think he's lying. What about you, Selah?"

Selah looked at Kavan and knew he was telling the truth. However, fiction was easier to believe. "Liar."

Kavan's eyes fell, and he started to shut the door. Firmin thrust it open and snatched his brother by the collar. "No more magic. Got it?"

Kavan locked his jaw and refused to say a word. "Got it?" repeated Firmin. Selah was frozen. All she could do was watch and see what her black-haired brother would do.

Kavan adverted his eyes. Firmin shoved him, getting his message across in the only way that boys seemed to know.

Selah broke from her paralysis and grabbed Firmin's arm. For some reason, she didn't want to see the brother she hated beaten. "Let's go, Firmin. Don't waste your time."

Firmin waited for a moment before dropping Kavan to the floor. "Fine. Come on." Her twin disappeared down the hall.

Kavan looked up at her, his sea green eyes asking an unspoken question. Selah turned away and followed Firmin outside.

*　　*　　*　　*

A squall broke her from the dream. One hand shot for the crystal cluster, tapping it once for more light, while the other groped blindly for the knife she kept close to her ever since the Dragonslayer.

The crystal flooded the room with light, revealing a small bundle of scales sprawled across the floor. Windchaser, delirious, had wormed out of Selah's grasp and fallen to the floor.

Selah retrieved her Chosen, noting with alarm that Windchaser looked at her with no recognition in her eyes. When the girl brought the dragonet into an embrace, she cowered in fear, fighting to get away. The next moment, she slashed wildly at things in the air that Selah could not see. She was hallucinating.

"Windchaser." Selah drew her closer. "It's me, Windchaser."

The dragonet bawled in confusion, weaving from side to side in fever. Selah had begun to stroke her head when she stiffened. Her ears pressed flat to her skull as her eyes squeezed tightly shut. "Windchaser!" Selah cried, but there was no reaction. *She's frozen*, Selah thought. *She can't hear me.*

Windchaser's breathing was ragged. She took up the dragonet, running for the second time to the infirmary. A new apprentice, older and female, took one look at Windchaser and lead Selah to Talmud's personal quarters.

The healer was less than happy at the sight of visitors in the middle of the night, but his expression softened when he saw Windchaser. "How long has she been like this?" he asked, referring to her tense and stiff position.

"A few minutes," Selah replied.

Talmud led them back to the infirmary. "If we can control her fever now, all will be fine." The unspoken "if not" lingered heavily in the space between them.

For an hour they fought to get Windchaser's temperature down, to no avail. It rose like a dragon mounted the air currents, and they could conjure no cure to make it fall. Talmud looked at Selah with deadly seriousness in his eyes. "If her temperature climbs anymore, she will die," he told her. Turning to an apprentice, he barked, "Bring me cold water!" The youths scurried away to perform the task—in the face of a crisis, the soft-spoken healer had transformed into a coarse commander.

Selah felt lost. Windchaser had ignored all of her pleas to wake; the dragonet had shut herself away from the outside world.

Windchaser, she thought. *Please, pull out of this.*

The dragonet stirred. Selah bent down, unheeding the stares of the apprentice healers, and touched her forehead to Windchaser's brow. *Windchaser, please live.* She closed her eyes to find the spark. Her Chosen's mind was easier to touch than Riveneye's. *Hear me.*

Her spine burned as she made contact with Windchaser. She felt hot and dizzy—by connecting with Windchaser, she was opening herself to her dragonet's most prevalent sensations and emotions. Selah struggled to fit her emotions into words, so she let her feelings spill into the dragonet; sadness, hope, anguish, and love streamed from behind her eyes and into the thoughts of her Chosen.

Windchaser, Selah pleaded, *you have to break the fever. You have to wake up.*

Finally she tried to send her strength, the energy she had in excess but her dragonet so desperately needed.

She opened her eyes, hanging on a precariously mental connection. Windchaser had not moved.

Hopelessness filled the girl. Her Chosen was slowly burning to death from fever, and there was nothing she could do. Selah closed her eyes to the world and reopened her mind. Reaching out, she grasped the sky blue spark with her thoughts.

Selah felt a sharp tug behind her breastbone as her heart skipped a beat. A wave of nausea rushed through her stomach, gripping her throat before she swallowed it back down.

Selah remaining motionless for what felt like hours, breathing deeply and slowly. Finally, she felt better and opened her eyes. Violet pupils, still glassy, stared back at her.

Talmud looked at her with a strange expression on his face. "Her temperature is receding."

Selah breathed a sigh of relief. Windchaser had broken her fever. The dragonet murmured, reaching out to grasp Selah's hand. Everything was going to be all right.

*   *   *   *

Selah awoke the next morning to a sharp rap on her door. It was the Master Healer; he asked if he could see Windchaser.

The dragonet was doing much better, although her eyes were still watery and she was a little warmer than usual. Talmud shook his head in disbelief. "I have never seen a dragonet recover this quickly. Did you feed her anything?"

"Just water. I was afraid that she would get sick."

Windchaser stumbled to her food bowl and whined. Selah pulled a strip of dried meat from the belt pouches that lay on the floor and handed it to the dragonet.

Talmud sighed. "She's only contagious on the first day—to be safe, skip morning classes and go to training."

The healer left, and Selah returned to bed and drifted off to sleep. She woke a second time to the servant that brought her breakfast. Windchaser ate half the meal—most of her energy and appetite had returned.

Selah rose and tidied up her room. She pulled on a fresh pair of clothes and carried Windchaser down to lunch in an empty quiver; the dragonet was too exhausted from her ordeal the night before to walk at all.

Her friends greeted her loudly when she entered the Mess Hall. "Where have you been?" asked Landon, pulling Indio off the table.

"Quarantined," said Selah; the boys immediately started sidling and shifting away from her. She laughed at the expressions on their faces. "Not me...Windchaser. She had the Cold Fever last night, and the healers didn't want her around your dragonets."

Bern rubbed the back of his neck uneasily. "Are you sure she's all right?"

Selah heard the unspoken request in his voice and decided to comply. "I'll sit somewhere else today, just in case she *is* contagious." The boys, although they protested, seemed relieved. The girl insisted and set her tray of food down at the empty table in the back of the hall.

Few dared to come near her—most of the fief, by this time, already knew that there had been a case of Cold Fever and no one wanted to be a carrier. Even as she ate, the servants were washing her sheets to remove the sickness from her quarters. Selah was not bothered by being alone; the Mess Hall was a pleasant change of pace from her room and the infirmary, and she was content to observe.

Talmud instructed one of the apprentice healers to watch Windchaser while Selah was training. The dragonet was still weak enough that a constant eye on her could do no harm.

Garrett, after taking a moment to ask how Windchaser was feeling, sent them into their daily workout of a run, push ups and sit ups. Selah found herself struggling, gasping for air at the end of a relatively easy run. *I was out for one day,* she thought. *How could I have lost that much conditioning in so little time?*

It was the middle of the week, the time when they focused the most on weapons—Garrett was still not satisfied with their fencing and instructed them to work on some freeform.

Selah was exhausted already, and her head felt wooly and overlarge. Her temples throbbed dully, but the girl shook it off and grasped the hilt of a blade that Garrett handed her.

Garrett, with any weapon, broke the pallons into three groups by skill level—Selah was placed in the top rank for archery and fencing, but the second groups for hand to hand combat and wrestling, and knife duels. In this manner, the pallons were situated with those at their own skill level, although Garrett liked to move pallons up a group to give them practice against stronger opponents. The pallons in the first groups sometimes battled against apprentices—the better ones, such as Landon or Renton, fenced against dragonriders from reserve Wings.

Thusly, each day in the first rank was challenging. Selah usually partnered with Aswin for fencing, and found him within a moment. The pain behind her eyes was increasing; it was becoming harder and harder to focus.

"Are you all right, Selah?" Aswin asked. Selah nodded obstinately—she was dizzy, nothing more. She had probably stood up too fast.

Garrett finished giving instructions to the first two groups and approached the best fencers. "Today we're going to do something different. When in single combat, it is best to be fighting from a height so that you have an advantage on your opponent. We'll do that today on the stairs and alternate fighting from an advantageous position." He made sure that the pallons were listening, and his eyes stopped for a moment on Selah. The girl had dug her sword point first into the earth of the training yard and leaned on it for support.

He caught up with her as they were making their way to the stairs. "Are you all right?" he asked.

Selah seemed not to hear him. He tapped her on the shoulder and repeated his inquiry. "Oh…yes, sir." A bead of sweat trickled down from her hairline. "I had a rough night—that's all." When Garrett raised an incredulous eyebrow, the girl protested. "I am fine, sir…honestly."

Garrett was not convinced, but the other pallons were awaiting orders and he needed to start the exercise. He placed Aswin and Selah on a small flight of stairs before moving onto the next pair.

A shout from the training master started the freeform. Selah was at the top of the stairs; it was all she could do to keep Aswin from overtaking her. The boy was everywhere, darting away from her blows and snaking in before she could react. Her headache was enough to distract her.

The dragonrider called for them to switch positions—Selah leaned against the guardrail on the staircase for a long moment before descending. She moved as though underwater, and each gesture seemed to take twice as much energy as it should.

Garrett instructed them to begin again; the girl realized that it was her turn to charge up the stairs. She did so and was thrust back by a sharp counterattack from Aswin. Selah swayed dangerously before righting herself.

Her sword was lead in her hands; lifting it was nearly impossible. The throbbing behind her eyes had escaladed into a roaring headache. Selah reached out and clutched the guardrail again, signally to Aswin that she needed a moment to collect herself.

"Selah, are you sick?"

"No," she lied. Her tongue felt thick and swollen in her mouth. "I'm fine. Let's keep going."

Aswin brought his sword up into the guard position, Selah a long measure behind him. Shaking her head to clear it, the girl charged again, Aswin leveling his sword in order to block her.

Another wave of nausea shot through her. Selah's knees buckled, and she swayed forward until her partner was bearing most of her weight. Aswin, thinking that she was trying to force him down, tore his blade free and slashed out at her in an effort to get her to back away. The girl was too delirious to block the blow. The sword's dull edge smacked hollowly against the chain mail that covered Selah's stomach.

Her vision went gray. Steel rang harshly against stone as her sword clattered against the steps. The girl doubled over in pain, swallowing down the bile that rose in her throat. Her foot sought the edge of the stone and found empty air; she tumbled down the steps that separated her from the ground floor.

Aswin called for Garrett, rushing to his friend's side. The girl moaned into the dirt. Her lungs seemed strapped in iron, cutting each breath's capacity in half. Aswin's blade had struck her just below the ribs, and her arms encircled the point of impact as if constant pressure could relieve the pain.

The panicked note in the pallon's cry for help betrayed the seriousness of the situation; Garrett wasted no time in getting to their side. Selah was shaking with more than the shock of a painful injury—something was very wrong.

Someone was trying to pull her arms away from her stomach; Selah wasn't strong enough to deny them. The world was unclear, then returned to clarity with a speed that only made the girl more nauseous. Garrett's face appeared above her—his fingers were gentle as he felt her forehead.

More hands peeled the chain mail from her shoulders and over her head. "Call a healer," Garrett said. His voice seemed very far away.

"Is she bleeding?" Aswin asked. There were more faces above her now, but she couldn't recognize them. Someone hissed as her shirt was lifted to reveal a scarlet welt that bisected her stomach. The edge of Aswin's sword appeared to have been branded into her skin.

She shivered, although uncomfortably hot despite the regular temperature of the air around her. The sharp blue of the sky above her faded to a pale gray with streaks of white, and finally black.

$$*\qquad*\qquad*\qquad*$$

Talmud paused for a moment to dip his quill into more ink as he scribbled away at his daily log of illnesses. He often consulted the large volumes of his predecessors when caring for his patients and his own experiences would someday be advice sought by those who followed him. He finished his paragraph on the adolescent dragon with the broken forepaw and stopped.

The girl in the bed across the room stirred, but returned to stillness when he looked over at her. Selah had not regained consciousness for several hours. Windchaser, curled into a tight ball at the foot of her bed, had long since fallen asleep. Talmud returned to the parchment in front of him. *Selah of Domar suffered a blow to the stomach during training and appears to have a fever as well. The wound was inflicted by a dull sword, but thanks to her armor she has nothing more than a bright welt that shall develop into a nice purple bruise in a day or so,* he wrote. *It is her fever that concerns me. Selah was found to have a draconic soul during the winter stay at Hadfoll and her dragonet recently contracted Cold Fever. The average recovery time is commonly three to five days for the normal fevers, but Windchaser has reached the second stage of the illness, sinus trouble and general weakness, in less than a full two days. At this rate, she will be fully recovered by moonrise on Thursday.*

The healer twirled his quill back and forth with his thumb and index finger, chewing the end thoughtfully as he sought the words to finish his report. *Selah can, on occasion, mentally communicate with dragons—that, coupled with her strange behavior when Windchaser was at the height of her fever, gives me the feeling that she has something to do with her dragonet's speedy recovery. How so, I am not sure, but I have learned to trust my instincts. There is a strangeness about Selah that should not be*—the soft knock on the door came just as he was about to write the final words. "Perfect timing," muttered the Master Healer, leaving his seat reluctantly and trundling to the infirmary entrance.

It was Garrett. The training master waited for Talmud to invite him inside before crossing the threshold into the room. His golden eyes lingered on the girl who lay prone and listless on the sickbed. "How is she?" he asked.

Talmud smiled. He had seen the comings and goings of several Dragonhold training masters, and Garrett, by far, was the most considerate. Whenever a pallon was a patient, he came by each day to check on their condition. "She still has not regained consciousness, but I think it is more sleep than anything else. The stomach wound is not too serious—we should be thankful that the pallon was off balance when he delivered the blow. It could have been much worse."

"Her fever?"

"I..." There was a second knock on the infirmary door. Talmud sighed. "Excuse me a moment." One of the apprentice healers entered the room, and whispered to the Master Healer urgently. Garrett, sensing that he was not welcome in the conversation, walked deeper into the room.

The open volume on the desk in the corner of the room caught his attention. Garrett pulled it forward, his golden eyes scanning the page rapidly.

Talmud finished with the apprentice and ushered him from the room. Shutting the door quietly, he turned back to the training master. "As I was saying..."

"Ignored," suggested the dragonrider, pointing to a spot on the page.

"I beg your pardon?"

"The word you want is 'ignored'." Garrett read aloud the sentence that Talmud had left unfinished. "*There is a strangeness about Selah that should not...*be ignored," he concluded with his own words.

"That was my line of thinking, yes." The Master Healer was a little flustered; he was not pleased that Garrett had read his report without asking.

Garrett, lost in thought, gazed at the girl. "You notice it as well." It was a statement, not a question.

Talmud nodded. "It is impossible for a dragonet to recover so quickly from so potent a fever. That Selah has developed a similar sickness so soon after is one too many coincidences."

Garrett sighed. "When she communicated with my dragon...Riveneye could not tell that she was not another dragon until she identified herself with a human title. She mind spoke as well as any adolescent dragon that is just learning. I would tell her myself, but..." he trailed off.

"Sean," finished Talmud.

"He fears her." Garrett could not help but notice how far from frightening Selah was in her current, weakened condition. The girl was pale, not as white as the sheets that wrapped around her protectively, but pallid enough that it bothered him. "He is afraid of what she is—dragon and human. Stormhunter has marked her, Talmud." His hands tightened on the backrest of the chair he leaned against. "We cannot sit by and hold her back from what she might be."

"Caution, my friend. We do not want a repeat performance of Hadfoll."

A rueful smile lifted the corners of Garrett's mouth. "That's what Sean said. He does have a point." He gazed plaintively at the ceiling. "That I could go out on a patrol again!" He shook his head. "I'm getting land fever, I guess. Life is so much simpler when you're on dragonback."

"Isn't everything." Talmud returned his attention to the girl that they spoke of. "Her fever does not seem to be too dangerous. She will be out for several days. No challenging work when she first returns, Garrett of Dalbrook." Talmud frowned in both mock and real severity. "I don't want her coming straight back here with something else wrong."

Garrett bowed. "Heard and understood, Master Healer."

"Good." Sensing that the conversation was coming to a close, Talmud held the door open for the man. "One more thing, dragonrider. Don't read my volumes again unless I ask you to or give you permission." The Master Healer smiled, trying to make his request with a lighter tone and still get his message across. "For all you know, I could have written about an illness that could be potentially embarrassing."

Garrett nodded. "I understand, Talmud. Good night to you."

"To you as well."

Talmud shut the door behind the dragonrider quietly as not to disturb the two sleeping occupants of the room. Selah did not move, too lost in slumber to notice. Talmud returned to his desk with a sigh....*be ignored,* he concluded, shaking his head in slight amusement. The volume closed with a soft thump and was replaced to its place of honor on the shelf. The healer tapped the crystals gently before leaving—the bright stones dimmed to a soft blue glow that barely illuminated Selah's motionless face. Her hand tightened on a fist-full of blankets once, and was still.

DARKNESS

*She and Firmin were arguing fiercely over who got to be King. "You can't be King,"
said Firmin haughtily. "You're a girl! Girls are Queens."*

*Selah frowned. "I don't want to be a Queen. I want to be the King! You were King
last time."*

"But girls can't be King!"

"Well...stupid people can't be King either!"

Firmin's eyes narrowed. "Are you calling me stupid?"

Selah stuck her tongue out at him. "Yes."

*He pushed her away from the stone that was designated as King's throne. "You
can't be King!"*

*"I can too!" Selah shouted, smacking him with the stick that passed as her sword. A
red line appeared on his cheekbone, and her brother yelped. Selah dropped the stick in
mortification. "I'm sorry, Firmin."*

*The red line was dripping blood down Firmin's cheek. Loud footsteps warned them
that Beda was on the prowl and had caught the sound of children getting into trouble.
It did not take long for their surrogate mother to reach them. "What's going on?" she
asked in a voice that made Selah tremble in her soft leather shoes.*

*"Nothing," the girl replied automatically. Beda had long since learned that 'noth-
ing' always meant 'something' and ordered Firmin to take his hand away from his
face. The boy complied and revealed a cheek that was stained with streaks of blood.*

"What happened?" Beda demanded. Selah braced herself for punishment.

*Firmin looked at her for a long moment before returning his attention to Beda. "I
hurt myself on one of the branches."*

Beda eyed the culpable looking Selah with an incredulous expression. "Are you sure?" When Firmin nodded, she led him off to tend to the wound.

Later, Selah asked him why he had lied to Beda. Her brother smiled at her. "Because," he said simply, "that's what you would have said if I had scratched you. Let's go play Dragonstones."

*   *   *   *

Selah's world, upon waking, was white. Snow covered hills and valleys rolled like waves upon the ocean, casting shadows that made parts darker than others. It took a moment for her to realize that the gentle texture around her was fabric. She was staring at the surface of tussled sheets, not a landscape.

The girl rose to her elbows, wincing as her stomach contorted in pain. She felt as though she had been kicked in the torso by an ox. A meadowlark sang somewhere in the distance, and it didn't hurt to listen; her head was clear of the dreadful ache that had plagued her earlier.

A cry of delight sounded from the foot of her bed. A sky blue streak slammed into her chest, knocking her back onto the pillows. Violet eyes stared deeply into her own. Windchaser was awake.

Selah protested that she couldn't breathe, and the dragonet clambered off her, permitting the girl to rise to a sitting position. Her stomach screamed each time she twisted one way or another. The girl finally stopped moving her body and craned her neck to look around.

She was in the infirmary, a place she was frequenting too often of late. A man in green robes hunched over a desk in one corner of the room; his hair had been arranged over a growing bald spot in the back of his head that defiantly refused to be hidden. He turned at the sound of Selah's moving about. It was Talmud; she had not recognized him from the back.

"How are you feeling?" he asked.

"Stiff," the girl replied honestly. She must have been lying still in one position for a long while. Selah had to clear her throat before continuing. "How long have I been here?"

"Two days...three nights, counting your first."

"Gods," Selah whispered. "How come? Did I ever wake up?"

"Once or twice," said the Master Healer. He seemed amused. "You had a fever—did you know that?"

Selah nodded. "It wasn't that bad, I thought."

Talmud chuckled. "Next time, consider consulting someone who knows how to diagnose illness, such as myself. You've been slipping out of delirium and consciousness for two days."

"Oh."

"'Oh' is right, young Rider." The Master Healer gathered a pile of papers on his desk. "Windchaser hasn't moved from the foot of your bed in all that time—we had to feed her there." The dragonet, knowing they were discussing her, looked at Selah with an expression of smug satisfaction. "Your Masters have dropped off your coursework over the past few days, as well the notes that your friends took during lectures."

He handed the pages to Selah. The girl flipped through the sections of mathematics problems and wind patterns, stopping when she came to a page of script written in Landon's tight print. *The Battle of the Five Armies...important, remember for essay...we lost because of tactical decisions made by the other side...watch for pikes in the grass, knights lost entire brigade to that one.* Some phrases were underlined to stress their importance. *Dragonriders didn't know how to fight from the air, lost twenty cause they didn't pull up in time. By the way, Selah, hope you're feeling better.*

The girl grinned and turned to the next set. This was written in Bern's wide and loopy scrawl. *If subtracting from one side of the equation you have to do it to the other side. Why do we have to know this? Same with adding, multiplying, dividing, or boiling, or frying in lard. This irks me—Selah, get better soon because I hate having to pay attention during mathematics. Want to switch places?*

The next page was from Aswin—the girl recognized his neat, flowing script immediately. *The swoop attack during battle is highly effective, but dragons have to learn to gauge distance well, low enough to hurt, high enough to regain altitude and high enough that the enemy can't hit them. Height is different for each dragon...Selah, sorry about what happened.* The girl's mouth lifted in another smile. *Get better soon.*

The last page was from Roswald; however, his were notes and nothing more. There were no messages for her intermixed with the information. Slightly disappointed, the girl set down the pages and returned her attention to the Master Healer.

A servant came in with morning tea—Talmud accepted the cup with a gracious thank you and offered Selah a scone. The girl shook her head—she wasn't hungry.

"When can I go back to training?"

"Not today," the healer decried nonchalantly, taking a bite into a pastry. "It's a little late for you to make morning classes, and training, after what you've been through, is out of the question."

Selah couldn't help but glower. After two full days of being gone, the other pallons would be miles ahead of her as far as training. She might have even lost her spot in the first groups. "I feel fine."

"That's what you said before you fainted." Talmud brushed crumbs from the front of his robes. Selah, chastised, propped herself up with pillows.

A moment later, she spoke again. "Can I please get up?"

Talmud waved her request away with a gesture of his hand. "Not until after lunch. You've hardly been awake for five minutes and you're already raring to get a weapon in your hand." He shook his head incredulously. "Dragonriders…"

"Aren't you a dragonrider?" Selah asked.

Talmud chuckled. "By title, maybe, but not by nature. Suntear and I don't like killing. Not all dragonriders are warriors. Suntear flies me from fief to fief as I am needed, and helps me when I'm healing large dragons that won't cooperate." The healer took a long sip of tea. "I think it has been years since I lifted a sword."

Selah felt trapped in a prison of sheets and Talmud's watchful eye. The girl yearned to get up and move about, even if it was only to walk.

Talmud finished his tea and set it down, looking at her intently. "I'm curious, Selah, as to how you contracted a fever. Do you have any idea how you got sick?"

The girl was instantly wary of the oddly direct question from a man who devoted his life to curing illnesses. "No."

"Are you sure? None of the other pallons were sick before you—besides yourself, the only other person who has contracted a fever is your dragonet."

Selah shrugged. "There's always a first person, right?"

Talmud nodded, but didn't seem convinced. "I have a question, and you don't have to answer it. When Windchaser was frozen in her fever, you reached down and touched foreheads with her. Why?"

Selah shifted, immediately made uncomfortable. "I…was trying to support her, I guess."

"Anything else?"

The girl waited a moment too long before replying. "No."

"Are you sure?"

"Yes."

"When Windchaser's fever broke, you looked like you were about to be sick…"

"That's was relief," Selah explained hastily. "I thought she was going to die."

"Indeed." Talmud rubbed his face with his hands, seemingly lost in thought. "All right. You were sick the next day…does that mean anything to you?"

Selah shook her head. "Just a coincidence, I suppose."

Talmud refrained from pointing out how many coincidences she had just described. If she was unwilling to discuss what had happened, he wouldn't interrogate her. He had other matters to ponder in the meantime.

"I'll make a deal with you, Selah of Domar—if you stay in bed until lunch, eat, and show me that you can walk the length of the room three times, then you can go watch training. Otherwise, you are bedridden for another night."

Selah nodded to show that she understood. She was quiet for the rest of the morning, asking only for a quill and some books from her room so she could do her coursework while she waited for the midday meal.

Selah ate her lunch voraciously, eager to show Talmud that she was ready to go outside. The infirmary could be smothering when one felt well. When she was finished, the girl cast aside her covers, almost regretting the action as the cool air of the room attacked her unprotected lower body.

Talmud turned his chair so that he was facing her. Selah eased her body over until her bare feet rested against the wooden slats of the floor. Bracing herself on the edge of the bed, Selah rose and crumpled back down to a sitting position. Her legs weren't working properly.

Talmud laughed at the frown that knitted her face together into creases. "Easier said than done, hm?" He quieted when Selah bit her lip in frustration. "Don't worry—your legs just aren't used to standing after two days of bed rest. Give yourself a moment."

Selah tried again, and was able to remain standing with the help of the bed frame. She felt strangely weightless as she took her first steps, although normal feeling gradually returned as she paraded about the room. It was more than three lengths of the infirmary before Talmud was satisfied. "Very well, you have proven your point. You may watch training today, although I'm not guaranteeing that you'll be back in top form tomorrow. You can go back to your quarters and change into fresh things before you go outside."

Selah had been dressed in the long white shifts that were given to patients of the infirmary—it had been made for an adult several inches taller than she and caught under her heels when she walked. Windchaser leapt into her arms, and Talmud escorted her back to the pallon's wing. Her peers were nowhere to be found—they had all finished the noon meal, changed into their exercise clothing and headed outside for training.

First was a long welcome wash in the large basin that had been placed in her privy. She submerged her head, ignoring the bite of the cold water as she washed her hair and face. Her skin felt gritty with illness. After she was finished, the girl changed, and examined the bruise on her abdomen. It had turned a deep shade of purple that reminded her of dragon's blood. With a shudder, the girl pulled on her shirt, tightened her belt, and made her way down to the training courtyards.

The walk took her twice as long as usual—she was tired, and was stopped often by servants or dragonriders asking her how she was. It seemed that her fever, and the injury that had come with it, had provided the fief with fifteen minutes of interesting discussion.

The spring sun was in full force, making any sort of jacket unnecessary on the ground. Garrett was midway through a demonstration on how to parry a straight on thrust effectively with a blade when Selah arrived. The training master acknowledged her briefly before returning to the demonstration.

The girl took a seat next to Landon. The boy was happy to see her awake and well. "How are you?" he asked.

Selah wasn't sure how to describe her condition, finally settling on, "Better."

Landon didn't comment on her pale and drawn features. The illness had obviously sapped his friend's strength. "Good to have you back."

"By the way, thanks for the notes."

"No problem."

Selah chuckled. "Did you take a look at Bern's?" When Landon shook his head, the girl smiled. "I'll have to show them to you some time."

"Landon of Boran?" The pallon's eyes snapped to the training master. "Unless you feel that you are a master of the sword, will you please pay attention?" Garrett sent an admonishing look in Selah's direction as well. "You too, Selah of Domar."

Selah, chastised and guilty that she had gotten her friend in trouble, sent Landon a look of apology. The boy shook his head, mouthing that it was nothing.

When she was training herself, the girl rarely stopped to watch the others. Now that she had no choice but to observe as she sat on the sidelines, she could not help but notice how impressive some of the pallons were. Renton and Landon, fencing together, resembled dancers wielding dangerous blades of steel—the two had graduated to the most challenging of sword work. Aswin had all the grace of a deer when he was running; he finished first on each sprint and distance exercise. Bern had a sense of balance that Selah could only hope to achieve—when Garrett had them work on wooden slats suspended several feet in the air, only the blonde pallon never looked down with a glance of apprehension.

Finally, they were finished, and the boys trudged past her with looks of exhaustion claiming each face. Bern grinned through a sheen of sweat. "Better?" Selah nodded. "That's good—if you don't mind, I'm going to go take a bath before my arms fall off." Selah struggled to keep from smiling; Garrett had put the pallons through a rigorous combination of pushups and other bicep tortures.

Bern staggered off past her, and Selah attempted to locate Windchaser. She twisted and gritted her teeth as her bruise screamed.

"It still hurts, huh?" Aswin's face was downcast and sorrowful. Selah instantly regretted her gesture.

"It's not that bad," she lied. "I've had worse."

"I'm sorry." Aswin looked as though a cherished relative had died.

"It's nothing, Aswin. I should have blocked the blow—it wasn't your fault." The girl had run out of things to say and cast about in her mind for a new topic of discussion. "Any idea what's for dinner?"

The boy shook his head, but the somber mood had been broken, and they talked of lighter matters. Selah had just scooped Windchaser into her arms when Garrett's voice stopped her. "Selah, a word, please?"

Excusing herself to Aswin, the girl approached her training master, who was adjusting the height of one of the balance beams. She bowed as was appropriate when a superior asked for private council. "How can I help you, sir?"

Garrett smiled, staring off into the distance. "How are you feeling?"

"Better, sir. Talmud forbade me from training today. I might be able to do some light work tomorrow."

Garrett sighed. "You didn't miss much while you were gone—some basic conditioning, sword review. Nothing you need to concern yourself about." He sat on one of the barrels that littered the courtyards and gestured that she do the same.

Windchaser, bored, leapt down from Selah's arms and began to examine the shadows behind the barrels, leaving Selah's full attention on her training master.

Garrett did not speak for a long while. When he did, it was softly. "There is something I need to know. When you mentally communicated with Riveneye," Selah stiffened at the mention of her dragon side, "what was it like?"

Selah rubbed the back of her neck. First Talmud, and now Garrett. Why was it so important that they know about her abilities? Selah would be content to leave her dragon soul locked in the dark recesses of her mind. It didn't help that the two kept bringing it up.

She opened her mouth with a lie fresh on her lips. Something inside closed them, leaving excuses reverberating through her skull. She couldn't be dishonest with Garrett. It had been hard enough to lie to Talmud, much less her training master. She owed too much to him.

"I...he was a spark, sir." Garrett raised his eyebrows—he was expecting her make some excuse. He had not expected to find honesty in her tone and words. "When you extend your arms out to the side," she demonstrated, "until you can barely see them out of the corner of your eye, until you're not sure if you see them, but you know they're there—that's what it was like. He was this spark that I wasn't sure if I could see. When I touched it—"

"With your mind?" Garrett interrupted.

Selah nodded. "I held on, and he asked me who I was. After that, it was the same as if a dragon had started the conversation with me, not the other way around. Windchaser was the same way."

"You mind spoke with Windchaser?"

Selah sighed. "I thought she was going to die of fever. I sent my strength to her."

"After Sean forbade you?"

Selah's eyes narrowed dangerously. "As much as I respect the Holdleader's wishes, there is a point where his thoughts no longer influence me. When I think my dragonet is going to die, I make my own decisions." The words of authority sounded strange from the lips of a thirteen year old. She could be so mature when the situation demanded it.

Garrett bowed his head to acknowledge her point. Had her eyes always been so intense? "Taken, Pallon Selah. When you spoke to Sean, you were vague on the details of how you made contact with Riveneye. I was curious."

Not curious, Selah thought. *There is more than you're telling me.*

"You know, Selah, a human with the abilities to mentally communicate could be quite resourceful. There are countless places that a Rider can go that her dragon cannot. It would not be so terrible, I think, to have such an ability at your disposal. Gifts from the gods are too few and far between to cast aside as useless. However, that is merely my opinion. I am not the one making the decision."

Selah immediately sensed the double meaning to his words. "Sir?"

Garrett clambered down from the barrel. "Dinner should be coming soon—you're probably starving." When Selah remained in place, eyeing the dragonrider intently, he shooed her away with his hands. "Go! Don't keep the table waiting."

The girl hastened to obey, her dragonet hurrying to catch up. Garrett leaned against the barrel, rubbing the corners of his eyes. Only then did he realize the repercussions that could come from what he had just said. The dragonrider stared at the fief, in the direction of the Great Hall and the Holdleader that was within. It was all up to Selah now.

*   *   *   *

Selah ate dinner in thoughtful silence. Her friends took her quiet state for exhaustion from her fever and did not bother her.

The girl returned to her room. Her masters, in a strange bout of kindness, had decried that she did not have to do her make-up work as long as she understood the concepts. It left Selah with plenty of time to think.

It would not be so terrible, I think, to have such an ability at your disposal. Selah could not help but repeat Garrett's words in her mind. She had proved that she could keep her control with Riveneye and Windchaser. She had relieved Windchaser of some of her pain when she was burning of fever. There was so much good that she could do with mental communication.

The girl turned to Windchaser. She closed her eyes. The blue spark that was Windchaser was instantly on the edge of her awareness. Selah opened her mind to the spark until her whole mind was concentrated solely on her dragonet.

Windchaser? Cloth rustled beside her as Windchaser reacted to the touch on her mind. *Windchaser, whistle if you can hear me.*

A low, piercing sound penetrated the blackness behind Selah's eyes. The girl opened them, barely keeping the spark from slipping out of her grasp as visual information assailed her senses. Windchaser was staring at her intently.

The girl reinforced her touch on the dragonet's mind before sending more. *Jump off the bed, please.* Windchaser complied, now gazing at Selah with a mixture of awe and confusion. Selah sent emotional traces of gratitude toward the dragonet. *If anything I do hurts, shriek as loud as you can.* When Selah asked her Chosen if she understood, the dragonet nodded, a human gesture that she had picked up from Selah. *All right.* The girl exhaled slowly. *Let's see what I can do.*

Mental communication proved to be exhausting. Holding on to Windchaser's mind for too long gave her a headache. Gradually, the girl conditioned her mind until she could interchange between verbal communication and mental without problems. As she ran during conditioning warm-ups, she would send Windchaser thoughts to keep her mind off her physical weariness. In a fortnight of intense and constant practicing, Selah got so that she could communicate while moving, with her eyes opened and closed, even when she was having a conversation with the twins.

However, Windchaser was so young that she could not send images back. Selah was only privy to the dragonet's emotions when she opened the connection between them as wide as her mind would allow. Selah rarely tried this; the fear of losing control and hurting the dragons was a constant pressure in the back of her thoughts.

April proved to be wet and dreary. Each day, the rain only seemed to intensify until it appeared that sheets of water were dropping from the sky.

It was one such day when Garrett called off training early, water dripping from his beard. "That's enough—if we stay out any longer, we'll drown." The pallons agreed with a low muttering of consent. Selah was soaked to the bone—her feet squished in her boots when she walked.

Sean had come to watch training and to mark the pallon's progress. He seemed impressed, although he had never approached Selah. The man walked over to Garrett once the dragonrider had dismissed the pallons. The girl could not help but overhear their conversation.

"The Fourteenth should have been in three hours ago," the Holdleader whispered fiercely. This was more than mere irritation at the delay in the Wing's return—there were valid strains of worry in the man's voice.

"It's all right," Garrett assured, although his voice held no conviction. "They were probably slowed by the rain."

Selah was slow putting away the weapons. Her eyes kept straying to the sky involuntarily. Averon was the Wingleader of the Fourteenth, and Aerin was a part of it as well. The memory of the Dragonslayer sprang up unbidden in her mind's eye. The girl shook her hand to dislodge her thoughts, but they refused to go away.

The other pallons filed into the fief, as did Garrett and Sean. Part of Selah wanted to follow, but the new part of her that she still did not understand rooted her feet to the dirt of the courtyard. Puddles gathered around her feet; the girl would have gone inside if Windchaser was with her, but the dragonet was safe and dry in her room.

"Dragon on the horizon!" shouted the men on the wall. Selah crossed the courtyard quickly in the long strides that were a by-product of her height. She clambered up the battlement steps, slipping once on the wet surface. The white-washed stone of Dragonhold resembled bone in the dim light shed by the gray and overcast sky.

Selah soon noticed the black speck on the horizon. It seemed irregularly shaped for a dragon, but what else could be so large and flying?

"That's not a dragon, Ben," scoffed one of the guardsmen.

"No," Selah heard herself saying as the figure became clearer. "That's a dragon carrying another dragon."

A black dragon swayed in the air, losing altitude rapidly between each wing beat. It was larger than most dragons, and held a blue in its great claws gingerly. The black dragon, instead of gripping the blue from the top, held the dragon from the side.

As the two beasts flew closer and cleared the cliff that lay several hundred yards from outer wall of Dragonhold, Selah turned away from the sight and rushed down the battlements.

Moments later, the guards ducked as the black barely cleared the battlements, breathing loudly in exhaustion. The girl ran to the middle of the courtyard, freezing in indecision as the dragons hovered over her. She dove out of the way as the dragons slammed into the dirt—the weight of the blue had prevented the black from making a proper landing.

Selah rushed forward. The blue was injured, although she could not tell how. There was a terrible familiarity to the body shape of the motionless dragon. She had seen the beast before.

The human strapped to the harness only confirmed her fears. The dragonrider lolled forward—Selah's stomach lurched as she recognized Averon's bearded face. The man made no further motion; it was the harness straps, nothing more, which kept him upright in the saddle.

She clambered up the side of the dragon, sick fear closing her throat as the beast that could only be Farsight made no response to her presence. She shook Averon's shoulder, calling his name. His face was pale and lifeless—he did not move. The girl struggled with the tight knot that secured him to the saddle. When her efforts proved futile, the girl drew her belt knife and cut away the strips of leather. Averon slumped forward, all of his weight on her.

Selah gritted her teeth, testing the limits of her strength as she lifted him from the saddle and bore him down the side of the dragon. She had to grip him around the midsection to get him down; when she laid him on the dirt of the courtyard, the white sleeve of her shirt was stained bright red.

The source of his bleeding proved to be a stab wound on the edge his lower torso. The guards on the wall top had come down to see what was going on. "Get a healer!" Selah shouted. "Bring Talmud!" There was no time to argue about whom gave orders—one of the guards rushed into the fief while the remaining one scanned the sky for attackers.

The black dragon rose—the impact of his fall had only stunned him. "What happened?" Selah demanded, pulling her shirt tails from the confines of her belt.

The black dragon staggered forward; he, too, had been wounded, and was limping heavily on his right side.—*Dragonhunters!*—His mind voice was wrought with pain.—*They had a camp on the east side of the Bearge River. We had split up—they were torturing Farsight and Averon when the rest of us got there. The others are coming—they were scouring the area for more dragonhunters when I left with Farsight.*—

Selah hacked large squares from the excess length of her shirt. She grabbed the white cloth by the handful and pressed it against Averon's side to stem the bleeding. "Why didn't they kill them?"

The black dragon moved Farsight into a more comfortable position.—*They prefer that their victims bleed to death.*—

Selah trembled as she remembered the Dragonslayer. She reached forward to check the dragonrider's pulse. Her hand was stopped as icy cold fingers wrapped around her own. Averon's eyes opened slowly. "Hermine?" he asked.

Selah's heart ached for the man who had saved her life. "No, Averon, it's Selah…Selah of Domar."

The dragonrider swore. "Dragonhunters got me, Selah." Tears leaked from the corners of his eyes. "They got Farsight. They got him."

"Hush, Averon," Selah's voice was choked. "Don't spend your energy talking to me. Hold on."

"Help Farsight, Selah. Please. Don't waste…on me."

Hands nudged Selah aside. Talmud had arrived; the healer knelt beside the dragonrider. "Averon…" he said sadly. Selah gestured to the wad of cloth she was using to staunch the blood flow. "It's a jab wound." She struggled to describe what she had observed. "The knife didn't go in sideways—it's not deep."

The expression on Talmud's face brightened. "There's hope, then." Selah withdrew her hands as the Master Healer took over. Her fingers were stained with blood. She rose to her feet slowly. She didn't want to leave Averon's side, but she could not ignore his request. She hastened to Farsight.

The scales of the blue were littered with scratches, cuts and wounds that were meant to cause pain and blood loss, not terrible injury. The dragon remained motionless as she approached. The dragonhunters had not attacked his wings—no doubt they wanted to hang an unmarred pair from the walls as a trophy. Selah's fists curled in anger, her fingernails digging into her palms until her own blood mixed with the blood of the dragonrider that stained her hands.

Selah knelt by Farsight's face. The dragon was breathing slowly. The girl reached out and touched the scales along his jaw. "Farsight?" she asked gently.

The dragon did not move. "Farsight?" she repeated, with the same result. When she called his name a third time, the dragon twitched, lifting his great head. Selah leaned back as his face drew even with hers. His eyelids fluttered open, and Selah thought she would be sick.

Purple blood streamed from Farsight's eyes. The dragonhunters, it seemed, were about to cut his eyes out but decided to merely slash them instead. The dragon was blind.

Farsight let out a great roar of pain, tightly sealing his lids and thrusting his head against the ground. Selah wrapped his head in an embrace, attempting to calm him. "Farsight, it's me, Selah. You're safe now."

Farsight roared again, his claws tearing great furrows into the ground. Selah closed her eyes and reached for the spark.

The moment she connected with Farsight's mind, she was struck by the intensity of his pain. *Let me help you,* Selah thought. *I can take your pain.*

The beast in Farsight was overwhelmed by the pain of his wounds and the pain of being blind. The part of Farsight that was still thinking, still reasonable thrust her away from him.

I can help you, Selah shouted mentally. *Averon is alive! Live for him!*

Farsight paused. Selah's eyes ached as a shot of pain jerked through them.

—*Selah?*—thought Farsight.—*Why are you...oh, gods, my eyes!*—

A wave of apprehension made the girl tremble. Swallowing her unexplainable fear, Selah touched her forehead to the dragon's.

Farsight roared in pain; it was echoed by the scream that tore from Selah's throat. Her eyes burned as though they had been branded with a hot iron. There was a second jerk behind her breastbone that sucked the breath from her body. She barely had the sense to swallow the bile that rose in her throat. Selah broke contact with Farsight, both hands covering her face.

Farsight's roar stopped long before her scream. The dragon felt the flow of blood behind his eyelids slow to a trickle and stop. Not daring to believe, he opened his eyes slowly.

The world was a gray blur, jumping in and out of focus. As if a shroud was lifted from before his face, his vision sharpened until he could see the raindrops. Healers surrounded him, their many colored robes in stark contrast with the dark brown mud he lay in. He could see.

Selah lay prone in front of him, rocking back and forth in pain. She was clutching her face and moaning in low tones that were worse to hear than her screams. Farsight shifted, wincing as the myriad other wounds he had received stressed and began to bleed again.

One of the healers rushed over to the girl, thinking that Farsight had struck her by accident. The dragon felt sick to his stomach, dizzy from the blood he had lost. Purple liquid oozed slowly from the many wounds that peppered his body, but they could wait.

Selah had stopped rocking back and forth. She waved the healer away from her, her motions wild and jerky. One hand was still clasped over her eyes.

She rose to her knees. The girl appeared all right; Farsight's thoughts went to his Rider, who lay several feet away, surrounded by the Master Healer, the Hold-leader, and the Training Master.

Farsight limped over the circle, craning his head over Talmud shoulder. His chest was tight with worry and pain for his Chosen.—*Averon?*—

The dragonrider lifted his eyes to the face of his dragon. "Farsight?" He tried to rise, but was shoved back down to the ground by Garrett.

"You'll live, Averon of Northford, if you would only stop trying to move!" Only the small tightness in the training master's voice betrayed how relieved he was that the man would survive.

Averon complied, allowing Talmud to bandage his side so they could move him into the fief. "Farsight...your eyes..." He frowned. "They were slashed..."

The dragon had not contemplated his newfound vision. He stepped backwards in surprise; his hind paw shattered a puddle. Farsight turned and stared into the mirror-like surface of the water. His face bent and stretched as raindrops struck the surface, but it was clear enough that he could see his eyes. The area above his cheekbones was stained purple with the blood from his eye wounds, but the source of the blood was nowhere to be found. His eyes, although red with irritation, were unmarred. The tinge of color that he could derive from the surface of the puddle made him stop and peer closer.

His eyes had once been the color of a southern sea, a pale green that made one think of blue. They were now the purest shade of gold.

A terrible thought locked in his mind. He had heard the rumors...he had heard the story of how his daughter, Windchaser, had been struck with the fever only to lose it as Selah contracted the same illness. He had felt the girl within his mind.

—*Selah!*—The girl was still on her knees, although the healer had coaxed her hand away from her eyes. At the touch of his mind, she lifted her face, looking around blankly.

Selah was not sure if her eyes were open—her hand had been peeled away from her face, but she still saw nothing.

Her world was black…utterly black. She brought her hand to her face, snatching her fingers away when they touched her open and unprotected eye. She rose to her feet unsteadily, brushing away the hands that tried to tug her back.

She took a staggering step forward. She had fainted; that's why she couldn't see. This was all a terrible dream.

—*Selah!*—called a voice in her mind. Selah rushed forward, seeking the comfort of another sentient being. Her body smacked into a rough surface that was hard and unforgiving—pressure caught her on the back and kept her from falling.—*Selah, are you all right?*—asked Farsight's voice, echoing through her dark cavern.

"I can't see!" she cried, clutching at the draconic arm that encircled her slender waist. "Farsight, I can't see."

The silence spoke volumes. Selah's throat choked with tears that her dragon soul prevented her eyes from shedding. The girl buried her face into Farsight's muscular shoulder. "You can."

She felt the dragon's muscles twitch as he nodded. Her chest tightened as she spoke the terrible truth.

"I'm blind."

*   *   *   *

Sean slammed the door of his office, making the training master wince. He sat heavily into the chair behind his desk, his long hair disheveled after running his fingers through it so many times in agitation.

"What is going on?" he demanded, his voice a terrible whisper.

Garrett sighed. "I don't know."

"Gonran's blade, man, tell me the gods-cursed truth!" The Holdleader trembled in outrage; his voice had skyrocketed from a whisper to a shout. "A dragon who just had his face slashed to pieces now sees perfectly fine, with a different colored pair of eyes. A girl who has a dragon soul now can't see. The dragon's moaning that it's his fault, and the girl won't talk. Now, I'll ask you again…what is going on?"

Garrett's jaw locked the way it did whenever he was about to be difficult. "I can't tell you."

"Can't or won't?"

"Selah might have traded her sight for his. Her eyes were bloodshot when I looked at them. It is similar to what she did when Windchaser had a fever."

"She healed her dragonet?" Sean's eyebrows snapped together like hawks diving for prey. "A human can't heal a dragon. It's magically impossible." When Garrett said nothing, he snatched a piece of parchment from his desk and began to twist it in his hands. "Why wasn't I informed?"

"We...I didn't think that it was worthy of your attention."

"So the girl has been disobeying me? Mind communicating." Garrett said nothing. For a transfer of dragon and human magic, she would have to make a mental connection. His words to her those weeks ago were beginning to haunt him.

Sean rose to his feet. "She could have killed every single dragon stationed here. Do you understand that? She could have killed thousands of dragons! Thousands!" His eyes were hard with anger. Only a man like Garrett, who had seen much of the world in his lifetime, could see the fear that hid behind the more dominant emotion of rage. "Where is she?"

Garrett could stand it no longer. "She didn't kill every dragon," he countered harshly. "Each one is alive and well—thanks to her abilities, a Wingleader's dragon will be able to fly again, and through the dragon, the Wingleader himself. You could've lost one of your best dragonriders and his dragon, but both will patrol again. Count your gods-cursed blessings when you see them, Sean."

The Holdleader was trembling in rage. "You forget your place, Garrett of Dalbrook."

The training master felt his throat close with disgust. "She's blind, Sean. She gave her eyes for Farsight."

"Get out."

The dragonrider needed no further urging.

✳   ✳   ✳   ✳

Talmud spread the paste of plant matter and ointments across the cloth that had been folded until it was only a few inches wide. Selah sat upright on the edge of one of the beds. She had refused to lie down.

Her eye sockets were badly bruised—even if she could see, it wouldn't have made a difference. Her eyelids had swollen shut.

Talmud placed the bandage across her eyes, ointment side down. Selah jerked back before she realized that Talmud was helping her. The balm felt cool against her tender eyes.

Selah's ponytail was right where Talmud wanted to make the knot on the bandage. He gently undid the leather cord that held her hair back from her face.

Selah took the cord from him and, brushing back her hair with her fingers, retied the ponytail until it was much higher than she usually wore it. It had become such a natural motion for her that she could tie a ponytail without the use of her eyes. Talmud, with a soft smile, knotted the bandage behind her head.

"Master Talmud?"

"Yes?"

"Will I see again?"

Talmud sighed, leading the girl over to the privy of the infirmary. He handed Selah a pair of clothes that had been retrieved from her room—the ones she was wearing now were soaked and stained with both red and purple blood. "You should change out of your clothes."

Selah fumbled for the doorknob. She was out several minutes later—the ties on her breeches had confounded her in her blindness. Talmud knew he could not avoid answering her questions for long.

Selah handed him her soiled clothing, waiting as he deposited them in the arms of a servant that had come to see if they needed anything. When she heard the door close, she turned her face in the direction that she thought Talmud was.

"Will I see again?"

"I don't know, Selah of Domar. I don't know."

Selah resisted the urge to itch the bandage. She placed a hand on the bedpost of one of the beds to steady herself and to find out where she was. "How are Farsight and Averon?"

Talmud pretended not to notice the quaver in her voice. "Averon is being tended to the best of anyone's abilities in the private infirmary for deeper wounds. Farsight is being treated by one of my apprentices in his den. Both are recovering well."

"That's good."

Windchaser had been brought into the infirmary. She sensed the note of terrible sadness in her Rider's voice and cooed lovingly.

"Master Talmud?"

Talmud put away the ingredients he had used for Selah's bandage. "Yes?"

"How can I be a dragonrider," Selah had to stop and swallow the knot of emotion that choked her words, "if I can't see?"

Talmud had no answer for her. Windchaser nuzzled the girl's hand, but it was a small comfort in a world of misery.

*   *   *   *

Selah wandered through the next three days in a haze of sorrow and the terrible weight of her loss. She could not do any sort of work, as much of her classes required them to read in some form or another. Thus, she was excused from morning sessions with her masters. The girl used an old spear pole to navigate her way through the halls of Dragonhold. Her dragonet would steer her away from possible obstacles by leaning on one of the girl's legs as she walked.

Training was out of the question. Garrett informed her that until she could see, there was no way that she could train with them. After she begged him, he allowed her to run during conditioning as long as Landon at her side the whole time.

Her third day back, they were sent for a run on the old deer trail that she walked before being trapped under the sapling. What had been a matter of weeks ago now seemed like years. She was at the back of the group of pallons, running much slower than she usually did; her inability to see limited her trust in her surroundings.

Selah's feet slid in a rough patch on the trail and she sprawled on the ground. Landon crouched at her side. "Are you all right, Selah?"

Selah's cheeks burned in shame. She was sick of her blindness, disgusted with her weakness. She rose to her knees, shrugging away Landon's helping hand. "I'm fine, all right! I can handle myself!" she shouted.

The boy backed away, giving her space. The girl rose, wanting to tear away the bandage that covered her eyes. She cursed the dragonhunters for injuring Farsight, cursed the dragon for letting her heal his eyes. Cursed the blackness. Cursed herself for bringing it.

*   *   *   *

Returning to training did little to change her outlook on life. She still hated the feeling of a hand on her back, even though she knew the person was only trying to guide her. She despised her blindness, and her mood was often just as dark as the world she lived in. Her friends took the brunt of her bitterness, often on the receiving end of harsh words. She apologized afterward and they forgave her. Selah hated it when they did—she knew they would not have brushed off her offenses so lightly if she were not blind.

Her eyes remained swollen, although she could now open them slightly. The bruises would not go away, no matter how many different concoctions Talmud tried. It was his fifth try with a different balm when she snapped at the Master Healer.

"It's not going to work," she growled as he placed a fresh bandage across her swollen eyes. "It never works."

Talmud merely raised his eyebrows as he knotted the bandage. "Keeping a civil tongue in your head would do you no harm, young Rider."

"It's no use!" Selah pushed his hands away. "The swelling isn't going to go down. Even if it did, it would make no difference. Why don't you just give up the false pretense that I'm going to see again and admit that I'm blind for the rest of my life?"

Talmud sighed heavily. "You have been in my infirmary every day, Selah of Domar. I tried every healing balm I know, read every volume for a clue to your blindness. I refuse to give up on your eyes—I wish you would do the same."

Selah could think of nothing to say in reply.

*   *   *   *

A week of despair followed. Each day seemed the same as the one before it, a terrible monotony of darkness and sympathy that left her lost in misery. The afternoon marking half a month of blindness found Selah meandering through the hallway, one hand trailing on the rough stones of the wall. Her heart ached and burned with what she had lost, and each step through her dark world was uncertain and forced.

Her hand left the coarse surface of the wall and slid over the smooth face of a hallway mural. Selah paused, finding a strange interest in the aberration in the routine of her walk. Her fingers traced the contours of the picture. Selah knelt, laying the spear pole that was her walking stick to the ground so she could use both hands.

From her first day at Dragonhold, the murals decorating the corridors had fascinated her. She had often stopped to gaze at them, and had more than once dared to touch the ancient artistry. Selah pressed her cheek against the cool stone. *Which one is it?*

Her memory could not connect the picture with the hallway she was in—the girl had often seen the murals in passing and her mind did not register specific images with certain corridors. Her fingers ran over the carved stone with all the delicacy she would reserve for touching a newborn child. She tried to take the grooves that curved around her hands and project them against the blackness that was her vision. Traces of gray lines flickered briefly in her mind's eye, but remained a broken jumble that meant nothing.

The girl had accepted that her only sight would be in her imagination. She had never contemplated that she could create a picture from her hands.

Time ceased to be a factor as she let the mural press against her palms. Windchaser, recognizing that the girl was deep in thought, sat quietly and rarely made a sound. Her fingers cast about the carving; Selah ran her hands over each groove, each projection.

Her knees had begun to ache when she dropped her hands to her lap. The girl was silent. She did not pay any attention to the soft cadence of footsteps until it stopped beside her.

"Selah?" The pitch of the voice swayed with male adolescence. The girl turned her face toward the sound, recognizing the words of her best friend. Landon's voice was still in the throes of cracking.

His leather boots groaned as he settled down next to her. Selah lowered her face to where she hoped his would be. The corner of her mouth twitched, her lips pulling back like a curtain to reveal her teeth. She smiled.

It was the first time she had worn an expression of happiness in a fortnight. She heard Landon's surprised intake of breath that he disguised with an inquiry. "What is it?"

Selah reached up and laid her hand on the mural. She turned once more in Landon's direction. The smile grew wider. "It's a dragon. The flying dragon." She thought for a moment. "*The Flight of Starcross.* That's what it was called."

"That's right." There was a touch of understanding in Landon's voice.

"Look," Selah said. The words that spilled from her mouth were free of the bitterness that had consumed her soul for the past two weeks. They fell like a healing rain on the wounds that no ointment could cure. "They even carved spray from the foam on the waves." She rubbed her hand across the minute etchings in the stone.

The girl felt Landon's hand beside hers. His callused fingers traced across the waves in circular motions. "They did." He was silent for a long moment. The boy recognized that her fascination with the mural had so much more meaning than a simple liking of the carvings. "I had never seen that before."

Selah brought her other hand to join the first against the wall. Her smile lingered in the slight pull on one corner of her mouth. "Neither had I."

*   *   *   *

For the first time in a long while, her sleep at night was sound. She dreamt of flying. She woke with a choked throat when she opened her eyes to darkness. Still, her sadness was a weighty burden that she bore with resolve, a far cry from the bitter, consuming presence that it had been earlier.

Touch became her comfort. In a state where the girl could never be sure if everything was where she thought it was, reaching out and feeling solidity reassured her greatly. Knowing the contours of her surroundings, whether it was a table or the edge of a volume, allowed her to 'see' in a way that, while not replacing her former sense, made her sadness seem somewhat lighter. When she crashed into a shelf, she paused to find what the furniture contained. She regained some of her interest in life.

She had not touched minds with a dragon since Farsight. It was not from fear—the girl had been too wrapped in her misery to think of anything more than her inability to see.

The swelling around her eyes diminished until she could open and close her eyes without any trouble, although her skin remained red and irritated. Talmud decided to keep the bandage over her eyes, hoping that his ointments would have some affect on her vision.

Sean called her to his office later that evening. Selah had come to associate the man with unpleasantness and interrogation—needless to say, she was not looking forward to a discussion with him. Even with the servant guiding her to the Holdleader's chambers, Selah was doubly as slow as she would have been with all of her senses whole.

The girl entered Sean's office with a heavy heart. The Holdleader spoke. "Sit down, please." Selah could imagine his expression; lips curved in distaste, his brow as furrowed as a Hadfoll field in springtime.

"You called for me, sir?" Her dislike for the man could not shake years of demanded politeness from Beda.

"Yes…Selah of Domar." The girl stroked Windchaser's wings for comfort; she was already bracing herself for what the Holdleader what might say.

"Dragonhold is not like Hadfoll or Domar—this is a place of training for warriors." Sean's voice cut through the darkness that was her world like a white-hot knife. "We cannot afford to harbor those who do not support themselves."

Selah felt a terrible nausea clench in her stomach. "What do you mean, sir?"

"Come now, Selah of Domar. You're an intelligent girl. You are irreversibly blind—there is no way that you, or your dragon, will ever be able to join any kind of fighting force. I cannot afford that my chief healer waste his time and energy trying to cure you. There are resources that you use here that could be put to better purposes. I cannot afford to carry burdens here at Dragonhold."

Selah rose to her feet. "Sir?"

"I have chartered a dragon to take you home in the morning. There is nothing for you here."

"Of course there is!" Selah shouted. "I...I could do something...here." *Leave Dragonhold?* her mind screamed. *I can't!*

"Like what, pallon?"

"I could..."

"Nothing. There is nothing that a blind person can do here at Dragonhold. Go home, Selah of Domar. It's where you belong."

"No, I..." Selah reached up and ripped the bandage from her eyes.

Sean jerked back in his seat. The girl was frightening to behold—her eyes and the skin around them were bright red with irritation. Plant matter from the ointment that Talmud had been placing on the underside of her bandage had smeared across her cheekbones and brow, crusting her eyelashes with green paste. Even though they were sightless, her hazel eyes betrayed the terrible urgency that was claiming her mind.

"My eyes are healing! Look—the swelling has gone down."

"To what end?" Sean snapped. He wanted her out of his office. "You still cannot see! Whether your eyes are swollen or not has no effect on your ability to work!"

"Please! I've been here a year...Dragonhold is my home," Selah whispered, shocking herself with her own words. They were true. She often thought of Domar, but it was the people she missed, not the place. The quarters that had been assigned to her, as cramped as they were, had become her room. The enormous fief with whitewashed walls had become her home.

Sean's words cut through her thoughts. "Go to your chambers, pallon. Pack your bags—a dragonrider will come for you in the morning." Selah opened her mouth to protest, but the Holdleader drowned her out. "I have nothing more to say to you."

Selah left the office in a daze. The Holdleader had banished her. Her body was trembling in disbelief, but a small part of her whispered that she should have seen it coming. Blind was the beggar—blind the dragonrider was not.

Windchaser, understanding that it was Sean who had pained her Rider, shrieked her rage at the Holdleader's door, her indignant whistles and trills reverberating through the stone corridors until the servants shooed the dragonet away.

The girl stumbled to the Pallon's Wing, a heavy knot in her throat. *It shouldn't matter,* she thought bitterly, one hand on the wall for support. *I can't tell the difference between Domar and Dragonhold anyway. They look the same to me.* Instead of bringing her comfort, the cynical words only made her want to cry.

She staggered into the commons room, running to a table. The voices of the other pallons came from all directions. "Selah?" "What's wrong?"

They stopped talking when she looked up. Like Sean, they were momentarily taken aback by her startling visage.

The groan of a chair as it scraped against the ground rang through the room. Landon was the first to speak. "What happened?" His footsteps were soft against the ground, as if he was treading near a fawn that was easily startled.

Selah swallowed the knot of emotion that smothered her words like a woolen blanket. "I'm going h…" she couldn't finish. The girl had to compose herself before continuing. "He's sending me back to Domar."

"Who is?" asked Aswin's light tenor in disbelief.

"Sean…the Holdleader."

"Bastard," growled Bern.

"He can't do that…can he?" Glenn's uncertain inquiry prefaced a long moment of silence.

Selah sensed, rather than saw, Landon nod.

Her throat was closing, sealing off with her pain and emotion. Her chest felt as though Stormhunter had reached in and ripped more of her heart away. She would be leaving them…all of them. Glenn, Renton, Aswin, Bern, Landon…she would probably never see them again.

She began to cry.

The liquid ran like warm honey down her cheeks. The pain her soul had carried for so long, like a storm cloud gray and swollen with raindrops, had broken into little pieces that were streaming out through her eyes. Each breath was shattered with a sob that racked her body until she had to grasp the edge of a chair for support.

Her head was bowed so that her chin rested against her breastbone—her head rocked gently as her crying drew on eternally. Gradually, the rhythm became steady, her breaths shuddering, but even.

Tears, tears she had not shed since Hadfoll, were still leaking out of the corners of her eyes. Instinctively, the girl wiped the moisture away with her sleeve, a habit retained from a time when it still mattered that her eyes were clear.

"Selah?" asked Bern's light baritone. The girl did not answer.

A white mote hovered in the air several feet away from her. Selah felt her eyelids close as she blinked in surprise—the mote disappeared for a brief moment before returning. Selah closed her eyes for a long period of time. The white glow returned when she opened her eyes.

The girl's fingers trembled in disbelief. As she moved forward, the mote grew larger. Selah reached out and felt smooth edge of a wall socket. Further exploration revealed the jagged edges of a crystal.

Selah cupped the light in her palm, drawing it to her. The mote was now marred with black lines—her fingers. It look a long while for the girl to tear her eyes from the crystal; when her hazel eyes lifted, she saw, rather than inky blackness, a dark gray blur.

"Gods," she whispered, her voice cracking with emotion.

The cool scales of her dragonet brushed against her hands. Selah returned her eyes downward and felt her heart skip a beat.

The crystal cast a muted light throughout her dim, gray world. The faint outline of a small face became firmer as it grew closer to the brightness in her fingers. When Windchaser was so close that she blocked out some of the crystal, Selah saw the vertical slits that were the dragonet's eyes staring deeply into her own. They were a dark gray—her world was colorless.

Violet, whispered her memory. *Windchaser's eyes are violet.*

"Gods," the girl repeated, feeling one last tear cut a trail of moisture along her damp cheek. "I can see."

RIFT

"What now?" Sean demanded when Selah, escorted by her friends, appeared at his door. "I thought we were finished."

"I can see."

Sean snorted. The crystal, a beacon of her newfound sight, revealed that the Holdleader was sitting at his desk. Selah could barely make out the contours that made up his face. "You left my office an hour ago blind as a sparrow at nighttime. Now you can see?"

Selah nodded, staring in fascination at the gray block that had to be his desk. Her tears had washed a film of blackness from her eyes, leaving her with a vision that, while reminding her of staring through murky water, was a vision nonetheless. Colorless, but a great improvement over her blindness.

"I already told you, Selah of Domar, you will be on your way home in the morning. You should go pack your things—I have no time to play pretend with you."

The gods had given her a miracle; Selah refused to stand around, wondering how her sight had come back to her, while the Holdleader kept her from her destiny. The girl walked forward until the edge of the desk prevented her from getting any closer to Sean.

She peered forward into the murky water. It was a long moment before she spoke again. "You're wearing a tunic. Embroidered."

"Yes, but that doesn't prove anything. Here…I'll humor you." Sean's superior tone grated against Selah's nerves, but the girl said nothing; staying at Dragonhold depended entirely on this moment. "Back up." Selah complied, stopping when she felt Landon's hand on the back of her shoulder. "Now…how many fingers am I holding up?"

Selah strained, squinting in hopes that it would focus her blurry vision. Up close, she had been able to make out the embroidered designs on Sean's velvet tunic. Farther away was another story. The whitish blur several feet up from the desk had to be Sean's face, which made the other, smaller blur beside it his hand. Try as she might, the girl could not make out any fingers. There was nothing but a round, white blur.

It was another minute before Selah realized the answer. "None," she announced with more conviction than she felt. Her vision was terrible, but there was no way that she could miss the Holdleader's long fingers at this distance.

A single white line lifted from the blur. "One."

Two more joined the first. "Three."

One more. "Four."

Two fell like soldiers in a battle. "Two."

Finally, all five of Sean's fingers extended away from his palm. "Five."

"How can you see?" Sean sputtered. "Did you find another Spring of All Tears in the pallon's wing?"

Selah gripped the edges of the crystal. "Somewhat." His words unleashed a torrent of questions in her mind. *Stormhunter's tears healed my burns. Did my tears heal my eyes?*

Will it always be tears?

"I can see now. It doesn't make sense to me either."

Sean sighed; although Selah couldn't make out the gesture, she heard the soft sounds as he rubbed his face with his hands. "No gods, this time? No flashes of light, magical disturbances?"

Selah shook her head, and her friends mirrored the motion. "I don't know why I can see. I just…can."

Sean's face betrayed little emotion. "Go inform your masters that you will not be departing. You can return to classes tomorrow."

When the pallons had left, Sean shut the door behind them. He felt old and tired. Just when he thought he had placed the girl in a box, a place where he could understand her, she broke out of it and threw another surprise at him. The Holdleader turned to his papers, a weary sigh escaping his lips. "How?" and "Why?" were not feasible or answerable questions when Selah was involved. Through the nature of her soul alone, she could make a fine dragonrider, or become a very dangerous one. Sean prayed to the gods for the former. He feared the potential of the latter more than he feared anything else in the world.

*   *   *   *

After many conversations that explained the new circumstances of her vision, Selah was allowed to return to classes and training. Her joy at returning the regular life of Dragonhold could not be tethered by the amount of catching up she had to do. The other pallons were a full three weeks ahead of her.

On her third day back, the tactics master assigned her three chapters on the series of battles fought in the foothills bordering Lon when the two countries were still at odds. Her eyes, although improving, prevented her from seeing the small print. She had to press the pages up against her nose in order to see the words. The musty scent that possessed all old volumes engulfed her face, and the girl had difficultly breathing.

After an hour, her eyes burned and watered with irritation. The text blurred in front of her eyes, and the girl had to set the book down. She pressed her cool fingers against her warm eyelids, wishing fervently for the vision she had once possessed.

Hands pried the book from her fingers. Selah looked up. Landon had taken the tactics book from her; even her misty sight could recognize the grin on his face.

He turned his chair so that he could stretch out his long legs in the open space beside the table. "Where were you?" he asked. Selah pointed to the spot in the text where she had stopped reading, bewildered by her best friend's actions. The boy cleared his throat.

"Commander Aides pushed the Lonian troops back to the river, but was slain in an ambush two days later. Alcaron, at a loss to produce similarly fine leadership, had no choice but to..."

"Landon," Selah interrupted. "What are you doing?"

Her friend only smiled. "Your eyes are bloodshot and red. Even a thick pallon like me can tell that if you try to read anymore, your eyes will pop out of your skull and start rolling around on the floor. I, for one, do not want to be the one who has to help you find them. Now, shall I continue?" Selah, dumbfounded, nodded. "As I was saying..."

Although the clarity of her vision sharpened each day, Selah still saw largely in shades of black and white. Some brighter hues, such as red and purple, showed up in pale strains that hurt her eyes if she looked at them for too long.

Landon continued to read for her until the girl was able to handle several hours of bookwork by herself—although her friends had told her a smattering of

what they had learned while she was blind, the masters required her to learn all
the concepts. Thus, Selah was often faced with three times the workload of her
peers. Sleep was soon sacrificed for the sake of her education; the girl was often
up late into the night toiling by crystal light.

Garrett, because of her troubling seeing, placed her in the third tier groups for
each weapon. Selah could not fault her training master—it was two weeks after
her blindness that she managed to see the target in archery enough to hit it.

It was not until the middle of May that she could see just as well as she had
before the incident with Farsight. Selah, late to Aviation, sprinted down the corridor, stopping when a mural caught her attention.

It was a carving of a dragon, stretched out in flight above a churning sea. The
dragon, large in all forms of the word, took up most of the mural, although the
waves had been masterfully carved with details that must have taken the artist
hours to include. Selah's lips curved in a rueful smile when she looked at the cap-
tion. *The Flight of Starcross.*

The mural was wonderful to behold. Selah reached out and placed her palms
against the surface of the mural. Touch, added to sight, allowed her to know the
art more than a mere glance could ever give her.

Still, Selah did not feel the vaunted joy that, when blind, she dreamed about
feeling when she would be able to see. It just wasn't the same as when she had
showed Landon the flecks of spray that had been lovingly textured into the stone.
The girl closed her eyes, touching her forehead to the stone. Instead of cursing
the darkness that came with shutting her eyes, she welcomed it. She allowed her
hands to trace the carving, let her fingers explore the grooves and indentations
that she already knew intimately.

It meant so more that way.

*   *   *   *

The wave of heat that arrived a week later announced the official coming of
summer. Summer was anticipated by the pallons for one reason—the long
awaited trip home. To ensure that the pallons would not lose focus in their training through the sheer monotony that it sometimes created, the masters gave them
July off. Garrett lectured them strongly on the importance of staying in shape
over the break. "I'll be able to tell those of you who haven't been working." The
training master's golden eyes were sharp with mock sternness. "I'll be working
those people twice as hard when we all get back."

Selah knew the training master wasn't as serious as he alluded to. All Garrett was truly asking them was that they retain their fitness until they got back. However, Selah was already behind in her training—a month of instruction from some of the warriors back home would help to close the gap between her and the others.

The last week before their return home flew by in an instant. Before Selah could really get track of things, her bags were packed, her room cleared, and Averon had volunteered to return her home.

On the first morning of July, the pallons wandered out into the bright sunlight of the summer sun. It was a Sunday, a day usually reserved for sleeping in, but the dragonriders that were to take them home required an early start.

Selah quickly caught sight of Farsight—he was the only dark blue with great scars down his haunches. The girl had not spoken to the pair since they had visited her when she was blind…she had not been overly welcoming.

Averon, upon seeing her, seemed at a loss of what to do. Selah, hoping that she was not being too forward, grasped his forearm in the manner reserved for close friends or comrades. The man had saved her life; in a much less literal way, she had saved his.

"I heard that you were seeing again." The man looked to her for confirmation; when she nodded, the dragonrider smiled. "Thank the gods. I am in debt to you for what you did."

Selah shook her head. "You saved my life during the Choosing, remember?" Averon rubbed along his jaw rather than reply. "Besides…" the girl paused, looking around at her surroundings. "You brought me here, to Dragonhold." Her voice took on a sentimental tone. "I could never repay you enough for that."

The dragonrider shook his head. "I think you would have gotten here regardless…whether or not I was the one who recruited you."

Selah, to save herself the embarrassment of coming up with an answer to his words, started strapping her packs to Farsight's harness.

—*We should start flying soon,*—suggested Farsight.—*Daylight waits for no dragon.*—He and Averon exchanged fond glances. Selah, knowing that she was on the outside of an inside jest, did not inquire as to their expressions.

Returning to Domar took them longer then it had leaving it. Averon and Farsight tired much faster due to the injuries they had sustained at the hands of the dragonhunters, and stopped in towns rather than risk an ambush in the wilderness. Selah could not complain—a bed was far more welcome than the packed dirt of a forest floor.

Averon seemed to be a bit of a local celebrity at each of the inns—each provided them with at least a free round of warm cider, although one innkeeper let them stay free for the entire night, meals included. "I ran off some men-at-arms who were threatening to make off with his livestock and woman if he didn't let them stay free for a week," the dragonrider explained when Selah asked about the innkeeper's generous gesture. The girl eyed the innkeeper, who was a portly man and would have had trouble with any kind of soldier, much less several.

"He was so grateful, he lets me stay without charge whenever I'm in town." The dragonrider lifted a mug to his lips, blowing on the contents to cool them. "Do favors for people, Selah...you'd be surprised how much it comes back to you."

They reached Domar on the fifth morning. "Who goes there?" shouted the guard. Farsight hovered over the wall, waiting for his Rider to provide Domar with identification.

"Averon of Northford, delivering Selah of Domar back for summer visit."

"Who?"

There had been a chilly breeze at flight level and Selah was eager to return to the ground. "Baldwin!" she shouted, knowing the voice of the guard. "It's Selah! Let us down please."

The guard waved with his hands to signal that they could come in. Farsight landed in an empty courtyard, folding back his wings once his claws were firmly settled on the ground.

Selah had barely slid down from the saddle when her arms were pinned to her sides by a massive embrace. "Flyn!" she exclaimed, catching sight of her guardian from the corner of her eye. The guard captain grinned, loosening his hold on her so that his charge could return his embrace.

Windchaser poked her head out from the front of Selah's flight jacket, whistling as she was squeezed between the two humans. Flyn took a step back. "Who is this?" he asked.

Selah undid the ties on her flight jacket and shrugged out of it—down on the ground, the extra layer was uncomfortably hot. "Windchaser—she's my dragon."

My dragon. Selah though with a stir of pride that she kept inside. At Dragonhold, having been Chosen by a dragon was standard—here, it was something special.

The girl bent down to deposit her flight jacket into one of her packs, blinking as she straightened. Selah had always been dwarfed by the man who had assumed the father role in her life; now, she reached his chin.

"Beda's out on the road with a supply caravan to Hillshire. Firmin has been here for a few days." Selah brightened at the mention of her brother.

Flyn turned to Averon, who had been watching the reunion quietly to the side. "Are you going to stay?"

Averon smiled. "Maybe for today, but we should be heading back to Dragonhold by tomorrow morning. Do you have any open dens that Farsight could stay in?"

Flyn addressed Farsight this time. "We have a few that you might find to your liking, although I'm afraid they're not full with fresh hay at the moment. If you want to stay out in the sun for a while, I could have someone prepare one of the dens." Selah could not help but notice that her guardian addressed the dragon rather than the dragonrider when he was discussing Farsight, something that was not common in non-dragonfolk. Her admiration and respect for the guard captain only increased.

Farsight nodded in thanks.—*That would be very welcome, as would a long rest in the sun. If you do not mind…*—the dragon's newly golden eyes sparkled with anticipation.—*I am going to go take a nap.*—

✳   ✳   ✳   ✳

The servants they passed in the hallway greeted her with warm smiles. Selah returned them, surprised by how many people she had left behind when she had gone to Dragonhold.

The acrid smell of the hallway torches, still smoldering from their nighttime existence, jarred against her nose. Although not too unpleasant, the scent reminded her that she was far from the crystal lit hallways of Dragonhold. The lack of artistry on the walls confirmed her feelings.

Flyn lead her to the main hall of Domar. The long table was filled with guards and freemen eating their morning meal. A cook with a pronounced paunch entered the room, bearing a steaming pot of more food.

Selah grinned when she recognized her old nemesis from childhood. Everyone simply called him "Cook" and she and Firmin had spent hours thinking of ways to sneak strawberry tarts from his kitchen without punishment. After their fifth crusade, Cook declared them enemies of the meal house and decried that they were forbidden to enter the room unless they were washing dishes. This, of course, only made the two redouble their efforts in a quest for sweets. Their vendetta had continued up until Selah had left for Dragonhold, and Firmin for Fief Chivalry.

Now that she was older, Selah thought making amends could be in order. When Cook placed the large pot down on the table, the girl broke away from Flyn and offered her hand to her old enemy.

The man raised his eyebrows at the profuse gesture. Selah, before Hadfoll, would have blushed. Now, she retained her composure when Cook did not immediately accept her hand. "I'm back on summer leave," she explained. "I know you probably haven't missed me terribly, but I'm glad to see you."

The man grinned, tugging twice on his beard before engulfing her hand in his own, massive one. "Truth be told, youngster, things around here have been quiet without you and that brother of yours. There have been others that try to snitch from my kitchen," Selah smiled at the thought of other children living on her legacy, "but none of them can get away with it like you could." Selah, now that she had made amends with the man, was eager to find her brother. She craned her head in either direction as far as she could without being rude to Cook.

A brown, shaggy head bent low over a small wooden bowl at the other end of the hall attracted her attention. Selah excused herself, nodding one last time to Cook, and walked over to where a boy her age sat, eating at a speed that rivaled Windchaser at mealtime.

Selah slid into the wooden chair next to him. Windchaser peeped in interest, but the boy did not look up from her meal. Even though her perception of colors was still poor, Selah knew that the shaggy hair that neared the point of falling into the bowl was the same color as her own had been before it had darkened in the Spring of All Tears.

"Hello, Firmin."

Her brother lifted his head, hasty passing a hand over his mouth in a quick effort to look presentable. It was a moment before recognition lit up his hazel eyes. "Selah!" he exclaimed. "I was wondering when you would be coming back." He frowned. "Your hair is shorter." Selah had cut her brown locks to shoulder length so that it was less of a hassle during combat.

"Yours is longer," the girl countered, eyeing his shaggy hair with a trace of amusement. His hair, somewhere in between short and long, was a fashion worn by those of common birth with noble status. While it looked good on her brother, Selah was more concerned about what it meant. Something told her that hairstyle was not the only thing that had changed about Firmin.

Windchaser clambered into Selah's lap. Firmin blinked in surprise before returning his attention to Selah. "Is that…"

"Yes," Selah finished for him. "This is Windchaser, my dragon." Terms such as "dragonet" and "adolescent" were words that meant little to those who were not familiar with dragonkind. "Dragon" would suffice for the time being.

Firmin nodded in acknowledgment of the dragon, offering one hand for Windchaser to sniff. The dragonet did so, eyeing Firmin with wary interest. She did not often meet new people and was cautious when she did.

Selah and her brother made small talk for an hour. Firmin told her about Fief Chivalry, about his friends there, and promised that he'd show her his future charger when it was old enough to travel. Selah spoke of Landon and the twins, training and the quirky personality of her mathematics master. Her throat closed when she came to the Choosing. In earlier times, she would have told Firmin everything—her burning, even Stormhunter's healing and the strange events that the incident had set into motion.

Her brother looked at her oddly when she was silent for longer than it was necessary just to gather one's thoughts. "Selah?" he inquired, getting the sense that there was more than his sister was telling him.

Selah broke herself from her reverie by shaking her head back and forth. "Sorry. Forgot what I was talking about there." The girl continued in her tale, but omitted any mention of gods, the Spring of All Tears, her dragon soul and the abilities that it gave her.

Despite the fact that most of the more dramatic parts of her year away were kept from her story, it was impressive enough that Firmin raised his eyebrows when she had finished. "You've been busy," he commented. "How's training?"

"Good," Selah replied. "I was in the first and second tiers for most weapons but when I was b…sick, I got moved down to the third until I recovered. We left for summer leave before I could truly try to move back up."

"We don't have tiers, but I am fairly good at fencing. I still have issues with archery, though. We have to learn how to fight on horseback, which makes everything more difficult."

Selah nodded—she would not learn how to fight from the back of a dragon until she was apprenticed to a dragonrider at the end of her pallonship. Regardless, the girl knew enough about weapons now to know that it would be challenging.

By the time they had reached a good point where their conversation could be set aside for the moment, the other occupants of the Main Hall had left. Firmin went outside, while Selah meandered through the hallways, trying to become reacquainted with the walls and passages she had once known as home.

*   *   *   *

Selah would have liked nothing more than to sleep uninterrupted for several days. However, her guardians had other things in mind. Once Beda returned from escorting the caravan to Hillshire, Selah was put to work organizing the armory, whitewashing the stables, dusting out the old dragon dens—various chores that had put off but could now be relegated to the extra pairs of hands that she and Firmin provided.

The two saved the armory for last, eager to have a look at the older and newer weapons as they put them in their proper places.

"Selah, look," ordered Firmin, spinning a ball and chain experimentally above his head.

The girl backed away in mock fright. "Don't come near me with that one." Her fingers brushed over the pole weapons, feeling how the wooden handles had been treated so that they did not give their wielders splinters. Her eye passed, uninterested, over the axes—the weapons were too brutal and awkward for her taste. She paused at the bows, stringing each one and pulling it back to make sure they were in good condition.

The sunlight lanced off the blades of steel and iron that hung from the walls. The swords, although cared for enough that they reflected the light, were not the ornate weapons that sometimes adorned the waists of nobles. The hilts, usually bound with black or brown leather, were for war...nothing else.

Selah chose one at random from its place on the wall. She cut through the air with half the speed that Garrett would demand, disliking the way the lighter sword felt against arms and shoulders that had been harden by long hours performing patterns with the training master's beastly long swords. Selah returned the blade to its spot, hefting a few before finally selected one to twirl experimentally in her hand.

It better suited her criteria. Selah slashed at an invisible enemy, flipping the sword and cutting down with the other edge. The girl was caught with the overwhelming urge to go out and practice; her relationship with Firmin had fostered a strong competitiveness that disliked being in the third tier. If she wanted to regain her place in the top groups, the girl would have to work for it over the summer.

Firmin eyed her twisting and turning with a measure of skepticism. "Is that what they taught you at Dragonhold?" he asked, the lighter tone in his voice betraying his desire to irritate her.

Selah frowned, facing her brother. "No. That's nothing."

The competitive gleam flared in Firmin's hazel eyes. "Really? Maybe you should show me some of your better patterns sometime."

Selah put on her most serious and sincere expression. "We dragonriders don't restrict ourselves to patterns," she countered, surprised by the intensity in her voice. "We fight freeform."

Firmin chuckled, taking an axe down from the wall to inspect it for chips or other flaws. "Don't get too big for your breeches, Selah. You're not a dragonrider yet."

Selah opened her mouth to argue, but shut it sullenly when she realized that she had nothing to say.

*   *   *   *

Summer was the most dangerous time of the year at Domar—the snows that kept Galdrid's Pass impenetrable during the winter were nowhere to be found during the hotter months of the year. Domar, seated at the hem of the mountains and the chief protector of the Pass, was often the first to be set upon by Cydran war parties or armies. However, the northern kingdom had been severely punished the last time they had attempted to take the border of Alcaron. The defeat a little over a decade ago had crippled them enough that they reconsidered any attack on Alcaron. Cydran was more apt to try a sortie into Doran or Lon rather than risk a second humiliation at the hands of Alcaron. The battle that had left Selah orphaned was the same fight that had brought Domar infamy. No man had ever attempted to breach its walls since a sand colored dragon had come down from the sky to save three babes.

Regardless, the men of Domar were often called upon to protect the neighboring towns and villages from raiders, bandits, and other woes that the people could not handle on their own. As such, the armory that lay untouched for the winter months became the most visited place in the fief as Flyn ran training sessions for the guards who had put on a little too much weight during the snows.

Selah, as Flyn's surrogate daughter and charge, received notice over dinner that attendance to these training sessions was mandatory to every able fighting man in the fief—a decry which included women.

"But we're on leave!" exclaimed Firmin. "You can't make us train!"

Flyn settled forward in his seat, his brows snapping down in a dangerous expression that usually meant a punishment when they were children. "I can, and I will. When I was at the Battle of the Shining, I was in the battalion that stormed the villages to flush out the Cydrans who were hiding in the houses. The freemen fought us. The men came at us with shovels, flailing wildly because that was the only way that they knew how to fight. We killed them. The women stepped over their husband's bodies, picked up their weapons, and fought us. We captured some, but most of them were killed. The children were too weak from starvation to pick up the shovels, but they threw rocks at us and scratched, bit, any way that they could fight. I still have nightmares about watching my men shoot arrows into the bushes and finding out that the boy they killed was only eight."

Selah and Firmin, stunned into silence by the grim story, waited to hear their guardian's point. The man sighed, rubbing his face as if to remove a bad memory from his skin. "It was hard enough being on the winning side of that battle. I don't ever want to be on the losing side. Every person in this fief will know how to fight. Every one. Even the children."

"We already know how to fight," said Firmin quietly. "We've been training for a year."

"That may be the case, but I know...knew...a lot of good men who trained for a year and got run through in their first real battle. It's worse for you two. Knights and dragonriders are the first into any fight. Selah, you may have a dragon, but it all accounts to nothing if you cannot defend yourself against others who have the same advantage. Whereas you, Firmin, don't always see as much action as Selah will, have no one but yourself to fight for you." The guard captain sighed. "That's why you will train with the rest of us."

The training sessions were not challenging for Selah—the guard captain and Beda showed the freemen how to handle a sword, bow, spear, and staff. Selah had already received good instruction with all of the weapons. She and Firmin were bumped up to the more advanced group that was headed by one of Flyn's sergeants. Seeing that the group already knew what they were doing, he let them loose into freeform, one on one combat that kept the fighters on their toes.

Selah and Firmin were not allowed to partner together—the sergeant preferred that they fight opponents older and stronger than they were in order to improve. Selah lost two for every three bouts—her body, having grown free of bruises and abrasions during her several weeks of blindness, soon remembered the feeling after a burly man the size of a small bear landed a blow to her side. The girl's gait became a hobble after a few more rounds with him.

Despite the fact that most of her battles ended in an undignified crash into the ground, Selah found the skill that she had possessed before losing her sight returned to her with the long hours of practice that Flyn's insisted they undertake. The guard captain was impressed by how much his surrogate children had improved over the year that they had been away.

Selah had matured enough at Dragonhold to understand that Flyn's desire for them to be able to defend themselves came not from his background as a guard captain or a strange urge to be unfair, but stemmed from his fear of losing them to the battles that they would certainly fight as dragonriders and knights. Firmin, although Selah suspected that he understood as well, did not respect his guardian's motives and complained whenever the man was not in earshot. A sharp cuff from Beda when he went over the line quieted the boy, but every training session was greeted with a sour face and grumbling.

✳   ✳   ✳   ✳

The rare day off found them nestled in the hayloft, seeking refuge from the stray guard that would ask them to run an errand. Firmin twirled a bit of hay between his fingers—Selah had closed her eyes and was seeing how close she could come to Windchaser's mind without opening herself up to emotion or pain. The dragonet was fast asleep in her arms, dreaming of flight; her wings jerked and twitched, accompanied by the occasional muffled whistle.

Firmin cast aside the fragment of hay in search of something more interesting. "I'm bored," he announced, a dangerous beginning to any of his conversations.

Selah broke away from the spark and looked at him with only mild interest. "That's nice," she replied. 'I'm bored' was Firmin's favorite ploy to attract attention from others. Kavan, away now at the Hollow, a city of mages and enchantment, learning to wield the magic that the gods had given him at birth, had once sarcastically described his brother as a concoction, which, if not shaken and stimulated enough, stagnates into sludge. Selah, although she did not particularly care for the description, had to agree that Firmin became cranky and grumpy whenever he was not interested in the situation around him.

"I'm thirsty. Selah, could you go get me a canteen?"

"No," the girl answered. "Get it yourself." After the disk had been placed between her soul and her mind, she had relied on Firmin for protection. Running the occasional errand for him did not seem overmuch compared to safety from hooded men with grimy fingers. Now, the request reminded her too much of servitude.

Firmin looked at her strangely but did not comment. A few minutes later, he said, "Let's go play a prank on Cook."

"Maybe later."

"Are you a coward?"

The accusation was half hearted, but Selah refused to treat it as such. "No. Don't call me a coward. Take it back."

"What if it's true?" Firmin, sensing that he had struck a nerve, pounced on the topic like a cat on a wood louse.

Selah stiffened. Her encounter with the Dragonslayer was fresh enough in her memory that she was still ashamed when she thought of the way that she had cried, giving the dragonhunter the pleasure of knowing she was terrified. Her lack of resolve still haunted her when she thought of battles to come. "It takes a different kind of courage, Firmin, to fight when you know you are going to lose than it does to dump a bucket of water on Cook's head. You should know that by now."

"What is wrong with you?" Firmin exclaimed. Selah, startled by the outburst, blinked in surprise and couldn't answer. It was just as well; Firmin continued to rant. "You and I used to play tricks on Cook all the time. Why can't you do it now?

Selah shrugged, struggling to come up with a good answer. "Because...it's other people's turn to annoy him."

"That's not why." Firmin stood, brushing the hay from his tunic. "You're different. Too different for a year. Just because you got Chosen by a dragon, you're suddenly a different person? You don't want to pull pranks, you're obsessed with training. You even look different! Your hair was the same color as mine. Now it's darker. Your eyes were the same as mine. Now, instead of just brown and green, they have amber in them. What happened?"

The words perched on the tip of her tongue. Try as she might, Selah could not begin to tell him what had really happened to her in that year. Firmin exhaled in disgust when she did not answer. "Something did happen to you. What was it?"

"You truly want to know?"

Firmin nodded. So Selah told him. She told him the entire story of the Choosing, throwing in explanations and knowledge that she had discovered during Hadfoll. It took a long time in telling—when she was finished, the girl's throat was a touch sore, and she felt as though a huge burden had been lifted off her shoulders.

Firmin frowned. "Stormhunter came to you? A god came to *you*?"

Selah disliked the tone in his voice as he spoke the words, but only nodded. The boy snorted. "I'm supposed to believe that? Believe that a god healed you and came to you in dreams? That you were Touched?" The Touched were people who had come into contact with a god for personal reasons. Some of the

Touched had become great heroes—others, messengers of fate or bringers of bloodshed.

Selah's shirt had laces, which, if undone, would reveal the scar beneath the nape of her neck. Despite the fierce heat, she kept them tied to reduce the exposure of Stormhunter's mark. Selah quietly undid the laces at the collar of her shirt, pulling the fabric back to reveal as much of her scar as she could without showing her breast band. Firmin's eyes widened.

The girl waited a long moment for his response. He shook his head. "That's not possible, Selah. You know it isn't. If you have a dragon soul, why don't I?" The girl could not give him an answer. "That scar is probably something that all dragonriders get when they are Chosen." Selah startled by his adamant refusal to take her words as truth, studied her brother closely. Staring into the hazel eyes that had once been identical to hers, Selah saw the understanding that his mind refused to acknowledge.

He turned away from her, beginning to descend from the hayloft. The words burst from Selah's mouth. "I'm not the only one who's changed, Firmin."

Her brother paused at the top of the ladder, looking to his sister for an explanation to her statement. Selah shifted Windchaser into a more comfortable position in her lap. "A year ago, you would have believed me."

The boy stared at her for a long moment before making his way down the ladder. He said nothing more.

*   *   *   *

Three days later, the trader came to Domar. The man came in with all regalia, bearing trinkets from various fiefs that would interest children with coppers to spend. Naturally, everyone in Domar came out to hear the news from the outside world that had not been relayed by the latest courier. Selah felt herself moved along like trout in a river current as people made their way to the courtyard.

Despite the fact that she was in the back, the girl was tall enough that seeing the trader was not a problem. The man was tall and muscular, bearing the appearance that he could carry himself in a fight. To be a traveler in the northern parts, one had to know how to handle fierce and unexpected combat. He was clean-shaven with long hair that defied the generally custom of commoners with shorter locks than nobles. A light blond that rivaled the color of Bern's, his hair caught the sunlight like spun honey. A dazzling smile only added to the general aura of charm, and the people of Domar flocked to him like bees to a sweet left in the summer heat.

He calmed his horse, a large stallion that stamped when the crowd got too close, but was quiet as his master addressed the inhabitants of Domar. "I've been traveling these mountains for weeks," he declared, taking on an expression of exhaustion, "just to bring my wares to you! A ring, silver pot, I have everything you could possibly need." He eyed one of the guards, who sported a beard that resembled a tangled nest more than anything else. "A comb, gentle sir?"

The crowd roared with laughter—the guard, Dwain, was the subject of many jokes because of his beard and had become a small celebrity for it. The fact that the peddler had been able to pick up on Dwain's oddity only made the people love him more.

Windchaser climbed onto her favorite perch on Selah's shoulder in order to see well. The man was slowly turning so that he saw each side of the crowd; at the moment, he was facing away from them.

"My name is Omar of Breveron, and I am a peddler of sorts. I bring things to sell to you, but—" He stopped. The man was facing Selah and Windchaser now, and his eyes were locked on the dragonet. The smile on his face flattened to a horizontal line of neutrality. Omar was silent for a long moment, and then seemed to realize his motionlessness. The smile returned in full force. "...what I like to do most is tell stories. Perhaps, if you will consent to let me stay for a few days, I can relate to you what is happening in our beautiful kingdom of Alcaron."

Selah, disturbed by the change that her dragonet had brought out in Omar, slipped away. The crowd did not notice her leaving, and pressed closer to the peddler until there was no sign that the girl had ever been there.

*   *   *   *

The trader was granted the seat of honor at the dinner table, and he spent the entire meal and well into the evening telling the diners the tales they wished to hear. Everyone seemed very charmed with Omar and his stories; Selah, although she had to admit to herself that the trader was a good storyteller, could not help but recognize her unreasonable dislike of the man. Omar, conversing with Flyn, ate heartily as was fitting for a traveler. The way he had stared at Windchaser unnerved her, and although Omar did not look at her dragonet a second time throughout the various servings, Selah did not let her Chosen out of her sight for a moment.

Selah was helping to clear the table when she felt a light touch on her shoulder. It was the trader, and he greeted her with a smile. The girl returned it half-heartedly, taking a moment to make sure that Windchaser was still at her spot at the table. "Can I help you?" Her voice was more courteous that she felt.

Omar brushed his blonde hair from his eyes. "I noticed that you have a dragonet. Are you back from Dragonhold on summer leave?"

"Yes," Selah said with measured slowness, surprised with the familiarity with which Omar referred to the fortress of dragonriders. "I have been there a year."

"It's Selah of Domar, isn't it?"

"How do you know my name?" The inquiry was too rushed, too forced—Selah regretted the words the moment they were out of her mouth. Firmin, seated at the other end of the hall, looked at her curiously but averted his gaze when he saw that his sister noticed him—the two had not spoken since their confrontation in the stable loft.

"I merely asked your guardian, that's all." Omar's face bore a patronizing smile that made Selah want to strike him. "Fascinating man. You see, I was selected to be a pallon." His eyes turned inward toward fond memories. "Stayed there for three months before I was rejected during the Choosing. I simply wanted to congratulate you on managing to get a hold of a dragonet."

"Oh..." Selah felt foolish now. She was not sure what she had considered Omar's motivations for speaking to her to be, but it had been far from what he had just told her. "Thank you."

"You're welcome. If you'll excuse me, I believe I am being called." Several at the table were waving the trader back. Omar nodded once in respect before answering their summons.

*   *   *   *

The trader seemed to be everywhere the following day—he told stories at breakfast, helped the little children with their chores, and a myriad of other things that placed him in public eye and earned him a few sales. He volunteered to teach the guards a few things about knife fighting during his stay. Selah came to watch.

Omar invited one of the bolder guards into the ring with him. The potential of combat transformed the trader—he seemed more catlike and focused the closer they got to the demonstration. A single knife gleamed wickedly in his hand. As Omar turned it in his hands, the sunlight reflected off the metal and shone on the ground. The knife seemed more like an extension of his body rather than a thing separate from it.

Omar beat every comer like he was taking a strawberry tart from a child. He threw one man over his knee and gave several more sharp raps with the hilt of his knife that the recipients would likely remember in the morning. It was not until the sergeant that instructed Selah's group challenged him that the audience actually had a fight worth watching, although Omar beat him in the end. The actual combat brought a stronger change in the man than the preparing for it—his eyes were wild and intense, and his face locked in a stony visage completely void of emotion. Selah found it more unnerving than him staring at Windchaser the day before. However, each person had their own fighting style, and Omar's certainly managed to distract his opponents enough to give him an advantage.

Someone from the middle of the watching mob called for Flyn to take up his knife and have a go with Omar; the crowd loved the idea and took up a chant. The guard captain shook his head, declining to go toe to toe with the trader. "I'd rather not place my dignity on the line, thank you." People moaned in disappointment, but Flyn was esteemed at Domar, and they respected his decision enough not to insist.

Omar, however, did not. "Are you sure you do not wish to challenge me, captain? I am eager for a worthy opponent."

Flyn only shook his head. "I've just eaten, and fighting so soon after digesting is unhealthy." He laughed, but Selah recognized the barest forced undertone that betrayed his mirthless feelings. "As men often do, I shall think with my stomach. I will have to decline for the time being."

Selah left the dinner table early—while Omar's story about his short lived pallonship was enough to refute his strange behavior when he had first arrived, he gave no explanation for his odd love for combat and the girl could not bear to listen to his stories for very much longer. The man had announced that he would be leaving in the morning, which brought cries of dismay from most but inward pleasure from Selah. She couldn't be rid of the man fast enough.

There was little to do besides eat at mealtimes—there was no one about in the hallways. Selah found herself wandering in the generally avoided sections of the fief, the old kitchen, storage rooms, and library.

The place of books was dusty with lack of use—before she had left for Dragonhold, the girl had only entered the room once or twice. After Kavan had claimed the space for his own, no one else cared to visit the library while he was there, which was most of the time. Now that he was gone, the room was unoccupied for many days out of the year.

Selah reached forward, taking a book from the shelf and opening it to the middle. The words were written in a script and language that she did not understand—nevertheless, she flipped through a few pages before closing the volume and returning it to its place of honor on the shelf.

A sound behind her made the girl stop and turn. Omar had entered the room without her knowledge and had purposefully made himself known by knocking on one of the tables.

"Didn't mean to startle you," he apologized.

Selah frowned. Nerves tingled up and down her arms at the sight of him—the man frightened her. "What do you want?"

"Nothing. Just wondering what you were doing."

Windchaser, at Selah's heels, began to growl. The girl shushed her dragonet with a warning look before returning her attention to the man in front of her. "I'm reading. You can go now." The dragon within her was threatened by the man's presence, and wanted him away—human demands of courtesy were moot at this point.

"Temper, temper. I'm not threatening you." Omar chuckled, and Selah felt her spine tingle as the sound, normally warm and welcoming, fell cold upon her ears.

"You must get that rudeness from the dragon side of you." Selah felt the contents of her stomach freeze. Omar smiled icily. "Yes, I know about your dragon soul. And Stormhunter—as well as your remarkable scar. We dragonhunters don't hold secrets from each other."

Gods! Selah thought. *That's why he stared! That's how he knew my name!*

"It will be satisfying being able to tell the Highslayer about the fear in your eyes as you died."

Selah, trying to control her panic, reached out and touched her dragonet's mind. *Run! Find Flyn and bring him here. Bring help. Run when I attack the bad man.* Selah struggled to place it into terms that her Chosen would understand. *Do not stop running. You must bring help.*

Selah reached for the belt knife that every person wore at their hip, and choked as she remembered how she had used it to cut the meat at dinner. It was sitting next to her plate.

Omar, if that was his true name, rotated one shoulder slowly, first one way, then the other. "I wonder if killing you will promote me to the rank of Dragonslayer, given the circumstances. Perhaps I would have to kill your dragonet as well to get such a reward."

Selah rushed forward, pushing Omar back before he had a chance to react. Windchaser bolted between the dragonhunter's legs, racing out the door and bawling as she reached the hallway. Omar paused, listening to the dragonet's squeals as she called for help.

Selah took the lull in the action to thrust the dragonhunter against the wall, starting to run toward the hall. An iron grip caught her by the back of the tunic and pulled her back into the library—Omar used his other hand to slam the door shut. Selah crashed against the floor when the dragonhunter pulled her back into the room—the hard stone banished the breath from her body upon impact.

Ignoring the dull ache in her back, the girl grasped a large volume from the nearest shelf and hurled it at Omar's head. The bound pages struck the dragonhunter in the face—the second projectile hit him square in the throat.

Selah grasped two more books, one in each hand. The dragonhunter wiped his bloody nose on his sleeve. His eyes burned in hatred so intense that it scared Selah far more than anything he had said.

The girl threw another book, and another. The man ducked the first and shrugged aside the second; he was upon her before she could do anything else. Pinning her arms to her sides, he pressed her against the bookshelves. The hard wood dug painfully into the girl's back.

Selah snapped her head forward, using the harder bone on her brow as a bludgeon. The dragonhunter only grunted when her forehead smashed into his jaw, refusing to loosen his grip. Selah's foot lashed out, catching him in the shin. A blade appeared in his hand from nowhere, and Selah stilled as the sharp edge bit into the skin on her throat. Omar used the back of his hand to wipe another stream of blood from his nose. "That's better." He smiled again—Selah had bloodied his lip with her head butt, and his teeth were stained red.

His blade slashed into the thick muscle on the back of Selah's arm—her cry of pain was muffled by the hand that Omar held over her mouth. Just like with the Dragonslayer, she was helpless. Omar was going to kill her, and there was nothing she could do.

The door crashed open, making Omar turn in surprise. Flyn, backed by five of his men, stood in the entrance to the library. Windchaser peered around the leg of one of them, whistling in horror when she saw Selah. Omar, knowing that he had to strike down the abomination now, thrust with his knife.

His blade buried itself into the wood by half its length. The girl, taking advantage of the distraction, had fallen to the ground to break free of Omar's grip. The dragonhunter whipped out his other blade, striking down and missing her torso by the barest inch—luck saved Selah a second time as she scrambled away to the safety of Windchaser's reinforcements.

Flyn placed himself between his charge and the dragonhunter, a blade of his own turning his hand into a deadly weapon. Omar turned to the next best target and feinted with his blade, twisting and cutting to the other side. The blade slashed a red line into the guard captain's shoulder.

Flyn, undeterred, cut at the dragonhunter's face. Omar dodged it easily, realizing his mistake when the captain's fist caught him under the heart. He reeled back, pretending hurt. When the captain rushed forward to finish him off, Omar kicked him in the stomach, using the art of unarmed combat that the dragonhunters had patented and mastered over their years of living in hiding.

Flyn fell back against the wall. The dragonhunter bore down with his knife, slashing him across the hand. The knife clattered from the guard captain's fingers as the tendons in his strong hand went limp. Flyn snatched one of the books Selah had thrown at the trader. Omar's thrust slid neatly through the bound pages, stopping at the hilt as Flyn caught the blow with the book. The guard captain twisted the volume over and down, wrenching the knife from the dragonhunter's grasp. Reaching out with his good hand, he retrieved his blade from the floor and buried it into the dragonhunter's chest.

Omar choked, his eyes misting over in death as his pierced heart slowed to a stop. Flyn, breathing heavily, rose to his feet as the dragonhunter fell to the ground. "I'm glad we could have our match," he growled. Omar didn't answer, and never would.

There was silence. Selah was the first to break it. "Flyn...your hand."

The guard captain eyed his wound with only mild interest. "It's nothing a good healing can't fix. Are you all right?"

Selah nodded. Flyn brought her into an embrace. The girl buried her face into his uncut shoulder, seeking the protection the cotton and muscle afforded her. "Was he a dragonhunter?" asked Flyn. Everyone in the kingdom knew about the dragonhunters—some were sympathetic to their ideals, while others hated them as much as the dragonriders did. Flyn fell into the second category.

Selah nodded, waiting for the tears that should come after her close scrape with death. They did not. Windchaser rubbed against her leg, mewing in support and relief that her Rider was still alive.

The girl knew she had to tell her adoptive father about the true reasons that Omar had come for her. She had to tell him about the mark of Stormhunter.

Now was not the time.

*   *   *   *

Beda made her way through the blackened halls of Domar. She had lived in the fief for most of her life now—she had memorized the corridors and passages so that she could navigate them in the dark if need be. Her destination was easy enough to find; she had often made midnight trips to the room when Selah was younger.

The woman opened the oaken door that guarded the entrance to Selah's room slowly, so as not to wake the girl. She had cared for Selah when she was a child, and knew that the girl slept lightly even when exhausted.

Beda peered around the doorway and was greeted by a pair of hazel eyes. The moonlight that shone through the slit window cast a narrow beam of light on Selah's face. The girl, although sitting on her bed, was propped up against the wall. Her eyes were wide open and revealed no trace of drowsiness.

Selah said nothing, staring at the woman who had become like a mother to her when Cassandra died. Beda felt uncomfortable under the review of eyes that were brown, green, and now, amber, all at once. "I know I saw you earlier," she explained, shutting the door behind her. "But I just wanted to make sure that you were all right."

"I'm fine. I just don't want to sleep." Beda, hurt by the curtness in Selah's voice, turned to go. She heard the girl sigh. "No, stay, please. I'm sorry."

Beda heard the bed creak as the girl rose to her feet. In the weak half-light that the crescent moon provided, Selah looked less like the child she had been and more like the woman she would become. She had grown much taller over the year she had been away, and already physical differences were breaking her apart from the sameness that had linked she and Firmin. A strange sort of sadness swelled in Beda's throat.

"He's gone, Selah," the woman assured, trying to make the girl feel safe. If Selah could not feel secure in her own room, what kind of home had they created? How had they not seen Omar's true nature? "He's dead, and nothing can bring him back from that."

Selah smiled ruefully, wrapping her arms around her body as she sought comfort from within. "There are more Omars, Beda. They just don't all have the same name."

"No, Selah, you're..."

"Right?" Selah gazed out the window to gather her thoughts. "I was helpless, Beda. There was nothing I could do. He was stronger than me, had a weapon, and caught me when I was alone. How am I supposed to defend Windchaser when I can't even defend myself?" There was more anger than fear in her voice as the girl glanced at the sleeping dragonet. It took Beda a long moment to understand that it was anger at herself. "I should have known to trust what I was feeling. Especially after last time."

"Last time?"

Selah shook her head. "I'll tell you in the morning. Now isn't the time to talk about it." The conviction in her voice belied her age, suggesting maturity beyond her years.

She's only thirteen! thought Beda with an aching heart. *Not yet a woman, and she's already been scarred like this.* Tears for the girl she had raised as her daughter welled up in her eyes, but the woman knew that it would do no good to have Selah see them.

Beda ignored the mother's voice within her that was telling her that what she was about to do was not right for Selah's age. The warrior that still resided within her, was still active when need be, countered that it was necessary. It was the fighter in Selah that needed reassurance, not the girl. "Come with me," she said. "I need to show you something."

The two walked through the corridors in silence, Beda trying to ignore the fact that Selah stared too long and too fearfully into the shadows. *How much has she lost?* the woman wondered. *How much faith in the world around her does she have left?*

The woman lead the girl to her room, still having lingering doubts that this was the right course of action. Beda's endeavors as a warrior had earned her one of the larger rooms in the fief—only Flyn's and the Lord and Lady's rivaled hers in size. The woman ignored the excess furniture that was there only to take up space and went straight to the locked chest at the foot of her bed.

It was a warrior's trunk, filled with chain mail, leather armor and weapons. Her plate mail resided in her dresser, as did her long sword, spear and bow, but the smaller items she kept in the chest. Beda dug through the contents, letting Selah admire some of the knives and dirks that she had accumulated over the years. She found it at the very bottom—she had never used it in her life, but sensed that Selah would put it to far better use.

The leather had not yet gone stiff—Beda had enough respect for her equipment that, no matter how little she used something, she never let it fall into disrepair.

"My father gave me this when he first realized that I wasn't going to turn away from being a warrior," she explained, handing it to Selah. "He said that there was rarely a blade as important as the little ones."

Selah peered at the leather—at first glances, it appeared to be little more than a fancy bracer. "It's a wrist sheath," Beda said softly. "A flick of your wrist and a blade is in your palm." The wide band of leather, when secured about the lower forearm, allowed someone to bear a dagger without revealing that they were armed. Drawing a blade from the sheath would be instantaneous.

The woman showed her how to tie it on, then selected a knife from her collection and slid it into the sheath. Selah favored shirts that were not overly tight about the wrists, which allowed her to easily get the knife into her palm without having to change the way she dressed. Beda showed her how to slide the blade out of its sheath while still keeping the blade concealed, how to flip the knife out quickly, and how to return it to its place. Once Selah had demonstrated that she knew how to perform each action, Beda led the girl back to her room.

"Now you'll always be prepared," Beda said, hoping that her words would comfort the girl. "You'll always be armed, and no one will know."

Selah reached up and embraced the woman. "Thank you," she said, and the two words were the sincerest that Beda had ever heard anyone ever say. The girl returned to her room, shutting the door quietly behind her.

Beda remained where she was. The silence of the night seemed to drain the life from the fief, and she felt uneasy surrounded by shadows. She listened intently, and heard the soft scraping of leather on metal, repeated over and over. Selah was practicing. The sound of bare feet against the floor filtered through the door as the girl spun around her room. Beda could envision the girl turning, flipping out her blade to confront an imaginary attacker. The steady sound of motion was interspersed with the occasional exclamation when the sharp dagger nicked skin.

Beda waited for the sounds of the girl returning to her bed. As the beams of light created by the crescent moon shining through the window grew longer, they did not come.

The woman went back to her room. It was not until her own door was closed behind her that Beda began to cry for the little girl child who climbed trees and dreamed that she could fly.

*   *   *   *

Selah sat them down the next morning and told them everything—the Choosing, Stormhunter, Hadfoll, her soul...all of it. Beda and Flyn listened in shocked silence, never interrupting her tale. They didn't have to; Selah's relating of her story was meticulous and exact, and not a single detail was excluded.

When she had finished, the girl took a long swallow of water—every time she went over the events of her year at Dragonhold, her throat always ended up sore.

Flyn wasn't sure whether or not he wanted to believe his surrogate daughter. The tale was incredible to say the least, but too much made sense for it to be ignored as pure fiction. "What does this mean?" he asked slowly, as much to give himself time to absorb the information as to inquire for more.

Selah rubbed her upper arm—like Flyn's hand, it was bandaged from the ordeal of the day before. The wound ached terribly, and moving the limb in any way was a painful process. "I have a dragon soul, and a dragon song." At the mention of the music, notes and melodies sprang into her mind, and the girl had to shake her head to physically return to the conversation. "When I was growing up, I was only half of myself. Now, I am, supposedly, whole."

Beda passed one hand across her forehead. Of all of her surrogate children, it was Firmin who she had suspected to be more than commonplace—Selah's later childhood days, with all their normality, had disbarred the extraordinary beginnings of her life. Now the woman understood why. "The…disk?"

"Gone," said Selah. "Stormhunter took it in exchange for my life."

"So, this dragon soul of yours…does it make you any different?" Flyn asked.

Slowly, Selah nodded. Telling her guardians that she was only half of what they had thought she was turned out to be far more painful that she had previously considered. "It…doesn't bother you…does it?"

"No, Selah." Flyn reached across the table and engulfed her hand in both his own. "Never. Did you think we didn't know you well enough to see that part of you was always somewhere else?"

Selah smiled as Beda grasped her other hand. Her eyes gleamed as they had twelve years ago, when a dragon had touched her brow and told the world that she would be different.

Dreams

Averon came to return her to the fief three days later. The girl was eager to go—for all that Domar was her birthplace, Dragonhold had become her home and she missed the company of her friends. Firmin, although he was willing to talk to her after her brush with death, provided none of the companionship that had once been so strong between the two.

Omar still haunted her like he had when he was alive—the girl could not walk down a corridor without craning her neck over her shoulder to reassure herself that she was not being followed. Selah welcomed the idea of sharing a fief with several thousand dragons; the great beasts still provided her with a sense of security.

They had to leave the same day the Wingleader arrived in order to make it back to Dragonhold in time for the girl's classes. Selah, knowing full well now how to tie her packs onto a dragon's saddle, was left on her own to secure her belongings as Averon spoke with Flyn.

The guard captain handed the man two letters. Curious, the dragonrider examined them closely without opening them—the red wax had been sealed with the stamp of Domar, two intersecting blades crowned by three stars.

"One is for you," explained Flyn. "It explains everything in detail. Long tale short, a trader that came to Domar attempted to kill Selah. He was a dragon-hunter in disguise."

Averon swore. "Was anyone hurt?"

Flyn smiled ruefully. "Just she and I—a gash on the back of her arm, and a slash on my hand and shoulder. Hers will take some time before she is back at full speed, but they were nothing serious."

Averon had missed how the captain favored his left arm and never closed his strong hand. Now he noticed them in detail—and saw the same guarded, wounded cautiousness in Selah's motions.

"She told us what happened to her…during the Choosing, Hadfoll." Averon had been included in Selah's tale—Flyn knew that the Wingleader was aware of Selah's unnatural qualities and experiences. "The dragonhunters know that she has been Touched by Stormhunter. They will be tracking her when they can."

"I will not let her out of my sight until we are within the walls of Dragonhold," promised the Wingleader. "Who is the other letter for?"

"The Holdleader and her teachers. Is Handuin of Mancrest still the training master?"

Averon shook his head. "Handuin stepped down after two of my year mates died in duels. Garrett of Dalbrook was elected into the position—not as experienced as Handuin, but a good instructor."

"Your letter details everything about Omar—the dragonhunter," Flyn added when Averon gave him a blank stare. "His clothes, his appearance, his possessions. He was the best knife fighter I've seen since the Cydran War; this was no grunt they sent. I thought you would appreciate the information."

Averon nodded in thanks. "That we do. We've fought the dragonhunters for over a century, and they still manage to surprise us daily."

"I would like you to share it with Garrett of Dalbrook. Teaching the pallons how to defend themselves against Omar's fighting style would do them no harm."

"How is she?" Averon's question had nothing to do with physical wellbeing.

"Shaken." Flyn looked very tired. "Wouldn't admit it for all the dragons in the world."

Averon watched as Selah smiled to a remark that Farsight had made, and wondered how far inward that expression shone.

*   *   *   *

Averon opted not to stay in the inns this time around. Previously, his fear of being caught in an ambush drove him to stay in populated places—this time, the people contained the danger. They made camp in a secluded grove and ate their meal cold.

Selah offered to take first watch and let the dragonrider have a few hours of sleep. Farsight claimed the second watch, which left the dragonrider with the early hours of the morning and Selah again until dawn.

Averon and Farsight fell asleep instantly—while only in the earlier parts of their lives, they had seen enough battles and campaigns to take their rest when it was given to them. The forest sounds that were eerie on Selah's ears did not seem to bother them.

Selah passed the time flicking the dagger in and out of her wrist sheath; having something to do comforted her. The darkness pressed in from all sides, threatening to overwhelm her if she let it.

Creaks and groans from the forest around her set the girl's teeth on edge. Her heart was pounding so loudly she was sure the wood creatures could hear it. *Coward,* she thought to herself. *Firmin was right.*

Time droned onward into the night. Selah felt no desire to sleep—the Dragonslayer and Omar cast enough of a shadow on her that she knew dreams would be nightmares. Sleep, and they would come. Sleep, and they would catch her.

The time passed with a surreal quickness; before she knew it, a light tap sent nerves racing down her spine. Golden eyes that shone in the moonlight softened when they saw the panic on her face.—*Your watch is done,*—said Farsight with a tone of apology in his voice.—*I did not mean to startle you.*—

"You didn't," Selah lied. She lay back, resting her head on the rolled blanket that served as a pillow. "Goodnight."

—*To you as well.*—Farsight watched as the girl tossed and turned; he had seen enough of the world to understand that her motion came from restlessness, not a search for a comfortable patch of the forest floor.

Several minutes later, Selah gave up the farce of sleep and rose to a sitting position, casting aside her blanket so that the folds of cloth would not hamper her legs in the face of an emergency. Sleep was out of the question.

—*Cannot sleep?*—asked Farsight, his golden eyes like small suns in the moonlight. Selah nodded, hugging her knees to her chest.—*Are you cold?*—

Selah smiled ruefully. The chill she felt came from within—no change in temperature could alter it. "No," she admitted, although his question would have been a good excuse for her behavior. "Just afraid of dreaming, that's all."

—*Why? Do you have nightmares?*—Farsight's voice was sad.

"I guess you could say that."

The dragon patted the dirt beside his side.—*You may help me keep watch if that makes you feel better.*—

The proud dragon inside of Selah kept her rooted to the ground. The girl inside of her needed the security that another, greater being would provide.

Scooping up Windchaser gently, the pallon walked over to Farsight's side, sitting down next to him. The dragonet, caught in a pleasant dream, only twitched before returning to motionlessness.

The spicy scent that Selah associated with dragons wafted around her, creating a ring of protection from the dank and musty smell of the woods. The girl, unconsciously, leaned against the dragon's side. The feel of scales against her back returned her to the realm of courtesy, and she glanced at Farsight to see if he was bothered. The dragon did not seem to notice.

She spoke with the dragon about neutral subjects such as the weather and the happenings at Dragonhold. As the night wore on, the dragon did more of the talking; her eyelids felt like lead. She fought to hold onto consciousness, but the girl was on the losing side of the battle.

—*What do you think, Selah?*—The dragon turned to see what the girl would say. She was too far adrift on the seas of slumber to hear him.

Farsight's golden eyes softened at the sight of the pallon.—*She sleeps.*— Reaching out with his limber tail, he dragged her blanket from where the girl had discarded it, pulling the cloth over her body. As he tucked the edges around her with a gentle claw, he met the violet eyes of the younger dragon.

Windchaser crawled from Selah's arms, chirping softly to the older dragon. Farsight listened with interest to the lost and sad words of Selah's Chosen. He replied in the dragon tongue so the dragonet would better understand him. *No, you are comforting her as much as you can. Do not blame yourself for her sadness.*

Windchaser seemed extremely comforted by the words of the older dragon. Farsight knew, however, that she needed more reassurance that she was not failing her Rider. *I heard how you ran and brought help when the dragonhunter came. You should be proud.*

Windchaser cheeped modestly. It seemed that her heroic actions had not been recognized, and the dragonet appreciated the attention from a full-grown dragon. She trilled and whistled more, softly so she did not wake her Rider.

Dragons did not smile with their faces—the emotion was read, mostly, from their eyes, and Farsight's golden ones gleamed with it. *I agree—you could not have made a better choice when you picked her.*

Both of the dragons turned their eyes on the girl. Her face was full of the peace that one can only find in a dreamless sleep. Shooing the dragonet back to the arms of her Rider, Farsight returned his eyes to the forest.

*   *   *   *

They made it back to Dragonhold in record time—the wind was with them, and Farsight had recovered fully from the loss and return of his eyes. They glided into the whitewashed walls of the fief with three days to spare.

Averon, as he had promised Flyn, delivered the two letters. Sean did not read his copy in front of the Wingleader; Garrett had no qualms with the dragonrider being in the room and read the guard captain's report three times before speaking.

"Have you spoken to Selah about this?"

Averon shook his head. "I thought it would be better if she didn't have to relive it so many times—I'm sure that you and the Holdleader would like to hear what she has to say."

Garrett nodded. "They aren't taking any chances. They don't even know that she can mentally communicate with dragons. All it takes is a scar and their assassins fall upon you."

"She would be dangerous without the scar. The dragonhunters don't want her to grow up," said Averon.

"True, but there are others with better training than she—the dragonhunters have not come knocking on the door of Landon of Boran, or Renton of Half Moon. They are the most talented pallons I have seen in my five years as training master."

Averon had to acknowledge the dragonrider's point. It took him a long moment to form his thoughts into words. "Selah's strength comes from her spirit, not from her arm. We saw it at the Choosing. If I were a dragonhunter, I would fear the day when Rider Selah of Domar accepts her sword."

Garrett sighed, scanning the letter one more time. "Captain Flyndain is right. I should teach them how to knife fight. I was hoping that the dragonriders they would be apprenticed to would teach them."

"That would have been right when I was pallon," said Averon sadly. "Now, it's too late."

*   *   *   *

The company of Farsight had banished her nightmares for the duration of the trip, but the specters returned with a vengeance when there was no dragon around her. Omar and the Dragonslayer had melded together into a dragonhunter with pale violet eyes and bloodstained teeth—each night, the girl had to watch as the dragonhunter slew her friends, family, Windchaser, and finally came for her. She woke each time, shaking and trembling with fear. She was disgusted with herself for her weakness, resolving each time to face the dream bravely and drive it away. It always reduced her to the verge of tears that her dragon soul would not let her shed.

Two weeks passed, and the dreams got steadily worse. To combat them, Selah threw herself into training, working until the sweat rolled down her face. She joined the Guild of Early Risers to satisfy her urge to be prepared.

September came and went with barely a nod of recognition. Selah left her bed each morning with dark shadows under her eyes and a hollow expression. Her exhaustion stemmed from only a few hours of troubled sleep and the limits to which she was pushing her body.

"Did you stay up late?" Landon asked her once.

"Just couldn't sleep," the girl replied, not bothering to expand on her answer. Landon had known her long enough to know that she was not being entirely forthcoming, but did not press her for more information.

Her fellow members in the Guild of Early Risers thought that she was crazy. "Why are you working twice a day if you don't have to?" Fagan whined to her during one of the wind sprints. "Do you have some kind of death wish?"

Selah glared at him, and the timid boy fell silent. His inquiry only troubled her further, and the girl worked twice as hard that morning. She staggered into breakfast—her friends didn't ask her any questions.

The dream refused to go away, staying with her throughout the middle of October. Despite the multiple times that she had run through the terrible images, they retained all of their terror. She woke each night, her body shaking with dry sobs. Only Windchaser's cooing could calm her. The dragonet would run her paws through Selah's sweat-soaked hair until she fell asleep, only to comfort her again when the girl broke out of the dream a second time.

Selah sought the only solution she had ever found to work—she threw herself into training to distract herself. One of Garrett's favorite exercises was a torture that the pallons had dubbed "Burning Bridges". The name came from the position of the exercise; pallons braced themselves on the flats of their arms and their toes and were forced to keep their backs straight, creating a human 'bridge'. The prefix came from the terrible burn that came when Garrett told them to go lower.

Garrett would time them, and give the pallons a few moment of rest before they continued on. The last set would always be a challenge to see who could hold out the longest. It often came down to two pallons, with the entire group cheering on one or the other, depending on where their loyalties lay.

"Up!" barked Garrett, leaning back on a barrel to watch. A few dropped out earlier than he had expected—the training master made a mental note to watch them during sprints and make sure that they were not slacking.

Those who were in the third tiers for weapons dropped out first—Selah had not stayed in that group for long and had returned to her former positions fairly quickly. The girl was still up.

One by one, the pallons dropped to the ground until it was Glenn, Selah, Landon, Bern, Renton, and Coyle. The group shrunk to Glenn, Bern, and Selah.

By now, Selah had trembled a few times, but managed to steel herself. She would not be the one to give. Giving in meant losing, and losing could mean her death.

Bern dropped a few seconds later—she heard the others congratulating him for holding out for so long. Glenn and she remained in the bridge. Sweat beaded on her forehead.

Selah thought of the dragon song to distract her from her exhaustion and give her strength. The music solidified her resolve and brought her comfort.

Glenn's voice cut through her thoughts. "Call it a tie?" he gasped. The boy was exhausted as she.

"You…first."

"That's enough," announced Garrett. Glenn and Selah dropped in relief—the girl's stomach ached like a pack of wolves had gnawed on her muscles and decided they didn't taste good enough.

She rolled onto her back, staring upward into a sky devoid of clouds. Garrett's face abruptly blocked her view. "Pallon Selah," he said. "I need to see you after training."

He was waiting for her when the others had headed toward the bathhouse. She wiped her face with a towel while the training master stared at the ground, gathering his thoughts. .

It was a long moment before Garrett's golden eyes met hers. "There is a line, Selah, between preparing yourself for what is to come and killing yourself. You have crossed the line."

"I don't want to be buried because I wasn't prepared," Selah retorted. The dragonhunter flashed in her mind's eye, and she shuddered. "He was a better fighter than I was. I never want to be that helpless again."

Garrett sighed sadly. "There is more than just a dragonhunter, isn't there?"

Selah nodded. "I don't sleep well at night."

Garrett had already heard everything that had happened to her at Domar when she had related the events to the Holdleader. Her friends knew nothing of the incident. Regardless, Landon had spoken to the training master about Selah's condition, and the dragonrider had agreed with the boy—Selah was pushing herself too hard.

"Your friends are worried about you."

"I know."

"You could take a herb from Talmud…it would provide you with dreamless sleep."

Selah shook her head. "This is something I need to deal with on my own. These are my own demons."

"That may be the case, but I want to you to stop coming to the Guild of Early Risers. Get your rest."

I wish I could, the girl thought as she headed toward the bathhouse reserved for the women of the fief. *Far more than anything in the world, I wish I could sleep.* Still, the dragon in her knew that an herb was not the answer. She would not spend the rest of her life dependant on a plant to give her rest.

That night, the girl tossed and turned as she usually did. The crystal by her bedside brought her no comfort. She closed her eyes, knowing that the rest her body so desperately needed would bring her terror.

*   *   *   *

The dragonhunter was far away, but that would not be the case in a few moments. A russet colored dragon leapt in front of the man with Omar's honey hair and was abruptly slain as the man spun daggers from his hands.

He was coming closer. Garrett stepped in front of the assassin. A flash of silver shot from Omar's hand and the training master fell with a knife buried into his side. Omar clubbed down Flyn and Beda with the ease of a mountain lion slaying a snow hare.

"That's not right!" Selah screamed. "Flyn beat you. He killed you!"

The dragonhunter stared at her with violet eyes. "There are more Omars," he hissed, *mirroring her own words.* "They just don't all have the same name."

Farsight and Averon met the same fate as her guardians. "No," Selah shouted. "Stop it! He wants me, not you!"

"Don't you understand, Selah?" *whispered Landon, one hand clutching a gaping wound above his heart.* "We have to protect you."

"No, you don't! I can save myself."

A gray dragon, scales crackling with lightning, launched himself at the dragonhunter. Stormhunter's claws were extended, and he slashed at the dragonhunter. His paw went through Omar like he didn't exist. A moment later, the dragon god lay, slain, like all the others.

Omar was coming for her now. Selah tried to flip the dagger from her wrist sheath, but the weapon clattered from her numb fingers. Windchaser leapt from her shoulder, diving for the dragonhunter's face. "No!" Selah screamed. "No!"

Windchaser fell.

Selah howled in anguish as Omar came for her, his violet eyes never leaving her face.

*   *   *   *

Selah's bare feet made little sound against the stone floor. She was trembling, and clutched Windchaser to her chest. The dream had never been so vivid, never been so terrible. Omar's face greeted her in every shadow; the girl brought the dagger into her palm and walked with the naked blade dangling at her side.

She made her way through the halls and outside, to the empty air that held the chill of fall now. Selah was barely aware of icy ground against her skin as she walked for the dragon dens.

The room was loud with the snores of dragons and considerably warmer than the outside air. Windchaser, awake, trilled a question that Selah did not understand. The green dragon on her right snorted and began move. The girl waited in apprehension as the great beast woke from slumber and regarded her with bright blue eyes.

—**What do you want?**—The dragon was clearly irritated by her intrusion into his dreams.—**It is the middle of the night.**—

"I'm sorry," Selah stammered. "I…"

The blue eyes softened.—**It is you. The dragon girl. Farsight told us about you.**—

"He did?"

—**Yes…about your nightmares. Do you dream of dragonhunters?**—

Selah nodded.—**I am sorry. I dream of them too, sometimes.**—The dragon rose to his feet.—**I am Jadewing. I think you have met my friend Riveneye.**—

The dragon that Selah had first contacted with mental communication was situated in the hay mound to the left of Jadewing.—**Hello, Selah. It has been a long time.**—

Selah was unsure how to react to the open hospitality of the dragons. Jadewing rose to his feet.—*I will bring Farsight.*—

—*No need.*—The dark blue dragon approached them along the path that divided the dens into two sections. Farsight's golden eyes bore a smile that was meant to reassure her.—*We sensed your distress.*—

"How? I just woke up."

—*When dragons are just learning to mind speak, they often transmit their emotions without meaning to. You were thinking of us, so we knew your thoughts before you reached here.*—

Selah began to shake. "It was so real, Farsight. I can't make him go away."

—*We can.*—

*   *   *   *

Averon wandered into the dens. He had been inside the fief for too long—the man was accustomed to a life in the flight harness and the whitewashed walls were suffocating him.

A wedge of Lonian Geese passed overhead, honking loudly as they flew to the warmer bays of the south. Averon generally welcomed the coming of winter, but he had been struck with fief fever quickly this year. Winter was the time of year for the reserve Wings—enemy activity was slow with the passes closed, and it was a good time for the younger dragonriders get some flight experience. As such, his Wing was not due for a patrol for several weeks.

A flight around the cliffs would clear his head. It would be unfair to ask someone else to tack up Farsight for a merely recreational flight; besides, the Wingleader preferred to do the job himself.

He rounded the corner into the den his dragon shared with three others. He stepped over the tails and claws of the red, green, and gold that lay sprawled about the large stable, tapping his dark blue on the shoulder.

Averon did not have to wait long; his dragon, with a great yawn, awoke quickly. "These walls are suffocating me," the Wingleader confessed.

Farsight held a claw to his lips in a human gesture for silence. When Averon looked at him in confusion, the dragon gestured to the hay beside him.

The dragonrider almost stumbled over the prone body that lay curled in the dried grasses. Her eyes were closed, her breathing steady. A sky-blue dragonet was wrapped in her arms. Selah slept.

"Why is she here?" Averon mouthed at his dragon.

*—She has been plagued by nightmares for months, Averon. When she was a child, a dragon named Sandrunner saved her life.—*The Wingleader raised his eyebrows at his dragon, an unspoken request to reveal his source. The dragon sighed.*—She told me the day you recruited her to be a pallon. It changed her, Averon. Dragons give her a sense of security. She saved my eyes, and my life. The least I can do is give her sound dreams.—*

Averon had to agree—the two of them both owed Selah far more than the girl would ever understand. "Dragons make her dreams go away." It was a statement, not a question.

Farsight chose to answer it anyway.*—Yes. Windchaser, when she gets older, should be able to make them go away as well. For now, she needs the company of adult dragons to be safe.—*

Averon turned to look at the girl again. Her right arm caught his attention.

The sleeve of her shirt had been pulled back from her wrist as the girl had slept, revealing the leather wrist sheath that adorned the skin beneath her cuff. The silver of a dagger blade shone in the early morning sunlight.

"She carries a blade?"

—Yes.—

A terrible sadness dropped the corners of Averon's mouth, the lines around his eyes all the more visible with his morose expression. "She's not even an apprentice."

Selah's unbound hair fell about her face in a brown halo. The lines of exhaustion on her face were fading, as were the shadows under her eyes.

Averon smiled as Windchaser shifted in the girl's arms. His flight could wait.

*   *   *   *

Selah woke in time to attend the last half of training. "Afternoon, Selah," said Garrett as the girl tried to sneak into the line. Selah only bowed and took her sword from the pallon's weapon rack.

She felt refreshed, and although she had only snatched a roll from the kitchen on her way to the training yards, better than she had in a long time.

Landon paired with her during freeform so he could talk to her. "Where were you?" he asked, parrying her blow.

Selah danced away from his counterattack. "Sleeping."

Her friend's green eyes begged her for more information, but the girl only blocked his strikes and dealt out her own. When the boy asked her again, Selah shook her head. "I'll explain later."

Landon followed her like a hunting dog on the scent until Selah would tell him. Her mood had greatly improved by a good night's rest, and she told him about the near assassination. He listened with a shocked expression.

When she finished, he rubbed the back of his neck. "Gods." The boy bit his lip. "Why didn't you tell me?"

"It was hard. I still have nightmares…"

"The shadows under your eyes."

"You noticed?"

"I'm your friend," exclaimed Landon. "You didn't think that I…we…weren't worried about you?"

Selah smiled, patting her friend's shoulder. "Thank you."

"You're welcome. Are you sleeping better?"

"Sometimes."

Landon, sensing that she had revealed more than she had wanted to in the first place, didn't press her for more than the vague answer she had given him.

Garrett began to teach them how to defend themselves against attackers when they were surprised. "Much of the time, dragonhunters or soldiers from the other side will try to attack you when you are unarmed. You've learned simple hand-to-hand combat, but there is a more advanced art, Korei, that is better suited to the caliber of opponents you will be facing."

Korei was far more effective than her previous instruction in weaponless combat and was exactly what Selah needed. Garrett showed them only the most basic moves, kicks and punches. He made an exception to his rule of "basic but understood" by taking the time during one training session to show how to throw an opponent over their shoulder.

Selah tried one night back in her room, away from the dragons—Omar returned, leaving the girl shaking and trembling. After Farsight suggested she move her pillow and blanket into the dens after three consecutive nights wrapped in nothing but hay, the girl gave up and went straight to the dens when it was time for her to go to sleep. She saw no alternative that would provide her with rest.

Somehow, the news of Selah's brush with a dragonhunter assassin got out, and the girl found the inhabitants of Dragonhold staring at her with pity. The fact that she stayed in the dragon dens at night to ward off her dreams only made her seem weaker.

Selah excelled at her Korei training, partly because she took it so seriously. She was the third person to master the basic blows to Garrett's satisfaction. The girl returned to weapons with newfound confidence—she didn't look over her shoulder so often when she was walking down the halls.

Corith, her old nemesis, watched the girl enter the fief with narrowed eyes. He had left her alone after the Choosing, but continued to bear a strong dislike for her. A smile touched his lips as a thought came to his mind. "Roswald," he barked. The boy looked up from his water canteen. "What did the Dragonslayer call Selah when you were captured at Hadfoll?"

Roswald's eyes turned skyward as he searched his memory. "Abomination, I think." He shook his head. "She started bawling the minute he whipped out his sword. Why?"

"No reason."

*   *   *   *

Selah had stopped to admire *The Flight of Starcross* and was torn away from the mural by the terrible growl in her stomach. Dinner should be soon.

The girl traversed the corridor at a relatively slow pace; she had not heard the roar that announced the beginning of a meal, and she had no other place to go. The hallway was deserted.

A muscular arm wrapped around her neck, restricting her air. "Die, abomination!" hissed a voice in her ear.

Selah reached back, seizing a fistful of fabric. Her attacker was wearing a baggy shirt; rolling her shoulder forward, the girl yanked down, sending her opponent to the ground. Her other hand flicked the dagger into her palm; the girl tackled her attacker, who was struggling to stand.

One hand pinned his arm to the ground; the other brought her dagger to his throat.

It took a moment for Selah's mind to catch up with the actions of her body—when it did, she stared down at Corith's frightened face. The razor edge of her dagger was a hairsbreadth from the knot in his throat. It bobbed up and down as the boy swallowed.

"What are you doing?" Selah growled.

"Get your knife away from my throat!" ordered Corith in a voice much higher than his normal speaking tones.

"Dragonhunter!" the girl spat, refusing to comply with his demand. All along, he had been here, and she had never suspected him.

"It was a joke, I swear. I just wanted to scare you." The boy's eyes flickered from side to side like startled deer, and sweat curled on his upper lip. There was real fear in his eyes. "I'm no dragonhunter."

Selah saw the truth in his eyes, and realized the folly of her train of thought. Corith could not be a dragonhunter—no dragonhunter would ever be Chosen by a dragonet, and if they had, it would have changed them. Regardless, her former bully had shaken her for a moment.

She brought her face closer to his. "If you think coming up behind me is some sort of sick, twisted way to get your fun, I hope this has changed your mind." She brought her knife away from his throat, but close enough that the boy was uncomfortable. "Don't *ever* pretend to be a dragonhunter again. It's low, even for you." Corith, seeing that she wasn't going to hurt him, began to flush in rage. "Besides—next time I might not recognize you."

The unspoken threat hung heavy in the air, and Selah was surprised that the words had come from her mouth. She let him up, returning the dagger to her wrist sheath with a quick movement—Corith probably hadn't seen where she stowed the blade.

"I'll be informing the training master that you drew steel on me." Corith's eyes were crackling in rage. "That you threatened my life."

"Go ahead," snapped Selah. "While you're at it, tell him about how you didn't do a thing as I cleaned the floor with you. I'm sure Garrett will be impressed."

Selah turned on heel and left, her ponytail swinging from side to side as she walked away. Corith trembled in shame and rage. He whirled, catching the eyes of the maid who had stopped to watch the spectacle. "Get out my way, wretch!" he shouted as he stalked off. Selah did not give him a second glance.

✳   ✳   ✳   ✳

Throughout the evening, Selah considered the repercussions of her actions. She could be disciplined for drawing metal on a fellow pallon, but she only gave those consequences the briefest of consideration. Corith was stronger than she was—the boy had made a point of proving it to her before he grew bored of picking on her and had targeted other pallons who gave in to bullying. Regardless, she had thrown him and made him yield to her. The action had been instinctual—those hours of flipping the dagger in and out of her palm, the small gashes in her hands, had paid off.

She was quiet and thoughtful during dinner. When it came time for the pallons to turn in, the girl, rather than making her way to the dens, headed to her bedroom. She did not bother to retrieve her blanket and pillow from the dens— there was a chance that the dream, being away from dragons, would reduce her again to the weak child that was still a part of her. It was long after the crystal had dimmed to blue that her eyelids closed and stayed that way.

*   *   *   *

Omar had returned, as did those who he killed, each night, as they tried to save her. "We'll protect you, Selah," said Farsight. "You will have sound dreams."

Omar was coming closer, leering at the girl. She had seen it too many times and knew the inevitable end of this dream. Windchaser chirped on her shoulder, her friends and family drawing their weapons as the dragonhunter approached them.

"There are more Omars," announced the dragonhunter, as he always did. "They just don't all have the same name."

Selah flipped the dagger into her palm. It stayed there.

The girl stared in amazement, but her fingers had locked onto the blade and would not let it fall. Her body, even in dreams, remembered the long hours of practice that had peppered her palm with white scars that would fade in a few years.

Selah felt her legs churn in a run. Windchaser fell from her shoulder. Landon reached out to her as she ran past him. Flyn and Beda called for her to stop. Averon and Farsight stepped aside. "Remember your dragon!" shouted Aerin.

Garrett blocked her path. He did not attempt to stop her as she maneuvered around him and loped toward the dragonhunter.

Omar smiled, not bothering to draw his own daggers. Selah was racing toward him, sprinting. "Temper, temper," he said. "I'm not threatening you. You must get the rudeness from the dragon side of you."

The human inside her was terrified, but resolute. Her dragon soul had been waiting for this moment. She slashed downward, drawing a great golden line from Omar's shoulder to his hip. Her dagger glowed white-hot.

The violet eyes he had stolen from the Dragonslayer widened in shock. Selah stepped back, feeling the dream world begin to spin. Landon, Flyn, Beda, Averon, Farsight, Aerin, Garrett, and Windchaser faded into the blackness.

Omar stared at his wound. His face had twisted into a horrible grimace. "I'm not afraid of you," Selah shouted. The truth rang through her, and shut out the lingering traces of fear.

The dragon song roared in her ears. The chorus of dragons bore down on the dragonhunter. Omar listened, his face melting into anguish. "I'm not afraid of you," Selah whispered.

Omar shattered, exploding in a thousand glittering pieces of glass. They fell like rain to fade away into the blue-black cloth of Selah's nightmares.

* * * *

Selah woke. Her body was soaked with sweat, but it was the moisture of exhaustion, not fear. Windchaser swarmed over her, worried that the girl had suffered again from the dream. Selah shook her head, and the dragonet backed away, sensing that her Chosen needed space to breathe.

The dagger was clutched in her palm. Selah slipped it back into the sheath, staring into the darkness that shrouded her room.

"I am not afraid," she announced.

The shadows did not contest her.

STRIPE

Selah awoke to the sound of the watch dragon's roar. The girl rolled over, wincing as her neck ached. Her head was sore from sleeping without any support the entire night. Selah sat up, staring around at the walls of her quarters. She had done it. She had conquered her dream.

The girl wandered downstairs, feeling the gentle happiness that comes from pleasant sleep. She ate a hearty breakfast and actually laughed at a few of the jokes made by her fellows—Landon asked her later if she was feeling better. The girl nodded.

It was good that she had controlled her fear by this time—Garrett, rather than instructing them which weapon they would be studying that day, asked them to sit down. Previously, this had meant a lecture on what it meant to be a dragon-rider—now, Selah sensed that it would be something different.

"Some of you might remember the beginning of your pallonship," he began, each word punctuated by a white cloud of mist that streamed from his mouth. Winter was upon them—the pallons now wore overtunics during training. "I mentioned that there would be a large tournament at the end of your second year."

The pallons gave him blank stares. Garrett sighed. "Does the word "Dragon-games" strike a bell with any of you?"

This time, a few of Selah's year mates nodded. "Isn't that the tournament where all the pallons from different countries come and compete with each other?" asked Quinn, adding a quick "sir" when he realized that he had spoken out of turn.

Garrett chuckled. "Don't flatter yourself. The pallons are only a small part of the Dragongames—still, you represent the future of Dragonhold and I expect that you will show a bright one."

Selah's heartbeat sped for a moment at the thought of fighting in front of judges or, gods forbid, a crowd. Were they to be put on display like circus performers?

"Thousands come to Dragongames—it is almost as popular as the Jousts the knights hold on the spring and fall equinoxes. Many people will watch you; I don't have to tell you that impeccable behavior is mandatory."

But you will, Selah thought to herself, moving into a more comfortable position on the ground. Something told her that they would be sitting there for quite a while.

"There isn't enough time for each of you to participate in every event—too many thirteen year old pallons waving swords wildly at each other tend to bore audiences and watching dragonriders. Therefore, I will select a chosen few—five or six, depending on the competition—to represent the group as a whole. I will make my decisions by the second week in May. We leave for the capital in June—they are held in Tora this year. You have several months to get ready."

A soft burn of anticipation made nerves race up and down Selah's skin. She was afraid of making the groups, frightened of fighting in front of so many people; at the same time, she dreaded not being a part of the tournament. Her normally competitive nature, coupled with the fear and disdain of losing that came both from her experiences and her dragon characteristics, made images of glory and defeat play out in her mind's eye. She imagined the pleasure of watching a Lonian pallon submit as she defeated him with the blade, or the Doranians heaving exhausted sighs as she out shot them with their bow. The girl smiled, shaking the pictures from her mind with a physical action. Delusions of grandeur would do little to help her now.

"There is…" The man stopped, and the pallons looked at him with renewed interest when they realized he had ceased speaking. His brows knitted together into a frown. "I'll wait," he thought aloud. "That can wait until later."

Although the pallons dropped questions and hints for the next three hours, the dragonrider would not tell them what "that" was.

*   *   *   *

The pallons threw themselves into training with a vigor that had not been seen since they had first arrived. They had tempered themselves against defeat—no pallon was perfect, and each had suffered humiliation at the hands of a peer or Garrett himself. Failing in front of the others was no longer as frightening as Selah had once considered it, but losing before thousands carried a considerable amount of shame. Her fellow carried the same thoughts with them, and fought doubly as hard during practice bouts.

The pallons were not the only ones to be struck by Dragongames Fever. If the young Riders doubled their efforts, Garrett increased his demands threefold. A mistake that usually went unnoticed now prompted a stern glance or even a reprimand if the situation called for it.

They were two weeks into the New Year when Selah first attracted Garrett's notice. She was dueling with Renton, having already been dispatched in her bout with Landon, when she left a wide-open hole making a thrust that was flimsy at best. Renton took advantage of it, and Selah backed away with several bruised ribs.

"Stupid," Garrett described, arms across his chest in a gesture of disapproval. "I don't ever want to see you do that again. In battle, that kind of mistake means death. Am I clear?"

Selah nodded, tightening her hold on her sword hilt. She returned to the fray, taking another beating from Renton and managing to make Hale yield in her next bout. Her victory over Hale did little to ease her bruises, both of body and dignity. Garrett's words, a repetition of what she already knew, did little more than rub salt into her wounds.

The girl did not evade the training master's notice for long. Two days later, the dragonrider berated her again for her fencing. Selah had considered the sword to be her strong suit, but was reconsidering the thought with all the criticism coming from her instructor. Her best friend was the best sword fighter of all the pallons—after training, she asked Landon if he could give her some help.

The boy was happy to oblige. Rather than putting their swords away at the end of training, they retreated to a back courtyard and practiced more.

Landon was as good as some of the guards and reserve dragonriders—fighting with him was like performing an intricate dance whose steps were a mystery to her. Selah relished the challenge; she had to depend on every trick and block she knew to keep up with her friend.

Landon's blows sent waves of pain running up her arms. Selah, already tired from the day's training, tried to ignore the terrible ache in her wrists and dealt out her own blows. Selah's body was ringing with bruises from where Landon had punished her mistakes—she had only managed to hit Landon a few times.

The girl saw the opening—reaching forward, she hooked her blade around Landon's and wrenched upward. It was a disarming move that Flyn had showed her when she back at Domar; Garrett had only brushed on disarming moves, hoping that they would be able to defend themselves with a blade before they thought of disarming their opponent.

Only a quick jerk by Landon saved the boy from losing his blade. "Nice," he exclaimed, genuinely happy for her. Selah smiled as they returned to the dance.

Her good mood faded as they continued their bout—besides that one small instance, Landon beat her each time, blocked each strike. It was frustrating, and the girl was soon at her wit's end.

They stopped after a half hour of intense work. Dinner was soon, and the two needed to wash up beforehand. Landon complimented her as they returned their swords to the armory.

"Are you joking?" Selah asked. Landon, taken aback, did not respond. "That was terrible. I hit you three times. *Three times.* We fought for half an hour."

"That was the best I've seen you fence."

"Then I'll make a swell dragonrider, won't I?" Selah's cheeks were flushed with irritation at her own lack of ability.

"Stop feeling sorry for yourself," replied Landon in an equally dark mood. Selah's poor feelings were contagious.

"Easy for you to say. You're one of the best fighters here. None of the pallons can touch you. None of us had a father that could afford a personal instructor for his sons."

That crossed the line. Selah regretted the words the moment they exited her mouth. Landon had been evasive about his father, and seemed ashamed of his nobility for reasons that Selah could not understand.

The boy's mouth was a hard line across the lower part of his face. "I'm sorry, Landon. I didn't mean it like that."

"Yes, you did." The boy looked off into the distance. "The fencing instructor was my father's idea. 'Teach my son to fight' he said…'make me proud of my youngest son'." The muscle along his jaw tightened. "He never came and watched me, never bothered to see that I had made him proud. Too much work, running a fief."

The corner of Landon's mouth curved in a rueful smile. "He just wanted something to keep me from getting underfoot. Everything comes at a price, right?"

Fighting prowess for a father, Selah thought, wondering if she herself would make that trade. Her father had died when she was young—Bendian meant nothing to her besides a deep voice that sometimes graced her memories. Flyn, her father's best friend, had taken the paternal mantle and done well. She often wondered if her life would have been different if the man who had given her brown locks had raised her.

She returned her attention to her friend. Landon had been silent for a long moment. "You know what your problem is, Selah?" The girl, thrown off track by the sudden change of subject, tried to catch up with her friend's train of thought. "You spend so much time staring at your weaknesses that you never fully appreciate your strengths. You're in the first tier for everything besides pole arms. You can react quickly when someone startles you..." Selah looked at him curiously, and the boy gave a slight smile. "We all know about Corith and how you 'cleaned the floor with him'." Selah felt the blood creep to her cheeks at the remembrance of her heated words.

"You're in the first tier for everything," Selah protested.

"I also started wielding a sword at age seven. Five additional years of fighting every weekend makes a difference."

Selah didn't know what to say. "Just then, when you came within a horsefly's eyebrow of disarming me? That was the closest anyone my age has ever come to ripping a sword from my grip. Renton hasn't even come that close. Count your stars, Selah, instead of staring into the black places where you think there should be more."

Emotion hung in the air between them. Selah realized what Landon had been trying to tell her. She had heard his words for quite some time; only now was she ready to listen.

"Thank you," she whispered.

"You're welcome."

Selah swallowed the knot of feeling in her throat. They continued toward the fief. She smiled mischievously. "Horsefly's eyebrow?"

"It was all I could think of," Landon protested.

"You know, I think we're a horsefly's eyebrow from the fief."

"Funny. You can stop now."

Selah grinned. "I get it. You're a horsefly's eyebrow from being irritated."

Landon sighed.

✳   ✳   ✳   ✳

Time passed with a speed that was uncanny. Days turned into weeks and weeks turned into months. At the beginning of March, Garrett announced a new training program. "You all know that the Dragongames are soon," he began. They were in one of the indoor training rooms, as the snow had fallen another two feet the night before. "There will be many dragonriders there to scout out potential apprentices. It is vital that you try to impress the dragonriders. If you can pass certain tests, a golden stripe will be on the sleeve of your uniform."

Landon raised his hand. "What is the importance of a golden stripe?" he asked.

"A stripe signifies that you are one of the best pallons of your school. Each and every dragonrider school, no matter what the kingdom, must follow the criteria for awarding a stripe. It is a universal symbol for dragonriders: a message that *you* are worth watching."

Selah leaned forward in interest. Garrett had finally revealed the elusive 'that' from several months ago.

At excited murmuring broke out at this news. Garrett cleared his throat to get their attention. "Earning a Stripe is not an easy task to accomplish. The training for those that are Stripe-worthy is much harder than the normal training. The tests are difficult, and you must have mastery of your body and your weapons to pass them. There will be a screening test to select those that are ready to earn their Stripe. The others will try to reach that point."

Selah envisioned some sort of weapons test for the screening when Garrett led them to the great gate of Dragonhold. The man beckoned for them to follow, receiving several nods of respect from the guards on the wall top as the men lifted the portcullis. Several dragons also came along, looking at each other as if they knew something that the pallons didn't.

A mile's hike through the forest brought them to the river. It was not too wide, but a distance that would be a challenging swim. The pallons eyed it uncertainly. What were they supposed to do?

Garrett faced them, his back to the river. "I trust you all know how to swim," he began, motioning to the river. Several of the pallons blanched. "If you run into any trouble, the dragons will pick you up. I will be waiting in a clearing further along on the trail. You have two hours to reach me." With that, he mounted his russet dragon, Riveneye. The dragon's claws dug deep furrows into the soft mud of the riverbank as he took off, carrying the training master across the river and to the east. The pallons watched until the evergreens blocked the dragon from view.

Several of the pallons immediately jumped into the raging water. Selah stared across the river, blanching when she saw the two trailheads that disappeared into the forest. The paths appeared to go in different directions. Which trail was the training master referring to?

Already, the pallons in the river had to fight the current. Quinn, one of the weaker swimmers, was being dragged downstream. Selah didn't want to waste that much energy on just the swim—who knew how far ahead Garrett had flown?

Selah grabbed Landon's arm just as he was pulling off his boots. "Wait," she said, feeling the beginnings of an idea in her mind. "What if we run upstream so that the current will take us down to the trail? That way we don't have to fight it."

Landon nodded, grinning. "When did you get brilliant?" Selah frowned in mock annoyance as they tried to gather the others. Aswin and Roswald were already too far ahead to hear their calls, but they managed to catch Bern before the blonde pallon waded into the river. The three ran upstream a ways before diving in.

Selah gasped—the water was frigid from the spring thaw. A childhood spent in the cold lakes and streams of northern Domar had taught her that the chill would soon fade to the back of her mind—she sliced through the river, ignoring the liquid that filled her nose every time her head went under the surface. Her clothes were dragging her down, and it took all of Selah's self control not to panic.

Too late she saw the rock that jutted out of the water. She tried to swim ahead, but the rock slammed and scraped against her foot. A streak of pain blazed on the top of her foot, coupled with a throbbing in her ankle. Gritting her teeth, Selah forged onward until she could feel the bottom of the river under her feet. Landon was waiting for her at the mouth of the trailhead to the right.

"Selah, what happened to your foot?" The girl looked down. Blood flowed from a nasty gash at the base of her toes. She had shed her boots at the beginning of the trail, leaving her feet unprotected—the rock had taken advantage of her situation and slashed a deep red line across the top of her foot.

Her wet shirt clung to her skin. The fabric was tight against her wrist sheath, the white cloth revealing the brown leather beneath. Selah pulled her sleeve away from the blade; fortunately, Landon had been too busy examining her foot to notice.

"It'll be fine," she assured him, realizing that her foot would have to support her through the long run to Garrett's position.

Bern, by this time, had struggled out of the river. "Hurry." He jogged past them. "We've only got two hours."

The trail was rough. Roots rose out of the ground like veins on the hands of an old man. At times it seemed like a straight, upward climb. Selah's foot throbbed with each step. Stones cut into the soles of her feet, and the pallons often had to pause to remove thorns from the soft arches. She knew it was the same for Landon and Bern, although they never complained. Selah refused to let herself be the first to break.

The pace never slacked, although the sun continued in its march across a sky that was the same color as Windchaser's scales. They had stopped to rest for a moment when they saw Roswald walking back along the trail. "There is nothing up there," he said quietly. "Garrett tricked us."

Bern was trying to catch his breath. "It has been more than two hours," he agreed.

Selah shook her head. "We can't stop. If Garrett said that he was on the trail, he will be. I think we should continue on. If night falls and we still can't find him, I can call a dragon for help."

The mention of her abnormal abilities prompted an awkward moment of silence, which Landon broke with a sigh. "I am tired, but I have to agree with Selah. There must be something more to this than a simple race. I vote that we continue."

Roswald frowned. "I already told you, there is nothing up there. Why can't you believe me?" He did not bother to restrain the affronted snarl from his voice—if anything, the acid edge to his words only made his former friends discredit them more.

Bern shrugged. "We just want to keep going."

Roswald's face darkened. "I'm going back. If you were smart, you would go back too." With that, he pushed by them, deliberately jarring Selah as he walked by. The girl ignored him, wrapping the cloth from her belt pouch around her gash. It had worsened. She knotted the bandage gently. The boy had once been her friend—ever since Hadfoll, relations between the two had been strained.

They continued on, but their pace was much slower than before and they often stopped to walk or rest. From the mere glances of sunlight that were peering through the trees, Selah reckoned that they had been on the trail for a good four hours. Her limbs burned with every motion—she had to force herself to jog. The girl could not bring herself to think that they had possibly picked the wrong trail.

The trail wrapped around a small hillside, reaching the other side only to snake up a steep slope that was nearly vertical. The pallons stopped to size up their newest challenge. The trail was devoid of switchbacks—the only way to go was straight up. Selah wondered if the makers of the narrow path had somehow constructed it so in order to spite them.

Selah paused to unwrap her foot, struggling to brush the grime away without irritating the wound further. She winced unconsciously, the relatively small injury bothering her more than she would have given it credit for. Bern helped her tend it, his training-calloused fingers gentle on the aching gash.

Selah knew that the massive hill would not stop the others. The look of determination on Landon and Bern's face was enough to prove that they would not be turning back. Neither would she.

Landon looked at her lame foot in concern. "Will it hold?" he asked.

Selah nodded. She hoped it did, or she may come to a harsh meeting with the ground.

They began to scale the slope. The stones that had troubled them the entire journey were now so coarse and sharp she had to bite her lip to keep from crying out when she misplaced a step.

She was halfway up when her foot gave out. The girl pitched backwards, arms flailing in a futile effort to restore her balance. Landon reached down and caught her before she fell. The girl's heart was hammering like a hunted jackrabbit. Landon held onto her arm until she had rested a hand on a sapling for support. "We're almost there," he told her quietly. Bern had almost reached small lip of hillside where ground met sky.

Energy renewed by her near-fall, Selah scrambled upwards, grasping her friends' outstretched hands when she reached the top.

"I don't even want to think about the trip back," the girl gasped, resting on beautifully flat ground. Landon and Bern agreed.

"Did you two see Aswin at all?" Bern asked. He had been worried about his twin all the while.

Selah shook her head. "I tried to get his attention at the start, but he was already too deep in the river to hear me. Maybe he took the other trail. I hope he's having better luck than we are." The girl winced inwardly at her own mention of their lack of success.

An awkward silence lingered between the three for a moment. "We should keep going," said Landon. "I know it has been more than two hours, but I think that we should try to move on as fast as possible, just in case."

Selah moaned inwardly at the thought of jogging again, but nevertheless, they had to keep going. Despite how long they had been traveling, they had still not seen hide or hair of Garrett, nor the clearing that he promised to be in.

Landon spurred them to a jog, moving along the trail at a fast clip. Selah was beginning curse her training master when she felt sunlight on her face. "Isn't that a clearing up ahead?"

Bern turned his eyes skyward. "Lady Aria, let our esteemed training master be in that clearing up ahead, and I swear, I shall speak nothing but respect to my mother for the rest of my time in this world."

Selah laughed. They raced down the trail, heedless of the tree branches that whipped at their faces like the blades of enemies. They were so close. *Finally this gods-cursed trail is over,* Selah thought. *I wonder if we are the first.*

The clearing was empty. Long blades of tan and pale green grass waved importantly in the wind, crassly announcing that the pallons should be pleased by the presence of greenery alone. Ignoring the irritating tallness of the weeds, Selah scanned the clearing. Not a single sign of Garrett or his dragon. The pallons slowed to a stop, their disappointment tangible in the air around them.

Bern kicked a tree stump in anger. "He told us that he would be here," he snapped. "I'm tired, my clothes are damp, and we are stuck here in the middle of nowhere!"

"Don't forget about our feet," Selah added.

"And my hands," Landon continued.

"And we don't have any food."

"No fire," said Selah. Their accusations punctured the still atmosphere like arrows, dissipating in both volume and vehemence as a breeze carried the sound away.

"The wind is blowing."

"It might rain."

"We have no boots."

"We don't know where we are."

The pallons paused, realizing that they had run out of complaints. Ranting in the open air had eased the pressure of pain and exhaustion, lightening their poor moods. However much ironic, the girl felt much better after their tirade. Landon and Bern's expressions no longer seemed so hollow, and she sensed that they, too, had benefited.

The sky above the little clearing was darkening rapidly into night. Landon miraculously found a piece of flint in his belt pouch and they soon had a large fire going. The question of food was harder to answer.

"Anyone have a blade?" Landon asked. Selah whipped her dagger into her palm, ignoring the stares of her friends as the knife came from nowhere.

"Where did you get that?" demanded Bern. "I took my belt knife off at the start of the swim." They had not been watching her when she drew it and were unsure where the blade came from.

"I kept mine," Selah lied, chastising herself for revealing her dagger. Bern stared at her belt, narrowing his eyes when he didn't see a sheath. He opened his mouth, but Landon elbowed him in the ribs, and the boy quieted. Selah, grateful for his intervention, turned away to avoid further confrontation.

The pallons were too tired to actively hunt for any sort of food, so they had to settle for several handfuls of blackberries gathered from a nearby bush. While not filling, it was enough to placate growling stomachs.

The evenings were still cold in March, and Selah hugged closer to the fire. Her clothes had dried, but her unprotected feet were feeling the effects of the chilly air. The girl was rubbing her arms for more warmth when she saw the figure. A shadow crouched behind a bush at the edge of the firelight. It waited, trying to see how many pallons there were. The girl watched the oblong blackness from the corner of her eye, not wanting to betray her knowledge of its existence.

Selah stood. "I need to relieve myself," she told her friends, purposefully speaking louder than normal.

Landon looked up, a little bemused by the interesting announcement. "Okay," he said, wiping at the blackberry juice that stained the edges of his mouth. "We aren't going anywhere."

Nerves on the alert, she headed into forest but doubled back so that she was behind the shadow. She was much slower than normal; the need for secrecy, coupled with her pronounced limp, had cut down her speed considerably.

A man was watching Landon and Bern intently. Selah's lame foot brushed a rock and the girl bit her tongue to keep from crying out. Wincing, she crept up on the man and grabbed his arms from behind.

With lightning speed, the man threw her over his shoulder in a traditional Korei move. Selah was struck by the irony of the situation in midair—it was the same move that had defeated Corith. Selah breath was knocked out of her, but she managed to flip the dagger into her palm. "Landon, Bern!" she yelled, tripping the man with one of her legs.

As her friends raced toward her, Selah leaped up and threw a punch as Bern raced toward them with a burning stick from the fire. The hilt of her dagger struck the man in the face, but he seemed to ignore it and pulled her arm behind her back. Selah stilled, feeling his strength and knowing that he could easily break the limb if he wished. Bern's torch lighted the forest, and he stopped short of where they were standing. "What are you doing?" snapped Selah. "Help!"

Bern began to laugh, as did Landon. Selah was bewildered until she heard the man that had her in an arm lock chuckling behind her. She turned her head so that she could see her attacker.

Garrett was already beginning to develop a black eye from her fist and dagger hilt. "I have to admit, Pallon Selah, that I am impressed at your ability to sneak up on someone. The blow was also in good form."

The girl was mortified. "Master Garrett, I am so sorry, I had no idea it was you..."

Garrett cut her off. "No problem, Selah. I should have been more cautious. It has been a long time since anyone ever caught me when I wanted to remain hidden."

Landon was wiping tears from his eyes. He had apparently derived great amusement from her situation. "Why were you spying on us, Master Garrett? We were looking for you."

Garrett smirked. "You wouldn't have found me. I wasn't on the trail at all until I saw your fire."

The three pallons sat there with their mouths open. "Not at all? We ran all this way for *nothing?*" asked Bern, his voice rising in a pitch slip that they did not dare ridicule. Selah slipped her dagger back into the wrist sheath while the attention was on her friend.

Garrett shook his head. "You misunderstand me. I didn't fly Riveneye to look for pallons until after nightfall. You see, the whole point of this challenge was to find those who didn't turn back and return to the fief. You are the first of three fires that I need to visit, but you are the one of the farthest."

Selah opened and closed her mouth, wanting to speak but unable to think of anything to say. Her first thought was of the angry Roswald they had encountered on the trail. "What about the others?"

"Those who went back to the fief were sent back to their rooms. They still do not know that they have failed."

Landon was shifting from one foot to the other to ward off the cold. "Sir, if nothing else is required of us, could we return to the fief? We have not eaten since noon and Selah's foot needs to be looked at by a healer."

Garrett's face changed to that of curiosity. "What is wrong with her foot?" Selah showed him. It was already swollen with infection—she had not been able to dislodge all of the grime, and the wound had begun to fester. Gently, the dragonrider pulled away her bandage to reveal the cut that had not clotted entirely. Garrett sighed.

"When did you get this?"

"During the swim through the river, sir."

Garrett looked at her oddly. "All those who managed to get this far are spending the night at the infirmary, partially for healing and partially so that your friends don't pester you into telling what happened tonight. Have Master Talmud look at this. You might have bruised your ankle badly as well."

He whistled sharply. What Selah had taken as a large boulder in the darkness reared up and revealed itself to be a gray dragon. "Shadewing, could you carry these three pallons back to the fief?"

The dragon was huge, bigger even than Blackwing from Averon's Wing. Selah had to crane her neck back to get a good look at his face.—*I once carried two horses across a river. Three skinny pallons shall not be any difficulty.*—

Selah smiled at the thought. She had never considered herself as skinny, but she supposed that a dragon would see them that way.

Garrett nodded. "Thank you."

Selah wanted to thank the dragon personally and started to look for the spark. She stopped. She had opened herself up to Farsight, and lost the use of her eyes for several weeks. The girl didn't want to expose herself to such pain ever again. The risks were too great.

"Thank you," she said aloud as she mounted Shadewing's broad back. "It must have been a pain to sit here, waiting for us." She stopped, wondering how much of the pallons' conversations he had been privy too.

—*No trouble, little one,*—said the great dragon as he took off.—*Mind that you don't fall asleep and slip off my back.*—

Despite Shadewing's warning, it was hard not to surrender to the weariness in her limbs. Her eyelids were drooping by the time that they landed.—*Thank you, little one, for being grateful,*—Shadewing said as she dismounted.—*Too often we are taken for beasts of burden.*—

Several of the servants were there with blankets and changes of clothes from their rooms when they entered the fief. They were lead to the infirmary once they had changed.

The healers were ready for them. Selah was sent straight to Master Talmud. He shook his head at the gash.

"You were lucky that the cut was only this deep. Still, it is remarkable that you were able to run on this." The Master Healer smiled softly as he tended to her wound. "How is that you always end up with the bruises?"

Selah returned the smile. "I have a knack for it, I guess. The cut has gotten worse than it was," the girl said, thinking that if it weren't for Landon and Bern's support, she would not have gotten as far as she had. "Could I see Windchaser? I haven't seen her for a while, and she is particular about that."

Talmud nodded, retrieving a bottle from the cabinet, pouring some onto a rag. "This will sting," he warned, placing it upon her foot. Selah winced. The liquid burned at the cut, and Selah resisted the urge to pull her foot away.

"What is it?" she asked when he removed the cloth to get a clean one.

"Turin. It is the juice of the leaves that stings. We use it to remove infection. Turin is usually found on hillsides. It's a little bush that has almond-shaped leaves."

While Talmud was tending to her cut, more pallons had filed in. Pomeroy, Hale, Ennis and Aswin were one group, while Coyle and Corith came in together after them. Selah was shown a small room in the back of the infirmary where she could sleep away from the boys. A female adolescent dragon served as a chaperone, sleeping in front of the locked door.

The dragonets of the pallons had been allowed to come in and Windchaser was livid. She scolded Selah harshly for leaving her behind and for gaining several new cuts and bruises. The girl scratched the dragonet beneath the chin to placate her, smiling. "Trust me, Windchaser, I would have taken you, but I didn't get the chance."

The dragonet, satisfied with the excuse, huffed and curled up on Selah's pillow. The girl was beginning to think about sleep herself when there was a knock on the door. She opened to reveal Aswin, Bern and Landon. "Can we come in?" asked Landon. "We need to talk."

Bewildered, Selah let them in, explaining to the adolescent that they were her friends and that they just wanted to talk. The dragon nodded, lying back down.

Selah shut the down behind her. "What is the matter?"

Bern frowned. "Do you remember what Roswald said to us on the trail?"

"How could I forget?" said Selah, folding her arms across her chest.

Aswin sat on the bed. "From what Landon and Bern have told me, I got the idea that he wasn't too pleased with you. It won't help that we found Garrett."

"Well, that he found us," clarified Landon.

"We were trying to figure out how to deal with people that are angry with us."

"I thought that you would be an expert in that department." Landon's eyes sparked with humor.

"Very funny," Selah said.

"Seriously, when…at Hadfoll, the others, we…didn't accept you because you had hurt our dragons." Selah looked down, still feeling the past twinges of shame from the incident that had stemmed from the discovery of her dragon soul. "Now that we are in the Stripe group, we may in the small sort of situation. How did you deal with that?"

Selah smiled, trying to shake off her morose thoughts. "I waited until you would see me for what I was."

"What's that?" asked Bern.

"Selah of Domar. Changing yourself to please others does little but sacrifice what you are for the sake of what someone else wants you to be. Fight as well as you can. Don't pretend to be just like the rest of us. Landon, you fight like you're dancing when you have a sword in your hand. Aswin, I've never seen anyone run like you can. Bern, you could do back flips on a dragon in midair and not break a sweat. Don't hide that just because people like Roswald will glare at you over lunch."

Her friends seemed overwhelmed by her praise. "Thanks," they said at once, breaking out of their surprise to show their gratitude.

The pallons bid goodnight and returned to their respective beds under the watchful eye of the female dragon. Landon stopped at the door. "Selah...I have a question."

"Ask," said the girl, heaving Windchaser into her arms and propping the dragonet on her hip.

"Did you ever figure out *why* you had a dragon soul?"

The girl was taken aback by the question. "N-No. I didn't."

Landon seemed to sense that he had overstepped his bounds, and appeared to be on the verge of apologizing for the forward question. "I should go to bed," Selah said hurriedly to avoid adding more awkwardness to the situation. "Goodnight, Landon."

The boy sighed, and the girl knew he was chastising himself. "See you in the morning."

Selah slid into her own bed once she had shut the door, painful thoughts troubling her mind. Windchaser cuddled up against her, comforting the girl until she fell asleep.

*   *   *   *

Breakfast was very quiet the next morning. Selah sat with Landon and the twins, while Roswald sat with several other pallons, never even glancing in their direction. It didn't bother Selah at all—she had not been on good terms with the boy for a very long time. However, the twins were friends with Roswald, and seemed to miss his presence at their table. Glenn, for all his cheeriness, would never be a member of their inner circle, a group that now consisted of Landon, Selah, Bern, and Aswin. The group of close friends had shrunk with the Choosing and the year and a half that had followed.

Classes were also very subdued. All of her teachers gave the assignment for the night at the beginning of class and allowed them to work on it for the rest of the time. Selah suspected that it had something to do with what would happen at training today. Windchaser discovered Selah's inkbottle and became fascinated with the stopper. She spent an hour amusing herself by corking and uncorking the bottle. Selah put an end to it when the dragonet spilled the black ink all over her hide, covering the desk and her papers as well.

Selah foot was healing well, thanks to the Turin juice and her friends' reminders not to push herself. Still, she had a pronounced limp, and often had to lean against the walls to rest the aching wound.

During training, Garrett asked them to line up. Selah stood next to Landon as Garrett went up and down the row, an unreadable expression on his face. "Nine," he said quietly. "Nine out of twenty-two pallons earned the privilege to train for a stripe."

The pallons looked at each other in confusion. Those that had returned to the fief had no idea that anyone had found Garrett, much less nine of their classmates.

"Nine were persistent enough to stay out after dark. Only nine of you were strong enough not to give up and return to Dragonhold. Why was it only nine?"

Collectively, the group hung their head in shame. Garrett sighed. "Those nine who managed to pass the test, I congratulate you. For those who did not, I suggest that you push yourself harder in the future.

"From now on, Haldwen, the blacksmith, will teach you on Tuesdays and Thursdays. On those days I will train personally with those who are earning their Stripes. Will those nine follow me?"

Somewhat reluctantly, Selah broke out of line and followed Garrett, thankful that she had Landon beside her. She could feel the eyes of the other pallons boring into her back.

Garrett led them to one of the side courts. "The stripe isn't easy to acquire," he told them. "Your training will be harder than that of the others; you will be forced to accomplish harder challenges than the others."

Garrett pulled out the sword at his waist. "Most of you have proven yourselves to be fast learners—thus, we will be moving a bit quicker than the other group. For example, your peers are only required to show basic mastery of the sword to become an apprentice. You will have to fence from heights, in tight spaces, against multiple opponents. You will have to be able to disarm an opponent."

Landon and Selah grinned at each other from the shared memory. When the girl turned away from her friend, she blanched. It was a formidable amount tasks to accomplish—and this was only the first part.

Garrett instructed them to do some freeform against each other. Because of her wounded foot, it would have been foolish for Selah to try to fight—instead, the training master showed her some more advanced patterns that she could try. While her fellow pallons received critiques of their fighting style, Selah worked the patterns until her arms learned them, and she felt that she could do them in her sleep. She increased the speed until the sword became a blur in her hands and her shoulders ached.

It took several weeks before Garrett was satisfied with her swordsmanship. Fighting from a height was the hardest; even as Hale was bearing down at her with a blade, open air was several inches from her foot. It was unsettling, but Selah was able to push the height to the corner of her mind. She was the fourth to move on.

She was returning to the inner fief when she saw the apprentice walking beside the adolescent. The dragon had a limp that rivaled hers following the screening test. Each step looked laden with pain. Part of her wanted to reach forward and heal the dragon, take away its agony. She turned away. Her mind was her own, and she would no longer share pain with the dragons. There was too much to lose.

When Garrett showed the group their next challenge, the girl couldn't help but think of the trick riders she had seen at home. He mounted a barebacked warhorse, urging the gelding to a fast gait. It was only then that Selah realized that he held a longbow in his hands. The graying man balanced, rising slowly until he was standing on the back of the galloping charger. Sighting down the bow, he loosed an arrow, firmly imbedding it in the center of a wooden target. Leaping down, Garrett rolled on his shoulder to ease his landing. He rose, looking for all the world as if he had simply taken a stroll through the woods. "So," he said, straightening his tunic, "who is first?"

No one made a sound. Garrett scanned down the row. "Selah, why don't you take a shot at it?"

She opened her mouth to protest, but shut it quickly. Everyone knew that she was the worst horse rider. Pulling her bow from her shoulder, Selah swallowed the dread that was rising in her throat.

The horse looked back at her as she approached it, a wicked twinkle in its eye. "Don't even think about it," she warned softly, mounting with difficulty. *I'll get it to trot,* she thought. *We'll move on from there.* Selah was just about to dig her heels into the sides of the massive charger when Garrett smacked it on the flank.

The horse took off at a gallop, leaving Selah bouncing like a rag doll. *I've got to stand.* Steadying herself, she shifted her legs so that her feet were resting on the bony spine. The girl pulled an arrow from the quiver at her hip and put it between her teeth. Harder still was releasing her steel grip on the mane and rising. The horse rocked like a ship on a stormy sea.

With speed born of desperation, she snatched the arrow from her mouth and set it to the bow. Sighting, she loosed, hoping that it hit somewhere near the target. Her balance shifted back, and the tip of the bow dug into the horse's side.

With a neigh of fury, the charger bucked her into the air. Selah turned so that her bow wouldn't break against the ground. The girl landed on her back, the compacted dirt of the practice courts banishing the breath from her lungs.

Garrett strode over to her, his infuriating smile grating against Selah's nerves. "What kind of landing was that?"

Selah tried to speak, but all that came out was a weak cough. She could hear laughter; no doubt Corith was having a great deal of enjoyment at her expense. The girl forced air into her lungs and managed to say, "Bow."

"Yes, it is a good bow. I can see why you wouldn't want it damaged."

Selah nodded, coughing again. The laughter grew louder, accompanied by several mocking repetitions of "bow". Garrett bent over. "Anything hurt?"

Selah sat up. "My pride," she admitted.

Her training master chuckled. "It was quite a dignified ride. If nothing is broken, return to the line."

Selah walked back to Landon and the twins. Despite themselves, they were struggling not to laugh.

"Great ride, Selah," chortled Aswin.

Landon's smile didn't fit under the hand he used to hide it. "They'll sing about that one for centuries."

"You were supposed to hit the target, not the horse, Selah." Bern's eyes were dancing in merriment.

"Oh, leave me alone," she said, her breath returning to her. "I just can't wait until it is your turn." Their smiles melted like frost under the spring sun. It was Selah's turn to laugh.

After two weeks, Selah had managed to overcome her fear of the horse and struck the bulls-eye of the target and got to the ground in a passable landing.

Some others were not so fortunate. By the time that Selah and five others had moved on, the remaining few were still struggling to hit the target.

As the Stripe training grew more and more intense, the regular training that Selah did with the rest of the group seemed to tire her less. Soon, the Stripes, as they had come to be referred to, began to stay after training and work on the task that Garrett had set before them. Some of the other pallons came as well, hoping to get into the group contending for a Stripe, but most left after the first few sessions. Roswald was not among them. Selah couldn't say that she was heartbroken.

After the horse challenge, Garrett had them run two miles in a quarter of an hour. It proved to be the easiest challenge yet, as they had already been in top form from their earlier training. Nearly all of the nine passed the challenge on their first try.

Next, Garrett instructed them on perfecting their Korei, forcing them to do the same simple kicks and punches over and over until they were almost flawless. Intermixed with the Korei was simple acrobatics such as handsprings and flips, which could be extremely useful when falling from a height.

Windchaser took it upon herself to train as well. While Selah was focusing on standing on her hands to focus her balance, the dragonet trotted around the outside of the training yard, building up her endurance. When Selah practiced her right and left kicks on a dummy, Windchaser fashioned her own dummy out of a pile of spilled straw and went after it with vehemence, teeth and claws bared. It was a source of amusement for the Stripes and pride for Selah. At water breaks, Windchaser would return with her tail held high, bits of straw in her teeth. Often they were all that remained of the dragonet's dummy.

Despite the intensity of her training, Selah realized that she was truly happy at Dragonhold. As the weather grew warmer, the pallons would often go out to the fields to play games from their homes. Selah favorite was one that involved the players stealing a leather ball from each other and throwing it through a hoop that they had tied to a tree.

Days blended into weeks with all the grace of a flowing river. It was the middle of April before Selah realized that she only had a few months until the Dragongames. Hale had earned his Stripe after completing the last challenge, but no one else had. Time was running out.

Hale declined to tell everyone what the last challenge was. Apparently it was a private test between Garrett and the pallon. Nor did he say what the Stripe would look like.

Landon and Pomeroy were the next two to receive their Stripe. Landon was bound by a promise to Master Garrett and could not tell them what the final challenge was.

Two days later, disaster struck. One of the apprentices had taken his dragon out to the cliffs, eager to prove to his dragonrider master that he could fly. The pair had flown too close to the ground and had crashed.

The pallons paused in their training to watch as the dragonriders bore the apprentice and dragon into the fief. The boy was pale and unconscious from a head wound, but the dragonriders said that he would survive.

His dragon was not as fortunate. The beast's white scales were stained dark purple from the abrasions and gashes that the rock face had opened up in his hide.

Selah stared, distracted throughout training by the grisly sight. Talmud would save the pair, but they would carry the lesson with them for the rest of their lives. Selah was certainly convinced that her first flight would be far away from the rocks.

An hour later, one of the apprentice healers approached Garrett, standing up on her tip toes to whisper in the graying man's ear. The training master frowned. As if to clarify, the girl pointed Selah.

The pallon felt her stomach turn to ice. Garrett beckoned for her to approach, and the girl obeyed, her hands hanging at her sides. "They need you in the infirmary," said her training master, staring at her eyes to see her reaction.

Panic closed Selah's throat. "I can't," she stammered. "Why would…"

"Halde!" shouted the training master. One of the guards on the wall turned and saluted to the dragonrider. "Could you watch the pallons for me?"

Halde nodded beneath his helmet, making his way down the battlement steps. He did not press the training master for a reason to his absence.

Garrett led her to the infirmary. The normally quiet room was humming with human activity. Healers raced back and forth, bearing cloths, steaming bowls of water, bandages, jars of ointments and balms. Selah's insides curled in fear—they wanted her to heal the dragon.

Garrett brought her to Talmud. "You called for her."

Talmud looked up from the side of the dragon. The white was in poor shape—while dragon blood was thick and clotted quickly, there were enough cuts that the dragon was losing significant amounts of lifeblood.

Talmud's hands were stained with purple and red. "I can't save him, Selah." The situation had tossed normal courtesies to the wind. Titles and phrases of society were a waste of breath and precious time. "If he doesn't stop losing blood, Highbreeze will die."

"I can't!" exclaimed Selah. "Last time I healed a dragon, I was blind for weeks. I could die with this one!"

Talmud sighed, his hands pressing a cloth to one of the dragon's wounds. "I know, and I understand if you don't want to help him. Sometimes, a healer has a hard time admitting that death is going to win."

"I can't." Selah repeated. Her heart hammered in her chest. The dragon in front of her was dying—if she tried to heal him, she would die as well. There was nothing she could do.

"I'm sorry," Selah whispered. "I can't."

"I understand," comforted Talmud. As a healer, he knew her turmoil. "You may go now."

Selah remained in her place. Her feet had turned to roots that anchored her to the infirmary floor.

"Count your stars, instead of staring at the black places where you think there should be more."

"You could have killed every dragon in this fief."

"Use your dragon song—you will need it in the hard times to come."

"You bear the mark of Stormhunter, abomination."

"Gifts from the gods are too few and far between to cast them aside as useless."

"Did you think we didn't know you well enough to see that some part of you was always somewhere else?"

"You'll always be armed, and no one will ever know."

"You're different, Selah. Too different for just a year."

"Changing yourself does little but sacrifice what you are for what someone else wants you to be. Don't pretend to be just like the rest."

"Guard this child well—she will leave a great mark upon the world."

The chorus of dragons that sang her song twisted around her, clouding her head with the notes and chords that encompassed her being. Selah listened, her music filling her ears and blocking out all other sound. This is what it meant to be a dragon. This is what it meant to be a human. This is what it meant to be both.

Highbreeze's scales were cool to her touch. Selah placed her palms along each side of his jaw, listening as her dragon song coupled with the ragged breathing of the dragon. Leaning forward, she placed her brow against his.

The skin on her back broke as phantom edges drew a pattern that mirrored the scratches along Highbreeze's spine. Her lip trembled as abrasions appeared on the unmarred surface of her arms, as scratches carved into her legs. Gouges broke the symmetry of her face.

Selah bore the agony with hardly a whimper. Her knees threatened to give way, but the girl straightened a little to steady herself, a cry of pain caught within her closed mouth as the wounds along her back and stomach stretched and bled anew. Dark crimson began to stain her white shirt.

Selah opened her eyes and stared into the green irises of Highbreeze. The part of her that was far older than her years whispered, "Better now?"

The adolescent nodded. A bruise along her cheek made Selah's smile painful. The coppery tang of her own blood clung to the corners of her mouth. "Get some rest, okay?" The girl was unsure if she was talking to Highbreeze or herself.

The green eyes closed.

Selah rose to her full height. Garrett and Talmud were staring at her in amazement. The girl swayed for a moment, steadying herself on the table. Her new wounds throbbed, and blood from the scratches along her arms dripped from her fingers.

"He's okay now." Her voice cracked with emotion. The dragon's wounds had stopped bleeding—all that remained of the life threatening injuries were scabs. The flesh beneath the dried blood was healed.

Talmud reached forward, supporting the girl. He had a new patient. Garrett got out of the way, staring at the red lines that were spreading on Selah's shirt. The color was too dark to be totally human in nature. The training master stared at the deep purple bloodstains on Highbreeze's white scales and the deep red on Selah's white shirt. The patterns were the same.

Garrett sighed, staring long and hard at the floor. The training master, seeing that he could do no more to help, left quietly and unnoticed. He had a new story to tell his pupils when it came time to discuss courage and bravery. It meant much more than his last one.

*   *   *   *

Stormhunter was waiting for her when sleep came to infirmary. His rain cloud gray eyes were sad and proud at the same time. "You have come full circle," he said.

Selah could still feel the pain of Highbreeze's wounds, even in dreams. "I almost didn't," she replied. "I almost turned away."

"*But you did not turn away. And by doing that, you accepted what you have been fighting with since Hadfoll.*"

Selah could hear strains of her dragon song. "*I have a question for you.*"

"*Ask, but I may not give you the answer you wish to hear.*"

"*Why do I have a dragon soul?*"

Stormhunter's eyes were truly sad now, and seemed to even bear shame. "*You are my mistake.*"

"*Mistake.*"

"*When it comes time for the creatures of this earth to be made, the souls that are destined to be great are taken before the gods to decide what kind of being they will become. Some in Dragonhold have been under such review—the treatment given to those who will be more than a footnote in the pages of history. Of course, none of this is definite. These are souls that have the potential to create change, affect history.*

"*Most souls like this would be best suited for a particular species—human, dragon, griffin—but you, you were different. You could have been anything. The human gods argued that you should be a human, I and the other beast gods were for you being a dragon, although there was one god that thought you should be a rabbit.*" The dragon god smiled. "*One by one, the other beast gods consented that you could do much change as a human.*"

"*Good?*"

"*Gods do not differentiate between good and bad when reviewing souls. We can only see the ability to change when they are in such a complex stage.*

"*I continued to demand that you be a dragon, but I was overruled. You were to be a human, and were sent to the Seer to see where she would place you. In my folly, I thought to break all the laws of creation and tried to make you both—a human with dragon characteristics, the ultimate blend of the two greatest races to ever walk this earth. I reversed you—a dragon with human characteristics, a human mind, a human body. The Seer, her eyes so focused on the future, has poor perception of the present and could not see you for what you were and placed you with two brothers that had the same qualities for change.*

"*The rest, I am sure, you know very well.*"

Selah didn't know what to say, searching her thoughts. She was surprised, and yet, it made sense. The fact that she was among a threesome that had the potential to enact change upon the world was a sobering thought.

She felt herself beginning to wake. "*One more question, Stormhunter, please.*" The dragon god nodded. "*Why did Windchaser Chose me?*"

Stormhunter smiled and began to fade away. Selah repeated her question. "*Why did she Chose me?*"

The dragon god had blended with the blue-black of her dreams. "*Because she loves you.*"

Selah watched until Stormhunter was nothing more than a memory.

*   *   *   *

Garrett called the girl into his office the next day. She was coated in bandages, and the pain of many wounds that she did not earn. The man smiled ruefully when she entered.

"Congratulations, Selah. You've earned your Stripe."

Selah sat, her eyes closing once in pain when the chair pressed on her wounds. It would take her at least a week to fully recover. "Sir?"

"A dragonrider's heart is much stronger than his sword. You proved that your own is quite powerful yesterday. I have fought two Wars, and the bravery you showed is only rivaled by two incidents I have observed in twenty-five years of being a dragonrider."

Selah lowered her eyes. Her actions didn't deserve the praise. Garrett was taciturn as far as congratulations, and this was overwhelming after two years with only a handful of compliments.

"Every one of those trying to receive a Stripe has already met the criteria. I am waiting for them to earn it with their character. You have. There will be a gold stripe sewn into the arm of your Dragongames uniform."

Selah, sensing a dismissal, rose to her feet. "Thank you, sir."

Garrett shook his head. "No...thank you." The man sighed. "I had almost forgotten..."

"Forgotten what, sir?" Selah prompted when the dragonrider was quiet for some time. Garrett smiled.

"I had almost forgotten what courage looked like. Thank you for reminding me."

Selah left with a blush of embarrassment on her cheeks. Garrett exhaled slowly, propping his head on his hands. Closing his tired eyes, the man let comforting silence fill the room.

DRAGONGAMES

The old, aching wheels of the cart groaned loudly, and Deracian cursed himself for his oversight. He laid a steadying hand on the withers of a pack horse as the beast in the cart hissed.

His boot stuck in the mud left by the summer rains, and he took the time needed to extricate it to look back at his entourage. Five other men followed closely behind, riding or walking beside the enormous cart. There were no open sides—the cart's weathered surfaces were topped by a roof of reinforced steel. It had been smeared with dirt to make it look battered and windswept.

Deracian's gray eyes scanned the night for any indication that their movement was being watched. The other dragonhunters paused, waiting for his instruction. Impatient, he waved them onward—the closeness of the beast, and the ramifications of its discovery, had every one of them on edge.

The train of dragonhunters was fast approaching the walls of the capital, and their first test of the infiltration. If they were discovered here, they had no hope of carrying out the rest of the plan. Deracian slowed his pace until he was even with the side of the cart; the creature within growled softly. The dragonhunter lengthened his stride until there was substantial distance between himself and the beast.

His boots sunk into one of the last puddles of spring. Deracian's breath escaped through his teeth in a low hiss as water seeped between his toes. The man swore, running a hand through his thick brown hair to center himself.

The great walls of Tora were within a stone's throw now. Deracian nodded once to his dragonhunters to remind them of their role. The size of the cart alone warranted a questioning from the wall guards.

It was not too long before heralding voices confirmed Deracian's convictions. "Who goes there?"

Deracian cast aside his dark brooding and sank into the persona of a traveling entertainer. "Weston of the Wandering Ballads, gentle sir. I've come to make some money at the Dragongames." It was an easy excuse for the dragonhunters—performers came from across the continent to draw in the massive crowds that came for the Dragongames.

"What kind of wares you carry?" came the reply.

"Simple entertainment. My band and I can sing, dance, juggle, you name it." He gestured broadly to the men behind him.

They were nothing more than grunts, Hunters that had not yet earned their hides. Fighting men that were too impressive would do nothing more than draw attention. Nonetheless, all of the dragonhunters could perform on a stage if called on to do so—not a single piece of their charade could be lacking.

"What's in the cart?"

"Dancing bears…a few monkeys, if the bears haven't eaten them yet." Deracian forced his voice to carry a nonchalant humor that his real personality did not contain. One of the riders near the cart prodded a side gently—on cue, the beast within growled in a terrible rumble that could only be attributed to a large animal.

The guard, without the protection of daylight and other human beings up and about, was almost as eager as Deracian to keep the beast inside the cart. "Go right on through, sir. Good luck at the Dragongames."

"Thank you, and a good night to you, sir." Deracian kept the false smile on his face until they were under the portcullis and out of sight.

Only then did he turn to his men. "Stick to the alleys. We are going to the Doe Hammersmith and Armory. You've memorized the maps, I assume."

His men nodded fearfully. Deracian did not allow an inner snarl to show on his face—such open fright was disdainful in a dragonhunter. He would make sure to report his opinions of these men to their commanders. "One man at a time will walk at my side. The others will take to the side streets. I will escort the beast the entire way to the armory. Do not fail, or I will personally ensure that you wish you had never been born."

His men scattered without another word. Deracian urged the carthorses forward, pausing when the beast inside rumbled once again. The magic that kept it partially subdued would have to be strengthened when they moved the beast from the armory to the final position.

Deracian eyed the streets without betraying that he was doing so. The hour was so late that only the homeless beggars or moonstruck couples were wandering around. The dragonhunter looked back at the cart, hoping that the years and resources invested in this animal would not be wasted. Over a hundred bribed, conscripted, tricked, or tortured mages had contributed to its creation. He refused to see that destroyed by a careless mistake by him or his men.

Deracian returned to scanning the streets.

*   *   *   *

The few weeks preceding the Dragongames fled like the birds that were returning north. Selah eyed the sky with a churning stomach. Not only were the Dragongames a matter of pride for her masters as well as herself, dragonriders would be looking for prospective apprentices. She would prefer that a dragonrider chose her as his or her apprentice than have the Holdleader assign one to her when none picked her. The prospect of Sean selecting her dragonmaster was more than a little frightening.

Garrett chose the pallons that would be representing Dragonhold in their matches. "Archery—Quinn, Glenn, Renton, Aswin, and Selah. Boxing—Landon, Bern, Roswald, Coyle, and Corith. Fencing—Landon, Renton, Ennis, Selah and Hale. Pole Arms—Coyle, Bern, Corith, Hale, and Pomeroy. Wrestling—Nolan, Coyle, Corith, Roswald, Pomeroy. Korei—Landon, Selah, Ennis, Bern, Renton." The training master rolled up his scroll. "That's all. If you have not been named, it is not because you have not mastered each category, but that the five showed proficient ability."

Selah could hardly contain her excitement. She would be participating in three of the six competitions. The girl was grinning from ear to ear as she paired up with Ennis for fencing practice. Only the morose faces of those who had not been named tethered her high emotions—they would be representing nothing at the Dragongames.

Two weeks disappeared like the last snowcaps on the mountains as summer came into full force. Selah lay awake the night before they left for Tora, the capital. She had sent letters home to Flyn and Beda, inviting them to come to the tournament. Flyn had written back, accepting. The thought of her surrogate mother and father in the crowd brought a smile to her face. Despite the fact that she considered them as her mother and father, the two were friends bound together by parenthood—nothing more. Flyn was ten years younger than Beda. They made an odd pair.

She woke early the next morning—her excitement had cut her dreams short. The fief greeted her awakening with silence. The girl dressed in the quiet, her bags packed and ready to go by the time the watch dragon roared.

"Wake up, Landon!" she shouted, pounding on his door.

"Leave me in peace," came a muffled voice. Landon had buried his face into his pillow to ward off the sound of her knocking.

"Landon of Boran, if you don't get up, you'll miss the Dragongames!"

"Go away," was the grumbled reply through the wooden door. "Five more minutes…" Landon's 'five minutes' often translated into an additional hour of sleep if no one roused him further.

Selah grinned. "I'll let Windchaser in."

"I'm up, I'm up." After what felt like hours, he was in the doorway, a pack and Indio in his hands. He yawned, glaring at her though bleary eyes. "That was unnecessarily cruel." Selah laughed.

It took some time to wake the others. Aswin was even drowsier than Landon, and Selah actually had to send in Bern to wake him up.

Several Wings of dragons waited for pallons and Masters in the courtyard. Selah was assigned, once again, to Firegem. Aerin grinned when she saw the girl. "Gods, are you going to stop growing sometime soon?"

Selah, unsure how to answer, shrugged. She was taller than most of the other pallons, although she was sure that it would change when they hit their later growth spurts. She came up to Aerin's nose.

They mounted up, securing their bags to the saddles. Selah fingered her bow for a moment before she slid it into its protective leather cover, tying it next to her sword.

Selah turned in the saddle, taking one last look at the fief that had changed her from a youth with dreams to a pallon with a dragonet, a girl that was so much more than what she seemed. The sun had cleared the horizon, and the white-washed walls looked much as they had when she had first seen them, flying in on the back of Farsight.

This time, Farsight was in front of her, Averon lifting his hand to signal take-off. The dragons began to pump their wings, running into the wind as their feet left the ground.

It took them several days to make it to Tora. When they broke through the low flying clouds and caught sight of the city, Selah was speechless.

The largest city that she had ever seen was Ranvaile—Flyn had taken her there once as a small child. Tora was easily threefold the size of Ranvaile. The palace loomed over all the other buildings, save the great Tower of Mages located at the northwest section of the city. Selah thought of Kavan, surprised when she realized that she could think of her brother without hatred or disgust. The years at Dragonhold had enacted a great change in her.

As they drew nearer, the girl could make out a great amphitheatre, the home of the Dragongames and all jousting tournaments. The large, flat field made a suitable landing zone for several Wings of dragons. The dirt lifted in heavy clouds as the wing beats of the great beasts stirred it to life.

Like Dragonhold, the amphitheatre was a remnant of the Golden Age that Averon had first mentioned to her when she had arrived at the dragon fief. The amphitheatre had been constructed from stone—the hardiness of the material had allowed it to survive in the weather for this long. The seats were, essentially, stone steps broad enough to sit upon. A wooden barrier separated the stands and the field of churned dirt. Even as they dismounted from the dragons, menservants were raking the surface smooth for an even playing surface. The field was large enough to contain a joust, a duel, and an archery tournament all at once—Selah felt lost in all the openness.

At the far side of the stadium, a large gate defended a dark recess in the stone. The gate, constructed of ebony metal bars, seemed to be an opening into a chamber housed within the stone that made up the outside edge of the amphitheatre.

Selah tapped Aerin on the shoulder, inquiring as to the gate's purpose. The woman thought for a long moment before answering. "I think that leads to the old beast pens. Back before King Aefric's great-grandfather outlawed them, beast fighters slaughtered wild animals for the thrill of crowds. That pen hasn't been used in at least a century." Despite Aerin's reassuring answer, Selah could not tear her eyes from the gate. The ebony bars reminded her of a gaping mouth. Any words that issued from it would be dangerous indeed.

Servants rushed over to them as they finished dismounting. "Dragonhold?" asked one in a deep voice. Averon nodded, patting Farsight. The servant straightened his tunic of royal colors. "You made good time. Welcome to Tora."

Another servant beckoned to the pallons. "Follow me," he said in a timid voice, racing off like a startled deer. They barely had time to grab their bags and dragonets. He led them through the empty stands and into a large building that was just outside the amphitheatre walls. The air smelled of horses—a stable bordered the building they would stay in.

A woman greeted the pallons as they entered. She was plump, but had a homely smile on her face that Selah couldn't help but return. The woman bustled down a flight of stairs, expertly hopping over a black dragonet that had made itself at home on one of the steps. "Welcome to the Green Dragon!" she exclaimed, dipping into a quick yet elegant curtsy.

Selah admired the well-lit entryway, her nose wrinkling once at the foreign, pitchy scent of the hall torches. Windchaser chirped in pleasure. She had spied a servant carrying a load of shiny silverware, and longed to touch it. Selah shook her head silently.

"You are Dragonhold?" Before anyone could answer, the woman, who Selah presumed to be the innkeeper, continued on. "Yes, well, boys' dormitories are to the right." She looked at Selah. "Girls' are to the left, up the stairs."

Selah nodded her thanks, trying to keep her worry from her face. She had not spoken to a girl her own age in two years. *What am I going to say?* she wondered as she trudged up the stairs.

Just as the girl reached the landing, someone else was rushing down. They collided. "Watch where you are going, oaf!" snarled a feminine voice.

Selah looked down. A girl about her age lay sprawled on the floor. The elegant green dress she wore sharply accented her tawny eyes, which burned in affronted anger.

Selah was suddenly and uncomfortably aware of her white shirt and brown breeches. Did all girls her age wear dresses now? Unsure, she felt herself blush. "Sorry," she mumbled, reaching down to help the girl up.

The blonde didn't take it, rising with an ease that suggested strength beneath the dress. "I'm fine," she snapped. Selah, puzzled at the girl's open hostility, struggled to find a source of her irritation besides their accident. She remained confused.

Windchaser growled at the girl's tone. Selah shushed her with a look. "I apologize. I was…thinking."

"Really?" asked the girl incredulously, eyebrows raised in mock surprise. She shouldered past Selah, walking down the stairs. Trying to ignore it, Selah walked to a door that had hastily been adorned with a sign that read 'Ladies'. Allowing herself another soft sigh, she pushed open the door.

The "dorm" was about the size of one of her classrooms, bunk beds lining the walls. In the center of the room was a circle of girls, all with dragonets in their laps. They all turned at the sound of the door opening.

Selah felt blood rush to her head, coloring her cheeks a rosy pink. "Uh…hello," she stammered, hand still on the doorknob. She had faced down two dragonhunters, but speaking to people her own age was beyond the measures of her calm composure.

One of the girls rose from the circle. "Did you just get here?" she asked kindly, her face framed by long brown curls. When Selah nodded, the girl continued. "My name is May. What is your name?" Her blue eyes held no scorn, merely curiosity.

Selah swallowed. "I'm Selah of Domar, from Dragonhold." A peep at her feet reminded her that she forgetting something. "This is Windchaser."

May smiled and pointed to a black shadow on her shoulder. "This is Swift-wing."

"Should have been named Lamefoot," muttered a voice from behind her. Some of the girls in the circle laughed, a high-pitched, false giggle that made Selah want to clap her hands over her ears. May's face deteriorated, the smile disappearing.

The speaker was the girl in the green dress, standing behind Selah, who was still in the doorway. Selah looked back at her, and the girl smirked.

Selah opened her mouth, and faltered. When she had fought with boys, it had been with punches and physical pain. This war of words was a battle that she had little skill in. Jesting with Landon and her friends had always been that—jest. She had no idea how to use her words to enact the same pain that blows could.

"Leave her alone," she finally said, settling on a simple command.

The girl laughed, raising her eyebrow at a few of her cronies. "It speaks!" The giggle came again, and Selah gritted her teeth. The girl returned her attention to Selah. "If you're not guarding the door, I suggest you get out of my way."

Selah didn't move. "Apologize."

The girl sighed. "I don't want to muss up my dress. You aren't fit to clean my boots, much less order me around. Just move, *now*."

Selah felt the dragon side of her stir at the insults. This girl irritated her more than anything the boys had ever said to her. The words, so quick to her tongue when jesting with her friends, finally arrived. "I'd comment on your dress, but that wouldn't be in the spirit of friendly competition." Selah's hazel eyes were terribly serious. "I'm not moving until you apologize, and I doubt you could make me." She eyed the girl's dress. "Probably trip on that skirt of yours."

Selah didn't like the nasty tones that covered her words, but there was nothing she could do to take them back now. Her opponent glared at her. "If the password is 'I'm sorry', I suppose that will do."

Selah, seeing that she would get nothing more from the girl, let her through. Selah turned back to the circle. May was gesturing for her to sit. Depositing her things on an unclaimed bunk, Selah sat down. Windchaser approached Swift-wing, inviting the black dragonet to come out and play. As Swiftwing came out from behind May, Selah watched for the "Lamefoot" that the girl in the green dress had mentioned. It didn't take her long to find it; there was a pronounced limp in the left hind foot.

"Selah?" asked May, snapping her out of her inspection. The girl smiled. "Thank you," she whispered.

"No problem," Selah murmured back, glad to have found a kindred spirit. "What is her name?"

"Vanessa."

Most of the girls in the circle were pleasant, smiling to Selah and introducing themselves. Windchaser, reflecting none of her Rider's shyness, trotted out to meet the other dragonets. "When do the Dragongames start?" Selah asked.

"Tomorrow morning," May replied. "After the Ceremony and the Naming."

Selah had never heard of either of the two. "Ceremony? Naming?"

"The Naming is where they introduce us to the public," explained another girl.

"Public?" croaked Selah incredulously. She had thought the fighting would take place in front of a small crowd. 'Public' sounded like a population, not an audience.

"I'm so excited!" continued the girl. "There's going to be a dragonet foot race, and well, everything! After we're finished, the apprentices go, and then the dragonriders."

Selah saw May's face fall at 'dragonet foot race'. It only confirmed her suspicions of Swiftwing's lameness.

The girl was still talking. "Weiss made the fencing for apprentices."

"Who's Weiss?" asked another girl in a coy tone.

The first girl blushed. "Well…"

Selah, not particularly interested in the conversation, let her mind wander.

The woman who had greeted them at the doorway poked in her head. "Lights out," she said cheerfully. "You'll need the rest."

May drew her aside as the others were getting ready for bed. "Thank you for standing up to Vanessa for Swiftwing. She gets teased because she has a lame foot."

Selah smiled. "Don't worry. She has the personality of a porcupine." Her tone, while not condescending, sounded too much like a reassuring mother for her taste, and Selah covered her words with a simple smile.

May returned the gesture, hoisting Swiftwing to a more comfortable position in her arms.

*   *   *   *

A sharp rapping on the dormitory door woke her the next morning. "Get up," called the innkeeper. "The Ceremony begins in an hour and a half. I have your uniforms, so come get them." Selah was the only pallon from Dragonhold, so she received hers from the innkeeper relatively quickly.

She pulled on the dark breeches, admiring the fine make. They were strong, but not coarse against her skin. Next came a shirt, white as new snow, which was tucked into her breeches. A golden stripe, running from the outside edge of her right arm to her neck, was sewn into the loose shirt. Her Stripe. Selah smiled, examining the thick belt that came with her uniform. Three vertical stripes were right next to the buckle. Two, blue and silver, represented the colors of Domar, her home. The third was Dragonhold crimson. The pattern was repeated on the other side of the buckle. Selah arranged her sleeve so that it would not reveal the wrist sheath she wore. Lastly, the girl pulled her hair in a ponytail—hers was higher than the other girls' because of the weeks she had spent tying them above a bandage around her eyes.

The innkeeper looked her over. "You do look right smart. The dragonriders asked me to have the pallons wear their swords, so go put yours on."

Selah buckled on her blade, fingering the sheath. She would be among those fighting with the weapon. Her sword, wielded by her hands, would represent the fencing prowess of Dragonhold. She hoped that she did not fail.

Windchaser whistled in admiration for the fine uniform, making Selah laugh. May had finished putting on her uniform as well. The girl was clad much the same as Selah, but for lighter breeches and a blue overtunic. "Where are you from?" asked Selah, realizing that she had neglected to learn May's birthplace.

May smiled, shifting her grip on Swiftwing. "I'm from Donus. It's a fief in Doran," she explained, naming a country to the west of Alcaron.

"I'm from Firemount," said a haughty voice behind them. Vanessa sneered. "It's the *better* fief of Doran."

"Shut up, Vanessa," snapped May, her cheeks reddening.

Vanessa, like May, had an overtunic, but it was a fiery red, true to her fief's name. Her white shirt had a red stripe down the right sleeve. The girl caught Selah looking and presented the stripe to the pallon. "What do think? Nice Stripe, huh?"

Selah crossed her arms across her chest so that Vanessa could take a good look at her own Stripe. "Indeed."

May, who had no Stripe of her own, blushed, and Selah thought of her new friend's feelings. "Just go away, Vanessa. I'm not in the mood right now."

Vanessa seethed at the casual dismissal. "Trust me, speaking to you is beneath my status. It will be my pleasure to part company." With that, she stalked off, not without a parting snap from her violet dragonet. Windchaser growled, but her Rider shook her head. The dragonet retreated to Selah's shoulder, grumbling.

∗　　　∗　　　∗　　　∗

The Ceremony was not what she thought it would be. King Aefric spoke a few words, the three Princes at his side. "You are privileged to watch the future in action," the King said, addressing the audience. "For these pallons *are* our future. Support them, for they will someday support and protect you. Let the Games begin!"

The Naming went in alphabetical order, with Dragonhold, the host fief, going first. At last it was Selah's turn.

"Selah of Domar and her dragonet Windchaser!" cried the Herald. Selah walked forward, bowing deeply to the audience, as the others had done. "Selah of Domar will participate in the Archery, Fencing and Korei competitions." Rising from her bow, Selah looked the section of the stands reserved for the family of the contestants. After a moment of searching, she saw them; Flyn and Beda waved to her, proud smiles on their faces. A broad grin on her own face, Selah returned to her place in line.

Once all the pallons had been named and introduced, the opener was announced: the dragonet foot race. It was a long lap around the outside edge of the field, with small logs for the dragonets to jump over. It wasn't hard to explain to Windchaser the idea of it. Already, there was a competitive gleam in her eye.

The pallons moved off the track, sitting on the benches that had been brought out for them. Selah sat next to Landon and May, strangely nervous for her Chosen.

With a bellow from the dragons on the field, the race was on.

Windchaser broke ahead of the group. The training she had taken upon herself when Selah was earning her Stripe was apparently paying off.

Selah's gaze turned to Swiftwing, who was lagging farther and farther behind. As the dragonet neared the first jump, Selah and May held their breath. Landon whispered softly to Selah, "She won't make it."

He was right. Swiftwing didn't get enough height and landed on the log, taking her full weight on the lame foot. The black dragonet shrieked in pain. May's eyes filled with tears and she hid her face in her hands.

Selah turned back to Windchaser. The dragonet had stopped, allowing the others in the race to pass her. Mewing softly, she trotted back to Swiftwing.

"What is she doing?" wondered Landon aloud.

Windchaser stood at the black dragonet's side, using her shoulder to get her to her feet. With Swiftwing leaning heavily on her, Windchaser headed toward the finish line.

Selah barely heard the scattered cheers for the dragonet that had won. All of her attention was focused on the two dragonets so far behind the others. When they came to the next jump, Windchaser carried the lame dragonet on her back, spreading her wings so that she wouldn't lose her balance.

Painstakingly slow, the two dragonets made their way around the track, matching each other step for step to the finish line.

The applause resounding through the amphitheatre was deafening. Selah and May raced down to the track to meet their dragonets.

Selah scooped Windchaser up into her arms, her eyes misty with pride. She wouldn't have been happier if her dragonet won the foot race by lengths. Windchaser trilled loudly, seeming to understand that the applause was for her benefit.

Selah felt a tap on her shoulder. A man stood behind her. She recognized him as the herald.

"Your dragon may not have the fleetest foot, but it certainly has the biggest heart. In all my years of heralding, I have never seen anything of the like. I wish the two of you well." He gave her a nod of respect and disappeared into the crowd.

Selah watched him leave, smiling. Windchaser gave a modest peep from her arms. Landon joined her, Indio clambering onto his shoulder. "What was that about?"

Selah shook her head. "Oh, nothing."

Without warning, she was engulfed by a massive embrace from behind. "Caught you," growled a familiar voice in her ear.

"Flyn!" she cried. The guard captain grinned at her.

"Gods, look at the size of her!" exclaimed Beda. She had never been a tall woman, and now looked up to Selah's considerable height.

Landon looked uncomfortable now that her family had arrived. "Should I go?" he asked her quietly, ready to leave.

Selah frowned. "Of course not. Flyn, Beda, this is my best friend, Landon of Boran." The smile that Landon gave her was worth a thousand words.

The herald's voice pierced the air. "Pallons and their dragonets, return to your training masters!"

"Sorry. Duty calls." Giving both a kiss on the cheek, Selah followed Landon to where Garrett was standing.

Flyn sighed, looking at Beda. "I wonder if she'll ever have to say that…"

"…and mean it," finished his friend. They watched their charge cross the amphitheatre with contemplative expressions.

Garrett paced in front of the Dragonhold pallons. "Attention!" he barked. The pallons moved as a unit, planting their feet shoulder-length apart, arms clasped behind their backs. Selah knew it by heart from the countless drills they performed before they left for the Dragongames. Even Windchaser was at attention, feet together and gazing at Garrett. The dragonets thought it was a game where you had to be as serious as possible in order to win. Windchaser hardly moved at all when she was at attention.

One by one, each of the schools came to attention. Selah noticed that other schools had different stances than Dragonhold. Firemount snapped their heels together and held their arms stiffly to their sides.

The first event was boxing; the pallons retreated into the stands, leaving Garrett, Landon, Bern, Roswald, Coyle, and Corith to face the wrath of the other schools. Selah sat with Aswin, cheering loudly when their friends were announced to the audience.

The herald explained the rules to the crowd and the pallons. "The training masters will judge the pallons based on blows with the fist. The winner will receive five points for their school. A loss will result in elimination. The pallon that remains undefeated at the end of the day will earn an additional five points for his school."

A circle was drawn in the middle of the field. The first match was between Bern and a pallon from Donus, chosen randomly. Bern left the field with nothing more than a slight bruise on his cheek—the Donus pallon staggered off with a bloody nose.

The next Dragonholder to go was Roswald, who won his bout on a matter of points. All of the other pallons from Alcaron won their matches—Selah's throat was already sore from yelling encouragement.

Coyle lost his next match because he struck the opposing pallon moments after the herald instructed them to stop. The judges disqualified him. The boy stalked back to the bench that had been dragged out for the participants, looking as if he would explode if anyone came near him.

Both Corith and Landon went on the sixth round. Landon lost his match, but Corith went undefeated, bringing in extra points with his victory. Selah couldn't help but feel a little jealous as her former bully became the hero of the moment.

Firemount was in the lead at the end of boxing, despite the fact that Corith had won. Dragonhold placed third, closely following Donus. Selah listened as the herald announced the next day's challenge. "Well done to all pallons who participated. Tomorrow will be Korei."

The apprentices came out next, and the pallons stayed to watch. Selah hated to admit it, but the apprentices were not as good as she thought they would be. Corith could have easily beaten some of the representatives from Dragonhold.

The tournament broke for lunch—Landon, one eye swollen and purple, treated them all to sugarbread sold by one of the merchants. The cinnamon and sugar coated pastry tasted like cloud in her mouth, and Selah licked her fingers thoroughly after the bread was long gone.

The dragonriders were worth the wait to watch. The ages ranged from fighters in their twenties to veterans of their forties and fifties. There were a few dragonriders she recognized from the fief, and she cheered for the ones whose names she knew. Dragonhold, once again, did not win, but made a solid place in second. The fief, with the combined efforts of the pallons, apprentices, and dragonriders, was situated in third, behind Firemount and Donus.

By now, the sun had sunk low in the sky. The pallons were not allowed out of their inn after nightfall—bidding her friends good night, the girl headed back to the Green Dragon. The boys were staying to find their families—Selah had already greeted Flyn and Beda and promised to meet them later the next day.

May met her halfway. "You didn't tell me that you were going to be in three of the events," she said. "I only made it into one."

Selah shrugged. "Well…" she trailed off, unable to finish her thought. They continued on in silence.

"Thank you," the girl said suddenly.

"For what?" Selah asked, somewhat bemused.

"For what Windchaser did. During the dragonet foot race. That was really nice of her."

"Well," Selah scratched behind Windchaser's ear, "Windchaser's like that." The sky blue dragonet murmured at the compliment, rubbing her head against Selah's arm.

May returned her attention to the ground in front of them as the sun sank low in the horizon. The Green Dragon was relatively empty, although the girl's dorm was fairly full. Selah sprawled across the cot that was her sleeping quarters. She could still taste the faint traces of sweetness from the sugarbread at the corners of her mouth.

"Selah," whispered May. The girl opened her eyes, turning her attention to her new friend. May pointed to the corner of the room.

Windchaser had discovered the remnants of the dinner that had been served to the room and was eating the scraps with the ferocity of a pig. The dragonet, her head submerged in a bowl of gravy, was blind to the fact that she had drawn the attention of her Rider. Her back facing Selah, there was no way that she could see her.

Get out of there! shouted Selah mentally. Windchaser scampered away from the dishes as if the cutlery had turned white-hot. The other dragonets in the room started—unwittingly, Selah had opened them to the order meant for her Chosen alone.

The girl, hoping to mask the strange behavior of the dragonets, frowned at Windchaser. May's eyes were wide, and Selah could almost see the conclusions that were rapidly forming behind them. "It's you!" she exclaimed. "You're the one with the dragon soul!"

The room became deadly quiet. "Selah of Domar!" cried Vanessa. Selah smelled trouble. "I wondered where I had heard your name before." Apparently, news of her dragon soul had spread to other dragonrider communities, if not entire kingdoms.

"I'm flattered that you remember me," Selah snapped. All the other girls were staring at her as if she had sprouted horns that dripped with poison.

"Tell me, Selah," Vanessa crossed her arms across her chest, "how did you come to get a dragon soul?"

Selah did not reply. The answer, even if she respected Vanessa enough to give it, was too personal of information to share with others. She was unsure that she would be comfortable telling even Landon the circumstances of her creation.

"It's easy to see that you're part dragon," Vanessa continued. She had pounced on the delicate subject like a rat terrier on its prey. "Your looks give you away."

Selah ignored her, unbuckling her sword and placing it on her bunk. Vanessa continued to goad her. "Maybe the dragon blood makes you stupid, and you can't talk. What's the matter? Did your mother have some kind of fling with a dragon, and you're afraid to admit it?"

The girl whirled, her hands balled into fists. "Get your foul mouth off my mother. Just because you're an illegitimate child doesn't mean everyone else is."

Vanessa blushed. "I am *not* illegitimate," the girl snarled.

Selah lifted her hands, palms outward, in an unthreatening gesture. "You brought it up. I don't want to talk about this anymore, and, I'm assuming, neither do you."

The girl's dorm was filled with silence and stares that night. Selah was the last to drift off into an uneasy sleep.

*   *   *   *

The next day's event was Korei. It was the first contest that Selah would be participating in—Landon, Ennis, Bern, and Renton would be competing against the other schools with her. Selah woke with nerves racing up and down her spine—she had almost forgotten the awkward events of the day before when the other girls woke and washed their faces without looking at her or speaking. Selah ignored them, leaving the room as soon as she had her uniform on. She left her sword; she would be fighting weaponless today. The girl did not remove her wrist sheath—she had learned her lesson with Omar, and made sure that her sleeve concealed the blade.

Selah was the first out the door, brushing past the innkeeper as the woman announced that it was time to move out. She bounded down the stairs, eager to see faces that would not stare in silence.

Her friends met her relieved expression with eyebrows raised in bemusement. "Have a nice dream?" asked Aswin.

Selah lowered her voice as the other girls came downstairs behind her. "I am so happy to see you all. The girls found out about my dragon soul."

"Ah," said Landon. "That could be awkward."

"Very," replied Selah.

Bern threw his arm around her shoulders, having to stand on his toes to do so. "No worries, Selah. We'll always stand by you."

The girl laughed. "Thanks. I'm moved, really."

The banter with her friends quickly lifted her spirits—not even May, kind as she was, could replace the camaraderie that she shared with Landon and the twins. Still, the Korei match loomed, and Selah's stomach began to twist into knots as they entered the amphitheatre.

There were people, but they were pockets of humanity scattered amidst the mostly empty stone steps that served as seats. After the opening ceremony, most of the audience did not come until the dragonriders, after lunch. Still, Selah was grateful for the people that had come to watch the pallons.

Once again, the pallons were brought to attention, and those who were not competing that day were sent to the stands. This time, Selah was on the other side of the wooden barrier that separated the crowd from the field.

Selah took a seat on the bench, between Landon and Bern. Renton and Ennis were on Bern's left.

Garrett stood in front of them. "Korei, in any sort of contest like this, demands that there are no weapons on the field. I need your belt knives." He went down the line, gathering the blades from the pallons.

He stopped when Selah gave him her belt knife. "The other one as well, Selah."

Selah hesitated, reluctant to give up her only defense. Garret extended his palm. "No one will try anything while you are here. You have no need for it during the tournament fights."

Selah flipped the dagger into her palm, offering it to the training master hilt first. "How did you know I carried a blade on my wrist?"

"The night you attacked me in the forest. I do have some observant qualities, Selah of Domar."

The girl blushed, averting her eyes as her fellow pallons stared at her. Landon seemed to know, or at least, was kind enough not to look at her wrist. Bern had been born without any sense of tact and asked, "You had a dagger on your wrist?"

Selah shook her head. "I'll explain it to you later, Bern." She felt exposed and vulnerable without the security of a blade at the ready. The girl thought of the dragon song to calm herself.

The first bout was a pallon from Firemount against a pallon from Broadriver. The two, while skilled, were nothing extraordinary, and Selah felt her mind wander through the next three bouts.

Renton was the first from Dragonhold to be called. He defeated his opponent from Alderstand with ease. The other schools, Firemount, Broadriver, Alderstand, Seacove, and Donus, did not have as extensive Korei training as Dragonhold. Part of Dragonhold's Korei experience stemmed from the assassination attempt on Selah, and the measures that Garrett had taken to be sure that none of the pallons would ever be in her position.

Selah's name was called. The girl rose, rolling her shoulders to relieve the tension that had been building since the beginning of the day. Anticipation sparked at the tips of her fingers.

Her opponent was a stocky boy from Seacove. "Begin!" commanded the herald.

Selah hung back, trying to get a measure of her opponent. He rushed forward at the sight of her hesitation, his fist curled into a ball.

Selah sidestepped the punch, delivering a sound blow into the Seacove pallon's back as he staggered past her. He turned, catching her on the shoulder as she danced away. He charged again. Selah's leg snapped out, catching him in the chest in a blow that made the crowd groan in sympathy for the Broadriver pallon.

They sparred for several more minutes, but Selah's skill at unarmed combat was superior. The judges named her the victor.

Selah returned to the benches, greeting the cheers from the Dragonhold section of the stands with a broad grin. It felt good to have a victory under her belt.

Selah's second fight drew more reactions from the crowd as she employed the same move that defeated Corith in the hallway—her opponent managed to get behind her, and Selah threw him over her shoulder with a force that left the boy momentarily stunned. Selah returned to the stands with five more points— Omar's scars did have their silver lining.

Her third fight proved to be her last. The boy from Alderstand seemed born into unarmed combat—although Selah put up a good fight, he was better than she was, and the judges awarded him the victory.

Selah trudged back to the benches with a sadness tugging at the corners of her mouth. Her friends instantly comforted her. "Don't worry about it," said Ennis. "I didn't make it past the second round."

Selah felt slightly better—none of the other Dragonhold pallons made it past the third round as the expert pallons from the other schools came out of the woodwork. Alderstand won the competition, bringing the total pallon rankings to be Firemount, Donus, Alderstand, Dragonhold, Broadriver, and Seacove in last place. Selah and her benchmates frowned. They thought they had put forth a decent effort, but there it was, Dragonhold in fourth. They dropped down a ranking.

It was a slightly subdued group of pallons that greeted those who had fought that day. Some even bore expressions of displeasure when the five who had participated in the Korei returned to the crowd.

Selah joined the other four as they went to retrieve their belt knives from Garrett's care. The training master returned them. He handed Selah both of hers with a sigh, watching with a gentle sadness as Selah slid her belt knife into the sheath and tucked the other into her sleeve. She felt much more secure.

Landon tapped her on the shoulder. "There is a meeting in the stables during lunch. Apparently, the others aren't happy with how we did today."

Selah sighed. "Excuse me if I don't leap for joy at the thought."

*   *   *   *

Selah was surprised not to see Garrett waiting with the others at the stables. When she asked Landon about his absence, the pallon shook his head. "I guess this meeting was arranged by us," he supposed. "Master Garrett probably had nothing to do with it."

Hale started the meeting once all the pallons had sat down. "So, we are in *fourth* place. I'm not really content with that. Is anyone else?"

Everyone shook their heads, some yelling out cries of dissent. "We have good archers and fencers," offered Landon. "Those events get more points than the others. And there is the final Battle of the Schools at the end of the competition."

Selah pulled a piece of hay apart, running the fibers through her fingers. "It doesn't matter. We fought terribly today," snapped Roswald. He knew that three of his former friends had competed that morning, and looked at them to see their reactions.

"I didn't see you fighting today," argued Selah. "Easy to criticize when you're sitting on your backside in the stands, getting fat on sugarbread."

Roswald frowned. "Watch your mouth, Domar. You didn't make it too far today in your rounds."

"Watch your own, Roswald." Landon's emerald eyes crackled with irritation. "She's right. We are trying. You didn't even make it past the first round in boxing yesterday, so I don't know why you're yelling at her."

Roswald flushed at the mention of his defeat. "We can't all be perfect like you, your nobleness."

"Then why are you asking her to be?"

"We all know she's your girlfriend, Landon, but you don't have to defend her like a buck during mating season."

Landon started forward, seething in rage. He paused as he felt an iron grip on his upper arm. "Let it go, Landon. If Roswald has to resort to petty insults to argue with someone, that's fine with me." Selah released her hold on her friend. "We're all a little tense right now. Tomorrow is pole arms. Those fighting tomorrow, we have some catching up to do. Those watching, perhaps some quiet is in order, or constructive advice. It's stupid to start attacking each other and make beating us that much easier."

She leaned back against the bale of hay. An awkward silence filled the stable. Even the horses stilled their nickering and quieted. "Sounds good," finished Hale hastily. "Good luck, everyone."

The pallons nodded, and hurried to leave the area. Selah was the first out the door.

*   *   *   *

Everyone was asleep by the time Selah returned to the Green Dragon—she had wandered about the streets of Tora for hours, avoiding both the eyes of the other girls and the gaze of her friends. She thought she had done well, but Roswald's words sent a stirring of doubt through her. Thankful for the reprieve from confrontational and fearful glances, the girl fell asleep quickly, comforted by the cooing lullabies of her dragonet.

Windchaser let her voice fall silent as Selah's breathing became steady. There always seemed to be a sadness within the girl that even her own dragon song could not banish. If she could, Windchaser would scratch and bite until everyone left her beloved Selah alone. Unfortunately, the dragonet had come to understand that the world was not that simple.

The air of the room was pleasant, heavy with the sweet aromas of perfume. Touching her muzzle gently to Selah's still cheek, the dragonet dropped her head until it rested on her paws. One of the other girls, a brunette from Firemount who had been tossing and turning for hours, finally swung out of her bunk and pried open the window to cool the dormitory.

Windchaser closed her violet eyes, letting her other senses explore her surroundings. A horse from the stables whinnied into the night, drawing a huff from the stallion in the paddock. Equine scents drifted over the dragonet. The brunette from Firemount began to snore as dreams overcame her.

A gentle breeze wafted in through the open window. A new smell, heavy with musk, made Windchaser's nose wrinkle. It was a living scent, terrible and...beast like. Windchaser's heart sped with instinctual fear.

The dragonet uncurled from the tight ball that was her normal sleeping position, dropping from the bed to the floor with a soft thump. Checking to make sure that Selah was still asleep, Windchaser padded across the wood slats of the floor. It was no small matter to hop to the windowsill, but Windchaser managed with a few well-timed flaps of her wings.

The night was peaceful. A bloated half-moon hung overhead, casting a dim glow on the city of Tora. Secluded as the inn was, Windchaser could only see the adjoining stables and the great outside wall of the amphitheatre. The paddock ran up to the outside of the inn—the stallion, intrigued by a pair of violet eyes gleaming in the darkness, approached her, nickering softly. Windchaser snorted at the horse, scornful of the pitiful creature with hard feet and no wings.

She returned her attention to the wind. The breeze came again, hot air billowing from the mouth of the stadium. The scent of the animal fell over her—it was acrid, dank, and foul to Windchaser's nostrils. The dragonet narrowed her eyes, venturing her head out the window to better determine the source of the scent.

A low clattering returned her attention to the ground. A large cart, drawn by two of the hard-foot creatures, ventured around the corner of the amphitheatre. Five men were gathered beside it, their footsteps making no sound against the ground. The brutish odor streamed from the cart, washing over Windchaser in a fetid wave.

Windchaser snarled at the cart, chattering the dragon spoke language. One of the men looked up at the dragonet. She batted the air with unsheathed claws, threatening him as best she could. Even her child-like mind could understand that these people were not friends.

The man hastily gestured to one of the others. His companion began to chant terrible words that made Windchaser tremble inside, his hands moving in gestures of magic. Breaking through her fear, the dragonet forced out a sound that would be a roar if she was fully grown.

Abruptly, the cart disappeared. Windchaser's eyes narrowed, peering at the place where the small entourage had been. There was nothing. A low rumble stirred in her throat, the dragonet's wings stiffening to make her seem bigger than she actually was. For a long while, Windchaser stared into the darkness. The cart did not return.

After an hour at the window with no sign of the group, Windchaser left the windowsill and joined Selah in sleep, convinced that she had driven away those who could mean her Rider harm.

Not even her keen eyes could see the two lines that curved around the outside of the amphitheatre. The lines, resembling wagon ruts, traveled across the gate and into the stadium as a phantom cart rolled across the field. Five sets of human footprints accompanied the pair of lines like guards, alternating on each side.

*   *   *   *

Selah woke early, preparing for the next day of the Games while the other female pallons were asleep. Windchaser did not rise early as she usually did, lines of exhaustion drawn on her sleeping face. Selah was especially quiet as she waxed her bowstring, not for the sake of the girls, but for her dragonet.

By the time the other girls had risen, Selah was out the door, a sleeping dragonet cuddled in her arms.

As she sat at the Dragonhold bench, waiting for the others to come, Selah's thoughts turned to her dragonet. The beauty of her shining scales put the pale morning sky to shame. Once again, the girl was struck by the emotional bond that had formed between them. Love didn't seem to be an appropriate word for what she felt for Windchaser. The girl wasn't sure if such a word existed.

Selah watched the sun mount higher into the sky as the pallons arrived. Those from Firemount were there first, Vanessa avoiding Selah's gaze, whether from fear or hatred for what she was, the girl couldn't tell. Perhaps both.

Landon was the first to arrive from Dragonhold. "Good morning," he said pleasantly. He would not be fighting that day and bore no weapons. Indio was curled up on his shoulder, yawning loudly.

Selah smiled. "Morning."

They passed a moment in comfortable silence, content to listen to the world wake. After a while, Selah spoke.

"Thank you, for yesterday. I appreciate the support." Selah shook her head as more of the female pallons arrived. "They think I'm…strange."

"Who's 'they'?"

"The other girls."

"Do you really care what they think?"

"No, but—"

"Never say 'but' when you're trying to convince someone of something. It erases everything you say earlier in the sentence." He craned his neck forward so that he could see her face better. "You *do* care."

Selah rubbed her forehead. "I'm not sure why, but I do. I don't want them to…it's…." she trailed off.

Landon scratched behind Indio's ears. "You want them to accept you." Selah nodded. Landon shrugged. "They will."

"How can you be so sure?"

Landon grinned. "You're a very acceptable person. A little rough around the edges, but acceptable." Selah returned the gesture, letting the smile erase the poor feelings that always seemed to follow an encounter with the other girls.

The pole arm contest went fairly well—Dragonhold did better than it had the day before as Coyle, Bern, Corith, Hale and Pomeroy showed their mastery of long handled weapons. By the end of the day, the pallons had pulled Dragonhold back into third place.

Selah stayed with the other pallons to watch the apprentices and dragonriders—she saw a member of Averon's Wing on the field but could not remember his name.

May, once again, met her halfway back to the Green Dragon. "I'm sorry—about revealing you in front of the others."

Selah frowned. Her patience with the girl was somewhat strained after the incident in the girl's dorm. "Why were you so surprised?"

May turned her head to the ground. "I didn't want you to be."

"What?"

"What you are."

Selah locked her jaw. "You say that like I'm some sort of..." she swallowed, refusing to use the word that the Dragonslayer had labeled her with, "monster."

May was silent. "Look," Selah began. "You probably don't have half of the right story. If what I am got all the way to you, in Doran, it doubtless got warped out of proportion."

May frowned. "You can't kill dragons?"

"No," Selah growled. "I can't."

"Can't conjure great winds and pain?"

"No."

"Go into wild fits of rage?"

"What do you think I am, mad? I can take on pain—I don't deal it out unless I lose control, and I've only done that once. I can mind speak and touch minds. That's *all*. No madness, no dragon rages, no murderous urges. I'm like you. Just...a little different."

May brightened. "Why didn't you say so? We all thought you were feral."

Selah's mood only darkened at the girl's cheery words. One corner of her mouth curved in a rueful smile that had no backing of humor. "Glad I left a good first impression."

$$*\qquad*\qquad*\qquad*$$

Deracian paced back and forth in the dank chamber. The hot, heavy breathing of the beast reverberated against the stone walls that boxed them in like a cage.

The other dragonhunters watched him pace. The grunts had been replaced with Dragonslayers—having sneaked into the city in pairs or groups of three, they had escaped detection and, one way or another, made their way to the final position.

Deracian eyed the multicolored scales of the Dragonslayer's armor. The muscles and hard, lean bodies of fighting men bulged under the gleaming hides.

He stepped over the tail of the beast in his pacing, unafraid to do so—the weight of chains and sleeping spells kept it motionless against the stone blocks that made up the floor of this place. The dry, arid smell of dust and age old air still clung to the corners of the chamber.

Deracian had shed his cloak in the heat of the room and ran a hand over the midnight blue dragonscales that coated his arm. "How did you earn your hide?" asked one of the less intimidating Dragonslayers, his face betraying his genuine curiosity.

Deracian closed his eyes for a moment, letting the memories take him back. "I laid traps on the bank of a river, in the reeds. I put snares in the water and waited for days. A dragon came to drink from the river." He shrugged; the rest of the story was obvious without saying so.

The Dragonslayer that had asked the question chortled. "You didn't fight it in battle?" When Deracian shook his head, the dragonhunter raised his eyebrows. "And they still gave you the rank of Dragonslayer?"

"I ran in five Hunts before that," Deracian protested, removing his glove to reveal the armband with five different scale colors. All participants in a Hunt got a bit of the hide—only the dragonhunter that made the killing blow was permitted to make armor from it. "I had also performed espionage for the Highslayer; the rank was justly rewarded."

"If you say so."

Deracian, eager to change the subject, turned to the commander of the Dragonslayers, a black-haired colossus with sun lines beaten into his face. There were several colors of hide woven into his armor—he had disposed of more than one dragon in his lifetime. The accomplishment was one to be respected, if not revered. "You are sure that no one can hear its breathing?"

The colossus nodded. "We hung blankets and furs several feet from the entrance—they should muffle the sound. One of our men is in position outside; he will tell us if he can sense anything."

Deracian nodded. "I will stay with the crowd for the next few days. The Highslayer named me as the messenger—I must be away from this place when the final battle begins."

The Dragonslayer smirked, a cold expression that was without humor. "I'm sure you must, little Slayer. We shall handle the fighting while you cower in the safety of the crowd."

Deracian bristled, but knew it would do no good to act on his anger. He resumed pacing as the Dragonslayers' laughter echoed through the chamber.

*   *   *   *

Over the course of the evening, May convinced some of the other girls that Selah was safe to talk to, and she actually had a few conversations with them. The following morning dawned much more optimistically than the previous one.

It was archery that day—Selah would be competing. The bow had once been her strong suit, but had been set aside as her focus when the sword had become more important to her. Regardless, her vision had returned to be clearer and sharper, even though she still had trouble discerning from similar shades of color. She was one of the best archers of the school.

Selah made her way down to the amphitheatre. By this time, most of the Dragonhold pallons had arrived, and the Dragongames were soon to be under way. Garrett appeared out of nowhere, bestowing advice on the pallons that would be shooting that day. "Make sure your breathing is steady…watch your stance…aim with both eyes open."

Before Selah knew it, the King had called the Games to order, imparting the same "Let the Games begin," that started each day of competing.

The targets were thick, wooden disks stood on poles. For the first shot, they were a good thirty paces away, but nothing that Selah couldn't handle. With each shot, the disks would be moved back another ten paces.

"Hit the inside three rings, or the pallon is out. When the pallon is finished, points equal to the number of paces of their last hit target will be awarded to their school. Archers ready…begin."

Selah took a second to aim and fired, smiling as the arrow buried itself into the bulls-eye. Looking around, she saw that none of the Dragonhold pallons left for the benches; Quinn, Glenn, Renton, Aswin, and herself were still in the running.

Their hitting streak continued up to sixty paces, when Renton coughed just as he shot. With each new target, more and more pallons walked to the benches, although Dragonhold was maintaining their four archers.

It soon became clear who the real archers were; Alderstand, a small but skilled group of born archers. None of them had missed yet.

By ninety paces, only a handful of pallons remained. Selah and Quinn were all that was left of Dragonhold. Three of the Alderstand pallons remained, one from Donus, and two from Firemount.

Once they passed one hundred paces, Selah knew that she was stretching her limit. She managed the second ring, but Quinn hit the outside ring. He was out. "Good shooting," she told him as he left.

Quinn sighed. "Good luck. It's just you now."

Selah looked around. The two from Firemount were gone, and the one from Donus had missed the target completely. All that remained was a single pallon from Alderstand. He wore his sandy blonde hair long, cutting it off at the top of his shoulders.

Selah shook out her arms as the groundskeepers moved the target to one hundred and thirty paces. The enormity of her responsibility as the last one left struck her suddenly, and she felt some apprehension as she looked at the distant target.

Time seemed to slow. *Breathe steady.* Selah raised the bow. The target seemed to sharpen in focus.

Selah loosed her arrow. It flew, too fast to see, and buried itself into the second ring of the target. Silence filled the amphitheatre. Then the Alderstand pallon swore, his arrow in the farthest ring toward the outside.

The cheers that burst from the Dragonhold benches sounded like a great roar. The pallons swarmed Selah, smacking her on the back and laughing out loud in triumph.

Selah was too caught up in the elation of her victory to do anything more than stare at the ground. Windchaser danced through the maze of feet to scamper to the top of Selah's head, trilling her pride to the entire world.

She wandered in a daze back to the benches, surrounding her cheering peers, quieting as they listened the new standings. With Selah's victory and their combined efforts, they had overtaken Donus and were now in close pursuit of Firemount, with only thirty points difference between them.

The herald blew his trumpet, signaling the end of the Dragongames day. Archery competitions for the apprentices and dragonriders required different targets, willow wands, and other things that could be put off until the next day. Landon tugged Selah's sleeve. "Let's go to the markets and celebrate. They have shops for everything here."

Selah nodded, still feeling slightly stunned. After grabbing their coin purses and changing out of their uniforms, Selah, Landon and the twins went to the shops.

Never had Selah seen such an array of items being sold. Everything imaginable, clothes, swords, sweetmeats, bread, jewelry, even horse and dragon tack, were on display. Whenever Selah would stray toward anything that she didn't need, Landon would gently pull her back, reminding her to save her money for the wonderful armories that filled the city.

Selah was glad for his advice. The famed Steelforge armory was located near the stadium, and Selah was amazed at the quality and precision of each weapon. She was also stunned by the price.

Selah settled for a fine set of sharpening stones. It was all that she could afford, although Landon bought a fine dagger. The twins did not spend their money. The pallons were examining a display of magic-attuned gems when a commotion distracted them.

A boy raced through the crowded streets, blindly shoving people out of his way. A loaf of bread was clutched to his chest like a treasured prize. Just a few steps behind the boy was a burly shopkeeper flailing a riding crop in the air.

"This be the last time ye steal from me, boy!" the man snarled, seizing the boy roughly by the shoulder, smacking him across the face with the crop.

Selah moved forward like a cat, belting the man across the nose. Shocked by the new attack, the shopkeeper reeled back, holding his nose. He glared at her. "Wretch!"

A steely glint had commandeered Selah's eyes. "Don't you *ever* hit someone like that," she growled, fists clenched in anger. Landon and Bern snatched the boy as he tried to disappear, a bruise already beginning to form on his cheek. His eyes, smoldering in hatred, held no tears, despite the pain the pallons knew he must be in.

"Don't get betwixt that varmint and me," the shopkeeper advised. "That un's stolen too much from me booth, an' I means to fix it." He pushed Selah roughly away and moved nearer to the boy.

Selah grabbed the front of the man's dusty shirt and slammed him into the side of a shop. The man winced, surprised by Selah strength.

"Apparently you can't hear me. I told you not to touch him." Selah's voice was cold and harsh. The twins looked at each other in amazement, surprised by the intensity in Selah's voice.

"Hawk?" called a young voice. A boy several years older than Selah and Landon raced to the boy's side, dressed in a tattered pair of breeches and shirt, similar to the first boy. Selah returned her attention to the man in front of her.

"Your name."

The shopkeeper struggled against her grip. "Hugo, Hugo the Baker."

"Hugo, you will never, ever touch this boy again, or any other like him. Do you understand me?"

Hugo spat in her face. She slammed him into the wall again. "Now do you understand?"

Hugo nodded painfully. "Good." Selah released him. She pressed a copper into his palm. "This should cover the cost of the bread." The girl turned away, walking back to Landon and the twins.

The shopkeeper could not leave and keep his face with his fellows. With a roar of rage, he lashed out with his fist, catching Selah across the cheek. She responded by hitting him in the stomach, driving the wind from his body. The chubby baker crumpled to the ground, clutching his abdomen. "Guards!" he shouted. The armored men only laughed.

One of them bent down and regarded the baker. "You deserved that, Hugo. Let them go."

Sighing, the girl left, her friends dragging the two boys behind them, ignoring Hugo's shouts of shamed rage.

Once they were far enough away that they could no longer hear the vicious shouts of the baker, Selah turned on the two boys. The youngest withered under her gaze. "Ma'am, I weren't stealin' fur fun, 'onest. I was 'ungry."

"Wasn't," corrected the older boy automatically. "Thank you for helpin' my brother. Hawk...he...well..."

The younger boy, Hawk, was staring at Selah in awe. "'Ow'd you learn to fight like that?"

Selah laughed. "I learned at Dragonhold. What's your name?" she asked, looking at the older boy.

He smiled timidly. "Robin."

"Where are your parents?"

"Don't have any. I've been looking for work, but no one wants to hire a boy off the street."

Selah's eyes were sad, but did not contain pity. "My name is Selah, and this is Landon, Bern and Aswin. We're from Dragonhold, in for the Dragongames."

Robin's jaw dropped in awe. "You're a dragonrider?"

Landon chuckled. "No. We're just pallons. You know, I'm sure you could find some food and a place to sleep at the Green Dragon."

Instantly Robin's face darkened. "We aren't looking for charity."

"I'm not saying that you'd get any. The innkeeper is a nice woman. I'm sure she would let you work off your meals."

Robin sighed, looking at his brother, who was gnawing at a corner of the bread eagerly. "All right. If this is some kind of trick, I'll stab you before you can make another move."

"I doubt you would find it so easy." Landon's eyes held an unspoken warning.

He drew Selah aside as they returned to the inn. "What made you attack that baker?"

Selah's hazel eyes burned intensely. "I'm training to be a dragonrider so that I can help those in need. I may as well start now. Besides, people like him make me sick."

Just as Landon predicted, the innkeeper fell in love with the two street children instantly. "Look at you," she cried, eyeing their rags. "You must be freezing." Selah declined to point out that it was the middle of summer.

Robin drew himself up. "Ma'am, I am prepared to work for food and a place to stay, if you have any room. The stable loft would be fine for us…"

"Stable loft! I'm not going to let two young men such as yourselves sleep in the stable loft. No, you shall have a nice bed, the both of you."

Selah saw a hint of a smile creep into Robin's eyes. Hawk was too blown away by the rapid reversal of their future to say anything—he just stared at the inn with wide eyes, gnawing on his hunk of bread.

The innkeeper caught sight of the small loaf. "Is that all you have to eat? Here, I'll get you a decent meal. Caldin!" she yelled, calling her husband. "Get these boys some food and clothing."

With a parting smile from Robin, the boys were ushered into the kitchen, disappearing down the hallway.

Selah started up the left staircase, the one that led to the girl's room. "Wait," called Landon. She stopped, turning slowly to face him. "That was a brave thing you did today. For all you knew, that man could have been an ex-soldier."

Selah smiled. "Thanks. See you tomorrow." She hurried up the stairs, leaving Landon behind her.

✴   ✴   ✴   ✴

The next day's event was wrestling. She did not compete and enjoyed the break from the large amount of pressure the day before. However, Nolan, Coyle, Corith, Roswald, and Pomeroy were competing, so she pulled on her uniform and prepared to cheer them on.

The pallons had taken the awkward confrontation in the stables to heart—the wrestlers pulled Dragonhold up even closer behind Firemount. Only a few points separated the two schools now.

Her throat sore from cheering on Dragonhold pallons, apprentices and dragonriders, Selah returned to the Green Dragon. Most of the other female pallons ignored Selah, and she they. They told stories of their homeland, and Selah couldn't help but listen in.

"Sometimes, we can get snowdrifts up to a horse's chest," said May, on the subject of winters.

"Winter is the safest time of year," Selah heard herself saying. The other girls turned to stare at her, but May gave her a surprised smile. Selah swallowed, then continued. "When the snow clears, the pass is open and Cydran bandits try to raid Hillshire and the other towns. Summer is the worst."

"Have you ever killed anyone?" asked a girl from Firemount. The others in the room leaned forward in interest, and Selah was tempted to launch into a wild story about how her dragon side had made her go into a murderous rage. Shaking her head, the girl opted for the more honest, but boring, side of events.

"No. I've been close to men when they died, and sometimes were the reason for their death, but I've never actually killed anyone."

"Were they simple bandits?" asked Vanessa with a trace of a sneer.

Selah shook her head. "They were dragonhunters. I...got lucky. Twice." She didn't want to tell them about the Dragonslayer's bright violet eyes or Omar's bloodstained teeth. The dream was a painful enough memory that she wanted to keep it buried in the dark recesses of her mind.

There was a touch of respect on Vanessa's face. "Dragonhunters?" Selah nodded.

Vanessa was the first to break the silence that followed. "I've slain a man." Her gaze seemed to turn to her memories. "There was a raid on a village I was visiting. He ran into my sword. I'm not sure that he deserved to die."

Selah propped herself up on her elbows. "You did as any dragonrider would have done. Think of how many more innocent people would have died if you hadn't stopped him."

For an instant, something like a smile passed between them. Then Vanessa turned away, looking down at her purple dragonet.

May yawned. "Well, I'm going to turn in," she said, crawling into her bunk. Selah too, closed her eyes as the other girls began to turn in. As Windchaser curled up in her customary place at Selah's chest, the girl drifted off into dreams.

*   *   *   *

Selah woke early, as was customary for her. Gently moving Windchaser to the side, Selah swung her legs over the bed, pulling on her uniform. Remembering that today was the final competition, fencing, Selah buckled her sword to her belt.

This time, Selah waited for May to be ready, choosing to walk down to the amphitheatre with her new friend. May smiled when she saw the reason for Selah's delay, Swiftwing trotting at her feet. "Thanks," she said as they walked down the stairs. Selah grinned.

Landon was waiting for them at the track. "Morning," he greeted.

"Morning," Selah answered, unable to contain a yawn.

"Hope you're not that sleepy during the matches today." Selah grinned to show that she, too, was trying to wake up. Landon noticed that Selah had a companion. "How are you, May?"

The girl blushed. "Fine, uh, good." She colored even deeper after her awkward answer.

For a moment, Selah was bewildered by May's behavior, and then she grinned inwardly. May had what Beda liked to call a "crush" on Landon. Now that she thought about it, Landon was attractive, as far as boys went. Still, he was her best friend, and Selah thought this new occurrence was extremely humorous.

Once Landon had excused himself to retrieve Indio from a food cart, Selah elbowed May, raising her eyebrows. "What?" whined the girl, blushing.

"You like him."

"Yes, he's a nice sort."

"More than that."

"Oh, Selah, be quiet. I just think he's...well...nice." May's blush turned an even deeper shade of red. Selah decided to stop her teasing.

"Don't worry. I won't tell."

"You better not. I know Korei, and I could tie you into knots."

"Don't forget I know it too." The trumpet sounded, calling the pallons to their separate schools. "See you later."

Selah first match was against a boy from Broadriver, one of the smaller schools. "Guard," called the herald, and the match began. The pallon was aggressive, slamming down on her blade with great force. Selah parried his next blow, leaping lightly back to get out of his range.

Deracian watched the girl intently. She had skill that rivaled some grown men. His gaze never moved from the pallon fighting below. She unnerved him, as much as he disliked admitting it. Still, she would not longer be a factor by the end of the tournament. Even her training and natural skill as a fighter couldn't save her from what was coming. Nothing could.

Just in time, Selah saw the complicated pattern that was meant to disarm her. Unable to stop it, the girl tightened her grip on the blade. The boy's sword locked with hers. It became a contest of strength as the pallon tried to force her to her knees.

He bore down, using his superior height against her. Selah rolled away, feeling the wind from the pallon's sword as he swung it into the dirt. The blade had been a mere inch from her face, maybe less. Selah sprang nimbly to her feet, blocking his second blow. He was attacking relentlessly, leaving his guard down as he forced her to defend.

He over-swung, and Selah was upon him, her sword flashing up to tickle his throat. "Yield," she snapped, irritated by his lack of concern for his opponent's safety. Their swords were dulled, but he could have killed her.

"I yield," growled the boy, dropping his sword to the ground.

Selah lowered her blade, looking at him for a moment before returning to the Dragonhold benches. There was no excuse for that kind of risk in friendly combat. Selah wasn't sure if this tournament could be considered "friendly" anymore.

Her next match was against a Firemount. Selah had to switch her sword to her left hand and back again. A Donus pallon was her next opponent; she beat her easily.

The girl was lowering her blade when her eyes were drawn to a man in the stands. He observing her intently, hands folded together, his elbows resting on his knees. As she moved about the stadium, putting away her blade and sitting down on the bench, his gaze did not leave her, his head turning to track her every movement. She stared at him, eyes narrowing.

Deracian started when he realized that she was staring back at him. His palms began to sweat, and he struggled to hide the uneasiness he felt under her gaze. Two men had died under the regard of those eyes, one who had earned the rank of Lesser Dragonslayer. It was strange how a mere girl already had the blood of her enemies, perhaps not on her blade, but on her hands. *No, not a mere girl,* he thought. *A dragon in a human body. It makes her that much more dangerous.* He continued to fix his eyes on her, well aware that she was sizing him up as well. Finally, she gave him a nod of acknowledgement, turning to talk to her friends. She didn't give him a second glance.

Selah tried to shake her apprehension and concentrate on her next match. It was a good hour until she was next called to the field. Her opponent was a burly pallon from Broadriver. He, too, had a Stripe on his right arm. "Guard!" called the herald.

From the start, Selah knew that her strength wouldn't help her in this match. He was much bigger than she was, and the girl would have to rely on quickness and speed.

He was not only strong, but quick. The girl was at her wits end—only her fight with Landon passed this one in difficulty. She kept the pallon at bay for several minutes before his sword tickled her throat. "I yield," she said.

The pallon lowered his sword and backed away. Selah sheathed her blade and returned to the Dragonhold benches. She should have been able to win that last fight. Still, her earlier bouts had been successes.

Landon was still in the running. He reached the final match, facing an opponent from Firemount. His bout became all the more important with the points situation between the two schools.

Landon fought like the Firemount pallon was nothing more than an unwanted dancing partner that would not leave him alone. Firemount blows fell on empty air or were parried by Landon's steel—Landon's blows, on the other hand, left the Firemount staggering for balance. The other boy, infuriated by his inability to waver Landon's defense, rushed forward in a blind, enraged attack. Rather than merely make the boy yield, Landon ripped the sword from his grasp in a beautiful disarming technique.

Landon's victory brought Firemount and Dragonhold to an even tie. The pallons moaned at their luck—"Why couldn't we have won just *one* more?" exclaimed Bern in dismay—but the Battle of the Schools was still to be fought. Everything would hinge on the final competition.

$$*   *   *   *$$

The final event was to be a battle between the six schools. The pallons chose Landon to be the commander of the Dragonhold forces. While it was to be treated as a real fight, the weapons themselves were not.

One of the mages demonstrated the new fake weapons they would be fighting with. The arrows were made of paint, drawn into the form of an arrow by magic. The mage asked Selah to take one of the strange arrows and shoot it at one of the stray targets. The red arrow felt chalky between her fingers, but it would fly well enough. When the arrow slammed into the target, it exploded, spraying red paint on the point of impact. "See," said the mage. "They won't hurt, but they will show if the hit is a 'kill'. Perfectly harmless."

"What about our swords?" asked Landon.

The mage pointed to basins of red paint. "Coat the edge of your weapons. They are dulled, but you must not strike too hard. That could actually hurt someone."

The pallons moved forward, doing as the mage ordered. Landon continued to question the mage. "Won't the paint dry?"

"No. We charmed it so that it will only come off on people."

"Thank you. Where is the battle to take place?"

"In a section of the city. We've cleared it out."

"What if someone continues to move after they've been 'killed'?"

The mage smiled delightedly. "They won't be able to. The paint has a numbing effect. If you are hit in the hand, you won't be able to move it. Hit in the back, and you won't be able to move at all. If it's a killing blow, the person is paralyzed until the mages release the spell."

Selah shuddered. Such preparation had been taken to ensure that it was realistic. The mage's expression at the success of the paralyzing spell unnerved her. The others were coating the edges of their belt knives—Selah treated hers with the paint, but did not remove her other dagger from the wrist sheath. She wanted a real weapon ready—just in case.

A good square mile of the city had been sectioned off for the battle. Landon looked around. "I don't like it," he admitted to Selah.

"Why?" asked the girl, readying her arrows.

"Too many alleys," he explained, eyeing the empty streets. "You could walk into this square and be fired on by three sides." He looked at her. "Could you round everyone up? I need to talk to them."

Once all the Dragonhold pallons were together, Landon spoke. "All the alleyways make us particularly vulnerable to ambushes, but we could use that to our advantage. I have an idea…"

A few minutes later, Selah found herself on the gently sloping rooftop of the centermost building, gazing out at the northwest corner of Tora. From her vantage point above the streets, she could see most of the other alleyways nearby. It was all a part of Landon's plan. With several of the other pallons on other buildings, Dragonhold would have advance warning of any attack that was coming. As well, Selah could pick off stragglers without giving away where she was. Setting an arrow to her bow, Selah waited.

The first to come within her sights was Seacove. Landon had situated the rest of the pallons in one of the larger alleys, and Selah shot an arrow against the side of their alley, hoping that the red paint would warn them of the nearby enemy. The signal sent, Selah returned her attention to the sortie below her.

It was a group of three, one archer and two swordsmen. Selah set her sights on the archer. The boy gasped as the arrow struck him in the back, exploding red paint. Panic rose up in Selah's throat as he staggered. Had she actually hurt the boy? The pallon collapsed to the ground as his fellows turned. Selah's second arrow caught one of the swordsmen in the chest. The third ran, sprinting down the street. He was down before he could turn the corner. Selah set another arrow to her bow, breathing out slowly.

The girl spent another hour picking off the occasional scout. As far as she knew, no one had discovered Landon's position, and he had not sent out any pallons. He was playing it safe.

She was startled out of her thoughts by the percussive cadence of collective footsteps. An entire Wing worth of Broadriver pallons marched down the streets, surveying the boys that had fallen to Selah's arrows. The leader, a burly pallon Selah recognized as the boy who had beaten her during the fencing competition, leaned over one of the fallen scouts. He eyed the red paint that coated the scout's shirt before speaking. "Where is the Dragonholder?" he snarled.

The scout coughed. The arrow had hit him in the lower back. It was enough to paralyze him, but not enough to numb his lungs. "Ro...roof..."

Selah ducked the hail of silver arrows that whistled over her head. The Broadriver pallons had panicked and shot in all directions, sending the chalky projectiles aimlessly into the summer sky.

Selah held her bow parallel to the rooftop, waited until they were reloading and loosed an arrow, retreating behind the safety of the gutter. A pallon cried out as red paint splattered his tunic, and the stocky leader swung around, having seen the arrow leave her rooftop.

"Samson, Brekk, on the roof, now!"

Selah swore under her breath, drawing her sword silently and laying it by her side. She readied another arrow, pulling back the string.

A Broadriver pallon poked his head over the gutter. Selah's arrow caught him in the collarbone. With a cry, he swayed back, sliding down the ladder he had pulled up to the wall.

Strong arms wrapped around Selah's neck, cutting off her air. One of the pallons had snuck up on her from behind. Selah drew her belt knife and sliced the painted edge across the pallon's hands. The girl broke free of the grip as the pallon's arms went slack. He reeled back, teetering on the edge of the rooftop. Selah snatched his shirt before he fell down to the street, pulling him back onto the roof.

He threw himself at her, driving the air from her in a full-bodied tackle. The pallon pinned her down, griping her neck again with his good hand. He did not seem at all troubled that the girl had just saved his life. Selah's hand scrambled to the side, searching for something she could use against him. His knee rested painfully upon the fist with the knife. Selah's fingers closed around an arrow and she swung it upward, the shaft dissolving as the point slammed into the boy's side. White with shock, his numb body rolled off her listlessly.

"Samson? Brekk?" yelled the leader, peering up at the rooftop. Selah sheathed her blades, racing to the edge of the roof. They would find her soon, but the streets were too dangerous. Taking a deep breath, Selah leapt to the next rooftop.

Hiding behind the slope of the roof, Selah quickly calculated her circumstances. If she wasn't seen, she could regroup with the others, but the risk of unsuspectingly leading the other schools to Dragonhold's position was too great. It looked like she was on her own.

Already Broadriver voices were drifting over. "Where'd they go?" "I don't like this." "What happened to Brekk?"

Selah nocked an arrow to her bow. Stepping out from behind the roof, Selah fired, taking down a Broadriver pallon. Before the others could react, she was on to the next roof, taking refuge behind the gentle slope. Silver arrows whizzed over her head, a reminder to be quicker.

Firing another arrow, Selah looked for an escape route. She was surrounded by streets too wide to leap across. The only way by rooftops was the route by which she had come.

Shooting one last arrow for good measure, Selah swung down, hanging onto the gutter for a moment to lessen the impact of her fall. By the time the remaining Broadriver pallons reached the roof, the girl was long gone.

*   *   *   *

Flyn watched his adopted daughter in the scrying mirror that had been provided for them. Selah had shaken off her pursuers and was now cautiously making her way through the Lower Alleys.

The captain smiled in pride as he saw her dispatch a scout that had discovered her position. Beda, beside him, nodded in approval. "I wonder what she'll do next," mused the black haired woman. "She can't go back to the others…"

"She'll think of something," insisted Flyn. "She's taken out almost half a Wing of Broadriver, and they have only three shy of two wings."

Selah was gradually heading toward one of the other sentry sights that Landon had set up, apparently trying to find one of the other Dragonhold scouts.

A sharp cry focused Selah's attention to the streets before her. A sortie of Firemount swordsmen spotted her, and Selah downed one with a quick arrow. As the others recovered and fumbled for their weapons, she backtracked to avoid being outnumbered. A threesome of Alderstand appeared around the corner. Selah, caught in the middle, drew her sword from her side and slipped her bow over her shoulder.

The Alderstand and Firemount pallons, losing interest in her at the sight of a bigger group, attacked each other. Selah was able to hack, shove and shoulder her way to the outside of the mob, breaking free without much notice. Dispatching an Alderstand pallon that stood in her way, she turned the corner.

A list of the remaining pallons hung constantly in the corner of the mirror. The numbers of most of the schools had been cut in half, although Dragonhold had only lost five so far. Broadriver had only one pallon left. Seacove was no longer on the list—they had been completely defeated.

Selah drew her sword, constantly looking behind her. Out of the corner of her eye, the girl saw a sword raise. She leapt to the side a moment too late. The Broadriver leader's sword slammed into her right forearm. Immediately, it went numb, and the sword tumbled from her senseless fingers.

The Broadriver pallon leered at her. "Coward. Too bad your idea of hit and run depended on never having to face someone."

Before the boy could recover from his speech, Selah dove forward, snatching her blade with her good arm. As she straightened, he smirked. "Please. You couldn't beat me with your natural hand. What makes you think you can beat me with your off-hand?"

Selah struck down, and he blocked it with ease. Pulling her sword back, the girl kicked him in the lower abdomen. He retreated, clutching his stomach.

"That's cheating!"

Selah leveled her sword at him. "Maybe in a tournament. Anything goes in battle. You should learn that before someone kills you for real."

She charged forward, striking with the sword. This time, it was he who punched out at her. She dodged back. He attacked, forcing her to parry constantly. He was growing angry, beginning to leave openings in his defense. He lashed out, catching her in the chin with a force that snapped her head back.

Blinking the spots from her eyes, Selah struck, the flat of her painted blade swiping across his chest.

The boy's face paled. "But, I was…" he coughed as he sank down.

Selah's lungs were burning in exertion. "Skill when you are safe counts for nothing…what matters is when your life is at stake."

"Selah!" The girl spun, already raising her blade in preparation. It was Landon with a Wing's worth of the others. "Thank goodness! I thought someone had got you."

Selah shook her head, lowering her sword with considerable relief. "No. I couldn't find Quinn or Aswin. I think all of Broadriver is down. I haven't seen much of Donus either."

Landon grinned. "Oh, we saw them. Took care of a good five some of their swordsmen two alleys back."

Selah breathed a sigh of relief. "You have no idea how nice it will be to have someone watch my back."

"Come on," said Bern. "We're going to sweep the rest of the city. We're the strongest force out there right now." He frowned. "What happened to your arm?"

Selah pointed to the motionless body of the last Broadriver pallon. "My luck ran out."

There were very few remaining pallons. The streets were littered with bodies; however, more unnerving were the eyes that followed them. They passed a Firemount pallon that had fallen with his body twisted into a painful position. Selah stopped and spread him out straight, dragging him to the side of the crowded street. "Thank you," he gasped.

"No problem."

Selah had just dispatched the last of a party of Donus when the darkening sky was set afire with the roars of dragons.—*The Pallon Dragongames are over,*—rang a deep voice in her mind.—*Dragonhold has won the Battle of the Schools. Pallons, please return to the amphitheatre.*—

Around her feet, the fallen were picking themselves up as the numbing effect of the paint wore off. Her arm burned as feeling returned, pinpricks dancing up and down her skin.

Bern whooped. "We won!"

Selah smiled as they returned to the amphitheatre. The Games were over and they had won; even though elation raced through her heart like a raging wildfire, the corner of her mouth pulled downward once before she joined the celebration. This was the end of her pallonship.

They returned the unspent arrows to the mages and washed the paint from their swords, dirks, and daggers. The sun had set by the time that everything was in order. A speckling of stars had appeared in the sky, grains of the sun scattered across a blanket of darkness. Windchaser rejoined her Rider, whistling in pride and joy.

After congratulating her friends, the girl returned to the dormitories, knowing that the other female pallons would not be happy to see her.

Contrary to her original thoughts, most of the girls were gracious when she came in. May even smiled. "Your fighting was amazing! I saw you on the rooftop—I had been downed by one of the Broadriver pallons."

"Thanks," replied Selah.

Changing into her sleeping clothes, the girl retired for the evening, battling down a small measure of foreboding she felt in her heart. Dragonhold had won the Dragongames, but her mind was clouded with a sense of uneasiness. Something felt unfinished.

$$*\qquad*\qquad*\qquad*$$

The next three days passed quickly—the apprentices and dragonriders continued their competitions. The dragonriders made up for the lacking work of the apprentices by pulling the final standings of Dragonhold into first.

The final ceremony was short and to the point. King Aefric spoke a few words before awarding outstanding pallons, apprentices, and dragonriders from each school. Landon earned the honor to stand beside the king and received a hearty cheer from the crowd that had seen his impressive final fight.

Aefric had drawn the ceremonies to a close when the herald stood, gesturing for the crowd to be silent. "Ladies and gentlemen," he declared. His voice, quite unlike the rich honey tones that had held the audience captive in the days beforehand, grated on Selah's ears. The girl looked up to behold a black haired man, so tall he was colossal, in the place of the herald that had complimented Windchaser. Sun lines seemed beaten into his face.

"Turn your eyes to the end of the stadium. Look at the ebony gates that have been shut for over a century—today, they shall open again!"

There were scattered cheers, but most of the audience sat in stunned silence as the herald continued. "You will be witness to the dawn of a new age, a time when the skies will no longer be restricted to a select few. A time when flight will be gifted to all of mankind, a time when the dreams of those who were deemed unworthy will not longer be quashed into earth."

Selah felt herself stand and break away from the others in the stands. The herald's words rang true with the ideals of dragonhunters—something terrible was about to happen. Windchaser, at her side, cheeped softly. Selah laid a finger to her lips. *You must stay out of danger if anything happens here,* she thought to her Chosen. *Do not get hurt.*

She vaulted over the wooden barrier and felt the soft dirt of the field give under her boots. "What are you doing?" hissed Bern behind her, but the girl ignored him. The herald's words held her in a terrible trance—she drew closer, her fingers drawing into a circle around the hilt of her blade.

"The dragonriders may do whatever they wish because they are tied to a dragon. I ask you, the common people, the backbone of our society, is that fair? Wise?"

Lies, Selah thought.

Garrett voiced her opinions. "Dragonriders must abide by the same laws that govern every citizen of this land. We uphold them, but are not immune to them. Do not confuse the two." The burn in his golden eyes revealed that he had come to the same conclusion as Selah. There almost seemed to be a trace of recognition in the training master's vision.

The herald smiled condescendingly, the expression almost lost in his wiry black beard. "I see. Is it true that you slew Orrin, the son of Lord Breveron, heir to the fief, and received no punishment from the Crown?"

Garrett's knuckles turned white as they tightened about his sword hilt. "Orrin had betrayed us to the Cydrans. He and I fought in a duel to the death that had not been sanctioned by a Lord, but was witnessed. Lord Breveron did not contest my actions."

"So you say. Enough with your sins...Selah of Domar!" The herald had caught sight of her as she had entered the field. "How long have you graced this world with your presence?"

Selah was silent, all her awareness focused on her surroundings, searching for anything out of the ordinary. Her eyes were drawn to the ebony gates—they seemed about to speak. A strange smell hung on the gentle summer breeze.

"Fourteen summers, are you not?" Selah did not reply, but the herald continued. "Not yet a grown woman, and you already have the blood of two men on your hands."

"I have never killed anyone," Selah growled. She resisted the urge to place her hand on her own sword hilt.

"Nevertheless, their blood is on your hands. You fought them, and they died, although maybe your hand did not make the killing blow."

"A Dragonslayer and a dragonhunter assassin! Was I not supposed to fight back when they held a blade to my throat?" Selah argued, feeling her blood rise at the herald's goading words.

"So a dragonhunter life is not worth as much as yours?"

"I didn't say that."

"I am through arguing with you, spawn of Stormhunter. You will meet your judgment soon enough." The colossus turned back to the crowd. "Standing before you is Selah of Domar. For the benefit of those who do not know of her, she is the girl who has the soul of a dragon, but the body of a human. An abomination, defying the laws of singularity which have governed the creation of mankind since the dawn of time.

"She is Touched. Remember Owen of Falran, and his connection to the gods of peace and love? Remember his treachery?"

Owen of Falran had died a generation ago, but the memory of the harsh and cruel tyrant had scarred the people of Alcaron irrevocably. Thousands had died at his hand. At the sound of his name, a low chorus of murmured anger swept through the crowd, passing over Selah like a wave and bearing away her confidence as it returned.

"Derrek of Molane!" countered Garrett. The whispers of anger shifted to a milling hum of confusion. Derrek of Molane, Touched by the god of honor, was fresh in the people's minds as an image of heroism from ballads and stories.

"Cretan of Landover!"

"Rorick of Half Moon!"

"Aekar of the Hollow!"

The shouting of names continued, good and wrong, right and evil, back and forth until both men were out of breath and the crowd almost drowned them out with the roar of collective muttering.

Selah was as lost and confused as the captive members of the audience. She was a pawn, shifting from side to side until her head spun with all that hung over her. The herald stopped, gazing at Selah for a long moment.

"Selah of Domar."

Garrett said nothing. The crowd had hushed into silence. They did not know whether to cheer or scowl.

The herald regarded her with eyes that were devoid of obvious emotion. He spoke. "The gods have failed by allowing this creature to walk the earth. It is time for man to take the beginnings of life into our own hands."

The ebony gates swung forward as two men pushed them outward from the inside. They were dressed in dragonscale armor, the red and purple hides shining brightly in the sun.

The herald smiled. "People of Alcaron, see the new beast of flight, one that will outshine the dragons for all their glory. See our creation…see the drake." A muffled roar came from within the stone chamber. Selah felt fear turn her spine to ice. The drake emerged from the shadows, blinking in the sunlight, and a child screamed from the mass of humanity in the stands.

The drake, at first glances, could be mistaken for a scarred, blunted dragon. Black hide that was pebbly rather than scales seemed to swallow the sunlight as easily as any shadow. Selah was too overwhelmed by the beast to do anything more than stare.

Horns protruded from the sides of its skull, curving forward until they ran parallel to the beast's jaw. The horns were only a few inches from the pebbly scales on its face, a natural barrier against attacks to the head. The drake was stockier than a dragon, muscle rippling visibly as three more Dragonslayers urged the beast forward. A thick, corded tail whipped restlessly. The jaw was broader and wider, opening and closing to reveal several rows of yellowed teeth.

"Selah of Domar," the girl tore her eyes away from the beast to regard the herald, "spawn of Stormhunter. Abomination." The man smiled coldly, and Selah was reminded terribly of Omar. "Meet your judgment."

With a roar, the dragons of the Riders that had been honored by the King launched into flight, bearing down on the drake. The beast was now surrounded by a battlement of Dragonslayers—they had been hiding in the animal pens. Each of them bore a long bow, and arrows whistled through the air.

The dragons swerved, flying higher to get out of range. At a close distance, a long bow could punch through their thick scales, even pierce bone. Attempting to charge the drake meant certain death.

Selah returned her attention to the beast. The roar of the drake reverberated throughout the stone stadium, trembling with a vibrato that the cries of dragons did not contain.

Selah drew the sword from her belt, shifting into the guard position. All of the courage of her dragon soul could barely control the trembling in her hands. The beast could kill her with a casual swipe of the paw.

The drake raced toward her, claws pounding into the dirt. Selah didn't move. Curling its hindquarters, the beast launched itself at Selah. The girl dove to the side, slashing with her blade as she fell. She felt the air whistle by her ear as the drake's claws missed her face by the barest inch.

The girl rolled as soon as her torso hit the ground, scrambling to get out of the drake's range. Selah ran several feet before realizing that the beast had not followed her.

Garrett weaved and dodged in front of the drake, his blade scoring light scratches in the beast's armor-like hide. Her training master was defending her. The drake snarled as Garrett's sword bit into its skin, lashing out with a claw.

The flat of the drake's paw slammed into the training master's side. With an exclamation of pain, the dragonrider crumpled to the ground under the force of the blow. The drake held one claw over the man, pressing him to the dirt as the beast attempted to see whether or not its attack had killed its opponent.

Selah bent, her hand scrabbling in the dirt until her fingers closed about a small stone that had been missed by the servants that tended to the amphitheatre. She hurled it at the beast. Her aim was good; the stone struck the drake in the ear.

Distracted, the beast turned its blood red eyes on her. Selah shuddered in fear, but her voice seemed to take a life of its own. "Come and get me!" she shouted, hoping to goad the drake away from Garrett. "Brute animal!"

The creature growled, stepping away from the fallen training master and hissing at her. Selah swallowed the fear from her throat, starting to back away from the beast. She fell into a Dragonslayer—he pushed her forward, sneering.

Leathery wings extended from the drake's back as the animal unfurled its means of flight. Selah realized her terrible mistake. Turning, the girl began to run to the other side of the amphitheatre, her panicked mind thinking of the safety of dragons.

She heard wing beats behind her—moments later, pain pierced her shoulder as the drake grasped her shoulders with its claws.

Selah cried out in pain as her feet left the ground, the sword slipping from her fingers as they opened involuntarily. Her hands pried at the claws that secured her to the drake, but to no avail—its grip was as powerful as a vise. The fetid breath of the animal engulfed her, and Selah choked.

Selah stopped struggling when the field below her shrunk to half its original size—a fall from this height would kill her. The pain in her shoulders was almost unbearable; liquid trickled down her skin as blood welled in the puncture wounds made by the drake's claws. Her feet dangled heavily in the air; Selah, normally comfortable with heights, was painfully aware of how far from the ground they were.

The grip on her shoulders jerked as a force slammed into the drake—the strain of her wounds made the girl bite her lip to keep from crying out. Green scales passed by her line of vision before disappearing behind the drake—the dragons, safe from bows at this range, had come to help.

The drake snarled, but it could not strike out at the dragons without releasing Selah. Somehow, the dragonhunters had placed her as the first priority in the beast's mind, and the drake was unwilling to let her go. A copper dragon slashed at the drake's side—the beast howled in pain, dropping in altitude to place itself within the protection of the longbows.

Arrows whistled by her as the Dragonslayers defended their beast, keeping the dragons at bay. More arrows, this time from the top of the stadium, rained down the on the dragonhunters. A handful of the city guards had replied to the screams and attempted to keep the Dragonslayers occupied. The pallons and their instructors, in the same predicament as the dragons without armor, hung back, a fair distance from the Dragonslayers. It would do no good to die uselessly.

Selah worked the knife from her belt, holding it in her left hand. The drake swooped low to evade the dragons, snarling as the motion aggravated the gashes in its side. Selah waited until the drake was at the bottom of its dive, close enough that a fall would not seriously injure her, before burying her dagger into its arm. The beast roared, releasing one of her shoulders. Selah, all of her weight on her right shoulder, winced in pain, clawing at the drake's other arm with her free hand.

The air rushed by her face as the drake released her. The ground rushed up to meet her with alarming speed, and Selah extended her arms to brace herself.

There was an audible *snap* as the girl struck the ground, the packed dirt banishing the breath from her body. Her right arm ached—her fingers barely responded when she asked them to move, and it was contorted into a position that defied the limits of her flexibility. It was broken.

Her other limbs did not seem to be snapped, but would not respond well; her body was stunned. The dirt felt rough and coarse against her cheek, vividly real—the texture kept her from losing consciousness.

Selah heard the heavy thump as the drake landed several feet away. Her eyes searched the crowd. They watched in shocked silence, making no move to flee or fight. They were still as statues.

The drake growled, trying to draw a reaction from her to see if she was alive. Selah scanned her surroundings, hope returning when a blinding flash of light burned her eyes. Her sword had fallen from her grip only feet from where she lay, reflecting the bright summer sun onto her face.

The girl tried to drag herself forward but collapsed when she placed too much weight on her broken arm. The drake was too close for her to make a lunge for the blade—it would be upon her before she made half the distance.

Her shoulder screamed in pain as she reached across her body, pulling her last defense from her wrist sheath with her left hand. Her strong arm was broken, and would do her no good—she would have to bear her dagger in her slightly weaker hand.

The sun beat down on her as heavily as rain. Beads of sweat coursed down her face, mingling with the blood from her bitten lip that gathered at the corners of her mouth. Her shoulders hurt so terribly, but the girl knew it would be over soon. There was no way that she could walk away from the drake alive. It was too powerful, too strong. She had to make sure that it hurt no one else.

The drake was almost upon her now, the rank odor of its breath falling upon her like a dank curtain of decay. Its red eyes examined her body, narrowing to slits when she did not move.

Now, whispered a voice in Selah's mind. *Strike now.*

She rose from the ground like a tidal wave from the sea, her dagger lancing in a silver arc through the space between girl and beast. Her blade glowed white-hot in the sun. Blue flecks stained her already blood-soaked white shirt as the edge of her wrist knife bit into the black hide. Her shoulder screamed at the motion. The drake lifted its head in a roar of rage and agony.

Selah hurried away from the drake, closing the distance between her and the sword. Grasping its handle with her left hand, Selah lifted it. Tears of pain clouded her eyes when her ripped shoulder only allowed her to raise the blade to her chest. She would be lucky to strike at the beast's forelimbs.

It was charging her now, terrible hatred in the red eyes. The drake snarled, claws beating against the ground in a deadly percussion. She would not win by running away. The same steely resolve that had made her jump through a raging firewall two years ago claimed her again, and Selah brought her broken right arm to join her left on the hilt of her blade.

The girl rushed forward. Dodging the strike of the drake's blunt head, Selah buried her sword into the beast. The blade embedded hilt deep into the hide just behind the drake's shoulder muscle.

The girl felt fire dig furrows along her ribs as the drake retaliated.

Selah slammed against the ground with both her momentum and the force of the drake's blow. She watched through misting eyes as the drake thrashed about, trying to dislodge the blade from its side. The Dragonslayers, stunned, fell as the arrows of the guard met their mark.

Blue blood streamed from the wound. It was a fatal blow, even for a beast the size of the drake, and the animal soon fell to its belly, the corded tail continuing to lash about as it died. The beast lifted its head to the sky and moaned. The sound was gentle, sad, and the heart of the drake cried for the loss of life. The blunt head dropped to the ground; the sound was lost in the cloud of disturbed dust that shrouded the red eyes in death.

Selah coughed in an effort to improve her breathing. The drake's claws had dug deep crimson gashes along her ribs, the marks curving around the left side of her torso. Blood seeped from the wounds, staining the uniform that marked her as one from Dragonhold.

The world faded in and out of focus. She couldn't breathe. Violet eyes brimming with love swam into her vision, and the distinct trills that she recognized as Windchaser seemed far and distant in her ear. She couldn't hold on anymore, and the world faded to gray, then the blue-black that was her nothingness.

*   *   *   *

She hung, suspended, in the blue-black. This did not feel like an ending, but it felt like death. Selah let her head fall forward to be cradled on her chest as the pain the drake had enacted on her body took its toll. She was so tired.

The blue-black swam around her; she could feel the currents, although the appearance around her did not change.

Her dragon song flowed around her on the currents of the blue-black, easing the pain of her wounds. Selah lifted her head and looked for the source of the sound, the singer of the song that defined who she was.

The chorus filled her lungs, sustaining her like air. A blue glow drifted down from above as the melody intertwined with the harmony.

A dragon flew down from the heavens, her sky-blue scales shining with a brilliance that put the sun to shame. Her violet eyes were brimming with the tears that dragons rarely shed.

"Windchaser," Selah whispered.

*The dragonet spoke, but the song did not stop.—**Selah.**—*

They waited in silence as the song ebbed and flowed around them.

"It hurts, Windchaser."

*Windchaser's eyes softened.—**I know.**—*

*The blue-black around her surged. Windchaser's pupils narrowed to slits in panic.—**Do not leave me! I cannot be alone!**—*

"I can't...reach you."

—Please…do not leave me here by myself.—Windchaser's voice was lost and choked with feeling.

"My shoulders…"

*—Please.—Tears leaked from the corners of her eyes.—Death comes only if you welcome it. You are not mortally wounded. You are **not** dying. I will not let you.—*

Selah reached upward, her arms shaking as the tears in her shoulders strained. Her broken arm could not grip Windchaser's scales, but the girl wrapped her left arm around Windchaser's paw.

The dragonet bore her upward, tears of relief streaming from her eyes. "I don't know if I can hold the pain, Windchaser," Selah confessed as they grew nearer to the present. "I don't know if I can keep going."

*Windchaser regarded her with eyes that were filled with a love that could not be measured with mere words.—I am your **Chosen**,—the dragon reassured.*

—I will not let you fall.—

＊　　＊　　＊　　＊

The sun was an unrelenting figure in the bright blue sky. Selah's fingers curled into her palm as color returned to her world. The hues came accompanied by sensation—her wounds made themselves known as the air flowed in and out of her lungs.

The sky was like a blue basin that had been placed upside down above her. Windchaser whimpered, tears streaming from her eyes. Selah reached up with her good arm and brushed the drops of moisture from scales that matched the color of the sky. Windchaser grasped Selah's hand with both paws and pressed it to her face, her body shaking with the fear that had claimed her when she thought Selah lost to her.

Selah smiled through the sweat, blood, and grime that obscured her face. "We won, Windchaser."

The dragonet trilled into her palm.

Green obscured the blue basin above her. The dragon that had helped her fight the drake bent over her, his eyes sad as he took in the enormity of her wounds. His claws were cool against her hot, battered body as he lifted her from the ground, bearing her weight in his forepaws.

He rose to his hindquarters, his cyan eyes burning with rage. The audience had not moved from their original positions—Selah could not have been unconscious for very long.

*—The drake is dead!—*declared the dragon, his mind voice trembling with contained anger.*—Selah defeated the beast of the dragonhunters. You all bear witness. That is all you can do—bear witness.—*

Selah clutched Windchaser to her chest with her good arm, gasping softly as another wave of pain flowed from the gaping wounds along her side.*—You sat here and watched while a beast attacked those who are sworn to protect you. You watched, as it was defeated.—*

The crowd murmured softly, but did not move. The dragon waited until the audience was silent before continuing.*—Remember the day that the dragonhunters came out of the shadows, to be driven back by the seemingly smallest of us. Remember the day that you watched and did nothing to help when your countrymen were beset. Remember the day that a girl, a young Rider, fought while you stared in silence. Remember the day that her courage put yours to shame.—*

Selah was too tired to feel embarrassed by the high praise that flowed from the mind of a dragon she barely knew. She was too exhausted to understand that the silence that filled the amphitheatre was respectful.

Windchaser began to sing, her voice ringing throughout the stone stadium. She sang the beginning of Selah's dragon song alone—when she reached the chorus for the second time, the three dragons that had tried to help Selah joined her. The green's arms trembled as his voice hit some of the higher notes, and Selah felt her eyes mist over with tears that she did not often shed.

The song fell over the crowd, the notes dancing through each row to reverberate across the field, past the pallons that were helping Garrett rise to his feet, around Selah's friends as they watched in silence, twisting through the foreign dragonriders and their charges, echoing against stone to return to Selah's ears.

Windchaser finished the song, letting the last note ring heavily in the air. The dragons had delivered their highest praise by honoring Selah with their voices. The girl held her broken arm to her chest as her left hand pressed her tattered shirt to the wounds along her side. Although it was a struggle to hold onto consciousness, the enormity of her song did not escape her. A tear slid down her cheek.

—Remember this day.—

*   *   *   *

Selah remained at the Green Dragon for the first two weeks following the attack by the drake. Her wounds had reduced her strength to that of a newborn kitten, and although the dragonriders were concerned with returning her to the safety of Dragonhold, her wounds would not permit her to travel—thus, every room in the Green Dragon was occupied by a dragonrider, and three dragons guarded each entrance. Few non-dragonfolk were permitted to enter the inn.

It was three days more before Selah was deemed well enough to receive visitors. Landon was the first to see her.

"How are you?" he asked as he settled into a chair that had provided by the innkeeper.

Selah had to swallow the dryness from her throat before replying. "Horrible. How do I look?"

Landon smiled ruefully, hesitating a moment before answering. "About the same." Selah was terribly pale, and the bandages on her shoulders were stained red again.

To his relief, his friend grinned. "I thought so."

"What you did…." Landon looked at the floor, having to force down his emotion. "That was the bravest thing I have ever seen in my life."

Selah had known her best friend long enough to recognize the self-loathing on his face that he had masked with a reassuring smile. "You would have done the same in my place," she consoled.

"I did nothing." Landon's knuckles turned white as he grasped the edges of the chair. "You were being attacked by this monster, and I did nothing."

"There was nothing you could do. The Dragonslayers would have killed you without blinking. Honor and legacy aside, you're more help to me alive than buried."

Selah winced as her side burned. "I'm alive. Garrett's alive. The dragons are alive. Stop killing yourself over a what-if."

"But…"

"Look, I'm a horsefly's eyebrow from standing up and beating you across the head, which would make my side reopen and we'd be stuck here for another two weeks. Will you please admit that I am right and stop berating yourself?"

Landon grinned at the old joke her words had reminded him of, and saw his smile matched on Selah's face. The boy knew that everything was going to be all right.

Garrett waited until the last of her friends had filed out of her room before visiting. The training master knocked once on the door before entering.

Selah had propped herself with several pillows so that she could better receive visitors. She gave a slight bow of her head when the dragonrider entered. "Master Garrett."

Garrett returned the gesture. "Selah of Domar." He took a seat in the same chair that Landon had rested in, grateful—his body was still sore from the blow of the creature. "I hear that you are feeling better."

"Better than I did, sir."

Garrett smiled, steepling his fingertips in thought. "The city guard captured the 'herald' as he tried to leave Tora. He was executed today, under King Aefric's orders."

"He's dead?" Garrett nodded.

Selah sighed. "Do you think he deserved it?" Her pale face was shrouded in her own uncertainty.

Garrett exhaled slowly, rubbing the corners of his eyes. "He was wearing dragonscale armor until his clothes. There were multiple colors—he was a higher Dragonslayer." He waited for her to speak.

"What he said…it made me wonder," Selah confessed. "Was he right? About me? About dragons and dragonriders?"

Garrett shook his head gently. His golden eyes were serene. "What he could not understand was the bond between Rider and dragon—how precious and strong it is. The dragonriders swore themselves into service of the kingdom in exchange for the bond—it is not a life many would relish. What happened, do you think, to the dragonriders who wanted to be explorers? What of those who could not stomach the killing when they saw war?"

Selah could not reply. Garrett answered for her. "The dragonhunters see only the glory of the dragonriders, and covet it like nothing else in the world. Yes, they have a few valid points, but every argument has some appeal to it. If they saw the sacrifice that we must make, how our very lives are forfeit for the love of a dragon, perhaps…perhaps they would understand."

The look of peace on the girl's face assured Garrett that he had calmed her inner turmoil. She lay back against the pillows with a gentle sigh, lines of weariness on her face, and the training master knew she was quickly running out of energy. However, he had another question for her. Clearing his throat, he spoke. "Why did you throw the rock at the drake?"

Selah shrugged, wincing when the motion stretched the wounds on her shoulders. "That was all I had to throw—I don't know how to throw daggers yet."

Garrett shook his head. "No…why did you draw attention to yourself in the first place?"

Selah turned her face to the ceiling, struggling to put her thoughts into words. "That's what you did for me when you attacked the drake." After another moment, the girl looked her training master in the eye. "That's what a dragon-rider is supposed to do, isn't it?"

Garrett smiled. "Yes...that's what a dragonrider is supposed to do."

The conversation turned to less interesting topics, such as recent happenings around the inn and the news that Selah's healer had not passed along to the girl. The training master had just finished a sentence when he realized that Selah was not answering him.

The girl was asleep, exhausted from a day of speaking, laughing, and consoling. Windchaser was curled at her uninjured side, guarding her Rider even in dreams. Garrett smiled, standing to leave.

"Well done, Selah of Domar. Very well done."

*　　　*　　　*　　　*

Selah grew stronger and stronger. Another week, and she was able to stand without assistance. A week and a half, and the healer the dragonriders had procured deemed her ready for three to four hour flights. They made it back to Dragonhold at a much slower pace than they had first come, and Selah had an awake and alert guard, dragon or Rider, wherever she went. Still, the girl was always too tired or in too much pain to truly care that there were always a pair of eyes on her, and she was relieved when they made it back to the comfort and safety of Dragonhold.

As they healed, Selah's wounds were becoming thick scars that would stay with her for the rest of her life. When Selah shed the cast that had protected her broken arm, Sean declared that he would dub the pallons apprentices in three days.

*　　　*　　　*　　　*

Selah shivered in the early morning air. The breeze, unusual for early fall, made her wounds ache, but the girl had wanted to see the sunrise. Windchaser and Selah watched the sun peek over the horizon, content with the comfortable silence between them. The two welcomed the sunlight on their faces.

The girl thought back to the words of Stormhunter as he had healed her in the Spring of All Tears. *The numerous scars you have collected are gone as well. Well, all but one.* She smiled—she had certainly done her very best to amass a new collection.

They were not all scars that could be seen on the surface of her skin. Selah's face darkened as she thought of Omar, the Dragonslayer, her dragon side, and Stormhunter. Each had left their mark on her in a less visible way. She was different now, far different than the girl who had left the battlements of Domar with nothing more than a dream and emptiness where a dragon should be.

Selah kissed Windchaser on the brow, laughing when the dragonet nuzzled her ear. Dragonhold had brought a great joy into her life, a happiness that revisited her each morning when violet eyes begged her for breakfast. Those same violet eyes were a promise that she would never be alone.

The ceremony was to start at the sun's zenith. Taking one last look at the sunrise, Selah made her way down the steps, heading for her room.

*   *   *   *

Selah looked around at her fellow pallons, decked out handsomely in the Dragongames uniforms. A new one had been made for her—the original was torn to shreds and stained with blood. The girl shook her head at the thought.

Selah smiled as Garrett presented Landon with a new sword. It was the greatest prize of an apprentice—each earned a fine sword made from Steelforge Armory. Garrett had provided input into each blade so that they would best reflect a new apprentice's fighting style. Landon sheathed the sword into his empty scabbard, bowing to his training master and Holdleader.

For each person, Garrett complimented on their greatest asset. He praised Landon for his ability as a leader, Aswin for his speed, and Bern for his strength. Finally it was Selah's turn.

"Selah of Domar." Selah knelt on one knee before her two masters, one hand clutching her empty scabbard, the other in a fist, knuckles resting on the floor in front of her.

"You have faced more than many grown men. Your strength and physical prowess is overshadowed only by the strength of your spirit. As a dragon once described you, 'Her courage puts all others to shame'." Selah bowed her head at the past words of praise coming once more from one she greatly respected. "I am proud to have been your teacher." Garrett bowed to her, deeply from the waist, like he had none of the others.

"Are you ready to become an apprentice?" asked Sean.

"Yes." Selah replied, no trace of doubt in her voice. She had waited two long, challenging years for this moment.

"Are you strong enough to face what will come?"

"Yes."

"Will you uphold the honor of dragonriders and never forget what you have been taught here?"

"Yes."

"Then rise, Selah of Domar. May you join our ranks as a dragonrider." Selah accepted the sword from Garrett, admiring it for a moment. A dragon rising in flight, the symbol of Dragonhold, was etched into the blade, near the wired hilt that fit her palm perfectly. She sheathed it, bowing to her masters.

When she returned to her seat, she felt no different than she had a few moments before. Her scars ached, but Selah the Apprentice felt the same as Selah the Pallon.

Landon extended a handshake of congratulations, but Selah ignored it and wrapped him in a massive hug. He returned it gently, careful not to hurt her wounds. "We've all worked hard to get here," he said. "You especially."

"You've saved me so many times. I owe you so much."

"Friends don't owe each other, Selah. I think we've both repaid each other with laughter and good times." He smiled. "If we don't get dragon-masters in the same Wing, I think I'll scream."

"Not any louder than I would." Selah released her friend from the embrace, a smile adorning her face. "I'm counting my stars, Landon."

The boy returned the expression. "Not staring at the black places?"

Selah grinned. "Speak for yourself. I don't have any."

"Of course. I'm glad you're counting your stars, Selah." Landon's emerald eyes shone with genuine happiness for her.

You're one of them, the girl thought, but only gave the boy a parting smile before receiving congratulations from Bern and Aswin. She didn't have to say anything; Landon already knew.

*   *   *   *

Selah wandered the halls of Dragonhold, Windchaser following at her heels. The wide corridors were so familiar to her that the girl was sure she could navigate them with her eyes closed.

The girl stopped at the mural. *The Flight of Starcross* stared back at her, the dragon extended over the waves just the same as before. Selah let her hands slide over the surface, smiling as Windchaser clambered to her shoulder and joined her in exploring the mural.

Selah thought she could hear strains of the dragon song resting on the breeze. The notes and melodies brushed against her like soft wings, her dragon's song twisting around her. Selah listened until the last sounds of her dragon soul fell away into silence. Selah felt Windchaser shift on her shoulder—the girl turned to regard her Chosen with surprise. The sound had been her dragonet, singing softly.

Selah reached up, letting her Chosen's paws intertwine with her fingers until it was hard to tell where human ended and dragon began. The girl stared into Windchaser's violet eyes. Their two years together had brought terrible scars and beautiful beginnings; there was no question that the future would bring more of the same. No matter what the battles, faces, and hardships their destiny would carry, their love for each other would remain. In the end, that was all that mattered.

978-0-595-34592-2
0-595-34592-1